SPIRIT LIGHT

The Spirit Song Trilogy | Book Two
Volume One

ROSS HIGHTOWER

Black Rose Writing | Texas

This is a work of fiction. Names, characters, businesses, places, events, and incidents are either the products of the author's imagination or used in a fictitious manner. Any resemblance to actual persons, living or dead, or actual events is purely coincidental.

ISBN: 978-1-68513-455-6
LIBRARY OF CONGRESS CONTROL NUMBER:2024932095
PUBLISHED BY BLACK ROSE WRITING
www.blackrosewriting.com

Printed in the United States of America
Suggested Retail Price (SRP) $27.95

Spirit Light is printed in Garamond

*As a planet-friendly publisher, Black Rose Writing does its best to eliminate unnecessary waste to reduce paper usage and energy costs, while never compromising the reading experience. As a result, the final word count vs. page count may not meet common expectations.

For an annotated map, character lists and more visit
rosshightower.com/argren

Praise for *Spirit Sight*
Book One of the *Spirit Song Trilogy*

"High fantasy mixed with mythic tale-telling, the author explores what it means to be a pawn in someone else's scheme. That is, until the pawn realizes the true extent of her power and the path it will set for the rest of the Empire."
–Eric Hoffer Award

"The story is packed with action, with plenty of twists and turns and lots of well-written dialogue. This is a captivating story that will take you away from the realities of life and let you wallow in magic and fantasy for a few hours."
–*Readers' Favorite*

"Hightower moves the story through this thoughtful environment swiftly and concisely, making it easy to grasp, and also provides scenes of action and adventure. Readers will likely be excited to see where the stories take them."
–*Kirkus Reviews*

"*Spirit Sight* blends its classic fantasy premise—the humble commoner comes into magical powers and is thrust into a grand destiny involving monumental forces—with themes of religious and political corruption, with an appealing focus on spirituality and the natural world."
–*IndieReader*

Praise for

Argren Blue: A Spirit Song Story

In Argren Blue: A Spirit Song Story by Ross Hightower & Deb Heim, readers are immersed in a gripping fantasy tale filled with resilience, self-discovery, and the pursuit of freedom.
–Literary Titan

The authors have created a vivid and compelling world.... I was immediately invested in the fate of Alar and his friends, aided by the skillfully described settings and circumstances. The writing is outstanding…"
–Sublime Book Review

"The world is vast and meticulously crafted, but it doesn't take itself too seriously to have fun. The plot moves swiftly… An expertly spun fantasy adventure featuring magic, combat, and art appreciation."
–Kirkus Reviews

SPIRIT LIGHT

Timeline

Year 1143 of the Imperial Era

Part I
Brennan

Part II
Argren

Month of Annenmon

Sera meets
Nicola

28

34

Minna arrives
at the Cut

Month of Ungemon

1

Harold flees

Macha heads
to Argren

Alyn has a
vision

Keelia meets
Karl

Minna learns
about Spirit Light

Harold meets
Nia

Flynn gets
her orders

Sera and
Nicola flee

34

Ulf meets the
rangers

Month of Heulomon

Minna gets
bad news

1

7

Alyn meets
her Spirit
Guide

The Storm Breaks

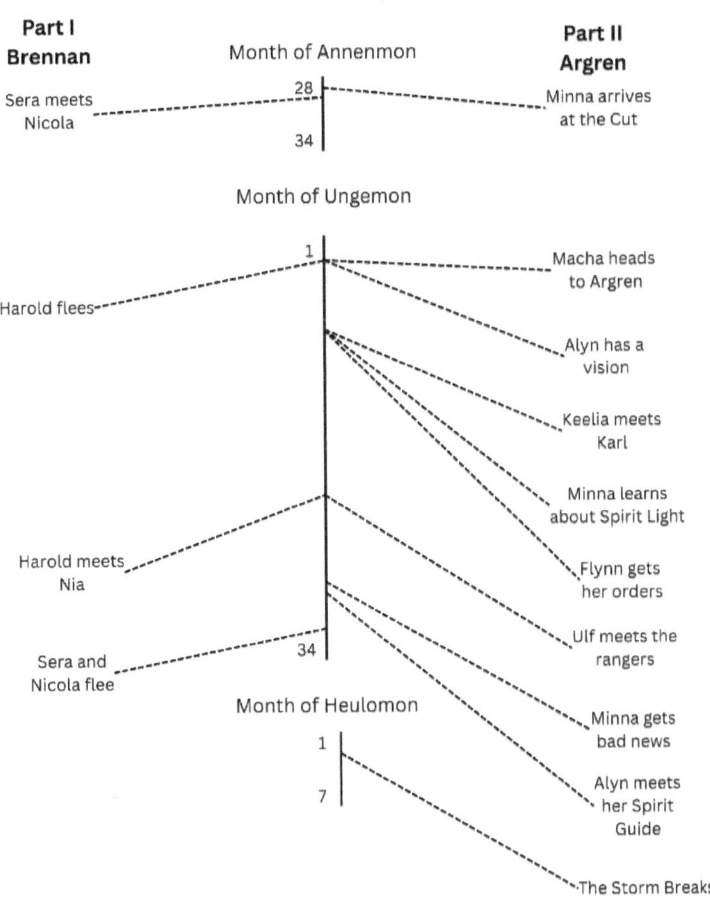

Prologue

Beadu

"What would you like to talk about?" Beadu asked the children crowded around her. It was the evening of Lindenlatha and this was her last class of the week. It was a mixed group that included the youngest children in *Helala*. Many of them still wore the trauma of their rescue from the Inquisition, but safe among other children who shared their experience, they showed signs of recovering.

"Tell us about Minna," one of the boldest girls said and grinned as others echoed her request.

Beadu couldn't guess how many times they heard the story of Minna's quest to rescue her sister from the Inquisition prison. But she knew from recent experience that what they really wanted to know was how likely it was the *Alle'oss* survived the war with the Empire. As children, they focused all their hope on the hero they knew; Minna Hunter.

"How many of you met Minna when she was here?" Beadu asked, amused at the hands that shot into the air.

One of the youngest girls, who arrived in *Helala* after Minna departed, said, "I know Alyn, her sister."

"Just so," Beadu said. "Alyn remained here while Minna left to —"

"Fight the Empire!" one of the few boys said.

"Why can't Alyn fight?"

Before Beadu could answer, Singa, one of the girls who had been in *Helala* longest, said, "Because she hasn't found her spirit guide yet." All the girls who could see the spirits looked up at the swarm of *lan'and* swirling above them. Their spirit sight was the reason the Inquisition hunted them. The Empire sought to capture them and twist them to their own ends before they grew into their power. It was why the *Alle'oss* rebels hid the girls in *Helala*.

"Just so," Beadu said. "Alyn has only eleven summers, but she is helping by translating Ragan's journal."

"That's Minna and Alyn's mother. Their *real* mother," Singa informed the group. "She could see the future, and she saw the Inquisition would kill her family. So she left home to try to change what would happen." Her eyes grew wide. "Minna and Alyn didn't even *know* she was their mother until last winter. Ragan saw how the *Alle'oss* could defeat the Empire, but she didn't tell anyone what she saw before she died."

"Not even you or Aron?" the first girl asked Beadu.

"No," Beadu said. "She left it to us to find the right path, but she had her reasons." Aron was Ragan's adopted son. It was the reason he commanded the *Alle'oss's* fledgling army, despite his youth. People assumed he understood Ragan's intent.

"Aron is a realm walker!" a boy said.

"Yes, he is one of two *Alle'oss* men who are realm walkers," Beadu said. It wasn't widely known outside *Helala* that Aron could enter the realm of the dead and return. But there were rumors, and she suspected that helped people accept him as their commander.

"Who is the other realm walker?" the boy asked with a frown.

"Alar," Beadu said. "He is the leader of the rebels who call themselves *Oss'stera.*"

"I'm going to be a realm walker," the boy said.

"Is it true Harold Wolfe is an inquisitor?" Singa asked.

"Yes, it's true," Beadu said.

"Why would Harold Wolfe help Minna rescue Alyn if he was in inquisitor?"

This part of the story was an endless source of fascination for the children. They couldn't understand how a man like the men who persecuted them could be anything but evil. The children grew uncharacteristically still as they waited for her answer. "He has committed crimes he regrets, but Ragan saw he had a good heart. It was Harold who allowed Minna to live long enough to become as powerful as she is. Ragan gave him hints that led Harold to the right place at the right time so he could help Minna."

"But he's *still* an inquisitor."

"Ragan asked him to remain in the Inquisition, at great risk to himself," Beadu said. "We don't know why, but we can only hope she had a good reason."

"Harold joined the *Alle'oss* just like Sister Keelia," Signa said. "She's helping us too."

"Yes, Keelia was a Seidi sister," Beadu said. The Seidi started as Imperial women with spirit sight. They were the reason the Vollen people were able to carve the Empire from smaller nations. But their power diminished in recent years. Now only a few sisters, Keelia among them, had true spirit sight. "Few people know that Keelia's mother was *Alle'oss*. When an inquisitor named Stefan Schakal betrayed her, she joined the *Alle'oss*."

"Is she as powerful as Minna?"

"No one is as powerful as Minna," Beadu said.

"That's how Minna defeated Aife!"

"Was Aife really *Alle'oss*?" a small girl asked timidly.

Beadu nodded. "Aife's real name was Ella. Malleus Hoerst, the leader of the Inquisition, kidnaps girls with spirit sight and tortures them until they fight for the Empire." She nodded solemnly. "It was Ella who killed Ragan, and Minna was forced to fight her." Beadu paused and scanned the faces of the children. They would have shared Ella's fate were they not rescued from the Inquisition. "We must not hate Ella for what she did. She suffered terribly at the hands of the Inquisition."

"Will we win the war?" a little boy asked after a long silence.

"Ragan believed we would win," Beadu said. "The Empire is powerful, but we must have faith in her vision. We must have faith that Minna, Alyn, Aron, Keelia, Harold and others can find the path Ragan left for us."

Chapter 1

The 15th Day of the Month of Annenmon
Year 1143 of the Imperial Era

She didn't dream. That's why she was sure she must be dead. She always had vivid dreams. So, she wasn't sleeping, but she always thought death would be different. She knew what the old sisters in the Seidi taught her was not true. She didn't expect to have to face Daga or his sons. Didn't expect to join the countless condemned in the Otherworld. No, she didn't know what to expect, but she assumed it would be something other than black silence. She had to admit, she was disappointed.

And then, out of the blackness, she felt a presence. She sensed determination, resolve. Exhaustion. She reached out, and the presence noticed. There was a flash of intense joy, then anger. Indignation.

I love you, too, and I'm sorry. She would have laughed at the spirit's joyful swoops. If she were alive. At least, if she were to be condemned to this dark place, she would have company. *Where are we?* But before the spirit could respond in its way, a voice echoed faintly in the darkness.

Gimlet, A Gravedigger

"Oi!" Gimlet set his shovel on the ground beside the half-finished grave and pressed his fingers to the neck of the woman's body.

"What are you doing?" Hawthen threw a shovel full of dirt on the pile next to the grave and paused to wipe sweat from his brow. "That's creepy."

"Hawthen, I think this one's alive."

Hawthen climbed out of the grave and bent over the body. "What's that you say?"

"Yeah, this one's alive," Gimlet said. "Pulse is weak, but she ain't dead."

The two men stood in the spring sunshine, looking from the body to the grave. "What do you think?" Gimlet asked.

"We *could* just bury her," Hawthen said. "That's what the brother, that Inquisition fella, told us to do. Maybe he knew. You know, letting us do the final deed."

"Yeah," Gimlet drawled. They looked at one another.

Discarding the shovel, Hawthen bent over and worked his hands under the woman's shoulders. "Here, you get the feet." They hefted the body and stumbled through the graveyard toward the wagon they left at the gate. "Not doing those bastards' dirty business," Hawthen said.

They placed the woman in the wagon and stepped back. "Where we takin her?" Gimlet asked.

Hawthen hesitated. "We'll take her to my place," he said.

"I think she needs a medic."

"We take her to the medics, they'll find her," Hawthen said.

They stared at the woman for a time, then Gimlet said, "She's a strong one. Might be she'll fight through it."

"Yuh," Hawthen said.

"We'll bring her to my place," Gimlet said. "Di will take care of her."

Hawthen chuckled. "She don't kill you first."

Hoerst

As Malleus of the Empire's Inquisition, Hoerst didn't normally have the time or patience to listen to complaints from those beneath him. He wanted to hear solutions to problems, not excuses. But the root of the current complainer's problems was Hoerst's fault, and he wasn't just any underling. Much of Hoerst's plans to resurrect the stumbling Empire relied on this man's expertise. Still, when Manfrid took a breath, preparing, no doubt, to launch from the beginning of his well-rehearsed speech, Hoerst had enough.

"Brother Manfrid," he said. The brother's mouth snapped shut at Hoerst's tone. Hoerst fixed him with a stare, then let a smile stretch his lips. "Do you think I am not aware of the problems I am causing you?"

"Oh, no, Malleus," he said with a quick shake of his head.

Hoerst overrode his next words. "Then is it your contention that I am mistaken?"

Manfrid's face stilled. His eyes shifted to the side, choosing his next words carefully. "Of course not, Malleus," he said evenly. "I'm sure you know how best to achieve our aims."

His emphasis on the last two words amused Hoerst.

"It's just…" Manfrid gestured toward the closed door of Hoerst's office. "I want to be sure you understand how these actions will slow our program."

"Don't worry," Hoerst said. "I will not hold you responsible."

Manfrid glanced at the other occupant in the room, Inquisitor Stefan Schakal. "Thank you, Malleus," he said, managing to convey his doubt despite his smile.

"Excellent!" Hoerst said and sat forward, folding his hands on his desk. "Tell us, how have you progressed in your methods?"

Manfrid's entire demeanor changed. Gone was the obsequious toady. Instead, the man standing before Hoerst was the one the Malleus found teaching Science of the Mind in the Inquisition Academy ten years ago. He stood straighter, hands clasped behind his back, a small smile playing at the corners of his lips.

"Fear is the key." He dipped his head and gave Hoerst a knowing smile. "Fear lays the mind bare, leaves it vulnerable to suggestion. But fear by itself is a blunt instrument, its effects unpredictable. It is fear's many corollaries — disgust, contempt, xenophobia, etc — that allow us to plant our narrative in the subject's mind. To construct a version of reality that serves our purpose." He lifted a hand, extending a finger. "First is the *anticipation* of unpleasantness, the erosion of the foundations of a person's reality. This, as you know, we accomplish by inserting the spirits of prophecy, the *sjel'and,* into the subject's mind. Fear of an uncertain future is one of man's most primitive drivers."

Hoerst glanced at Stefan, gauging his response. The inquisitor had been his closest assistant, one might say, his fixer, since before he became Malleus. He knew of Hoerst's efforts to make use of Brochen witches, but Hoerst never confided to him the true extent of his blasphemies. The Vollen Church considered consorting with spirits the worst kind of sin. Hoerst wasn't worried Stefan would object on moral grounds, but he was curious how he would respond. Stefan sat rapt, staring at Manfrid. Smiling to himself, Hoerst returned his attention to the brother's lecture.

"None of our subjects has shown an affinity for the *sjel'and,* so the results are often… unpredictable. Fortunately, the spirits have a grasp of what would cause the most trauma, and they seem to enjoy their subject's torment. The results would be more reliable if we could direct them, somehow, but so far, we have not been so lucky.

"However, we *have* recently discovered one of our more successful subjects has a gift that allows her to plumb the depths of a person's subconscious. Past traumas, dread, phobias, anxieties…" he said, twirling his hand as he enumerated his tools. After falling silent for a moment, looking thoughtful, he shrugged, and said, "Well, you can imagine how much more reliable it is to use a person's most deeply held fears. For the first time, we can exploit a subject's vulnerabilities in a targeted fashion." He gave Hoerst a satisfied grin before continuing.

"Of course, once you strip the subject's reality from them, you must help them construct something new. Something that allows them to feel safe in a dangerous world. We need merely feed them the narrative we wish them to believe. Something that allows them to feel safe. And then we repeat it until it becomes their truth." He clasped his hands behind his back again. "At some point, not even direct evidence can sway them from their new truth. The human mind is really quite remarkable."

Manfrid fell silent, looking from Hoerst to Stefan, a satisfied smile on his face. Before Hoerst could compliment him on his progress, Stefan spoke.

"But aren't they dangerous?" He looked away from Manfrid and spoke to Hoerst. "This… procedure, though it might be effective… Well, it sounds like it would leave their minds broken. How can we be sure they will conform to our wishes?" His eyes flicked to Manfrid, then he leaned toward Hoerst and spoke with a quiet urgency. "I was there. The night that black-haired witch wrecked the fortress. I saw what she can do." He shuddered visibly. "She was sane, at least."

It was a good point. Hoerst had to admit, he often felt uneasy around Aife, the first *graduate* of Manfrid's program. He often wondered what recourse he would have if the sullen witch decided she didn't need him. He looked at Manfrid, expectantly.

Manfrid's smile widened. "Well, this is the best part. You see, people…" His head waggled from side to side. "Many people, anyway, have a deep-seated need for a paternal figure. Someone they can rely on to tell them right from wrong, truth from lies, and this is especially true if they perceive the world as uncertain and dangerous. Once their mind is made vulnerable, one need merely implant such a figure."

"The emperor," Stefan said.

Manfrid stared in horror at Stefan. "Daga, no!" He gestured to Hoerst. "The Malleus." He shrugged and adopted a dismissive tone. "They might seem dangerous. Are, in fact, quite dangerous. But I can assure you, they will do anything to please their father figure. The Malleus."

Hoerst could tell Stefan wasn't convinced, and he was sympathetic. But what choice did he have? "Very good, Brother Manfrid. I see you *have* made significant progress. I'm sure I can expect that to continue." Manfrid almost shivered at the praise. "Now, can we meet them?"

Manfrid became businesslike again. "Yes, of course. Your message said you wanted the most powerful, the most reliable subjects. Those criteria are often at odds, but in weighing various considerations, I chose these three. Although, as I mentioned, they are instrumental in our programming efforts and their absence will set us —"

Hoerst lifted a hand in a placating gesture. "I have said, I understand." He gestured to the door and dipped his head.

Manfrid gave him a quick nod, opened the door, leaned out into the outer office and stepped back.

The three women who prowled into his office reminded Hoerst of Aife. There was a feralness about them. It was in the way they moved, like wary predators entering an unfamiliar den. They wore short tunics and leathers tucked into calf-high boots. The garments were like those worn by many of the Brochen caste from mountainous regions. But isolated in their remote fortress, these women obviously developed a unique identity. The sides of their heads were shaved, leaving a wide strip of hair. Intricate tattoos, similar to those worn by the Sisters of the Seidi, adorned their scalps. Leather torques ringed their throats, and they wore intricately wrought silver bands around their upper arms.

Wide eyes roved his office warily. When they found Stefan, subtle predatory shifts in their posture sent a thrill of fear through Hoerst. Seeing Stefan's discomfort, one of the women laughed. Her blond hair fell in a braid down her back. Hoerst was startled to see she wore the manacles the Inquisition recently designed to disarm witches. Iron mittens encased the hands, forcing the fingers to curl into fists, preventing the witch from channeling spirits.

She lifted her hands and rattled the heavy chain that connected the mittens in Stefan's face. "These are my *muzzle!*" Stefan nearly fell backward off his chair, sending the woman into gales of laughter.

Hoerst didn't blame him. No matter how often he worried about Aife, she was never so volatile as this woman. The other two watched the exchange with small grins. Gathering his courage, he cleared his throat. The women's heads snapped around to glare at him. His breath caught, and though he maintained an outward composure, there was a frightening moment when he saw all his plans falling to ruin.

And then the women recognized him. They seemed to shrink, their coiled menace melting away. They turned to face him, dropped their heads, and peeked up at him. Hoerst let his breath whisper out between parted lips. Not for the first time, he looked forward to the day he could rid the world of these creatures. But not yet.

Manfrid, a smug smile on his face, said, "Malleus, may I introduce my most successful subjects? In truth, they are like daughters to me." Hoerst was sure he saw a curled lip on the woman standing closest to Manfrid. Manfrid rested a hand on her shoulder, eliciting a small flinch he didn't appear to notice. "This is Macha." Manfrid leaned forward. "She is the only one I have who can insert the *sjel'and* into our subject's minds."

Ignoring the faint note of accusation in the brother's voice, Hoerst said, "She's Andian." The woman's eyes came up and met Hoerst's for a moment, before she dipped her head again. Her skin was the rich mahogany of Hoerst's desk. Her hair fell down her back in long dreadlocks.

"Yes," Manfrid said. "As you know, despite the purge, there are still scattered pockets of Andian in the western swamps." Manfrid patted her shoulder. "As many Andian witches have, Macha has an affinity with animals, most especially birds."

"Birds?" Stefan blurted and seemed to instantly regret it when the women's heads pivoted toward him.

Ignoring Stefan's outburst, Hoerst nodded to the woman in the middle, whose long black hair hung loose. "Vollen?" he asked.

"No," Manfrid said. "Neiman is Ferol." One eyebrow climbed his forehead. "One of Neiman's gifts is the ability to induce fear, as I described earlier."

Hoerst's eyes slid to the blond woman wearing the mitten cuffs. "You assured me they were not dangerous."

"And they are not. To you… or me, that is." He nodded to the blond woman, who was peeking at Hoerst, a small grin curling her lips. "Eriu can be volatile. The cuffs are only there to keep her out of trouble." He paused, then spoke slowly. "She will obey you and Macha, but you must be very clear in your instructions." He cleared his throat. "She can be mischievous."

"She's *Alle'oss*," Hoerst said and noted the twist to her mouth when he said the word.

"Yes," Manfrid said.

"What is it you want of us?"

Surprised, Hoerst met Macha's gaze. She stared at him, obviously fighting the urge to drop her head again. The other women, their heads still tipped forward, watched her out of the corner of their eyes. Perhaps the one wearing the cuffs wasn't the one he had to worry about, after all.

"I want you to hunt down and kill three *Alle'oss* witches," Hoerst said.

Chapter 2

The 15th Day of the Month of Annenmon

Minna

"I have a surprise for you," Ulf said.

They were walking along the road that led from the village of Fennig to the stables Ulf's family owned. There was still snow in the shadowy places, but spring's warm breath was in the air. Minna smiled up at him. "A surprise, huh?"

"Do you want to guess?" Ulf asked, then waved his hands and said. "No, never mind, you'll never guess."

They walked shoulder to shoulder, speaking of small things, aware they were both ignoring the looming clouds of war. It was an unspoken agreement. They would not discuss what happened the previous winter or the uncertainties of what was to come. Not yet. The *lan'and*, spirits of the land flitted in and out of the trees, though only Minna could see the small luminous orbs. Linea, her spirit guide, zigzagged across the road in front of them, greeting her fellow spirits.

The stable and attached corral came into view on the left side of the road. They climbed through the rails and Minna looked across the road to the Lothan's home. Smoke rose from the chimney, but no one was in the yard. She spent almost as much time in their cozy home as she did in her own since returning from *Helala*.

"Stop," Ulf said. He stepped in front of her, blocking her view of the interior of the stables. "Close your eyes."

She leaned out to peer past him. "Something in the stables?" Linea swooped past Ulf into the dim interior.

"Yes! Just close your eyes. And no fair using Linea to peek."

When she complied, he took her arm and led her inside, then turned her. Remembering the layout in her mind's eye, she guessed she was facing one of the stalls.

"Okay, open your eyes."

Minna opened her eyes to find a familiar horse regarding her. "Edda!" she exclaimed. It was the horse she rode when she and Ulf left Fennig the previous winter, the one she thought lost for good when the Empire attacked the *Alle'oss* camp where she met the old *saa'myn*, Beadu. She extended a hand and let Edda nuzzle her palm. "Where did you find her?"

"My brother, Tamas, was checking the snow in the Breakheart Pass. He met some others and one of them was riding Edda." He patted the horse's neck.

"How did he get her back?"

"He was sketchy on the details," Ulf said. "You can ride her when we leave, if you want."

There it was. Minna sighed and turned to face him. Without a word, he pulled her into his arms and held her. "What did Tamas say about the pass?" she murmured into his chest.

"Another week," Ulf said. "We're leaving on Freienlatha. I was going to tell you. I just wanted…"

"I know." They held one another quietly. "I wish this was all there was. This moment."

"Yeah," Ulf said. "But it can never be the same. I mean, it's all the same. The house, the people, the chores. But nothing is the same. It's all so…"

"Empty."

"Meaningless," Ulf said at the same time.

They fell silent again until Minna asked, "Do you think we'll ever be able to have a normal life?"

Ulf chuckled. "What would a normal life be like for you?"

Minna pulled her head back so she could look up at him. "A house in the forest. A cozy, warm house. Two children, a boy and a girl." She looked at his chest and gave a small laugh. "Hunting, teaching my children to hunt. Festivals, stories by the fire, crisp autumn days and those snowy winter days when the forest is so quiet." She fell silent, her smile fading. Then she laid her head back on his chest. "All of that."

"That sounds wonderful," Ulf said. After a moment, he asked, "Are you worried about… what will happen?"

"Yes. I keep replaying what Ragan said, trying to figure out what she wanted me to do." Her birth mother, a powerful seer, worked for years to manipulate the future. All she told Minna was she hoped to bring about a future free of the Empire's evil. Unfortunately, she died before she told Minna her plans.

"Are you sure she wanted it to be you to figure that out?" Ulf asked. "Maybe Aron and Zaina know what the plan is. They knew her a long time."

Minna nodded against his chest. "That's what I'm hoping."

"You know you don't have to win this war all by yourself," Ulf said. "I know you're really powerful and all, but the rest of us will help you fight. You aren't alone."

Minna stiffened, but pressed her lips shut before she said anything. Of her many fears, her biggest was for Ulf. He had let hints drop he wanted to join the fledgling *Alle'oss* army. Minna had said nothing, hoping, by not bringing attention to it, he would forget it. She didn't know what Ragan wanted her to do, but she was sure she wouldn't be able to protect Ulf and do what she needed to. She half hoped he remained in Fennig, but that was unrealistic. Instead, she determined to steer him to ways to be useful other than fighting.

"Is something wrong?" he asked.

She pulled back, leaving their fingers entwined. "No," she said with a sad smile. "This is nice. It's just… I can't let anyone else, especially my parents, see me worry."

Ulf nodded and gave her that lopsided grin she loved so much. "You know you can be yourself with me. Always. If you need to worry… and I don't know anyone who has more right to… you can do it with me."

"I know."

They turned toward Edda, and stood close, enjoying the peace, surrounded by the comforting scents of horse, hay and whiffs of the forest coming to life after a long winter. "My ma made a pie with the last of the winter apples this morning," Ulf said. "It's a little mealy, but still good. You want a piece?"

Minna let a grin grow on her face. "No cherry pies?"

"You know what they say about beggars and choosers," he said, taking her hand and leading her toward the exit.

Minna put her worries away once again, determined to enjoy their last carefree days together.

Alyn

Alyn sat back, picked up an ink-stained rag, and absently wiped the nib of her quill. With a sigh, she let her chin drop to her chest, stretching the knot that tightened as she bent over the translation. The happy voices of children, freed from their schoolwork for the day, drifted through an open window. It must be later than she thought. The children were playing in the large communal space at the center of *Helala*. The village was founded by Ragan, Alyn's birth mother, as a sanctuary for the Empire's young victims. A group of *lan'and*, drawn to the children's happiness, swirled in the air above them, their glittering light illuminating the long shadows cast by the mountains that cradled the village on three sides. Most of the girls could see the small orbs of light because they had spirit sight. The *Alle'oss* brought the girls here to hide them from the Inquisition, which would twist them to their own ends. Or kill them if they found them wanting.

That would have been Alyn's fate if she hadn't escaped the Inquisition prison the previous winter.

A smile lifted the corners of her lips as she watched the girls leaping up, as if they could catch the small spirits in their hands. The *lan'and* seemed to enjoy the game, swooping down then dodging away, though no one could actually touch them. Her smile faded as she wondered if one of the spirits would choose to be her spirit guide. A spirit guide introduced the *saa'myn* to the spirits in the other realms. Not everyone was chosen. She knew it was foolish to worry about it. Minna had thirteen summers when Linea chose her. Alyn had only eleven summers now. Still, while Minna would be defending Argren from the Empire, Alyn was stuck going to school in *Helala*. It was hard not to feel left behind. She wasn't a child. After all, she nearly escaped from the Inquisition on her own, before Minna arrived. She caught herself biting her lower lip, then shook her head and pressed her lips together. She never noticed that habit until someone suggested it made her look like Minna.

Sighing, she cupped her hands in her lap and let her gaze drop to Ragan's journal, which lay open on her desk. The old *saa'myn*, Beadu, told Alyn her mother was the greatest seer who ever lived. Alyn didn't know if that was true. All she knew was that her mother left her family so that she might change the future. Before Alyn was born, Ragan had a vision of the Inquisition killing her family. Instead of accepting her fate, she determined to steer the future to one in which her family survived and her daughters helped rid the world of the Empire's evil. Now, Minna was off helping to fulfill Ragan's vision and Alyn was stuck in *Helala*, doing nothing useful.

Ragan told Minna she hoped her journal would help her understand. Minna accepted Ragan's explanation for why she left, had even adopted their mother's cause as her own. But Minna met Ragan, talked to her, watched her die at the hands of the witch, Aife. Maybe that made a difference. To Alyn, Vada Hunter would always be her mother. Ragan was the woman who abandoned her not long after she was born. Nothing she translated in the journal, so far, changed her mind.

"I'm just bored," she said to the empty room. "And worried."

Not that her days weren't full. She spent her mornings with Beadu, learning the lore of the *saa'myn*, which turned out to be a lot more than spirits. Before the Empire came, the *saa'myn* were her people's spiritual leaders, healers, judges. There was so much to learn. Though it was dry, she could see the importance of learning the law as the *Alle'oss* saw it. The herb lore was fascinating and she could understand the necessity of learning the history of the *Alle'oss*. But though the mythologies her people held dear before the Empire came were interesting, she couldn't see the purpose of learning about fairies, sprites and the like. Beadu told her the myths held lessons, but if they did, they were lessons beyond Alyn's understanding.

She spent the afternoons in the school taught by Deirdre and Brother Xander. Being the oldest student in the school, and Minna's sister, gave her a sense of what Minna must experience. With Minna gone, the children turned their adoration on her, whispering when she passed and rarely leaving her alone. Though she tried to accept it all with the same grace as Minna, something about being Minna's substitute didn't sit right with her. She wasn't Minna, couldn't call forth wind spirits or fire spirits. She might never be able to.

She let her gaze drop to the parchment on which she wrote her translation. She and Minna never learned to read while growing up. They were excluded from the school in Fennig because of Minna's spirit sight. Learning to read was easy for Alyn, but Ragan wrote her journal in Ancient Vollen. The archaic language was complex, so translating it was a slow process. She read the last paragraph she translated.

Thomas was thrilled when I told him he would have another daughter. I don't know what to do. I'm now confident the future the sjel'and are showing me will come to pass, and Beadu agrees. It is long past the time I should tell Thomas what I've seen. But how can I when he is so happy? He takes Minna with him for walks in the forest, already wanting to teach her everything he knows. She's too young to understand, of course, but their shining faces when they return speak of their happiness. I will tell him, as Beadu has been urging. I just want to give him a few more days without worry.

Alyn touched her father's name with her index finger, then lifted it when the still damp ink smudged. "Zut," she murmured, picked up the rag and wiped her finger. Ragan must have been talking about Alyn when she wrote another daughter. She smiled at the thought her father was thrilled when he found out Ragan was pregnant. The smile fell away and her brow wrinkled as she imagined how devastated her father must have been when Ragan told him he would have to raise his daughters alone.

Standing, she picked up the journal. She hesitated, looking down at the translation, then turned away, leaving it on her desk. After returning the journal to the cabinet behind her desk, she left the small room Deirdre gave her to do her translations, and made her way to the front door of the empty community building. She paused in the shadows inside the front doors, looking out at the villagers gathering for the evening meal. Then, with a sigh, she hitched a smile onto her face and stepped into the sunlight.

Harold

Harold slipped around the corner of the Monk's Habit, into a shadowy alley, then peered back into the street, searching for purposeful movement among the few people out this time of night. From the outside, the seedy alehouse wasn't much to look at, but that was the point. There was little to connect him to the place beyond the short time he wallowed here after his former lover, Karl, betrayed him. The last time he was in the Monk's Habit, Aron appeared, bringing Ragan's cryptic message. His fingers rubbed the scar left by Aron's knife and chuckled softly. You couldn't say he didn't have an interesting love life.

The few people on the street had the look of long-time Fallows residents, a neighborhood that never failed to place its stamp on anyone unlucky enough to reside there. Confident he wasn't followed, he entered the alehouse. He paused inside the door, letting his eyes adjust to the dark interior. It was strangely comforting to find it exactly as he left it. Even the aroma of stale ale was welcoming. He could swear the same people occupied the same tables, as if time froze when he last left. Louisa, the barmaid, smiled when she saw him and wove through the tables to join him, bantering with the patrons as she came.

After admonishing him for being away so long, she leaned in and said in a conspiratorial tone, "Someone sitting at your table." She glanced over her shoulder. "Looks official like. Got people nervous. You expecting someone?"

"Yes, he's with me," Harold said with a grin. "Your finest ale, Louisa."

"Of course," she said with a wink, and turned away.

Harold made his way toward the shadowy tables along the right wall and found Henrik where Louisa said he would be. Watching the taciturn brother, Harold understood why he made the people in the room nervous. The sergeant lifted his ale stiffly to his lips, and let his eyes scan the room over the rim of the mug, looking like a villain in a Styrian melodrama. When he noticed Harold, he slammed the mug down, sloshing ale on the table, and stood up.

"Sir," he said, then shut his mouth. "Uh, I mean, Harold." His eyes darted around at the people watching them and said loudly, "Finally. I thought you forgot."

Harold dropped into a seat and motioned for Henrik to sit. Louisa set a mug in front of him, glanced at Henrik with a lifted brow, then left. Harold took a sip of the brown ale, set it down, and wiped his lips with his hand. "Not your cup of tea, Henrik? This clandestine stuff?"

Henrik hesitated, then an affronted frown appeared. "I was careful coming here." He folded his arms on the table, his indignation doing much to ease his awkwardness. "Not that your directions were easy to follow."

"I sent you around a bit to throw off any tail," Harold said, grinning.

"Well," Henrik conceded. "I think it worked." He looked out across the room. "Not sure it's going to do any good. This lot made me as soon as I came in. They must not get many strangers in here."

Harold returned the wave of Renard, the proprietor. "Don't get many tourists in this neighborhood. It doesn't look like much, but the Monk's Habit is probably the safest place to drink in the Fallows. It has a loyal clientele, who like to keep it that way. I'm counting on the fact they won't want to bring unwanted attention to the place."

Henrik grunted and the two of them fell silent, sipping their ale.

Finally, Henrik glanced around, leaned forward, and said, "So, what do you think we should do?"

Harold tapped the table with his knuckles. Wasn't he in the exact same predicament the last time he was here; waiting for Ragan to tell him what to do? It was Ragan who brought Harold and Karl together, though Harold didn't know it. It was all so Karl could deliver Ragan's cryptic hint. When Harold followed it, he discovered Malleus Hoerst was kidnapping *Alle'oss* witches for some unknown reason. He had no idea what to do with that information, so he waited to hear from a mysterious woman who turned out to be Ragan. It was Aron who delivered her message. The brief memory of Aron draped across this same chair brought a flush to his cheeks. Aron's hint sent Harold on a quest which culminated in the dramatic rescue of Minna's sister from the Inquisition prison.

As far as Harold could tell, the others escaped, but Harold remained behind at Ragan's request. He told her it was a crazy idea, but she assured him she had a good reason. The only problem was, she didn't tell him what that was, and he and Henrik hadn't heard from her. What was so important that they risk their lives?

He trusted her. After all, hadn't she earned it? Unfortunately, their time was running out. He told Ragan the Malleus would never believe the wild story they concocted to cover their complicity in the rescue. Ragan told him it wouldn't matter. So far, she had been right. The Malleus, and his stooge, Stefan, gave them some rope, hoping to glean information about the *Alle'oss* resistance, no doubt, but how long would it be before they lost patience? If Ragan didn't contact them soon, it would be too late.

He looked at Henrik, who was watching him expectantly. "I don't know," he said. Henrik looked as if he expected that answer. "We wait, for now, but let's come up with an escape plan. Just in case."

"Right," Henrik said and stood. "I have those reports to finish before tomorrow." He took one more swallow of his ale, set it down and said,

"Soon as you hear something." Harold nodded, and Henrik made his way to the door.

Harold watched heads swivel as Henrik passed, their eyes turning his way after he left.

Chapter 3

The 15th Day of the Month of Annenmon

Aron

Aron watched the carpenters working on the wooden stockade the *Alle'oss* were erecting across the highway at the top of the Wollen Cut. The Cut rose from the lowlands below the long escarpment that separated the southern Vollen Empire from the *Alle'oss* homeland of Argren. Sheer granite walls bordered the highway as it climbed through the Cut. Other than a frighteningly narrow set of stairs carved into the cliff face, the Cut was the only way to reach the top without traveling leagues to the north or south. The stockade wasn't much of a barrier, but the Empire would have to spend men and time to break through. He pulled his cloak tighter against a chill westerly wind, turned and walked along the edge of the Cut toward the rim of the escarpment.

Zaina and Keelia were waiting at the point where the Cut opened out into the lowlands. Their posture suggested the camaraderie that grew between the two warriors in recent weeks. Morning sun brought out the ruby highlights in Keelia's hair, a bashful reminder of her *Alle'oss* heritage. The two women didn't turn as he approached, but gave him grim nods when he joined them. He looked out at the Imperial city of Hast visible in the distance, just on the other side of the brown ribbon of the Odun River. But what drew his attention was the Imperial soldiers spread across the plains east of the river.

"What have we here?" he asked.

"The vanguard of the Ninth Legion," Keelia said. "I expect the rest of them will arrive over the next week."

Aron grunted and watched in silence. The wind lifting his hair away from his face brought whiffs of wood smoke. "Looks like they're getting settled."

"Imperial doctrine," Keelia said. "A legion makes the same camp everywhere they stop. By the end of the day, they'll have the road network laid out and a moat dug. It's like a small village."

Aron stared at her, then caught Zaina's eye. "Road network?" Keelia nodded. "How… how many we talking about?" he asked as casually as he could.

"Ten, twelve thousand, depending," Keelia said with a shrug. "Last I heard, the Ninth was in the thick of it with the Kaileuk. I doubt they've had time to replace their losses."

Most of the villages in Argren had a population a fraction of what the Ninth Legion would bring to their borders. Zaina must have noted the concern in Aron's expression, because she said, "We knew it wouldn't be easy."

Aron glanced over his shoulder at the handful of *Alle'oss* archers watching the Imps with more confidence than he felt. Not easy and impossible were so close as to be nearly inseparable. Chance. A bit of luck. Not for the first time, he lamented his mother's death. He became so reliant on her visions of the future, he felt blind since she died. When Zaina looked away, he returned his gaze to the west. "Yes, we did. We knew that," he said. "But I guess my questions are why a whole legion and why here?"

Keelia took a breath and blew it out. "As to the first question… that is curious, isn't it?" She lifted her gaze toward the southwest horizon. "They rotate the legions out of the front line to rest them. I can only assume the Ninth was in reserve when the emperor recalled them. Even so, if the Kaileuk figure it out, they'll take advantage. If they break through like they did near Ulm last year, the Empire will have no reserves to plug the hole." She shrugged. "Seems to me the emperor is taking an unnecessary risk, especially when you consider…" She glanced back at the *Alle'oss* archers, bringing the tattoo that covered the left side of her face into view, the mark of a sister of the Seidi. As one of the more powerful members of that magical sisterhood, Keelia fought against the Kaileuk for the Empire. That was before the pull of her *Alle'oss* heritage overcame her loyalties to her Seidi sisters. She didn't continue, but she didn't have to. More *Alle'oss* were arriving to join the fight every day, but the Ninth Legion would dwarf their army and few *Alle'oss* were experienced fighters.

"It's Minna," Zaina said. "Powerful she may be, but with that many men, they hope to overwhelm her."

"But the cliffs are easily defended," Aron said. "Once we fortify the Cut, it will be nearly impregnable with Minna here. Which brings me back to my second question. Why not north or south, beyond the cliffs?"

"The legions are trained to fight on open ground or to attack fortified positions." Keelia turned around and swept her hand toward the mountains. "Argren is too rugged for cavalry. Infantry would have a better chance, but to be most effective, heavy infantry need to maintain their tight formations and close with an enemy. Neither of those is possible in the mountains. The Imps learned lessons in the mountains of Styria. Infantry formations loosen on uneven ground. The Styrians would pick them off from a distance or wait until the formations stretched out on narrow roads and ambush them. Once they did as much damage as they could, they would melt away. The Imps could never get close enough to use their advantages." She looked to the west again. "They'll use the Imperial Rangers in the mountains. They're trained for that."

"This is how it will play out," she said and gestured toward the soldiers making camp. "The Ninth is here to keep most of the *Alle'oss* army, and Minna, pinned down. I expect they'll start probing our defenses soon after they're all here. They'll want to find out what they're up against and they don't mind spending a few lives to do it. If they can force the Cut and take out Minna, so much the better. They'll use the rangers in the north and the south to keep us spread out and wear us down. When they're sure of the situation, they'll attack en mass on all fronts. We need to survive that. Somehow. It will give us some time for… whatever we're going to do."

They watched men digging a moat around the Imperial camp in silence for a while. "It's a good plan," Aron said finally.

"When is Minna getting here?" Keelia asked.

"Breakheart Pass is still snowed in," Zaina said. "Another two weeks, maybe."

"Who's covering the gap north of the Cut?" Keelia asked.

"*Oss'stera*. They're a resistance group that has been fighting the Empire in northern Argren for nearly ten years," Zaina said. "They have a lot more experience than we do."

Keelia's eyes narrowed. "Oss…"

"Our struggle," Zaina said. "It's an old *Alle'oss* construction. They're easily a match for the rangers in a standup fight. It's just a numbers game. We have to kill ten for each one we lose."

"*Oss'stera* is sending some people to stiffen our resistance and help us train new recruits. Our biggest worry is the Imps will infiltrate south of the escarpment and find *Helela*," Aron said. He got Keelia's attention. "I'm making it your responsibility to make sure that doesn't happen. Take two hundred archers south and cover the land between the end of the escarpment and the coast. Keep them from finding *Helala*."

Keelia studied him. As a veteran of the Empire's wars, Keelia had more military experience than anyone in Argren. She knew what an impossible task he was handing her. "Two hundred?"

"It's all we can spare," Aron said.

She looked out toward the vanguard of the Ninth without answering. He thought she might refuse, but finally, she nodded and said, "I pick my people."

"Of course."

She returned his nod, then watched the Imps making their camp in silence. After a short while, she asked the question Aron was dreading. "Did Ragan give you any hints for how we can win this war?"

Aron blew out a breath and dropped his gaze.

"I take it that means no," Keelia said. When Aron didn't respond, she said, "Seems like an oversight." She gestured toward the west. "She sets all this in motion, then conveniently dies, leaving us to pick up the pieces."

The virulence of the rebuke was so unexpected from the taciturn Keelia, Aron didn't react at first. But the question fanned the barely contained anger he felt toward his mother. From the time she adopted him when he had ten summers, she relentlessly pursued an impossible goal; to rid the world of the corrupt Empire. A former novice of the Seidi with the gift of prophecy, she used her glimpses into the future to manipulate events. For years, he ran her errands, often committing questionable acts for her without complaint. He did it because he loved and trusted her and because he believed in her goal. She repaid his trust and loyalty by abandoning him, leaving him with nothing to tell him how to carry the burden she left him. That Keelia was right didn't temper the anger her question unleashed. He opened his mouth to respond with ill-chosen words when Zaina interrupted.

"She didn't leave us a plan," she said, her usual calm blunting the hot tip of his anger. "But she would not have set everything in motion without having a plan." She and Keelia gazed at one another. "We just have to find out what she intended."

Keelia looked to the west. "She leave you any clues how we do that?"

Precious few, but Aron wasn't going to admit that. "Some," he said. Keelia gave him a quizzical look. He started to tell her they were still working on it when he glanced at the Imperial camp and was suddenly reminded of something Ragan mentioned shortly before she died. "Ragan told me not to take the loyalty of the Imperial military for granted. Is there any truth to that?"

Keelia shrugged. "Grumbling among the rank and file is rampant. They've been fighting this war for years and there's no end in sight. Many of them are conscripts from the Brochen caste. It wouldn't take much to foment rebellion among them, but if they refuse to fight, the Kaileuk will sweep across the Empire. You don't want that."

With the appealing image of Kaileuk hordes burning Imperial cities in his mind, Aron was about to disagree when Keelia spoke again.

"There is one man who might be a possibility," she said. "Victor Storm. He's a General of the Imperial Cavalry. The emperor made him a marshal for the duration of the war, so he's in overall command. A brilliant tactician. Probably the only reason the Empire is still holding its own."

Zaina caught Aron's eye. When Keelia noticed, she asked, "What?"

Zaina cleared her throat. "Ragan never mentioned Victor Storm, but she mentioned a Sera Storm."

"Sera? That's Victor's daughter. What did Ragan say about her?"

"There are two realm walkers we know of alive today," Aron said. Realm walkers could enter the realm of the dead. While in that bleak world, time in the physical world appeared to slow so that the realm walker could disappear and appear at another spot in an instant. Aron was one of those people. "But there will soon be one more."

"Sera?" Keelia asked.

Aron nodded, and they all fell silent, each considering the possibilities.

"The Storms would have to live in the Imperial District, wouldn't they?" Zaina asked.

"A stone's throw from the palace," Aron said. "An experienced realm walker could easily find their way past security and into the emperor's private chambers."

Keelia eyed him. "I know Sera. She's a good person. I would hate to put her in jeopardy."

"The life of one person against thousands," Aron said. "Besides, if she's clever, she can get in, kill the emperor and get out alive."

Keelia's lips pursed. "I'm not sure she's the kind of person who could do that. Killing someone is a hard thing. Most people can wield a blade against people trying to kill them, but not everyone can commit murder. Especially in cold blood. Besides, killing Ludweig wouldn't end the war."

"No, but it would sow chaos," Zaina said. "Might take the pressure off and give us time."

"When is she supposed to get this ability?"

"Maybe she already has," Aron said hopefully. "How would we contact her?"

"Someone we know who has access to the Imperial District," Keelia said.

"Harold Wolfe," Aron and Zaina said at the same time.

"You in touch with him?" Keelia asked.

"We're working on it," Zaina said after a pause.

"Sera is a smart girl," Keelia said. "She can make her own decisions. You just make sure you let her know what she's getting into."

"Don't worry," Aron said with a wide smile. "If what you say about Victor Storm is true, we wouldn't want to get on his bad side."

She gazed at him for a long moment, then nodded and said, "I'm going to get organized. I'll be leaving for the south in two days." When Aron nodded, she turned and walked back along the edge of the Cut.

Zaina watched her go. "You sure about using Sera like this?"

"Why else would Ragan let slip that Sera will be a realm walker?" Aron asked. He met her skeptical gaze and said, "Speak up if you have a better plan. Until and unless we have something better, we use what we have."

Zaina nodded, and they turned to watch the Imps making their village.

Part I

Brennan

As one who has spent too much time among the *sjel'and* of *annen'heim*, it has always astonished me how Ragan sifted through the limitless possibilities to identify those few people who held the threads of her plans in their hands. Harold Wolfe was such a person. When Ragan left him in Brennan, he couldn't know he would be the catalyst who set so many on their proper courses.

From Alyn Hunter's commentary on The Book of the Witch by Ragan Hunter

Chapter 4

The 28th Day of the Month of Annenmon
Year 1143 of the Imperial Era

Victor

Marshal Victor Storm walked along the parapet that overlooked the training yard. He returned the salute offered by a guard patrolling the alure atop the wall, then edged over to the crenelations along the outer wall. As he drew close to the training yard, the thock of practice swords rose above the sounds of the Imperial District. The sound stopped suddenly, then after a brief pause, a female voice shouted, "Not fair!" He smiled. That tone of outraged indignation was one he had become quite familiar with the past eighteen years.

The roof of the armory extended above the training yard, providing a vantage point from which he could look down without being observed. It was one of his favorite places to escape from the pressures of command when he was in Brennan. The scene before him was one he watched many times. Only two people were in the yard. The older one was his chief weapons instructor, Werner.

Werner, a veteran of many conflicts, was laughing. "What do you mean, not fair? What's fair got to do with fighting?"

The other person in the yard was Victor's daughter, Sera. Ignoring Werner's offered hand, she picked herself up from the sandy ground. After brushing herself off, she snatched up her sword and turned to face her instructor. Eyes narrowing, she said, "You said we were practicing advanced pairs form one. There are no leg sweeps in that form."

Werner chuckled and nodded. "You are correct, Sera. The form one has no leg sweeps and, as usual, your execution of the form was impeccable."

Sera threw her hands out to her side and scowled.

Werner turned serious and said, "Unfortunately, real fights are not forms. The forms train your body, they give you strength and facility with the blade. But that is all. Your form is always immaculate, Sera. Still, you must continue to practice the forms, as there is always something more to learn from them. For example, when you become so skilled at the form that your body is performing while your mind is elsewhere, you might get your legs swept." He cocked his head and grinned.

Sera stared at him, incredulous, then glowered and grumbled, "I still say there are no leg sweeps in advanced pairs form one."

Werner threw back his head and laughed. Then, taking a ready position, he shouted, "Again!"

Victor couldn't help smiling at the familiar scene. Sera was a bright, energetic young woman with a boundless curiosity. Yet, she had a heightened sense of injustice that constantly led her into trouble. He supposed she earned it the hard way. From her point of view, the fact she was a Volbroch, the daughter of a Volloch father and Brochen mother, wasn't her fault. So, when the Volloch children taunted her as a half-breed, she took umbrage. Victor didn't blame her, but no matter how often he counseled her to avoid fights she couldn't win, she wouldn't walk away.

He thought back to the day eight years before, when Sera came home with yet another black eye. In a moment of inspiration, he handed her off to Werner. He reasoned learning to use a sword would give her focus, let her burn off her inexhaustible energy, and allow her to feel less helpless.

And it worked. He worried Werner would object to teaching a girl. Women who were not sisters of the Seidi didn't fight in the Empire. But those worries proved unfounded. After a wary start, Werner and Sera took to one another like long-lost friends.

Watching the two sparring, it appeared to his trained eye that Sera was very nearly the old veteran's match. She made remarkable progress in the year since he last watched them practice. He came back from the front only at the insistence of the emperor. Ludweig II said he wanted to honor him with a ball to celebrate a recent victory over the Kaileuk. If the past was any guide, the emperor would be sure to offset any honors bestowed on Victor with petty slights. Victor almost ignored the summons. Recalling him at such a precarious time was just another in a long line of foolish decisions by the emperor. He hoped there was something resembling stable lines when he returned. Giving his jacket a quick tug to straighten it, he turned crisply and returned along the parapet.

Sera

Sera untied the straps that bound her practice leathers, watching Werner out of the corner of her eye. Losing patience, she said, "Well?"

Werner glanced her way and returned to organizing the practice swords. "I swear I've told this new batch of recruits to keep this neat a hundred times."

Sera rolled her eyes. Forgetting her leathers, she stood and faced him. "You can try to ignore me, but you know I won't shut up until you answer me. You might as well tell me now to save us both the bother."

Werner threw his hands in the air and stepped back. "Why am I doing this? This should be their job." Dropping his hands to his hips, he turned to face Sera and adopted his instructor expression, which told Sera he was serious. "I've considered your request, Sera."

Her heart fell.

"And I think you are right. You need to spar against others to learn different fighting styles."

Sera opened her mouth, ready with her rehearsed rebuttal, then froze.

Werner gave her a satisfied smile. "Now close your mouth and get a move on. You're expected to attend the banquet tonight with your parents."

Sera was about to leap for joy until he mentioned the banquet. She frowned for a moment, then her face lit up. "Who? When?" she asked.

Werner turned, preparing to leave, but stopped and said, "I'm not sure yet. I'll let you know next week."

Sera watched him receding down the hallway, then sat to continue removing her leathers. "I still say there are no leg sweeps in advanced pairs form one." She mumbled it, but made sure it was loud enough for Werner to hear as he walked away. She couldn't see his face, but she knew it wore a smile.

Hoerst

The emperor sat back in his desk chair, gazing at Hoerst. The Malleus was curious how he would react. On the one hand, Ludweig made it clear he didn't want to know what Hoerst was doing with the Brochen witches. On the other hand, it wasn't often one had a chance to glimpse the future. Not in recent years, anyway. There were sisters of the Seidi with the gift of prophecy hundreds of years in the past, but the Seidi sisters were no longer as formidable as they once were. That was the reason Hoerst was forced to commit his sins. It wasn't so much that the emperor was a devout man. It was just that he didn't want his reputation tainted by rumors of blasphemy. He would prefer to let Hoerst do the dirty work. The Malleus also preferred it that way.

Ludweig sat forward and fixed Hoerst with a stare. Hoerst had to suppress his smile. The emperor was an imposing man, with a powerful presence. This stare was intended to show Hoerst who was in charge. He had seen men wilt under the emperor's regard. Hoerst met the emperor's eyes and remained silent.

After long moments, the emperor looked away. "You're saying this…" He waved a hand. "This Brochen witch had a vision of my future."

"Yes," Hoerst said. "Although, it is more correct to say she witnessed the vision the spir —"

The emperor slammed his palm on the surface of his desk. "I don't want to hear about your blasphemies. Just tell me what the vision revealed."

"I suggest you let her tell you what she saw," Hoerst said.

"You want me to talk to the witch?"

"I assumed you would wish to question her."

Ludweig sat back, his eyes roaming the office. Finally, he said, "Yes, I suppose that is wise." He looked up at Hoerst. "But you know what she saw?"

Hoerst hesitated. Given the subject of the vision, he couldn't guess how Ludweig would react, but if he asked the witch whether she told Hoerst, she wouldn't lie. When in doubt, the truth was the safest course. "Yes, Your Eminence."

Ludweig studied him, no doubt trying to glean the nature of the vision from Hoerst's expression. "Is she here?" he asked finally.

"No. Your office would be much too public. She's waiting in your drawing room. We can go down right now."

"No. I must listen to the blood traitor's complaints first." When Hoerst lifted a brow, the emperor said, "Victor Storm." He motioned toward his office door. "We'll go see the witch as soon as this is done."

Hoerst opened the door and found Marshal Storm, hands clasped behind his back, studying a painting of Ludweig's coronation. The marshal turned when he heard the door open and froze when he saw Hoerst. Quickly regaining his composure, he said, "Malleus. This is a surprise."

"Yes," Hoerst said. "It has been a long time. Not surprising, you being away at the front, keeping the Empire's enemies at bay." He smiled and said, "Congratulations on your victory at Ulm. The ball tonight is well deserved."

"I'm afraid we owe more to Sister Keelia for that victory." Victor watched Hoerst's face for a moment. "It's rather curious that Sister Keelia is not invited to the ball, is it not? In fact, considering how instrumental the sister has been in keeping the Empire safe from the Kaileuk, I'm surprised no one seems to have heard from her in months."

"Yes, quite. I suggest you take this up with the Malefica."

"I have. Visited the Seidi personally, but Malefica Briana would not see me."

Hoerst noticed the slight emphasis on Briana's name. So, Marshal Storm was suspicious of Briana's rise to the leadership of the Seidi. Not surprising. The former Malefica, Deirdre, was a favorite of the military. "The emperor will see you now," Hoerst said and gestured into the inner office.

Victor walked past him and stopped in front of the emperor's desk. "Your Eminence," he said with a slight bow.

The emperor, busying himself with a stack of papers on his desk, glanced up but didn't respond. Finally, after making the marshal wait for a full minute, he sat back and said, "Marshal Storm. What can I do for you?"

"As I have been summoned to Brennan for this… ball in my honor, I wanted to take advantage of the opportunity to reinforce the warnings I included in my latest reports."

The emperor didn't respond.

"You have read my reports?" Victor asked.

"I have heard of them," Ludweig responded.

Victor's face tightened. Hoerst fought the urge to intervene before the marshal said something stupid. He had no more love for the blood traitor than the emperor, but they would need all of his brilliance to keep the Kaileuk at bay until this matter in Argren was settled. To his relief, Victor calmed himself. When he spoke, his voice was measured.

"Then perhaps you *heard* the absence of the Ninth Legion has put the entire front at risk. The only reason it hasn't collapsed yet can only be put down to the Kaileuk's ignorance of their disappearance. But, I can assure you, they will discover it soon. Our patrols have turned up evidence of a major offensive. We will not be able to withstand the onslaught."

The emperor erupted, "They are savages!" He leapt to his feet and jabbed a finger at Victor. "You will find a way, or —"

Hoerst had to give the marshal credit. He hadn't even flinched in the face of the emperor's rage, but his voice had an edge when he cut the emperor off.

"What is the point of sending the Ninth to Argren?" Victor asked. "They are unsuited for the terrain, Argren is sparsely populated and the *Alle'oss* are not the Styrians. They have no history of warfare."

Red in the face, the emperor looked as if he would leap across his desk, so Hoerst hurried to intervene. "Your Eminence, if I may." Ludweig's surprised hesitation gave Hoerst time to speak. "Marshal, there are factors which you are not privy to that necessitate the Ninth's presence in Hast. Believe me, we understand your concerns. The legion will be returned to you as soon as possible."

Victor didn't look mollified, but before he could respond, the emperor spoke. "You just do your job, Marshal. Otherwise, you might find I'm not as tolerant of your personal choices."

Victor went still. His eyes flicked to Hoerst. The Malleus nearly reached out and put a hand on his shoulder to restrain him. Fortunately, the marshal merely asked, "Your Eminence?"

"You know what I mean," Ludweig said. "I only tolerate your Brochen wife and her half-breed spawn as long as you are useful. If that changes…"

Hoerst held his breath as Victor and the emperor stared at one another. Finally, Victor gave the emperor a slight bow. "We understand one another," he said. He nodded to Hoerst, spun on his heel and left the office. The Malleus let his breath sigh out, listening to the emperor fuming as he stalked around his office.

•   •   •

By the time they were standing outside his drawing room, the emperor had regained his composure. Ludweig had a towering anger, but the storm usually blew through quickly, allowing his reason to resume control. He took Hoerst's arm and stopped him before the Malleus opened the door.

"You are absolutely sure we need the Ninth in Hast?" he asked.

The lamp Hoerst carried cast deep shadows in the rugged terrain of the emperor's face. But even so, Hoerst could see something he never saw before in the man's expression. Fear. What was he going to think when the witch told him of the vision? Hoerst never expected the need to reassure Ludweig II to be among his many concerns. Not so soon. This too, he could lay at the feet of the black-haired witch. The attacks on the Inquisition and Seidi led by that witch affected the emperor more than Hoerst would have expected.

Hoerst nodded slowly. "Yes, Your Eminence," he explained once again. "The *Alle'oss* will have to defend the Cut. The legion's presence will fix the witches where they will be easy to find."

Hoerst kept his face blank as the emperor gazed at him. "And you're sure these…" He waved his hand at the door to his drawing room. "Your creations can kill the *Alle'oss* witches."

"Absolutely," Hoerst said. "The *Alle'oss* won't expect them. Their appearance will be masked by a surprise attack." The emperor already knew this, but he also knew that Victor Storm was right to be worried about the Kaileuk. "The presence of the Ninth on their doorstep is necessary to keep their eyes to the west. They will not expect an attack in their rear."

Ludweig wiped his hand across his mouth and looked to the side. "I'm forced to trust you in this matter," he said, "but wrap it up as quickly as possible. The sooner we can return the Ninth and deploy your… experiments to the front, the sooner we can rid ourselves of people like Victor Storm."

"Of course, Your Eminence."

Ludweig nodded to the door. "Let's get this over with."

Macha

Macha studied the portrait of the royal family set above a massive, cold hearth. The Malleus left her with only one lamp, but her spirit guide hovered by her shoulder, casting his light on the painting. The emperor and his wife sat in the center, the daughters sitting at their feet, the sons standing next to their father. Despite the family resemblance, the impression she got was of a group of strangers. Turning away, she let her gaze travel over what the Father called Ludweig's drawing room.

Macha supposed she must have had a family. Before. Her memories of her early life were fragmentary and fleeting. Not even her spirit guide could weave them together. The first memory she was reasonably sure of was the day she arrived in Narvik, the fortress where Manfrid and his staff raised her and her sisters. She didn't know how old she was, just that she was too young to be alone in the world. She arrived near death, starved, shivering in Narvik's harsh climate. Terrified by the ordeal that brought her there. Manfrid greeted her, wrapped her in his warm cloak, fed her and introduced her to the woman who would be her mother for the next ten years.

She shook her head, trying to rattle the disjointed memories of the ensuing years into some recognizable narrative. Vague memories of terror, anger, disorientation eclipsed long stretches of her life. But there was always Mother, Manfrid or one of the others to comfort her, to dry her tears and remind her she was loved.

She focused again on the drawing room, its obscene opulence revealed as her spirit guide drifted silently. She couldn't help comparing it to her spartan cell in Narvik. There was something not —

The door opened, and the Father entered, followed by a man Macha saw in the portrait. The emperor. She stood absolutely still, hands clasped in front of her, peeking at them from lowered eyes.

The emperor drew up when he saw her, a surprised expression chased by disgust. "It's Andian!"

The Father met her eyes and gave his head a small shake. "Yes, Your Eminence," he said.

The emperor stared at her, looking as if he might turn around and walk out, but then he spoke to Hoerst. "Tell her to tell me her vision."

Macha spoke before the Father could say anything. "It was not my vision."

Startled, the emperor glanced at her, then said to the Father. "What does she mean?"

Hoerst lifted a hand to Macha in a placating gesture. "Macha has the ability to force others to see visions, so technically, she is correct. The spir

— The vision was shown to another. However, she sees the visions, so she can relate its content."

The emperor studied Hoerst, glanced at Macha, then motioned for her to proceed.

"The vision showed a large room, white marble, rows of columns along the sides and a great chair."

"The throne room," the emperor said, his interest finally piqued.

"You were sitting on the raised platform on which the chair sits," Macha said.

"What was I doing?"

"Cowering," Macha said, careful to hide her glee at the flush that blossomed on the man's cheeks. She glanced at the Father. When she saw his disapproval, she dropped her eyes before continuing. "There was another person there. You were arguing. She held a sword."

"She?" the emperor asked.

"You lunged at her, and she thrust the sword into your heart." Macha lifted her head to look directly at the emperor's stunned face. "You died."

The room was silent for a moment, then the emperor erupted. "What does she mean?!" he asked Hoerst, throwing a hand toward Macha. "How do I know she isn't just making it up?"

Hoerst got Macha's attention. "Do you swear this is the vision you saw, and you have left nothing out and added nothing?"

"Yes, Father," Macha said.

Ludweig gaped at her. He shook his head and said, "I don't believe it." But then he asked, "Is it something that *will* happen, or can it be changed?"

"The sisters with the gift of prophecy lived long ago," Hoerst said. "But I have taken the liberty of having Malefica Briana study the archives. It seems it *is* possible to change the future. You merely need to avoid the circumstances revealed by the vision."

Ludweig considered this, his eyes darting between Hoerst and Macha. "Who was the woman?" he asked Macha. "In the vision. Did you see who it was?"

Macha smiled and nodded. She turned toward the painting of the emperor's family and pointed. "Her."

Chapter 5

The 28th Day of the Month of Annenmon

Sera

Sera tugged on the sleeves of the gown her mother forced her to wear to the banquet.

"Stop fidgeting," her mother whispered.

"I'm not fidgeting!" Sera mumbled. "It's just so tight around my shoulders."

"Unfortunately," her mother said, "gowns are designed for young women who don't swing swords around all day." Sera sighed, and her mother conceded, "Don't worry, we'll stay for dinner and then you and I can escape."

Victor, standing behind them, dipped his head so that only they could hear. "I'm sorry, Lyra, but we must all stay until the dancing begins after dinner."

Sera snagged a champagne flute from a passing server. Catching her father's disapproving frown, she said, "What? I'm eighteen. There has to be something to make these things tolerable." She took a sip and suppressed the urge to spit it back into the glass. Her eyes flicked up to her father's knowing smile. "Mmmm."

She let her gaze travel across the gathered Volloch elite waiting in the entrance hall of the palace for the arrival of the emperor and his family. The white uniform of an inquisitor among the dark formal suits drew her eye. She never met an inquisitor before. Curious, she watched him and was surprised he was nothing like she imagined. He laughed and smiled warmly. When he reached out and touched the arm of the person he was talking to, Sera nearly dropped her glass. She tugged on her father's sleeve to drag him away from the men he was talking to. Ignoring his exasperated scowl, she asked, "Why is Mom talking to an inquisitor?"

Victor glanced at the pair and leaned forward so he could whisper. "That is Harold Wolfe." He paused, causing Sera to look at him. "He's Volbroch."

Sera hesitated, letting her mind reassure her she heard correctly. Her head snapped around, and she watched the inquisitor throw back his head and laugh at something her mother said. "How is he an inquisitor?"

"A lot of people ask the same question," her father whispered. "Very mysterious."

"Do you know him?"

"Oh yes," her father said. He was quiet for a moment, then said, "Sera." When she looked at him, he said, "Inquisitor Wolfe is a good man. If you…" He glanced at his wife. "Or your mother ever run into… problems while I'm away, go to Harold Wolfe."

"What are you talking about? Are you worried something is going to happen?"

"No, of course not. Just… it's good to have someone in authority who can help when… *if* you need them." Her father looked uncharacteristically uncomfortable.

"Right, Dad. Harold Wolfe. I'll remember."

"Good. Yes," he said. "Well, I think I'll join them. You stay here so we can find you to enter the banquet hall together."

"Sure, Dad." She watched him walk away. It was rare for her father to be so… vague, and he sounded worried. She watched him carefully as he joined her mother and shook the inquisitor's hand. He laughed and kissed her mother on the cheek. Nothing out of place in that interaction. Deciding she was overreacting, she let her gaze drift.

Harold

Harold watched the marshal lean down to kiss his wife on the cheek and couldn't help smiling when she batted playfully at him. Such a simple gesture, nothing one wouldn't expect from two people in love, but he could almost hear the disapproving hisses from those standing nearby. A Brochen wife, public displays of affection. The marshal sure didn't seem to care what the other Volloch thought of him.

"Harold," Victor said. "You're just the man I want to see." He stepped closer, gazing at nearby groups. When he spoke, his relaxed stance was at odds with the intensity in his low voice. "I looked for you last winter. After the storm?"

Harold watched his profile, waiting for him to continue.

"I was told you were in the infirmary," Victor said and glanced at Harold for confirmation, before resting a hand on Harold's shoulder and pretending to laugh at something Harold said. "I've heard some unsettling rumors."

"Rumors?"

As Victor started to speak, the doors to the emperor's private wing opened, interrupting him. The arrival of the Imperial family was imminent. Giving his head a small shake, he stepped closer to Harold and dipped his head so he could murmur into Harold's ear. His wife stepped closer to block the view of anyone paying attention. "The Inquisition asked me to provide troops that night to patrol the harbor and guard the exits from the Imperial District."

"The exits?" Harold asked. He and Henrik already knew the escape did not go according to plan. The girls, Aron and Zaina, were supposed to go straight to the harbor after exiting the tunnels in the Great Cathedral.

The destruction at the Seidi was evidence they took another route. They concluded the escapees found their way to the Seidi through the tunnels, though they couldn't guess how that happened. Victor's furtiveness suggested he knew something.

"Yes," Victor said. "I thought it odd as well. Who would be trying to *escape* the Imperial District?"

"And did anyone attempt to escape?"

Instead of answering the question, Victor said, "There was apparently some conflict at the Seidi the same night. Something substantial. When I dropped by to see the new Malefica this week, they were still repairing the damage to the Great Hall."

"And with all those sisters there." Harold couldn't help a small grin. "Hard to imagine." After seeing what Minna was capable of, he was surprised the tower still stood.

"Yes. One would think they could protect their own house," Victor said. He glanced past Harold, then over his own shoulder. "But the oddest thing I saw that night was Sister Keelia, two brothers from your escort and a group of *Alle'oss* girls leaving through the postern gate. I would put that only minutes after the altercation at the Seidi."

Harold nodded, careful to control his expression. "*Alle'oss* girls in the Imperial District? Not something you would expect to see."

"And then there was the damage to the harbor the same night," Victor said.

"Too bad no one was guarding the postern gate or the harbor," Harold said.

"It was a fluid situation," Victor said, waving a hand. "Confusing, contradictory orders and there was that storm."

"Easy for a small group to slip through."

Victor caught his eye and held it for a moment, then he straightened and spoke in a normal voice. "I can't help feeling the recent concentration of forces on Argren's border is related, somehow."

"I'd say your intelligence branch is top-notch, as always."

"I would also say the *Alle'oss* won't stand a chance against the forces arrayed against them," Victor said. He turned to face Harold for the first time. "Yet, I'm wondering what's taking so long. An entire legion and every ranger company in the Empire should have swept through Argren by now. It's true the terrain isn't ideal for a legion, but the *Alle'oss* are few and peaceful. They are not the Styrians."

Harold studied Victor's carefully controlled expression. Did he know something, or was he just probing? He gave Victor's wife a significant look, then said, "Are you not concerned for the welfare of that peaceful people? The *Alle'oss*."

Victor glanced at his wife. "I'm concerned for the welfare of *all* the Empire's people. Regardless of caste. If the southern front were to collapse, no one would escape the Kaileuk's fury." He paused. "Is that not what we should all be concerned with?"

Ragan said she wanted to transform the Empire, without unleashing widespread devastation. During their trip to Brennan the previous winter, Harold quizzed her about what that entailed. She was, as usual, frustratingly terse, but one thing they both agreed on; the Kaileuk wouldn't simply recede into their swamps if they somehow managed to displace the Empire's authoritarian order. To transform the Empire, they would need the Imperial military's cooperation. Or at least their acquiescence. Harold studied Victor and his wife standing shoulder to shoulder, waiting patiently for his response. If there was anyone in the Imperial military he could trust, it would be Victor Storm.

Harold turned casually and surveyed the nearby groups. When he was sure no one was close enough to overhear, he leaned in and said, "There may come a time when you have a choice to make. When that time comes, just remember, there are people who are as concerned for *all* the Empire's citizens as you are."

"People?" When Harold didn't answer, Victor glanced up at the activity presaging the royal family's appearance on the balcony overlooking the entrance hall. "I would like to think these… people would feel comfortable approaching me on topics that concerned the welfare of the Empire."

Their eyes met and Harold said, "Understood."

"On another matter," Victor said, speaking quickly. "I'm returning south tomorrow."

Harold nodded.

"I wonder if I might ask you to keep an eye on Lyra and Sera for me," Victor said. "Nothing overt. Just keep your ear to the ground. If they are in need, I've asked them to seek you out."

Harold's response was interrupted by a fanfare announcing the arrival of the emperor and his family. They turned to watch the Imperial family appear on the balcony. He glanced at Victor. Was this the reason Ragan left him here? To make this connection? He didn't need prophesy to know Victor was a man they needed on their side. He looked down as Lyra entwined her fingers with her husband's. It would be hard to build a relationship with the marshal while he was at the front, but Harold would make it his business to ensure his family was safe.

Chapter 6

The 28th Day of the Month of Annenmon

Sera

Most of the Volloch of any consequence were already in attendance. The room was full of the banal banter that seemed to be a requirement for these affairs. Sera sipped her champagne, watching the pompous elite and putting words into their mouths.

"Oh yes," she said under her breath, watching the minister of the exchequer. "Of course, it's the gold toilets that really make the new summer house. Only the best for my bum."

Growing bored, she idly considered the empty flute. It wasn't as bad as she originally thought. She was considering tracking down a server for another glass, when a fanfare finally announced the arrival of the emperor's family. The crowd hushed and turned as one to watch them descend the stairs from the balcony. The emperor was in the lead, of course, his wife, Crysta, on his arm. Ludweig was tall and athletic, though she noted considerably more gray in his hair than she remembered. He paused at the top of the stairs, smiling and favoring a few special people with waves. Gracious as always, but something was off. When he looked back at his family standing behind him, his face hardened for a moment, and the smile that returned before he descended the stairs seemed forced.

The emperor's wife was tall and thin, with black hair piled artfully on top of her head. No gray in her hair. She was twenty years younger than the emperor. Speculation about their relationship, or lack of relationship, was one of the most popular sports among the Volloch aristocracy. Unlike the emperor, Crysta wore a pinched expression that never seemed to change. Sera's mother said it was as if she smelled something disagreeable once and the expression stuck.

Behind the royal couple came the royal children. The first one Sera noticed was Roderik, the heir apparent. He paused at the top of the stairs and surveyed the room. Sera supposed he was attractive in a brooding sort of way. At least, that was what the other girls said. Sera thought his haughty expression made him ugly. He would be emperor one day and she presumed that contributed to his attractiveness to many girls. When his gaze reached the side of the room where Sera stood, his eyes seemed to settle on her for a moment, before someone called his name and he turned away. When they were children, Roderik never stooped so low to harass her himself, but the members of his entourage were relentless, and Sera was sure it was with his approval.

Roderik moved out of the way, revealing another person standing behind him. Nicola, the youngest daughter. Her hair was arranged like her mother's, but her simple dress was out of place among the billows of lace and tulle most Volloch women wore. The tattoo of a Seidi novice at her left temple was new. She must have recently been elevated from initiate. A little older than usual. Like her brother, she stopped on the top step and surveyed the room. When her gaze fell on Sera, she paused, and her smile shifted into a mischievous grin. Sera looked to the side to see who she gave that smile to, but there was no one near. When she looked back, Nicola was watching her, an eyebrow hitched up.

A covey of girls interrupted the moment, calling the princess's name and rushing up the stairs to meet her. Nicola's smile broadened as she ran down to join them. Before they disappeared into the crowd, Sera was sure Nicola threw her one more look. Okay, that was odd. Sera fidgeted with her dress and nonchalantly looked down to make sure everything was in order.

Her parents appeared, and the three of them joined the flow of the elite, making their way into the banquet hall. Her mother, walking behind her, tapped her on the shoulder and whispered, "Stop fidgeting."

Sera scowled, stepped aside and ushered her mother ahead of her, then followed, pulling her sleeves.

The royal family sat together at the head table at the far end of the hall. Their table was elevated and perpendicular to the others so that everyone could see them. Sera sat with her parents near the door to the entrance hall, as far from the royal family as possible. A place that was decidedly not an honored one. Sera looked to the other end of the room and noticed Nicola sitting quietly, her gaze unfocused.

When a latecomer blocked her view of the princess, Sera examined the surrounding terrain. Her mother sat on her left, so she was safe there. She looked to her right and was relieved to find a boy who appeared to be about six years old. He looked up at her with a frank, open expression. "Your name's Sera, isn't it?"

Sera smiled and said, "Yes." The little boy nodded, looked away, and seemed to lose interest. The boy's mother, busy with her own conversation, didn't notice the exchange.

She looked across the table. An older woman, obviously a lower level Volloch, didn't bother hiding her disapproval at being seated so close to the Volbroch. Sera shot her a sweet smile and looked away.

Her gaze wandered the hall until she found herself looking at the head table again. Unfortunately, dozens of servants serving the first course blocked her view. She frowned, strangely disappointed.

The rest of the evening was interminable stretches of boredom punctuated by the arrival of elaborately prepared courses. Sera took a single bite from each and still felt stuffed after the second soup. When she noticed her mother was no longer engaged in conversation, she leaned over and whispered, "Why are we having this banquet?"

Her mother whispered back, "To celebrate the Empire's victory at Ulm."

"But wasn't it father who won the battle of Ulm?" Sera asked.

Her mother shifted around to look directly at her, but didn't say anything.

"What I'm asking is, why are we, why is father, sitting all the way back here in the lousy seats?" Sera asked.

Her mother gave her an exasperated look. "Sera, surely you don't really find that hard to understand, do you?"

No, Sera understood perfectly, but she found it difficult not to express her outrage, and her mother was the unlucky target. Giving her mother a perturbed look, she turned and found the little boy staring at her again. Sera glanced at his mother, and finding her distracted, she smiled at him.

The little boy frowned and said, "You fight with swords, don't you?"

Amused, Sera said, "Yes, I do."

The little boy glanced at his mother, his brow furrowed, then he looked back up at Sera and asked, "But why?"

Sera gave him a serious look and said, "Because I like it."

"But you're a girl." His eyes dropped, as if to confirm his conclusion.

Sera laughed. "Yes, I'm a girl, but girls can fight just like boys."

His frown deepened as he considered this, then his expression cleared, he nodded and lost interest, again.

That may have been the longest conversation with someone outside her family Sera ever had at one of these affairs. She looked toward the head table again, a smile still on her face. Nicola sat back in her chair, arms crossed, a pensive frown on her face. While Sera watched, the princess looked up and their eyes met. Nicola's gaze lingered for a few moments, then she looked away. Sera licked her lips, her mouth suddenly dry.

After the last course, Sera was ready to sprint from the room. Anticipating her daughter's intention, her mother whispered in her ear, "Remember, we have to go to the dance, at least for a short time."

Sera sighed, but fortunately, people started to rise from the table. She stood so fast, she knocked her chair to the floor. While she was retrieving it, her mother caught her sleeve. "Meet us in the entrance hall in one hour. If you aren't there, we're leaving you."

Sera nodded and joined the crowd heading to the ballroom. As she shuffled along, she looked in the direction of the head table again, but the royal family was gone.

When she entered the ballroom, she slid sideways, out of the flow of traffic, and put her back to the wall. She was preparing to spend the entire hour in this spot when she noticed the wide doors opened to the Imperial Gardens. Edging along the wall, she made her way to the nearest door and gazed out at the elaborate gardens with a heavy sigh. *Maybe I could just leave.*

"What are you looking for?"

Sera spun around, guilt warming her cheeks. It was the princess.

"Oh my," Nicola said, that mischievous grin returning.

"Ummm." Sera's brain froze. Why was the emperor's daughter talking to her?

"I see," Nicola said. She looked over her shoulder and walked through the door into the garden, taking Sera's hand as she passed. Sera barely got her feet moving in the right direction without falling. Nicola pulled her into a lane formed by lilac hedges along the eastern edge of the garden. Once they were out of sight of the door, she stopped and turned to face Sera. Moonlight, reflected by the white marble of the palace, illuminated her face. She was standing very close, holding Sera's hand in both of hers. Turning Sera's hand palm up, the princess ran her finger along the callouses at the base of Sera's fingers. Terrified, Sera stood frozen, watching the finger's slow progress.

"Your hands are so strong... and rough," Nicola murmured.

Sera jerked her hand free and hid it behind her back.

Nicola watched the hand disappear, then clasped her hands behind her back and lifted her eyes to peer at Sera's face. That enigmatic grin was back.

Sera was flummoxed. "Ummm," she said, again.

Nicola laughed. Not the twittering giggle so common among her type. This was a throaty chuckle that Sera felt deep inside. She stared at Nicola in wonder, as if at a creature she had never seen before.

Nicola looked up at her, her expression serious. "I watch you when you're training." The crooked grin appeared briefly, then she became serious again. "I've never seen a girl fight like you do. You're like a boy." She looked quickly at Sera's eyes, uncertainty or fear flashing across her face before she dropped her eyes again. "I mean… you're *not* a boy, you're a girl," she stammered, then showed Sera an uncertain frown.

Slowly, what was happening filtered through Sera's daze. But it couldn't be, could it? She felt her neck flush and hot prickles spring up all over her body.

"I'm sorry, I thought…" Nicola said, and pushed past Sera.

Alarmed, Sera tried to engage her mouth, but it only worked soundlessly. Nicola was hurrying away before Sera could blurt, "Wait!"

Nicola stopped, facing away, unmoving.

Sera's brain careened around, searching for something to say. Finally she was able to stammer, "I… uh… I mean, when did you watch me?"

Nicola peeked at Sera over her shoulder.

Sera attempted a smile, though she wasn't sure what expression was actually painted across her face.

Nicola's eyebrow quirking up rendered Sera weak with relief. The princess turned slowly, searching Sera's face, then a small smile appeared. Not the mischievous grin she used before. This was a shy, intimate smile.

Several small steps brought Nicola close enough for Sera to breathe in her scent. Cinnamon and sweat. Not the overpowering flowery odors the Volloch girls of Nicola's age preferred.

Nicola looked into her eyes, searching, then took Sera's hand and said, "Come with me." She led Sera deeper into the gardens.

They walked, hand-in-hand, until Nicola pulled her through a gap in the hedge onto a small, secluded balcony overlooking the Imperial District and the city of Brennan beyond. The Eastern City Gate was visible at the far end of the Empire's Way, illuminated by immense braziers.

"This is my favorite place in the palace," Nicola said, her hands alighting on the balcony rail. "I don't get to leave the district very often. I come here and imagine the places I read about."

Sera watched her for a moment before stepping up beside her. "Where would you rather be?"

The princess pointed to the east. "Way over there is Hast, and beyond it are the mountains of Argren." Leaning toward Sera, she whispered, "The *Alle'oss* call their mountains *na'lios*." She looked up at Sera. "It means our home." She returned her gaze to the east and said, "Imagine that, a whole people who call their mountains our home." She chuckled softly. "I've lived in Brennan my whole life, and it still doesn't feel like home."

They fell silent for a time, then Nicola said, "I've never been anywhere, really. I'm here, at the palace, at our summer home, or in the Seidi." She touched the tattoo on the left side of her face with a delicate fingertip. "I was so happy when I entered the Seidi. I thought they would have to let me out into the world once I became a novice." She let her hand drop to the railing and looked out into the night. "But a princess can't leave the Imperial District. It's too dangerous."

Sera watched her, noting the distracting pout of her lips. "You watch me?"

Nicola glanced up at her. "Yes, my fa — Someone mentioned there was a girl who trained like a boy. I was only eleven then. At first, I thought it was odd, a little funny." She gave her head a small shake before continuing. "But I couldn't get it out of my mind. The images would come to me at odd moments. A girl fighting with a sword." A hand went out as if flourishing a sword, then she smiled shyly at Sera and said, "Of course, the girl always won in my fant…" Her voice trailed off. "When I turned thirteen, I was allowed a bit more freedom, and I decided I had to see for myself. I was afraid to ask anyone about you." A quick, worried glance. "So, I decided to go see. Well, not entirely by myself. I had to bring Maeve. She's my maidservant. I don't think it would be allowed, really, but what they don't know, you know."

She paused, and Sera was about to prompt her to continue when she spoke again.

"We found a room in the War College. You know the building next to the training yard?" Her eyes flicked up to Sera to make sure she understood. "The first time, I just couldn't believe it! You were so strong and fast. I watched for an hour, at least. I was cheering when you won and hissing when you lost." She laughed that throaty chuckle that vibrated Sera's insides. "The man you were fighting said something funny that made you laugh, and I laughed too." She smiled at the memory.

She turned to face Sera, and Sera turned until they were almost touching. The situation was completely beyond Sera's experience. She was never interested in boys the way the other girls were, and who would she share those secrets with in any case. The only thing she had to draw on was the stories in her parents' library, the ones her mother called romance stories. Searching her mind for some reference point that might help her decide what to do, she breathed cinnamon and sweat.

Nicola looked up into Sera's eyes and whispered, "I try to watch you whenever I ca —"

Before her brain could interfere, Sera put her hands on Nicola's waist and pulled her close. It was madness. She had her arms around a princess. Feeling as if she was careening down a precipitous slope out of control, she held her breath, waiting for Nicola to scream or run away. Instead, the princess gasped and gazed up at Sera with wide eyes, her lips parted.

Sera bent down and put her mouth on Nicola's mouth.

Nicola melted against her. The tip of her tongue fluttered against Sera's lips and ran along her upper teeth. Sera touched Nicola's tongue with her own. With a low growl, Nicola reached up, wrapped her arms around Sera's neck, and pulled her body against Sera's.

Sera never experienced anything so completely overwhelming in her life. Her entire world collapsed into the raw physicality of the moment. An eternity passed, not long enough. Dimly, she heard bells. The last remaining rational part of her brain answered with echoing alarm bells. She pulled away suddenly. Nicola, her arms still held aloft, looked alarmed.

"No, the bell," Sera said hastily. "I have to meet my parents." She grimaced. "Sorry!"

Nicola's face relaxed. "Go on, Sera Storm." She stepped up to Sera, reached up and kissed her lightly on the mouth, then stepped back and said, "I like to walk in the gardens at four every afternoon."

Sera nodded, turned, and sprinted through the garden. The world had taken on a dreamlike state. Plants, statues, people all sailed by as if behind a veil. Her mind buzzed, overwhelmed. Her parents waited for her at the great doors in the entrance hall. As she grew close, her mother's exasperated expression melted into a look of concern. "Sera, are you alright?"

No, she was anything but alright. She stared at her mother, sure her guilt was obvious. Her skin felt hot and prickly. The uncomfortable dress stuck to her sweaty skin, and she was panting. Finally, she stammered, "Alright." All this did was to bring alarmed expressions to her parents' faces. She attempted a smile and said, "Yes. Fine."

Her father gave her a speculative look and said, "I'd say that was a guilty look, wouldn't you, dear?"

Both of her parents looked at her expectantly. Sera took a deep breath. Her face tried for innocence and remorse but got stuck in between. She pointed back toward the ballroom, but realizing she didn't know what to say, she stood motionless, her hand extended. Then, without another word, she dropped her arm, marched past them and escaped into the night.

Chapter 7

The 29th Day of the Month of Annenmon

Sera

Sera opened her eyes. Something was different. She lay still, trying to decide what it was. Normally, waking up was a struggle for her, but not this morning. She fell into bed the night before without closing the curtains of the wide windows in her bedroom and dawn's gray light painted her room in muted colors. Other than the pile of silky fabric that was her gown piled beside the bed, nothing was out of place.

And then she remembered. Nicola. That was it. Sera kissed a princess the night before. Didn't she? Letting her eyes unfocus, she replayed the previous evening, forcing herself to linger over the dreary banquet, lest she discover it was a dream.

The moments played out in her mind, details she was too overwhelmed to notice the night before revealed. The small white circles on a red field painted on the nail of the small finger that traced its way across the calluses on her palm, the way Nicola's face shown as she talked about the mountains of Argren, the flutter of her eyelashes as she peered up at Sera just before they kissed. Sera focused on the canopy above her bed, a vestige of her mother's fantasies of what her little girl would become.

But not all of her mother's fantasies were in vain. Last night could have been ripped from one of her mother's romance stories. A princess. Forbidden love. The roguish object of the princess's desire; Sera. Yes, that was what was different.

She rolled out of bed, scooped up the gown, and stuffed it in the bottom of her armoire. After drawing on her practice leathers, she sat to pull on her boots, then sprang up and raced from the room.

Victor

Victor loved the silence of the house early in the morning. It was one of the only times he could be alone with his thoughts. He sat at the kitchen table, drinking coffee and replaying his meeting with the emperor the previous evening. Victor had no illusions about what the emperor thought of him. Not since he defied the emperor's wishes and married a Brochen woman. Forcing him to return to Brennan to attend the banquet, then relegating him to the worst seat in the room was a pointed reminder to the Volloch elite what the emperor thought of him.

But the threats to his family were new. Victor always assumed the worst the emperor would do would be to exile his family from Brennan. He never entertained the thought they would be in danger. Especially after his service to the Empire. He considered having his family leave the capital, but they would be no safer elsewhere in the Empire. They would have to leave the Empire. But where? It would take some thought, but it was the only way to ensure their safety.

At least he had the comfort of knowing Harold would keep an eye on them while he was away.

Lost in thought, he was staring vacantly at the door on the far side of the kitchen when something flashed past. *Was that Sera?*

As if summoned, Sera entered the kitchen, returning from the direction she was heading a moment before, fairly bouncing as she walked to the table.

"Morning, Dad," she said. "Forgot breakfast."

Victor eyed her warily. Seeing his daughter smiling so early in the morning was unsettling. She was never late to training, but everyone in the household got out of her path, if at all possible, before she left for training. "Good morning, Sera. You're awake early," he said.

Sera, busy stuffing a muffin smothered in honey into her mouth, hitched an eyebrow and gave him a quizzical look. "I always have training this early," she said through a mouthful of muffin.

"Oh, I know. I didn't say you were out of bed early. I said you were *awake* early."

She gave him a blank look, then snorted. "That's funny, Dad. I've always said that about you. You are a funny man." She chortled to herself while she drizzled more honey onto her muffin.

Victor shook himself and tried again. "You seem to be in a good mood this morning. What's this all about?"

Sera froze, then swallowed, nearly choking herself. When she was able, she said, with exaggerated nonchalance, "Just ready to train this morning, that's all."

Victor stared at his daughter. "I guess we should let you drink champagne more often, huh?"

Sera stopped mid-chew, returning his gaze. Finally, she chuckled and said, "Yeah, maybe that's it." She grabbed another muffin, twirled, and headed to the door. "See you later, dad!"

"Sera!" When she paused in the door, he said, "I'm leaving today."

"Oh, right," Sera said and came around the table. Victor rose and let his daughter give him a hug and a sticky kiss on the cheek. When she stepped back, she said, "I'll see you at lunch, right?"

"Yes, of course," Victor said. "However, in case we don't get a chance to be alone again…" He paused, looking into Sera's eyes. "Remember what I told you about Harold Wolfe, the inquisitor your mother was talking to last night?"

"Right, the mysterious Volbroch inquisitor."

"That's the one," Victor said. "If anything happens while I'm away, if you or your mother feel threatened in any way, you can go to Wolfe."

"Why? What's going to happen?"

"Almost surely nothing. But… just in case." Victor gave her a smile he didn't feel. "Now, aren't you going to be late?"

Her worried gaze lingered on his face for another moment, then she nodded. "Right. I'll see you later." She backed slowly away, turned and jogged through the door.

Sera

"Is that clock right?" Sera asked, pointing at the pendulum clock on the shelf behind Werner's desk. True to his word, Werner found sparring partners for her. After their afternoon session, he met with her in his office to discuss how it went. From Sera's point of view, she mopped the floor with her opponents. But Werner had a long list of *suggestions*. She was so absorbed in their argument, she forgot the time.

"Of course," her instructor said without looking.

"Gotta go," Sera said. Without waiting for an acknowledgment, she rose and raced from the room.

"Sera, wait!"

Sera kept going. Nicola said she walked in the garden at four. It was already half past and it would take Sera ten minutes to get to the gardens. Deciding it was too late to change and wash up, she sprinted through the narrow streets of the Imperial District, grimy and wearing her practice leathers. Ignoring the scandalized glares of the Volloch pedestrians, she crossed the lawn in front of the palace, angling for the stairs that led up to the gardens. Pausing at the top, heart thudding more from anxiety that she might have missed Nicola than the run, she scanned the gardens, a breeze ruffling her short hair.

There she was, standing with her back to the gate, talking to another woman. When the other woman saw Sera, she pointed. Nicola spun around. For one terrifying moment, Sera was sure the princess would laugh at her for coming. It was all another elaborate joke the elite played on the strange Volbroch girl. But then Nicola's face lit up, sending Sera's heart soaring.

Feeling as if she forgot how to walk, she crossed the narrow space and stopped in front of Nicola, then realized she had no idea what to say. Her cheeks warmed, nervous sweat sprung up on her back. Her eyes wandered, briefly finding the amused smile on the other woman's face, before she found her courage and looked into Nicola's twinkling eyes.

"You came, Sera Storm," Nicola said.

"Yes —" Not knowing how to continue, Sera snapped her mouth shut.

Far more gracefully, Nicola turned without commenting on Sera's awkwardness and gestured to the other woman. "This is my maidservant, Maeve." She leaned toward Sera and winked. "My partner in crime when I sneak away to watch you practice. Maeve has a question for you."

"Princess!"

"Now, don't be shy, Maeve," Nicola said. "You know you want to ask."

Maeve pressed her lips together, a blush reddening her cheeks, then she said in a rush, "When you change into your practice leathers, do you change with the men?"

Sera's mouth fell open. It had to be a joke, right? But when she noticed Nicola grinning at her expectantly, she realized it was a serious question. She blushed, imagining the two of them speculating about her changing her clothes. "No, of course not," she blurted. "I change by myself."

Maeve looked disappointed, but Nicola laughed at Sera's discomfort. "Come, Sera. Let's walk." She took Sera's arm and led her into a path between hedges. Maeve followed in their wake.

The next hour passed in a blur. To her surprise, once she got over her initial embarrassment, Sera found herself chatting easily with Nicola. It wasn't until they were returning to the entrance that she realized how skillfully Nicola orchestrated the conversation. She put Sera at ease, asking her questions that let her talk about topics she was enthusiastic about. The sophisticated royal woman, trained since birth in the subtle arts of social discourse, entertaining the smitten tongue-tied rube. But it wasn't that. As Sera looked down at Nicola's smiling face, she knew, for some inexplicable reason, the princess was sincere. And she also knew she was in love with Nicola.

The princess took Sera's hand, glanced furtively around, then reached up and kissed Sera's cheek. "Until tomorrow, Sera Storm," she said. Then she and Maeve slipped past Sera and entered the palace.

Sera watched the door they disappeared through for a moment. Yes, something was different. She turned, glancing around to make sure no one saw the princess kiss her, then strode toward the exit.

Hoerst

Arriving early for his meeting with the emperor, Hoerst wandered to the large windows in the anteroom to Ludweig's office and gazed out over the gardens. He barely noticed the three people standing near the exit until one of the women turned her head, revealing a tattoo on the left side of her face. Hoerst got Stefan's attention, pointed at the trio and asked, "Is that who I think it is?"

Stefan stepped up beside him and looked down as the woman reached up and kissed the cheek of the person standing in front of her. "It's Princess Nicola," Stefan said, as the princess and a third woman disappeared from view below them. When the person Nicola kissed turned to watch her go, Stefan and Hoerst exchanged incredulous looks. "It's the half-breed," Stefan said. "Sera Storm."

They watched Sera turn and disappear through the gate.

"Do you think the emperor knows?" Stefan asked.

"I can't imagine he does," Hoerst said quietly, his mind racing. What would Ludweig do if he knew? The half-breed would be dealt with. Given how amusing the Volloch elite found the idea of a woman training to fight, she would probably find herself bundled off to the front to be die fighting the Kaileuk. Unfortunately, Victor Storm would react rashly. That could be disastrous given the precarious situation at the front.

And what would the emperor do with Nicola? After Macha's revelation, Hoerst could see Ludweig struggling with the idea that his favorite child would be his executioner. Ludweig didn't want to believe the vision, but Hoerst knew the outcome of his struggle was already determined. The emperor was a paranoid man. The image of his youngest daughter standing over him with a sword would eat at him, dragging him along a dark path to an inevitable conclusion. Nicola would die. It would break the emperor, but his love for Nicola would not stay his hand. Hoerst counted on it. It was the reason he revealed the vision to him. But it was too soon. He needed the emperor to remain in control until the situation in Argren was resolved. If Ludweig discovered his daughter's dalliance with the half-breed, there was no telling what he would do.

"Perhaps if the Volbroch girl and her mother were to disappear," Stefan said. "After the marshal leaves for the front."

"Risky," Hoerst said. "Someone would get word to him and Nicola would demand to know what happened to them." He clasped his hands behind his back and gazed at the Seidi tower, which rose beyond the gardens. "But perhaps…" He only needed to offer the emperor an alternative, to dangle a hope he might retain his daughter's love. The door to the emperor's office opened. As Hoerst turned, he whispered to Stefan. "Put someone on the half-breed. I want to know what she and the princess are up to."

Chapter 8

The 3rd Day of the Month of Ungemon

Sera

Sera opened her eyes. *What a weird dream.* She stared up at the hated canopy above her bed, trying to assemble the fragmentary images into a whole. A dark tunnel, a bright light. Ripping. None of it fit together, and even as she grasped after it, it slipped away.

"Strange," she muttered as she rolled out of bed and stood still for a moment. Something was different. Her mind felt… cool… loose. Those were the only words that fit. She bounced on the balls of her feet, wobbling her head back and forth. When nothing rattled around inside, she shrugged, grew still again, closed her eyes and listened to the house.

The predawn quiet of the big house had its own feel. The sigh of air moving in the empty halls, mice scurrying back to their nests in the walls, stray, unidentifiable sounds from the city beyond the walls of the Imperial District. Sounds so subtle and familiar, they were indistinguishable from the quiet. Unless you paid attention. But this morning, there was something new. A tone, a single sustained note, like the last fading notes of a bell's peal.

She turned her head from side to side, but couldn't locate the source of the sound. It was coming from inside her own mind. Pressing her hands to her ears, she swallowed and opened her mouth in an unsuccessful attempt to pop her ears. She gave her head a vigorous shake. Nothing changed. Jumping straight up, she pulled her knees to her chest, landed in a crouch, then sprang up and started bouncing again. Everything else seemed to be working. Shrugging, she drew on her practice leathers, snatched up her boots and padded out into the hall.

• • •

Werner wasn't in his office or the training yard when she arrived, so she busied herself by practicing forms. An hour later, sweat running down her body, she was bouncing on the balls of her feet, waggling her shoulders and letting her arms swing when she heard the door to the dressing rooms open. Spinning around, she dropped into a ready stance, practice sword extended, and gave the newcomer a fierce glower.

Werner stopped in his tracks. Popping up, Sera resumed bouncing and said, "You're late."

"I've been rounding up your next opponent," he said, studying her as he approached. "You've been busy, I see."

"Feel… energized," Sera said with a grin. She shook her head, sending drops of sweat flying.

While Werner was wiping his face, a second man entered the yard. Sera's heels came down with a thud. It was the inquisitor. He wasn't wearing his uniform, but it was unmistakably the inquisitor with the gray eyes. The one her mother was talking to at the ball. The one her father told her was a good man. Harold Wolfe.

Werner, grinning at her reaction, said, "Sera, this is —"

"Harold Wolfe," Sera finished.

The inquisitor lifted his practice sword in a salute and bowed. "Sera," he said. "Your father told me a lot about you."

"Huh," Sera said. She paused a beat, then added, "My father told me about you, as well." She wiped her brow, hiding the disappointed scowl she threw at Werner. In recent weeks, her trainer brought a series of swordsmen from the Imperial Military Academy to spar with her. At first,

Sera was pleased to discover she was more than a match for the best of them. She was feeling pretty good about herself until Werner let it slip that few of the elite swordsmen would consent to spar with her. It was disappointing and infuriating. How could she measure her skills unless she fought the best? She examined the inquisitor. Inquisition brothers wore swords, so they must have some training, but they weren't renowned for their martial skills. After all, how much skill was required to kidnap little girls?

Werner took up his usual position, readying himself to judge their bout. Sera watched as the inquisitor took his position and returned her regard with an annoyingly cocky grin. Maybe there was a silver lining. After all, how often were you given license to beat up an inquisitor? A good man he may be, according to her father, but he was still an inquisitor. Giving him an exaggerated smile, she took her place across from him.

She took a breath and sighed it out, letting it relax her and take stray thoughts with it. In the resulting silence, the tone emerged from the clutter that masked it while she trained. Even though they were the only people there, the training yard was still noisier than her bedroom before dawn. The tone was so faint that, even now that she focused on it, it was barely perceptible. She gave her head a shake and tried to ignore it.

"You both know the rules," Werner said, looking from one to the other for their acknowledgment. "Ready."

Sera dropped into a ready stance and eyed the inquisitor, expecting his opening stance to reveal much about how he fought. He didn't move. Looking as if he were out for a stroll in the gardens, he stood casually, sword hanging loosely by his leg. Still, the infuriating grin. Sera glanced uncertainly at Werner, who looked as if he was suppressing a smile.

Exasperated, she was about to ask what the joke was, when he dropped his hand and shouted, "Fight!"

Sera feinted, expecting Harold's reaction to reveal something. He didn't move. She shrugged inwardly. *His funeral.* She took a breath and exploded across the space between them. With his sword down, she expected to land a solid whack on his arm. Not enough to break a bone, but enough to leave an educational bruise.

Incredibly, he slid backwards, pivoting only enough so her sword sliced air.

Swordplay was all about initiative, balance, and momentum. These were the principles Werner drilled into her since she was a child. Sword fights ended quickly and usually the winner was the person who managed their momentum and maintained the initiative. When she started as a child, she joined a class of elite Volloch boys for whom learning the art of the sword was a social necessity. Though they were the same age as Sera, they were all bigger and stronger. And they were intent on putting the Volbroch girl who dared pick up a sword in her place.

She hid the livid bruises decorating her body from her parents, but she couldn't hide what was happening from Werner. When he suggested she give up for her own health, she begged him to allow her to continue. He relented, and Sera persevered.

Unable to compete on strength and speed, she vowed to use technique and guile to best her tormentors. Every bruise, every defeat, every humiliation was an opportunity for a lesson, and she hung on Werner's every word. It wasn't long before she was holding her own. When she became the one inflicting the bruises, the boys refused to spar with her.

Sera was so intent on wiping the smug grin from the inquisitor's face, she forgot her lessons. When she missed unexpectedly, she should have followed her sword, stepped outside her opponent's body, and maintained her momentum. Instead, she reversed her stroke, bringing her sword to a stop in order to block his counter stroke. It was all Harold needed.

He sprung at her, thrusting for her chest. She just managed to block, but as she backpedaled, trying to regain her balance, he drove her backward, his sword a blur. She worked furiously, just to keep him at bay, barely blocking attacks that seemed to come from impossible angles.

When he finally made it through her defenses, it was so fast, she wasn't sure how it happened. The light tap of his sword on her chest was almost nonchalant. He stepped back, bowed, and saluted.

Dumbfounded, Sera looked past the inquisitor to a laughing Werner.

"Inquisitor Wolfe was the Inquisition champion for ten years straight," Werner said. "They finally tired of a Volbroch winning every year and forced him to retire from the competition." He lifted a finger. "Point Wolfe."

Harold, grinning smugly, retreated to the center of the yard and took his starting position again.

Rolling her shoulders, Sera followed, eying her opponent with new respect. She wouldn't underestimate him again. This time, it would be different.

But it wasn't. Time and again, Harold snatched the initiative from her, driving her across the training yard and forcing her into increasingly desperate blocks. Clack. Clack. Clack. Point Wolfe. Clack. Clack. Clack. Point Wolfe. Point Wolfe. After the tenth humiliating defeat, she trudged, panting, back to the center, took her position and wiped away the sweat pouring down her face. Only a light sheen troubled the inquisitor's brow. *He's playing with me!*

"I think that's enough," Werner said.

"No!" Sera said rather more loudly than she intended. "Sorry. Just one more. Please."

Werner looked at Harold, who shrugged. "I'm fresh," he said.

Pompous ass. Sera ground her teeth, racking her brain for some opening gambit that might throw him off balance. But when Werner gave the signal to start, Sera's mind went blank. Neither of them moved. They watched one another in silence. Suddenly, Harold dropped into a ready position. Startled, Sera skittered backward. When he didn't attack, she scowled and resumed her position. As a child, she would occasionally visit her father in the field with the Imperial Cavalry. It was the Empire's finest who taught her the colorful insults that so shocked the Volloch children who bullied her. Distracted as she recalled a few of the choicest of these, Harold's attack nearly surprised her.

She only just parried his initial thrust, but rather than retreating as she had before, she stepped past his extended sword and attempted to sweep his leading leg. He leapt back, lifting his foot out of the way. There was a brief pause as they reset, then they were trading blows. He advanced, but she was still in control, causing him just enough uncertainty to prevent him from overpowering her as he had before. For the first time, the grin fell from his face, replaced by a quiet concentration. A small bit of her usual confidence returned, quieting the clamor of her frustration and anger.

And in the silence, the tone rose and fell, weaving a melody that mirrored her movements, as if her sword were her baton and she the conductor. Distracted by the song, she let her body take over and slowly she began to take the initiative. Her hands anticipated his moves, almost as if they had their own mind. Then, with a leap of faith, she let her mind go blank and gave in to the song.

The smallest adjustment in her stance, a parry, a flick of her sword, and she was driving the inquisitor backward. So captivated was she by the ecstatic harmony of her body flowing with the song, that when her sword struck her opponent's chest, she startled, as if pulled suddenly from a dream. She blinked and stared at the inquisitor, seeing in his face her own surprise reflected back at her. But there was something else as well. Respect.

He grinned, lifted his sword in a salute and bowed. "That was the finest swordsmanship I've ever seen."

"Thank you," Sera said numbly.

"Sera."

She turned to find Werner staring in astonishment.

"That was… unprecedented, to say the least."

She hitched an indignant brow and lifted her arms to her sides. "Well?"

A blank look came over Werner's face. Then he smiled, lifted a finger and said, "Point, Storm."

•   •   •

It turned out Harold Wolfe wasn't the arrogant jerk he seemed at first. A little full of himself, maybe. He seemed genuinely interested in Sera, asking questions about her training, her parents, her schooling. It was all very pleasant, and she began to see why her mother enjoyed his company.

Fortunately, he didn't press her about what happened in the last bout. After an hour, he left, promising a return match.

Werner was another matter. While Sera watched the clock, Werner pressed her to explain what happened. She was sure he didn't believe her when she waved it off as her just getting tired of the inquisitor wiping the floor with her. She dismissed the idea of explaining the song in her head. At least, not until she understood it better.

Promising to discuss the bout in detail the next day, Sera fled his office with only five minutes to make her rendezvous with Nicola.

Nicola and Maeve were waiting for her when she entered the gardens. Despite the fact, they had been meeting for some time, there was always the nagging sense of doubt that the princess would be there. That she had a change of heart. But today, as every day, Sera's appearance brought out the smile that took Sera's breath.

"You wore your practice leathers," Nicola said, the mischievous grin making an appearance. She caressed Sera's biceps, sending shivers up Sera's arm.

"We finished late," Sera said. "Hi, Maeve." Normally, Sera allowed the princess to take the lead, but flush from her victory over Harold, she took Nicola's arm and led her between the lilac hedges.

"Oh, my," Nicola said, grinning.

"I'd like to see you in private."

Nicola rearranged their arms and took the lead. When they arrived at the invisible opening in the hedge that led to the balcony where they first kissed, she turned to Maeve and said, "Maeve, I hate to ask, but —"

"I'll keep watch," Maeve said, glancing back the way they came. "Just… don't be too long."

Sera took Nicola's hand and pushed through the opening. She approached the railing and looked down. The gardens were eight paces above street level. They should be safe from observation. She turned around and would have taken a step back if the railing wasn't at her back. Nicola was standing so close she was almost pressed up against her.

The princess looked up at her, closed her eyes, and breathed in through her nose. When she opened her eyes, she grinned up at Sera, twisting slowly left and right. "So, Sera Storm," she said. "You have me in private."

All Sera's questions about the song fled her mind, and her arms slipped around Nicola's waist. She looked into the princess's eyes, asking a question, then they were kissing. They had stolen quick kisses in the days since that first night. But they were not the only couples who strolled through the gardens in the afternoons. Though they never discussed it, Sera assumed Nicola understood how scandalous their relationship was. A princess and a Volbroch, and not just any Volbroch. They couldn't risk discovery.

At least, that's what Sera told herself. The truth was, she was carried away that first mad night and hadn't worked up the courage since. Lying in her bed at night, replaying their conversations, Sera heard all the hints she missed when they were together. Still, the next day, she walked along beside Nicola, once again deaf to her gentle seductions.

Alone on the balcony, safe from discovery, Sera gave in to a desire she never imagined before that first night. She slid her hands tentatively down Nicola's back. Encouraged by Nicola's moan, she let her hands explore the contours of the body she imagined every night. The princess's hands kneaded the thick muscles on Sera's shoulders, then slid down and squeezed her arms.

Permission. To caress, to squeeze, to kiss, to share their passion. The barriers between them dissolved and an urgency Sera could barely contain wiped all thoughts away. All except the demands of her body, thrilling to Nicola's urgent response.

And just like when she was sparring with Harold, her song rose.

"Nicola!" Maeve's voice, muffled by the hedge. "Someone's coming."

Nicola stepped back, looking up at Sera with wide eyes. "Sorry, Sera," she said, breathlessly. "We better go." She took Sera's hand and pulled her through the hedge.

They walked down the lane, careful to keep a chaste distance. Sera had to remind herself how to walk. Nicola kept up her usual conversation, but without her usual grace, and the flush on her cheeks gave her away. When they turned the corner in the lane and found it empty, Nicola peeked at

Sera and gave her a small, private smile that sent Sera's heart fluttering against the cage of her ribs.

Chapter 9

The 3rd Day of the Month of Ungemon

Stefan

Stefan approached Hoerst's office, the rapid click of his boots on the stone floor in time with his heartbeat. The Malleus would finally have to see reason. When he burst into Hoerst's outer office, the Malleus's new assistant looked up, startled.

Stefan came to a stop, hands clasped behind his back. "Brother Eckehart," he said. "Please inform the Malleus I wish to see him."

Recovering from his surprise, one of Eckehart's brows rose. "Do you have an appointment?"

It was all Stefan could do to stop himself from leaping across the desk when he caught the twitch at the corner of the man's mouth. It was the same with all the rank-and-file brothers after Fennig; barely contained insolence. Even from the likes of Eckehart, who only transferred to the Inquisition from the Imperial Infantry months before, a man who nearly fawned over Stefan the day they set out from Brennan for Fennig the previous autumn.

That all changed after Stefan and his escort made their dash from Fennig to Brennan in hopes of catching Harold Wolfe conspiring with the

Alle'oss. Like all the Inquisition brothers, the men who accompanied him to Fennig were jealous of his swift rise to be the Malleus right hand and were quick to interpret events in the worst light possible. It didn't take long for tongues to start wagging. Now, everyone believed it was Stefan who alienated Sister Keelia, a rare hero of the Empire's wars, driving her into the arms of the *Alle'oss* rebels. They also blamed him for allowing the black-haired witch to escape.

It was all lies, of course. Sister Keelia was a traitor, and despite being one of the most powerful women in the Empire, Stefan subdued her, single-handedly. It wasn't his fault his idiot sergeant couldn't finish the job. And the black-haired witch, Minna Hunter, escaped because the citizens of Fennig foolishly attacked her before Stefan arrived. For Daga's sake, he captured her sister. No, none of it was his fault, but the idea of stooping to defend himself to men beneath his contempt ignited a rage within him only a session in his workshop with a heretic could quell.

Stefan took a moment to be sure his voice wouldn't shake, then he said, "Tell the Malleus it's about Wolfe. He will want to see me."

He might have imagined the shadow that crossed the brother's face, but before he could examine him more closely, Eckehart rose, tapped on Hoerst's office door and entered. When he returned, he held the door open in invitation, then closed it behind Stefan after he entered.

Hoerst barely looked up as Stefan entered. "I have news on Wolfe," Stefan said.

That caused Hoerst to lay his quill aside, sit back, and focus on him.

"He sparred with the half-breed — the other half-breed, Sera Storm — this morning," Stefan said triumphantly. When that news didn't produce the reaction he hoped for, he added, "And then they met away from observation for over an hour."

Hoerst's head swiveled toward his office's tall windows. He gazed at the rain pattering the glass. "I was quite confident the *Alle'oss* left Wolfe behind as a spy," he said, "but it's hard to see what good he is to them. The Ninth Legion is keeping the black-haired witch busy, and Chagan will soon be in position to spring the trap. With any luck, that will mean the end of Minna and Alyn Hunter. Then it's only a matter of time."

Stefan waited, barely breathing, while the Malleus considered.

When Hoerst spoke again, it was with a musing quality. "It's hard to imagine what Harold could possibly do to prevent it."

Stefan felt his prize slipping away. But before he could offer a counter, Hoerst spoke again.

"Still, your men have had little success keeping him under observation when he disappears into the Fallows." He sat up and gave Stefan a cold smile. "You finally get your wish. Arrest him, and Brother Henrik as well, but do it quietly. Tonight at their apartments. Tell everyone you sent Wolfe on assignment in Argren."

Stefan stood frozen, his momentary triumph tarnished by Hoerst's last statements. He opened his mouth to protest, but Hoerst retrieved his quill, a sign he was done with the conversation. "Yes, Malleus. Thank you."

He left the office, throwing a sneer at Brother Eckehart on his way through the outer office. He had been looking forward to parading a shackled Wolfe in front of the brothers who treated Stefan with such contempt. They would have to see he wasn't to blame, that the half-breed who should never have been an inquisitor betrayed them all. Still, a half victory was better than none, and he would ensure he had a full complement of assistants when he extracted a confession from Harold. Harold would take responsibility for everything, Stefan would make sure of it. Gossip would take care of the rest.

Harold

Harold read the same sentence three times, and it still didn't make sense. With a sigh, he lay the duty roster on his desk, sat back and gazed at his open office door. It was long since he recovered from the knife wound Aron gave him, part of the cover story that allowed him to remain in the Inquisition. He should have been returned to field work, especially after Minna and Keelia's intrusion into the Inquisition fortress thinned the Inquisition's ranks. The Malleus obviously didn't trust him with anything more significant than the kind of clerical work normally performed by low-ranking officers.

He stood, stretched and stared at raindrops pattering the windows. The incandescent hope ignited by the successful escape only flickered sullenly now. Ragan told him she didn't reveal her plans because the knowledge would change people's choices. As soon as that happened, the schemes she so carefully wove together would fall to ruin. Even the smallest change could be disastrous. Could it be his brief interaction with Marshal Storm was the only reason Ragan left him here? Were Ragan and Aron done with him? Having made the nudge Ragan wanted of him, had they abandoned him and Henrik to an uncertain fate?

He could believe that of Ragan. She seemed a woman unafraid of hard choices. But the thought that Aron abandoned him hurt far more than Harold cared to admit. He thought back to when Aron pressed his lips to Harold's while he thrust the knife into his lung. He told Harold, "I wanted to make sure you had something to live for." Was that just to ensure Harold didn't change his mind and flee before he fulfilled his purpose?

He refused to believe it, and in the absence of guidance, he would do what he could to pursue Victor's loyalty. Harold agreed to spar with the marshal's daughter to get to know her. He found her bright, engaging, talented and a little full of herself. But who wasn't at that age? He planned to pay a social visit to the marshal's wife, Lyra, later, just to let her know he was available if she needed anything. He wasn't sure how it helped the *Alle'oss* cause, but with no word from Ragan or Aron, it was the best he could do.

He sighed, let his chin drop to his chest and kneaded his forehead with his fingertips.

"Excuse me, sir."

Harold jumped, his thoughts leaving him feeling vaguely guilty. He turned and found a young brother standing in the doorway. "Yes, brother."

The man held out a folded piece of paper. "A boy arrived at the gate with a message for you."

Harold's heart leapt. Was this it? He stared at the piece of paper. Pretty careless, sending a message so openly to the fortress. He was sure someone already informed the Malleus. His eyes flicked up to the man's perplexed expression, then took the message.

"Did he say who sent it?"

"No, sir," the brother said. "Just said it was for you."

"Thank you, brother," Harold mumbled.

After closing the door, he sat at his desk and examined the message. The tissue thin paper was folded on itself, so that it would be difficult to unfold without tearing it. There was no writing on the outside. Sitting at his desk, he carefully unfolded it and laid it flat. Rows of runes, organized into even blocks, covered the page. If there was a message, it was encoded. The handwriting was familiar, but he couldn't place where he saw it. He sat back, staring at the runes, popping his lips softly in time with his finger tapping the paper. It wasn't Aron or Ragan. It didn't seem their style, and besides the folding and the use of encryption had an Imperial aroma about it. Henrik? Not likely, since he saw his friend from time to time.

Whoever sent it, they assumed Harold could decipher the message. So, it was an Imperial code, one Harold should know. He sat forward and examined the text of the message, focusing on the shape of the letters. He had seen this writing before. The runes were carefully formed, the rows straight and evenly spaced. All the more reason to wonder at the small, irregularly shaped ink splotches spattered across the front and back of the page. It was as if the author never used a quill before or never learned to manage the flow of ink.

Not being directly involved in the intelligence arm of the Inquisition, most of Harold's exposure to Imperial codes came from a rather dry class in the Inquisition Academy. He held the page up to the lamp on his desk. A memory from that class swam up from where he stashed it after the final exam. "It couldn't be," he murmured. Still… Standing, he turned the paper, so he was looking at the encoded message and held it up to the window. Even the dim light leaking through the clouds shone through the thin paper, revealing the ink spots lined up with specific runes. It took him a moment to find the pattern, but stringing every fourth rune together revealed the message.

Stefan arresting you and Henrik tonight.

He stood with the paper aloft, eyes losing focus. He expected it every minute of every day since he awoke in the Inquisition infirmary after the escape. Yet, now that his arrest was eminent, his reaction surprised him. There was fear, of course. Stefan and what he called his workshop, his torture chamber, featured heavily in Harold's nightmares. But beneath the fear, relief warred with excitement. Waiting for the hammer to fall was exhausting. Stefan might still get his wish, but at least someone, whoever sent this message, gave Harold and Henrik a fighting chance.

He wasn't sure how long he had been struggling with the duty rosters, but a glance out the window told him it was the middle of the afternoon. If Hoerst or Stefan knew about the message, it wouldn't look good if he left suddenly. Deciding it would be best to follow his normal routine, he sat and dipped the corner of the paper into the flame of his lamp. Holding it up, he gazed at the burning paper, contemplating the identity of his benefactor.

The code was an old one used by the Imperial military in the rough-and-ready conditions in the field. It had to be someone currently, or formerly, in one of the branches of the military. The list of people he knew who fit that description was short and would be much shorter if he only included those who wished him well. Victor Storm, maybe. But he was down south, at the front, and how would he know Stefan's plans? No, it would have to be someone privy to the Malleus's and Stefan's secrets.

Watching a curl of white smoke rising, the wispy memories of a conversation from months before came to mind. It was in the Siren's Song, the tavern to which Aron directed him to put Joseph and Nia in his path. One of Ragan's breadcrumbs. Joseph told him Stefan was traveling to Fennig to arrest a witch, who they thought might be Minna. Joseph knew a man going with Stefan. A friend recently transferred from the infantry who Joseph thought might ensure the witch reached Brennan alive. Eckehart. That was why the writing was familiar. As Hoerst's new assistant, Brother Eckehart wrote the orders issued from the Malleus's office.

He shook the paper to extinguish the flame, dropped the remnant in the waste bin, then sat back and considered his next course of action. He and Henrik had a plan, of course. In the unlikely event they had enough time to act when Stefan made his move, they would leave Brennan through the harbor and take a boat north to Maintz. After that, the plan was rather vague, but they stashed enough supplies in a small apartment in the Fallows to get them far from Brennan. The question they struggled with was how long they should linger in the capital.

His fingers rubbed absently along the thin scar Aron's blade left between his ribs. To leave would be to abandon any hope Ragan or Aron still had a use for him in Brennan.

He was considering how to warn Henrik when a light tapping at the door brought him to his feet, heart lurching.

Taking a breath, he blew it out and chuckled. A tap was not Stefan's style. Rounding the desk, he gathered himself, then pulled the door open. Henrik stood in the hallway. Though most people would describe his sergeant as inscrutable, Harold recognized the subtle signs of fear immediately. Henrik turned without speaking and disappeared down the hall.

Snatching up his jacket, Harold left the office without a backward glance. Whoever warned Harold must have warned Henrik, as well. If Stefan knew they both received mysterious messages, he wouldn't wait to act.

Harold's office was on the second floor of the administration building, across the inner bailey from the prison complex. He hesitated at the top of the stairs, then walked to the end of the hall and peered down into the inner bailey while he pulled on his jacket. There was only the normal hustle and bustle of the fortress. No squads of brothers waited for them. Henrik emerged below him, walking stiffly across the lawn toward the middle gate. No one appeared to arrest him, but as soon as Henrik disappeared through the gate, two familiar-looking men emerged below

Harold and jogged after his sergeant. His tail. They would have to be dealt with.

He hurried down the stairs into the entrance hall, trying his best to keep his steps slower than his racing heart. He was halfway to the open door when a voice brought him up short.

"Inquisitor!"

Harold stopped, a chill crawling across his skin. His hand went to the knife strapped to his lower back as he turned toward the voice.

The young duty officer stood behind his desk, smiling uncertainly. "You forgetting to sign out?" he asked.

Relief weakening his legs, Harold nearly laughed out loud. "Right," he said. "Of course. Getting absent-minded." He crossed to the desk, wondering where the men assigned to follow him were hiding.

After scribbling his signature in the ledger, he bid the man goodnight and exited the building. It was no longer raining, but the air was heavy with moisture. The sun, breaking through a small gap in the clouds, lifted wisps of vapor from the warming cobbles near the middle gate. He couldn't help glancing at the entrance to the prison. No one burst out to arrest him, but as he stepped into the shadow of the middle gate, two men he recognized exited the Administration building.

As soon as he was out of their line of sight, he threw caution to the wind and sprinted across the outer bailey toward the main gate. Emerging from the barbican, he slid to a stop, ignoring the startled exclamations of the guards. He spotted Henrik just before he disappeared behind a line of wagons trundling north on Lachlan Boulevard. Harold swore. Henrik was heading to the Fallows. He was following their plan, but if the men tailing him discovered the small apartment where they hid the supplies they prepared for their escape, all would be lost.

Having learned how difficult it was to follow them in the Fallows, when Henrik turned down a narrow lane into that neighborhood, his pursuers abandoned all pretense at stealth and raced after their prey.

Ignoring the puzzled queries from the brothers guarding the gate, Harold took off after his friend. By the time he dodged through the traffic on the broad thoroughfare, there was no sign of Henrik or the men following him. He jogged down the lane where he last saw them. He had given Henrik directions to the apartment that followed a convoluted route designed to lose a tail, but the men following Henrik were following too closely for that to work. Unfortunately, Henrik didn't know the Fallows well enough to improvise.

Harold needed to give himself time to eliminate Henrik's tail before the men following Harold caught up. Gambling Henrik would take the path Harold gave him, he took a right and sprinted through a series of streets, stopping, panting, at an intersection he hoped was near Henrik's route. He peered around the corner and was rewarded by the sight of Henrik crossing the street a block away. Before he disappeared, his sergeant glanced back at the two men following him. They apparently no longer cared whether they were seen.

Harold pulled his knife and followed, waiting for them to turn onto Thieves Lane. Knowing he would only have moments to act when his chance arrived, he closed the gap, relying on the fact they, determined not to lose their quarry again, were focused on Henrik. As he hoped, Henrik turned onto the narrow street. As soon as the two men disappeared after him, Harold broke into a sprint again.

Why Thieves Lane had a name was a mystery. Harold's broad shoulders nearly scraped the walls on either side. Sodden refuse littered the street, deadening his footsteps. The men didn't hear him coming until it was too late. As the trailing man turned to look behind him, Harold dragged his blade across the side of his neck, opening his carotid artery. His strangled cry alerted his companion, who turned and drew his sword. Harold retrieved his victim's sword before he fell.

He was considering the best way to get past the still-twitching body when his opponent lunged at him, trampling his companion's corpse. It was quickly clear Harold was a more accomplished swordsman, but the confined space narrowed his advantage. After a flurry of clashes, the two men eyed one another. Harold needed to end this quickly, before the men following him arrived. He let the tip of his sword sag, inviting a lunge his opponent was only too happy to make. Rolling his wrist, Harold trapped the man's sword against the wall with his blade and thrust the knife in his other hand into the man's wide eye. Harold let him fall, letting go of his knife.

"Watch out!" Henrik cried.

Harold whirled, bringing his sword up just in time to bat aside the sword thrust at his back. The men following him had caught up. The narrow alley prevented the two men from attacking him together, but also allowed the one in the back to escape. He shouted to Henrik over his shoulder, "Don't let them get away!" He heard Henrik answer, but was too engrossed in saving his own life to listen to the words.

Though he wasn't on Harold's level, this man was no novice with the sword. Harold tried to back away to give himself room, but his heel caught on the body of the man he just killed. Seeing him stumble, his opponent lunged. Falling backward, Harold swiped desperately at the sword aimed at his head. Searing pain in his forearm forced his fist open. His sword clattered against the wall and disappeared into a pile of garbage.

He sat, his legs draped across the body, bloody forearm cradled against his stomach. His opponent loomed over him.

"Looks like we don't have to wait until tonight," the man said. "Inquisitor Stefan says he had to be alive, but he didn't say we couldn't soften him up a bit."

His companion's face appeared over his shoulder. "Right. Why let the inquisitor have all the fun, Lar?" he asked. "He resisted arrest. Couldn't be helped. Not our fault he got tore up a little."

"I like the way you're thinking, Shem," the first man said.

When Lar glanced over his shoulder at Shem, Harold jerked his knife free of the body sprawled beneath his legs and thrust it into his tormentor's abdomen, driving it under his ribs toward his heart. The man grunted, looked down in surprise, and dropped his sword. As Harold scrambled backwards, the man wrapped his hands around the hilt of the knife, dropped to his knees, then flopped forward and lay still.

Harold looked up at Shem, who was staring down at his dying comrade in shock. Noticing Henrik approaching Shem from behind, Harold grinned, and said, "Goodbye, Shem."

Shem looked at Harold, rage giving way to incomprehension, then realization, but before he could turn, Henrik crushed the top of his head with a brick.

Henrik dropped the brick on Shem's body, nodded at Harold's arm, and said, "You want me to stitch that up?"

A small grin touched the corners of Harold's mouth. "Won't be the first time."

.   .   .

They dumped the bodies down a coal chute into the basement of a moldering tenement building. Not that the residents of the Fallows didn't know perfectly well what they were doing. Harold caught sight of some of the locals drawn by the commotion. Hoping to have the first crack at looting the bodies, no doubt. But none of the Fallows denizens would volunteer the whereabouts of the bodies to the Inquisition. The stench would eventually give away the location, but that was common enough in the Fallows that it might be a long time before the Inquisition found them.

By the time they made it to their apartment, the brightest stars were appearing between gaps in the clouds. Harold dropped onto a sagging sofa while Henrik peered out the second-story window into a nearly deserted street.

"How long before they come looking?" he asked.

"Not long," Harold answered, wincing as he pulled his shirtsleeve away from the drying blood on his arm. "The guards at the fortress gate saw where we went."

"Here, let me do that," Henrik said. Retrieving a water jug from the provisions they stashed, he sat and dribbled some on Harold's arm. Setting the jug aside, he worked the fabric free of the wound, and mumbled, "You've had worse."

"Not recently," Harold said with a strained grin. With the fabric free, he let Henrik pull his arm from the sleeve and remove his shirt. "I expect we're safe tonight," he said, watching Henrik thread sinew through the eye of a needle. "The question is, what do we do next?"

"What are our options?" Henrik asked as he prodded the edges of the cut.

"We could stick to the original plan," Harold said. "Make for the harbor and take a boat up the river to Maintz. Once we're there, we'll have a day or two to come up with a plan."

"But…" Henrik said, flushing the wound with alcohol.

Harold sucked in a breath and gritted his teeth while he waited for the burn to diminish. "I hate to leave without knowing what Ragan wanted from us," Harold said. Noting the twitch of Henrik's lips, he added, "From me." When Henrik looked up and met his eyes, Harold said, "You should leave. Get away from Brennan. I doubt they'll chase you far."

Henrik lifted the lamp from the end table and handed it to Harold. "Hold this." When Harold had the lamp situated so the light fell on his arm, Henrik pinched the edges of the wound together and began to stitch.

After tying off the end of the sinew, Henrik retrieved Harold's shirt and tore the undamaged sleeve into bandages. "I'm not going anywhere," he said. He retrieved a pouch of calendula herb from their supplies, mixed it with water to form a poultice, then spread it on the wound and bandaged Harold's arm. "My guess is the *Alle'oss* have forgotten we're here. Or whatever plans they had for us have changed," he said. "I could be wrong, but even if I'm not, how would they even find us now? And as far as Marshal Storm's family goes, it's hard to see how you can help them."

Harold squeezed his fist experimentally. Henrik's technique had improved dramatically since the first time he stitched one of Harold's wounds the day they met. "I've been thinking about that," he said. Henrik finished tying off the bandage and Harold stood and used the remains of his shirt to wipe away the sweat that sheened his torso while Henrik stitched his arm. He retrieved clean clothes from the pack he left weeks before. "Inquisition intelligence reports there are *Alle'oss* hiding in the city. The Inquisition knows some of them, but they suspect there are others they don't know, wearing disguises."

"Do you know any of them?" Henrik asked, watching Harold work his injured arm into the sleeve of the fresh shirt.

"No, but I still have a few contacts in the Fallows." Harold dropped onto the sofa. "We find a safer place to hide, then we put out the word."

They sat in silence for a few moments, then Henrik asked, "How long do we wait?"

Harold shrugged. "Until someone gets in touch, or we feel like the Inquisition is getting too close."

Chapter 10

The 16th Day of the Month of Ungemon

Nia

Nia's eyes fluttered open. Only profound weariness dulled the surprise she felt at being alive. Too weak to move her head, she let her eyes roam the small unfamiliar room in which she found herself. The only furnishings were the narrow bed on which she lay, a crude bedside table and an old rocking chair in which a woman slept. The woman's hair, falling loose around her shoulders, was more gray than black. Her chest rose and fell rhythmically. From her dress, Nia guessed she was quite poor. Nia knew she should rouse herself, find out where she was and how she came to be here, but the bliss of unconsciousness tugged at her. She closed her eyes and drifted off to the woman's soft snores.

· · ·

When she woke again, the rocking chair was empty. She was alone but for her spirit guide, drifting slowly above her. She let her eyes close again and tried to stitch fragments of memories together. The red-headed *Alle'oss* woman, one of Hoerst's witches, attacked her. She should be dead, but her spirit guide found her in the moments before life left her. Her spirit guide kept her alive, drifting on the edge of the abyss, for how long she didn't know. She thought she must have dreamed, but the memories were too vague for her to be sure which were real and which were dreams.

"She's awake."

Turning her head was far more difficult than it should have been. The older woman she saw before stood in the doorway, looking back over her shoulder. As Nia watched, she came into the room and eased herself down into the rocking chair. A man of similar age followed. He had the hard, leathery look of a man who worked a strenuous job in the hot sun, but when he saw she was awake, his face split into a grin that showed a lot of teeth.

"Well, now," he said. "We'd almost given up on ye."

Nia tried to speak, but could only manage a strangled croak.

The woman pushed herself up out of the chair, squeezed past the man and left the room.

"Now, you don't need to be talking yet," the man said. He lifted a hand, knobby with callouses, in a calming gesture. "Name's Gimlet." He leaned a shoulder against the wall and gestured after the woman. "Di's my wife. We both been seein to you." He leaned forward in a confidential gesture. "But she's taken care of the…" His eyes cut to the side, then he crossed his arms. "Well, we've been proper is all I'll say."

Nia felt a small smile touch the corners of her lips

The woman appeared again with a small pitcher and a chipped teacup. She poured a small amount of water into the cup, handed the pitcher to Gimlet, and settled onto the bed beside Nia. "Help me get her up," she said to Gimlet.

Gimlet set the pitcher down on the bedside table, worked his hands under Nia's back and lifted her as easily as a down pillow into a sitting position.

"Small sips," Di said. Her voice was gruff, but though she didn't smile, her face was not unkind.

Nia sipped the blessedly cool water.

"Fresh from the well," the woman said.

After a few more swallows, Gimlet let her lay back.

"How long?" Nia managed to ask.

While Di settled back into the rocking chair, Gimlet leaned against the wall and gazed up at the ceiling. "Well, now, let's see," he said. "Don't know how long fore we found you, though I spect it wasn't long." He glanced at Di and concluded, "Near two months."

The old woman nodded. "That's about right."

Two months!

"We dribbled porridge and water into your mouth," Di said. "Kept you alive, but I imagine you're weak as a kitten. It'll be a while fore you're up and about."

"Why?" Nia asked.

Di and Gimlit exchanged a look that told Nia this had been a much discussed question between the two of them.

"Is there someone we should contact for you?" Gimlet asked. "We would have let the Seidi know you was here, but seein as someone tried to do you in, we didn't know who was safe."

"Deirdre," Nia said.

The man and woman looked at one another, then Di said, "Malefica Deirdre disappeared. The new Malefica is Sister Briana."

"Disappeared? Where?"

"Well, now," Gimlet said with a smile. "If we knew where she got to, she wouldn't be disappeared."

Suddenly, the weariness she felt since waking was too much to resist. Hoerst must have moved against Deirdre soon after his witch tried to kill Nia. Deirdre was probably dead. Who else could she trust? "Joseph," she muttered, but so low, she doubted either of them heard her. Joseph was a brother of the Inquisition, but they found in their short time together, they were kindred spirits. They recognized the rot at the heart of the Empire. She heard Gimlet and Di whispering as they left the room. When she was alone, she extended her connection to the spirit realms just enough to welcome her spirit guide into her mind. *Thank you.* The spirit swooped.

Suddenly, Nia was thirteen, a newly initiated novice in the Seidi. She smiled, knowing why her spirit guide was showing her this memory. The younger Nia walked through the Imperial Gardens, thinking of her father. Would he be proud of her? Did he expect his plan to hide her to be so successful when he left her with the Volloch family? Lying in the small bed, Nia felt her eyes prickle, though she had no tears to moisten her cheeks. She knew what came next in the memory.

The younger Nia turned the corner in the maze of lilac hedges and found a spirit hovering a few paces away. When she entered the Seidi, the sisters asked her if she could see the spirits. Not knowing better, she proudly said she could. The cleansing she underwent to rid her of her spirit sight was brutal. It took her five years to shrug off the effects. A private rebellion, a way to reclaim the secret of her heritage. She retained the guilt and fear the cleansing instilled in her, even to this day. It was Deirdre confronting her about her spirit sight, who set her on the path to recovery.

In the memory, the spirit hovering in the path before her glided toward her. She didn't know how, but it was as if she and the spirit knew one another. On instinct, she let herself open and, for the first time, allowed the spirit into her mind. No one at the Seidi would teach her what it meant. They would have executed her, had anyone discovered her secret. But from the spirit, she discovered her many gifts. It wasn't until Deirdre took an interest in the *saa'myn* that she learned the *Alle'oss* called it a spirit guide. She told no one, not even Deirdre. In the difficult path to sisterhood, she hoarded the joyful secret as a talisman against the evil she was forced to ignore.

The memory faded, and the room returned. *Thank you. You need to go be with your kind. I'll be fine until you return.*

The spirit appeared above her, swooped once, then flitted through the door.

Nia tried to bring her father's face to mind, but only his gray eyes remained of her misty memories. The eyes of a Ferol.

"*Oliana, nalana* (Thank you, father)," she whispered. As she drifted toward sleep, she considered how she could get in touch with Joseph.

Harold

"Who are we meeting?" Henrik asked.

"No idea," Harold said.

"Our long-awaited contact from Ragan?" Henrik asked.

Harold lifted a brow.

"Right," Henrik said. "You have no idea."

"They're very shy," Harold said. "All I've been able to glean is that they have an axe to grind against the Empire."

"That narrows it down," Henrik said, staring down a group of men who stepped off the narrow walkway into the street to get out of their way. "Would have preferred to meet them somewhere outside the Fallows."

"I agree. You can almost taste the tension here," Harold said. "It was getting bad before we fled. The Inquisition stirred an already turbulent pot, searching for us."

After the night they fled, they found a vacant apartment in the narrow residential district that ran along the northern city wall. A few extra coins bought the landlord's silence. At least they hoped so. At night, they returned to the Fallows and put out the word they were looking to contact *Alle'oss* hiding in the city. Then they waited, through long, tedious days hiding indoors and late nights roaming the streets. They played cat and mouse with the brothers searching for them and the city guard attempting to tamp down unrest. After a week, the Inquisition expanded their search beyond the Fallows, but had not made it as far as their neighborhood yet. It was only a matter of time. Though neither of them said it aloud, if this contact didn't pan out, they would have to leave the city.

Harold led them down a dark, narrow alley, stopped at the intersection and peered into the cross street.

"That our contact?" Henrik asked, looking over Harold's shoulder. A man slouched twenty paces away, hands in his pockets. He was looking through the open door of a decrepit alehouse, a small smile on his face barely visible in the low light coming from the alehouse. The unmistakable sounds of a brawl emerged from the interior.

"That's him," Harold said.

"What's his name?"

"Torsten."

"Volloch?"

"I don't think so, but it's hard to get a read on him," Harold said. "I've only seen him in the dark. His hair is black, but he's careful about letting me see his eyes. My guess is he dyed his hair."

"How do you know him?"

"I don't know him," Harold said. "Louisa, from the Monk's Habit, introduced us."

When Henrik noticed Harold grinning at him, he asked, "What?"

"Just want to make sure you had all your questions answered before we proceed."

"Not likely," Henrik said, returning his attention to their contact. "You don't seem to *have* many answers."

"Fair enough. Let's go get some," Harold said and stepped out of the alley.

Torsten reacted instantly. Half turning away, he looked as if he was ready to break into a sprint.

Harold stopped two paces away and glanced into the alehouse at what looked like a melee that threatened to spill onto the street. "Torsten?"

Torsten's gaze flicked to Henrik standing behind Harold. "You bring any weapons?"

Harold lifted his arms, turned slowly, and Henrik did the same.

Torsten nodded, turned without another word, and walked away. It didn't take Harold long to determine he was trying to get them lost. It would have worked if Harold hadn't spent his youth on these streets. After nearly a half hour, they ended up two blocks from where they started, near the southern border of the Fallows. The tenement they stopped beside was in good shape by the standards of the Fallows. Though most of the windows were covered by oilcloth, some still had glass and based on the lights coming from the interior, most of the apartments were occupied by people wealthy enough to afford lamps.

Torsten motioned for them to wait while he climbed the steps to confer with two men perched on a low wall that surrounded the stoop. Their studied casualness was obviously a pretense. Guards.

Harold turned slowly, studying the neighborhood. Up and down the street, groups of men and women gathered at strategic spots, trying and failing to appear as if they weren't paying attention.

"A lot quieter here," Henrik muttered.

Harold nodded. He could still hear the chaos in the surrounding streets, but here, it was almost peaceful. "Someone has taken charge," he said, turning toward the stairs when he heard the scuff of a boot.

Torsten stopped on the bottom step, pointed at Henrik and said, "She didn't agree to see him."

Harold's heart stuttered. She? Ragan?

"Oh no," Henrik said. "He goes up, I go up."

"You can come up," Torsten said to Henrik, "but only Harold talks to her. You wait in the hall."

Harold's head rocked back. He hadn't told Torsten his name and asked his contacts to keep it to themselves. "You know me?" he said.

"Never met you," he said. "But she has." He turned and led them up the stairs.

The guards watched them warily as they entered the building. They followed Torsten up a dark stairwell to the third floor, then down a hallway. Torsten knocked on the last door. After a moment, the door opened a crack. Harold couldn't see who answered and couldn't make out their low conversation, but after a few moments, the door opened wider.

The man who stepped into the hallway was big. Even in the low light in the hallway, Harold could tell it was a man who labored many years in the sun. Though he was obviously years older than Harold, the arms that protruded from the short sleeves of his threadbare shirt were knotted with muscle and ended in the knobby hands of someone used to hard labor. He eyed Harold and Henrik from eyes set deep in a leathery face.

"Up to me, wouldn't let you in," he said. "But she insisted." Before he turned away, he said, "She's still pretty weak. I see you taxing her, I'll toss you out." He glared at Harold until he nodded. He pointed at Henrik and said, "Bit tight in here. You stay in the hall with Torsten."

The inside of the apartment matched the exterior of the building. Though the modest means of the occupants was obvious, the room was tidy. When Harold appeared, two men rose from an old sofa. The one closest to Harold was taller and broader than Henrik. The other was short, but wide, and had the scarred face of a dedicated brawler. An old woman, sitting at a small table, peered at him through squinty eyes. Even with Torsten and Henrik remaining in the hall, the small room felt crowded.

"This is my missus, Di," the man who met them in the hall said.

"Hello," Harold said. "My name is Harold."

The old woman only said, "She's waiting, Gimlet."

The old man, Gimlet, Harold assumed, grunted, pulled a door open, leaned in and said, "He's here. You still want to see him?"

Harold heard a woman's voice answer in the affirmative and Gimlet stepped back. As Harold passed the giant, he glanced up and stopped. They were standing so close that even in the low light, Harold could tell the man's eyes were the same color as his own. He was Ferol.

"What you looking at?" The man's rumbling voice bounced around the small room.

Before Harold could speak, a woman's voice drifted from the other room. "Harold."

The voice was familiar, but it wasn't Ragan. Glancing once more at the giant, Harold squeezed between the shorter man and Gimlet and entered the other room. The shorter man's eyes were identical to the giant's. Harold never met another Ferol in his life, and here were two.

The room he entered was a bedroom. Besides a narrow bed, there was a small table and a chair in which a woman sat. He only recognized her from the tattoo on the left side of her face. She seemed somehow shrunken from the woman he met months before. Hollowed cheeks testified to how much thinner she was, her hair hung lank and she molded to the chair as if she were a child's rag doll. "Nia?" he asked.

"Harold," she answered. "You've no idea how surprised I am to see you again."

Harold's head tipped to the side while he studied her. "What happened to you?"

"Hoerst," Nia said. "Or his witch, anyway. Turns out you were right about what he was doing with the witches. I ran afoul of Hoerst and an *Alle'oss* witch. A very powerful witch."

Harold studied her. "How…" He gestured vaguely around the room. "How did you end up here?"

"It's a long story, but it boils down to the kindness of strangers." When Harold started to question her further, she lifted a hand that trembled noticeably. "I'm afraid I'm still very weak. We have only moments before I tire, and I have questions."

Harold nodded and settled onto the bed. He only met her once, but that was enough to make an impression on him. He would never forget hearing his spirit joining her in a haunting duet. The moment did more to convince him the spirits were real than anything he heard or saw since. Like Harold, she was Volbroch, a half-breed. To most, she could pass as Volloch, but Harold saw the truth the moment he met her. It wasn't anything specific about her appearance. Her eyes and hair were as black as any Volloch. It was the recognition he saw in her eyes.

He glanced at the open door, where he could see Gimlet making no effort to pretend he wasn't listening, and thought of the two other men. "You're Ferol."

"Half," Nia said with a smile. "My father was Ferol, my mother Volloch. My mother was killed by the Empire. When my father realized I had spirit sight, he gave me to a Volloch family so I could become a sister. He thought it was the only way to be sure I lived."

"I didn't know there were any more Ferol."

"Oh, yes," Nia said. "It would be very difficult to exterminate an entire people. Most of the survivors fled into the mountains. They scratch out an existence not far from where the Vollen originated. Ironic, don't you think?"

"But I grew up on these streets. I never met another Ferol."

"They haven't been here long," Nia said.

"Why now?" But before Nia could respond, Harold remembered the men on the street outside the building. "You're organizing them." When Nia smiled, Harold asked, "For what?"

With a visible effort, she leaned forward. "Haven't you felt how explosive the Fallows are? It's a powder keg. It will explode soon, as it does from time to time, violent and angry, but unfocused. And like the other times, the Empire will squash it, taking the opportunity to rid themselves of hundreds of the poor."

"You hope to channel their fury," Harold said.

"That is my hope," she said. Despite her weakened state, her voice conveyed a fervor their previous meeting hadn't prepared him for.

"I fear it is a vain one," Harold said. "The Empire has always been good at stoking divisions among the Brochen. And then there are the gangs and Sefiliad. They have their own rivalries. There is little time to overcome that distrust before the pot boils over."

Sefiliad was the Vollen name of the criminal organizations that flourished in the Empire. Most of them had ties to powerful Volloch lords and the Desulti. Harold didn't see how Nia expected to convince the notoriously antagonistic groups to work together. Even if she succeeded, he was sure the Empire would make quick work of them, but he kept the thought to himself.

"But if we *were* able to channel that fury," she said.

From her expectant expression, he guessed why she brought him here. To forestall that conversation, he asked, "So Ragan and Aron didn't send you to contact me?"

Confusion flitted across her face, followed by what looked like annoyance. Instead of answering immediately, she settled back in her chair with a sigh, her gaze roaming the room as she composed herself. "I don't know either of those people," she said.

Harold glanced into a dark corner of the room. Now what? To give himself time to consider, he said, "I'm sorry, you said you have questions."

She folded her hands in her lap, pursed her lips for a moment, then cocked her head slightly, and said, "You can start by telling me why you're hiding and putting out feelers for *Alle'oss* in the city."

"We're traitors to the Empire, Henrik and I," Harold said with a wry smile. "We helped the *Alle'oss* break some of Hoerst's captured witches out of the fortress."

"You rescued *Alle'oss* witches from the prison?"

He told her about the former Seidi novice, Ragan. About the spirits of *annen'heim* and prophecy. About Ragan's quest to save her daughters, Minna and Alyn, and destroy the Empire. Though he left out the shameful details, he told her how she manipulated him into taking charge of the rescue. He fell silent, smiling at the memory of the moments in the garden of the Shrine of Eidolon when he finally met the young woman Joseph called Harold's angel. Minna. "Ragan wanted us to stay when they escaped. Well, me, anyway. Henrik stayed of his own volition. For what reason they wanted me here, I don't know. I presumed they wanted a spy, but they haven't been in touch, so even if I had useful information, I have no one to tell. I was hoping you were their contact."

"No, sorry," Nia said. She grew quiet for a moment, absorbing what he told her. "So, Ragan has a plan to end the Empire?"

"To *transform* the Empire, without the chaos one would expect if it fell apart."

She gazed at him for several moments, before her eyes unfocused and she looked past him. "Hard to imagine." Before Harold could agree, she said, "Someone told me Briana is the Malefica. They said Deirdre disappeared."

"Deirdre is well," Harold said. "Or she was the last time I saw her."

"Where? Where did you see her?"

"Before the rescue. Ragan and Deirdre were friends when they were novices in the Seidi," Harold said. "The night of the rescue, Ragan convinced Deirdre to leave before Hoerst forcibly removed her. Deirdre told us about the tunnel into the fortress the girls used to escape." He let his gaze drop to the floor. "At least I think they escaped. I suspect we would've heard if the Inquisition captured the former Malefica or the culprits who devastated the Inquisition and the Seidi. They would make sure the trial would be on everyone's lips for months."

"Where did they go?" Nia asked.

"I don't know," Harold said. "Argren, I presume. The Ninth Legion is camped out on the border of Argren. I can't think of any other reason they would still be there unless Minna was stopping them."

Nia's brow furrowed. "She's that powerful?"

Harold chuckled. "Hard to believe someone so small could be so…" He waved a hand, searching for the word. "Destructive."

"Why?" Nia asked. "What did she do?"

Harold shook his head. "I'm not sure I believe all the rumors, but I did see her first hand once. We were trapped in the prison. Needed someone to clear the way. She… Think of the most violent tornado you've heard of." He glanced up and read disbelief on Nia's face. "It was only wind, but it stripped the roofs from all the buildings in the inner bailey. Shattered every window. Dozens injured and dead. If the buildings weren't made of stone, I think she might have leveled the entire fortress." He paused. "Apparently, she put a significant dent in the Seidi as well."

"I heard a lot of those same rumors. People on the street are talking about her as if she's Ione, come again," Nia said, her eyes unfocused. "Many of the sisters in the Seidi regard the stories of Ione as myth now, but Deirdre insisted the old sisters were as powerful as the histories say." They sat silently until Nia came back from her memories. "So, that's what Hoerst wants with the witches."

"I would guess so," Harold said. "Hard to understand how he plans to control them, but if you met one of them, I suppose he found a way."

"I only saw her for a moment," Nia said, "but I saw madness in that brief glance. Hoerst may be playing with fire."

"If they truly are insane," Harold said, "can you imagine what would happen if Hoerst lost control of them?"

"You think there is more than the one I saw?"

"Hoerst has been shipping witches north for years." Harold shrugged. "I'm afraid we have to assume the worst."

Silence fell again until Nia said, "Hard to see what this Ragan had in mind. How could the *Alle'oss* defeat the Empire, even with a witch as powerful as Minna?"

"Yes, I had the same thought," Harold said. "But Ragan didn't strike me as someone without a plan."

"It would be comforting to believe that. But for those of us not privy to her plan, we have to make our own way." Nia sat forward, and Harold could see her gathering herself. "You don't *know* she intended you to be a spy. Maybe… maybe she left you here to help us. You're Ferol. I'm Ferol. We're both on the run from the Inquisition and both of us ended up in the Fallows." She paused for a moment. "Seems an unlikely coincidence, doesn't it?"

Harold gazed at her. "Yes, it does," he said slowly. "Still, I'm sorry, Nia. I know your heart is in the right place, but even if you were to organize all the Brochen and Volbroch in Brennan, the Empire would brush them aside as easily as a gnat."

"That is true. Or that's how it worked in the past," Nia said. "*But*, if Ragan did have a plan to transform the Empire, what place would the Inquisition have in this new Empire?"

"The Inquisition. You're going after the Inquisition."

Nia nodded. "Whatever else must happen to bring the Empire down, the Inquisition must be dealt with. Plus, I have a personal reason to see Hoerst humbled."

"That's suicide. Even if by some miracle, you could organize the poor, *and* hit the Inquisition, the Imperial Guard are stationed in Brennan. It would not be pretty."

"I expected as much," Nia said. "I was hoping to do enough damage before they reacted to make a difference. But perhaps this plan of Ragan's, whatever it is, offers us an opportunity. She would have to account for the Imperial Guard, wouldn't she?" Nia waved a hand and glanced to the side. "Maybe the guard will be otherwise occupied at the critical moment."

"Perhaps, but —"

"If the opportunity arises, a chance to strike a death blow to the Inquisition… Shouldn't we be ready?" Before Harold could reply, she said, "And even if there is no plan, if that moment never comes, organizing the Brochen and Volbroch can only help the poor scratching out an existence in the Fallows." When he didn't answer, she asked, "What are you doing while you're waiting to hear from Ragan? Anything useful?"

Harold gazed at Gimlet, listening to the conversation from the other room. He thought he understood the loyalty Nia earned in such a short time. Gimlet and Di were like many in the Fallows, making a life in the shadows of the Imps and the gangs. Good, honest people who, by accident of birth, found the world stacked against them. There were many who would fight for a chance at a life free of violence and exploitation. They just needed someone they believed in to lead them.

Harold stood, crossed to the small window that looked out on the street in front of the building, and pulled the curtain aside. It was still peaceful. Was that even possible in the rest of the Fallows? Even if it wasn't, did it matter? Nia was right. He had no idea what Ragan had in mind. It could be she did leave him here to help Nia. How would he know? Whatever the outcome of Nia's efforts, it couldn't be worse than hiding in their apartment waiting for something that never came.

He let go of the curtain and turned to face Nia. "What can we do to help?" he asked.

Nia sagged back into her chair, blew out a breath, and said, "You said you know a tunnel into the fortress?"

Harold nodded and returned her smile.

Chapter 11

The 29th Day of the Month of Ungemon

Harold

Harold walked through a neighborhood he barely recognized. The tenement on the corner where he often found refuge as a boy burned to the ground a few years before. The gaping craters in the cobbled street where rainwater pooled had multiplied. But it wasn't the physical changes that left him disoriented. It was the quiet. Though Nia had only been able to impose order on a narrow strip along the southern edge of the Fallows, this neighborhood was testament to her progress.

The gangs resisted, of course, as Harold thought they would. But Nia's resourcefulness surprised him. Before he met her, she put out a call to the Ferol living in the mountains, and they came, harboring a cold fury and seeking vengeance. They were a hard lot, toughened by the same circumstances that made the Vollen such formidable fighters when they emerged from the mountains to build the Empire.

Where Nia met resistance, she negotiated. When that didn't work, she imposed her will, using tactics the gangs understood. Once she took charge, her word was the law, and she enforced it ruthlessly. Like the other bosses, she allowed the gangs to operate and took her cut. The difference was she didn't tolerate the victimization of the weaker members of the community. Watching her deal with the more recalcitrant, it was hard to remember her as the enchanting siren he first met.

As Nia's notoriety grew, she attracted those who always gravitated to power. In effect, Nia was becoming the leader of one of the bigger gangs in the Fallows. But Nia had an advantage over the other gang leaders. Though they kept her identity as a former sister of the Seidi a secret, her gifts were tailormade to the task she set herself.

Harold and Henrik stepped into the shadows of a small alley and watched for anyone who might be following them. Nia was as savvy with propaganda as she was with people. Her growing network spread rumors that he and Henrik escaped the city and headed north to Maintz. And it worked. Few brothers ventured into the Fallows in the past week. Though he and Henrik remained cautious, it was much safer for them, at least at night, when the city guard avoided the Fallows.

A woman exited the building across the street, herding two rambunctious children onto the walkway ahead of her. He stared at them. In the quiet neighborhood, the children's piping voices triggered his hard-earned alarms. It was a sight he would never have believed a month ago; a mother and her children out after dark in the Fallows. Some questioned the morality of Nia's tactics, but in Harold's mind, the results couldn't be questioned. He watched the trio until they disappeared into the next building, then said to Henrik, "Wait here," and set off down the alley.

Having grown up on these streets, it didn't take Harold long to find the children who moved like ghosts through the shadows. They slept in the same basements he used to, ate at the same mission, begged on the same street corners. They didn't trust him at first, but he knew their lingo, was familiar with their secretive ways. Once they learned he worked for Nia, a few opened up to him. They feared the gangs as much as anyone.

The boy he was meeting tonight was an enigma. A loner who seemed to know everyone. His quiet demeanor led most to dismiss him, but Harold recognized a penetrating intelligence behind his preternaturally calm gaze. Harold wasn't sure how he did it, but the boy seemed to know everything that was going on in the Fallows.

The boy was waiting for him halfway down the alley, back to the wall of an old brewery. The caramel scent of boiling wort wafted through the open windows. Light leaking through the window illuminated the boy's matted hair, but left the rest of him in shadow. His head turned when he heard Harold approaching. Harold stopped two paces away, put his back to the bricks of the brewery, glanced back toward the entrance of the alley, and asked, "What do you hear?"

The boy's head tipped. A gesture Harold knew meant he was thinking. "The Red Dragon are getting ready to move."

"But they agreed to the truce," Harold said.

"They're lying. They're going to hit the Lions tomorrow night."

"You know where?"

"Grimmard Place. You know it?"

Harold chuckled. "Used to sleep in the basement of that old warehouse on the corner of South Street."

The boy's head turned as he looked up at Harold, revealing his eyes. "Yeah," he said. "That's a good place."

"Dry. Or at least it used to be."

"Still is," the boy said, his face disappearing into shadows again. "You just have to get used to —"

"The smell."

"Yeah."

The boy's head bobbed as he nodded. Harold fished a loaf of bread from a satchel and handed it over as the boy turned to leave.

"What's this?" the boy asked, not taking his eyes off the bread, despite the question.

"You look like you could eat."

"I don't help you to get paid," he said, his eyes still glued to the bread.

That was another difference between this boy and the other children. Their first question was always what Harold would give them. The boy stopped in the light, giving Harold a rare unobstructed view of his face. His eyes were definitely black. So he had Vollen or Styrian blood. He couldn't be Andian or Tituun. His skin was too pale. Unfortunately, his hair was so filthy, it was hard to tell in the dim light what color it was. All

Harold could be certain of was it wasn't black. He was not Volloch. When Harold didn't say anything right away, the boy's gaze rose from the bread to Harold's face. "Then why do you help me?" Harold asked.

His lips twisted. "Because you're making things better," he said with a tone that suggested he thought Harold daft.

"Still," Harold said with a small grin, offering the bread. "You look like you could eat."

The boy gazed solemnly at him for a moment, then nodded and took the bread. "Thank you," he said, turned and walked away.

"Be careful, Lika," Harold called after him.

Lika glanced over his shoulder, but didn't stop.

•   •   •

Harold peered into the nave of the small chapel they chose for the meeting. Nia waited nervously behind him. She still bore signs of whatever she suffered before he met her, but she put on weight and gained strength in the three weeks since their first meeting.

"You heard anything back from the people you sent after Joseph?" he asked her. Joseph, a brother who was once on Harold's escort, was with Nia when Harold met her. Harold's impression was that they were in love, an impression confirmed by Nia's attempts to contact him in recent weeks. The last Harold heard, Joseph was posted to Hast, but they couldn't be sure that was still the case.

"Only that they haven't seen him," Nia said with an annoyed twist to her lips. "Hast is on a war footing. Locked down tight. It might take a while."

"Sorry," Harold said. "Shouldn't have brought it up."

"No, that's okay."

"You ready?" he asked.

She took a breath and blew it out. "Yes." She turned the left side of her face to Harold and asked, "How do I look?"

Harold leaned in and examined the makeup they applied to obscure her tattoo. "Looks good," he said.

She gathered herself, gave him a nod, and said, "Ready."

The Ferol giant who took offense the night he met Nia stood behind her. He gave Harold a small nod, the corner of his mouth twitching, as close to a smile as Harold ever saw on his face.

"Let's go," Harold said, and stepped onto the small stage at the front of the chapel.

The room grew instantly quiet, all eyes turning to focus on Nia as she stepped up to the altar. It took Nia and Harold three weeks to get these men and women to agree to listen to her plan. They were the leaders of many of the Sefiliad on the east side of Brennan. Though they accounted for a quarter of the organized crime in Brennan, by the standards of the Empire, most of them could only be considered small-time crooks.

All except one. The big man sitting in the last pew. Royce Canon, the third most influential man in the criminal underworld of Brennan. Perhaps the richest man in Brennan, outside the Volloch elite. The only reason he was here was because he owed Harold. The rest of them were here because Nia was affecting their bottom lines by taming the street gangs. Their first instinct was to react violently, of course, but finding a more formidable opponent than they were used to in Nia, they were persuaded to come listen to her.

Harold nodded a greeting to Royce's bulk, though his face was lost in the shadows at the back of the room.

"That man is an inquisitor!" The man who spoke stood and pointed at Harold. "I've seen him in his uniform. He thinks the beard hides who he is, but it doesn't."

Harold sighed and exchanged a look with Nia. It was only a matter of time before someone recognized him, but they hoped to earn some trust before it happened.

"Is that true?" a woman with frizzy blond hair asked. She ruled the organization whose territory was most affected by Nia's efforts and only agreed to come after Nia ruthlessly repulsed her raid on Nia's headquarters.

"Yes, it's true," Nia said. There was a moment of stunned silence, then everyone rose and scrambled toward the single door at the back of the room. Before they could exit, four of Nia's Ferol enforcers moved to block the exit. Nia insisted the crime lords could only bring one body guard to the meeting, and no weapons were allowed. Still, they outnumbered the Ferol. Only their ingrained distrust of one another prevented them from uniting and overwhelming the men blocking their way.

"No harm will come to you," Nia shouted over the clamor. "Just listen to what I have to say, then you can go in peace."

They didn't return to their seats, but they grew silent and turned back toward Nia and Harold with baleful stares.

"Explain what he's doing here," a man who controlled the northern neighborhoods in the Fallows said.

"You've heard rumors of prisoners escaping from the Inquisition prison," Nia said. There were glances exchanged and grudging nods. "It would not have been possible without the help of a man on the inside. An inquisitor. That was this man."

"You think that makes up for all his crimes?" the woman asked.

"No, it doesn't," Harold said before Nia could respond. "Listen, if I still worked for the Inquisition, we wouldn't be talking." There were frowns of incomprehension at this. "I wouldn't need you to listen to Nia. I've got everything I need right here in this room." Fear wiped their frowns away. "I round you up, I decapitate a quarter of the criminal organizations in the city."

"Man's got a point," Royce said in his booming voice. He hadn't risen from his seat.

"Okay," the blond woman said. "You got us here and won't let us go until you tell us what you got to say. Let's hear it."

"Please, have a seat," Nia said. As everyone found their seats, she gave Harold a relieved smile. They worried what would happen when someone recognized him. Now they had, and no blood was shed.

Harold felt Nia opening herself to the spirit realms a moment before she appeared to grow slightly taller, her eyes brightening, her shoulders squaring. When she spoke, her voice resonated in the small room. It was one of her gifts, from the same spirits that called out to his spirit when she sang and allowed her to detect lies. Even though he knew what she was doing, Harold felt himself drawn to her. It wasn't foolproof. It only worked on those whose spirit was receptive, and if he concentrated, he saw her for what she really was. But if she could sway some of these men and women, they would bring the others along in their wake.

Harold let Nia's words fade into the background and studied the faces in her audience, guessing which of them were falling under her sway. One man, sitting near the front, grimaced and shook his head, signs he was affected by Nia's spirit sight. But few in Brennan encountered sisters and if they did, they would not have experienced a sister opening herself to the spirits. They would not recognize the symptoms. Fortunately, most occupied pews near the back of the room.

"And what's his role in this plan?"

Harold came back from his thoughts. The man who spoke was the same one who recognized him. "I know how they operate," Harold said. "I can help us prepare without them noticing."

Accusation on the faces turned to speculation.

"We won't reveal the plan right now, but remember, this is the man who helped prisoners escape the fortress."

"I'm sure you have a clever plan," Royce said into the silence. "*If* this attack on the city comes. I assume you're talking about the *Alle'oss*. Who else could it be? What makes you think the Imps won't do to Argren what they did to Styria, Ferol and Andia?"

"Minna Hunter."

The voice from the back of the room was the same that haunted Harold's dreams for months. Bodies shifted as they turned to see who spoke, opening a gap which revealed a man Harold hadn't noticed before. It was too dark to see his face, but Harold felt his breath catch when the man spoke again.

"The *Alle'oss* will come eventually because of Minna Hunter," he said.

Though he spoke to the room, Harold was sure he stared straight at him.

"And who are you?" Royce asked.

"Karl Siegling," the man said, rising and striding down the center aisle.

It was Karl, the man who was Harold's lover for years before his betrayal sent Harold on his quest to rescue the witches in the Inquisition prison.

Karl stepped up onto the small stage, his eyes catching Harold's as he turned to face the room.

"Okay, but who *are* you?"

"I'm here representing the *Alle'oss* army," Karl said.

"The *Alle'oss army?*" the blond woman scoffed amid the laughter.

"Yes," Karl said. "The army holding the Ninth Legion camped outside Argren."

The laughter petered out. Though no one knew what was happening inside Argren, the question of why the Ninth Legion remained outside Hast was a frequent topic of rumor and speculation.

Harold should have been watching their reactions, but all he could think about was Karl's familiar scent.

"Minna Hunter," Royce said. "Where have I heard that name?"

"You've probably heard the tales —" Karl said.

"The battle of Minna and Aife," the blond woman said. "A tall tale if I ever heard one."

There were chuckles until a thin man who was a vassal to the powerful cartel that ruled the Harbor District spoke. "I was there the day after, at the harbor," he said. "I can't say the story is true, but *something* happened at the harbor that night."

"Listen," Nia said. "We know putting aside your differences, working together rather than against one another, is a big ask. But wouldn't the chance to bring the Inquisition down be worth it? If the opportunity never comes, what have you lost? Old animosities. Feuds stoked by the Volloch that harm your profit and cost you people."

"I suppose it wouldn't hurt us to try cooperating for a time," a woman said. "As long as no one takes advantage."

Even with his mind numbed by Karl's presence, Harold couldn't help thinking the woman was quick to acquiesce because Nia already subsumed most of her territory. She was only trying to hang on to what was left.

"What's the chance of that?" Royce asked with a bitter chuckle.

"Common cause," Nia said. "Against a common enemy."

"And what if we say no?" someone asked from the back. "What are you going to do? Common cause, you say, against a common enemy. Maybe you're the enemy?"

Despite Nia's gifts and the arguments she and Harold constructed to convince these people, Harold could see in their faces, their opportunity was slipping away. If they left without agreeing to their plan, it would likely mean a complicated and costly war among the Sefiliad and Nia's organization.

Then Nia lifted her hand and produced a small flame that danced above her palm.

•   •   •

They hoped to keep Nia's gifts a secret, but her dramatic gesture had the desired the effect. Once the furor died down, they were able to convince the crime bosses to agree to another meeting. Long tedious negotiations later, most of the men and women rose and filed out of the room, eying one another distrustfully as they left. Two of the leaders of smaller organizations lingered to complain to Nia about some perceived slight. Harold's eyes were on their conversation, but his attention was entirely on the man standing next to him.

"That was impressive," Karl said under his breath. "They'll probably be at each other's throats within a week, but at least they appeared to listen."

Harold turned toward Karl, but couldn't think of anything to say, even if he had the breath to speak.

"Aron sent me," Karl said. "We need to meet."

"Meet," Harold said mechanically. He was back on his balcony. Not the night Karl tore his life apart. No, it was one of the countless nights they held one another, murmuring their love.

"Come on, Harold, " Karl said. "Pull it together."

Harold sucked in a breath. The anger he thought he left behind roared up, clearing away the befuddlement. "Aron? Why would Aron send *you*?"

Karl chuckled softly. "Ah, I thought there was something off about his reaction when he realized it was me," he said. "Listen, Harold, are we really going to do this here?" He glanced at Henrik, who stood just within hearing range of their quiet conversation. "Is there a place we can talk?"

"Why not now?" Harold asked.

Karl gestured to windows illuminated by morning's light. "I've come a long way, and it's been a long night," he said.

Harold readied an angry response, but before he could hurl it at his former lover, he noticed Henrik frantically shaking his head. This was what they had been waiting for. A message from Aron and Ragan. He'd let fatigue and his own hurt feelings blind him to that fact. "Monk's Habit, tomorrow night at midnight," he said. "You know it?"

Karl nodded to Torsten, who waited nearby. "Torsten will show me." His eyes met Harold's for a moment, then he turned away. Perhaps it was only because he wanted it to be so, but Harold saw something in that small glance he had only seen in their most intimate moments.

Chapter 12

The 30th Day of the Month of Ungemon

Harold

"Why the Monk's Habit?" Nia asked, peering down the hill at the Inquisition fortress.

"I panicked," Harold said. He, Nia, and Henrik stood just outside the alehouse with two of Nia's Ferol bodyguards.

"We could have met him last night. He was right there."

"It was past dawn when you finished up," Harold said. "I needed some sleep before…" Harold let his voice trail off, trying to ignore Henrik's suppressed smirk.

"The sooner we're out of here, the better," Nia said. "The only reason I agreed to this was because he might know something about what Ragan had in mind."

"You think it's a coincidence they sent Karl?" Henrik asked.

"No," Harold said, "But it's more likely it's because Karl knows Brennan than for any darker reason."

Henrik looked skeptical, but he nodded.

"Why?" Nia asked. "What other significance could it have?"

Harold exchanged a look with Henrik. "Karl and I…"

"It ended badly," Henrik said when Harold couldn't finish.

Nia looked from one to the other, turned away and mumbled, "This should be fun."

Harold cleared his throat and said to Henrik, "I expect you to keep me straight in there. We've been waiting a long time for this. We want to make sure we find out what they expect of us."

"Yes, sir."

"Good," Harold said. "You ready?"

"Let's do it."

Henrik pulled the door open and stepped back to allow Harold and Nia to enter. Harold hesitated inside the door, nodding to a few of the regular patrons. He didn't see Karl. He waved to Louisa, the server, standing next to the bar at the back of the room. Louisa returned his wave, then nodded to a table hidden in the shadows along the wall.

Harold picked a path to the table that would allow him to approach, hidden by one of the columns spaced regularly around the room. He told himself he wanted to make sure Karl was alone, but the real reason was he hoped to find Karl was as anxious as he was. Unfortunately, Renard the proprietor greeted Harold loudly before he was halfway across the room.

Hearing Harold's name, Karl leaned out and their eyes met. Harold paused, forcing Nia to pull up behind him. "Sorry," he mumbled. He pasted what he hoped was a nonchalant expression on his face and sat stiffly in the chair across the table from his former lover.

Henrik and Nia took their seats. The body guards took up positions on either side of the table, looking awkward and staring balefully at patrons on nearby tables. Harold saw people nodding in their direction and talking excitedly. They undoubtedly guessed who Nia was. He motioned to one of the bodyguards and murmured in his ear, "Make sure no one leaves." The man nodded, made his way to the front of the alehouse, and squeezed himself into a chair at a table by the exit.

Henrik nodded and said, "Karl."

"Sergeant," Karl responded, tearing his eyes away from Harold. "It's nice to see you again."

Henrik looked as if he didn't know how to respond.

"And Nia," Karl said. "That was an impressive performance last night."

Henrik asked, "How did you get to Brennan?"

"Been living here since…" Karl caught himself, glanced up as Louisa set drinks in front of them. Eying the bodyguard, Louisa gave Harold a nod and left without speaking.

"Anyway," Karl said. "Sister Keelia helped me get out of Argren and over the Odun River. I've dodged Imp patrols for two weeks, crossing the plains, then a week finding a way into the cit —"

"You look Imperial," Harold said. He nodded to Karl's dyed hair. "The hair. I wouldn't have known you were *Alle'oss*, if I didn't know you."

Karl hesitated. Shifting in his seat to face Harold, he gazed at him with a guarded expression. "I have dark eyes." It was true, though bright sunlight brought out green flecks.

"And a darker complexion," Harold said. "I mean, than most *Alle'oss*. Makes it easier to fool people. Imperials, anyway."

"Sometimes deception is necessary for survival," Karl said. Harold started to respond, but Karl overrode him. "Who are you deceiving now, Harold? Who are the men searching for you?"

"Inquisition thugs —" Harold said contemptuously, then froze. He stared at Karl as a sad smile touched his lips. Feeling his face heat, Harold looked away, but then he took hold of his courage and forced himself to return Karl's gaze.

In the silence, Henrik cleared his throat. "Yes, well, I think what Harold meant to ask is, if you look Volloch, why couldn't you just walk down the Imperial Highway and through the city gate?"

Karl blinked at Henrik and hesitated. Harold wasn't sure he heard the question until he answered, "The Imps are checking the papers of anyone traveling the highway between Hast and Brennan."

"Not surprising," Nia said, throwing a quick frown at Harold. "But if we can get back to business, we came to find out why Ragan left Harold and Henrik here."

"Right," Harold said. "Has Ragan revealed her plans?"

"Ragan is dead."

Harold gaped at him.

"That witch, Aife, the one Minna fought. She killed Ragan on the docks before they all escaped."

Harold sat back, his hands falling into his lap.

Nia recovered first. "So, what does this mean? Surely, she told someone what she intended. Who's commanding the *Alle'oss* army?"

"Aron Hunter is," Karl said.

Aron? Harold thought of the night he met Aron in this tavern. There was a lightness to the man, a carefree spirit a much more guarded Harold found irresistible. There was no doubt he was intelligent and resourceful, but did he have the experience and ruthlessness it took to command an army? Would it destroy what Harold loved about him? Harold came back to the present to find Karl watching him with an unreadable expression. "Did he have instructions for us? Aron?" Harold heard himself ask.

"He did," Karl said. His gaze lingered for a moment, then he sat up, his eyes cutting to the side. "But it has the stink of desperation about it."

"What is it?" Henrik asked.

"Do you know Victor Storm?"

"The marshal?" Henrik asked.

"That's right," Karl said. "He has a daughter. Sera."

"I know her," Harold said, the unexpected direction of the conversation clearing some of the fog from his mind.

"Aron says she's a realm walker."

Harold exchanged a look with Henrik. "Like Aron," he said.

Nia's brows rose. "Aron's a realm walker?" She glanced at Henrik for confirmation, then at Karl, who shrugged. "But Aron's a man. Right?"

"Nevertheless," Harold said.

"You've seen it?"

"Yes," Harold and Henrik said at once.

"So, Sera is a realm walker?" Harold asked before Nia could pursue the topic. "I assume no one else knows this. I don't know what the Inquisition would do if they knew, but I'm sure they wouldn't turn a blind eye to a Volbroch realm walker."

"Ragan told Aron about Sera," Karl said. "He's thinking it can't be a coincidence."

"Seems we're not the only ones trying to read meaning in coincidences," Nia said.

"It's possible Sera doesn't know it yet," Henrik said. "Ragan may have seen it in a vision."

Harold thought about his sparring match with the marshal's daughter. She displayed remarkable skill with the blade, but he didn't see anything that suggested she disappeared into *annen'heim* the way Aron did. Noticing Karl watching him, he asked, "And Aron wants to use her somehow?"

"To assassinate Ludweig." They stared at him. Before anyone could respond, Karl said, "I told him you wouldn't like it."

"And you were right," Henrik said and glanced at Harold for confirmation. "Sorry, sir, but that would be crazy. I can't believe that's what Ragan had in mind. You remember she wanted to *transform* the Empire. In a controlled way. If Ludweig was assassinated, there's no telling what would happen."

"Rule would fall to the heir apparent," Karl said with a shrug. "It should be a smooth transition."

"The emperor's son is vain, self-indulgent… completely unsuited to rule," Harold said. "Ludweig has his faults. Getting the Empire involved with the Kaileuk was foolish, but he *has* managed to hold the Empire together. I would hate to see what happens with his son on the throne."

"Not sure he would actually be the one calling the shots," Nia said. "He and Hoerst are very close, and you know who has the upper hand in that relationship."

"Hoerst would manage the military situation better, but do we really want to elevate that man?" He glanced at Nia. "We still don't have any idea what Hoerst is up to. He must have some plan for those witches."

"Do we have a better plan?" Karl asked. "I'm not sure what you know about what's going on in Argren, but I don't see the *Alle'oss* holding out much longer."

"Not even with Minna?" Henrik asked.

"Minna can't be everywhere," Karl said. "The rangers are doing a lot of damage up near Richeleau."

"And even Minna can be overwhelmed if you don't care how many lives you spend to do it," Nia said.

"But is this *really* Ragan's plan?" Harold asked.

"I got the impression they have no idea what to do," Karl said. "Aron wouldn't tell me much, but the scuttlebutt around the campfires is that no one knows what Ragan wanted."

"So, we're *all* trying to figure out what Ragan wanted us to do?" Harold asked.

They were quiet for a time, each with their own thoughts, until Nia voiced Harold's fear. "It's always possible she had no plan."

"Or she died before she told anyone," Karl said.

"I can't believe that," Harold said. "If that is so, we have no hope. Argren will be another Ferol."

"Maybe she was hoping Minna would win the war all by herself," Karl said. "That's obviously what the *Alle'oss* are hoping."

"You think that's what Aron is hoping?"

"I don't know what he thinks, but Argren is abuzz with the story of the battle at the harbor."

"One of Hoerst's witches," Harold said. His eyes met Karl's briefly, then he looked away.

"Ragan was right about that, at least," Nia said. "The witches and Hoerst."

"That's right. I just can't believe she went to all the trouble she did, years of her life —" Harold gestured and cast about, then leaned forward and said in a firm voice. "It would be the lunatic quest of a mad woman. I can't believe she fooled us all so completely. There's something we're not seeing." He sat back, fingers drumming on the table, eyes wandering the room. After a moment, he focused on Karl. "You spent a lot of time with her, while she was…"

"While she was coaching me to betray you."

"Yes," Harold said. He shut the others out and focused on Karl. "Let's get that out of the way. Like Nia said, she was right about the witches, and as painful as it was, it got me moving in the right direction. I don't know what else would have." Something shifted in Karl's expression, something subtle, and suddenly, the man Harold spent so many intimate moments with sat across from him.

Henrik cleared his throat.

Feeling his cheeks warm, Harold broke eye contact and glanced toward the door to the alehouse. "In any case…" he said and cleared his throat again. When he returned his attention to the others at the table, the tension that existed before was gone. He leaned forward, and the others did the same. "In all the time you were with her, did she say anything that indicated what she expected us to do?"

"No," Karl said, shaking his head. "I've racked my brain, but I can't think of anything. I was curious, of course. I mean, it seemed she was going to a lot of trouble for that simple hint she wanted me to deliver. Frankly, if I didn't have another reason to stick around, I —" His eyes flicked up to Harold, then he cleared his throat and continued. "Anyway, she obviously had a bigger plan than just me and you. But she was very guarded about all of that." He paused, his eyes losing focus for a moment, then he tapped the tabletop with a knuckle. "There was one odd thing."

"What?"

"Before you and I met, she wouldn't let me out of her sight. Afraid I would have a change of heart. For good reason. We made trips into Argren. Nothing unusual. But on two occasions, we headed north."

"To go where?"

"To an Eidolon monastery north of Lachton in the Northern Mountains."

"An *Eidolon* monastery?" Henrik asked.

"Why?" Harold asked.

"No idea. When we arrived, the monks kept me busy and away from her," Karl said. "The only time I saw her while we were there, she was talking to a woman."

"A woman?" Harold asked. "Did you recognize her?"

"She looked familiar, but I don't know who she was. She looked Volloch."

While they sat, quietly pondering, a song started and soon most of the people in the alehouse joined in. Nia leaned forward so they would hear her. "It *must* be significant," she said. "From what you told me about her, she worked tirelessly on her plans. Why go all that way if it wasn't important?"

Harold sipped his ale, set the tankard down and gazed at the bubbles on the dark surface of the liquid. It was absurd, trying to read the mind of a dead woman, jumping at shadows, grasping after the smallest hints. But that was what they were left with, and what choice did they have?

"It's not much," Henrik said, "but it's something. Should we go check it out?"

Harold was about to agree when Nia wrapped her hand around his forearm.

"No!" she said. "Even with the progress we've made, there is still too much to do. The meeting last night was only a fraction of the people we'll need to persuade. And as suspicious as they were of you at the beginning, your presence lends credence to the plan." She gestured to the patrons in the tavern. "You've seen the good we're doing for the poor." She let go of his arm and pressed her palm flat to the table. "Maybe this woman in the Northern Mountains is significant, or maybe not. But what we're accomplishing here is real." She paused, glanced at the others, then said, "How do you know what we're doing isn't part of Ragan's plan? If we're supposed to transform the Empire, we will have to deal with the Inquisition and bring the people along with us."

It was a good point, and the wildly circuitous path that led Harold and Nia to one another was just the sort of thing he would expect of a plan Ragan conceived. He glanced at Henrik and recognized the look his sergeant gave him. He was waiting for his commander to make a decision. Harold took in Nia's fierce frown, then his gaze settled on Karl's face and saw sympathy and something else.

"I refuse to get Sera involved in this assassination plot," Harold said. "Even if she succeeded, I doubt the outcome would be what Aron expects. You're right, Nia. Hoerst would be the de facto emperor and there's no reason to think he would suddenly become sympathetic to the

Brochen. We don't know what he has in mind, but until we do, we should do anything we can to thwart his plans." Harold put his elbows on the table, leaned forward and lowered his voice as the song petered out. "We can't leave right now, but this monastery is the only lead we have to find out what Ragan's intent was. We'll find someone else to investigate."

"I can go," Karl said.

"That's an idea," Henrik said. "He knows where it is."

"No," Harold said before he realized he was speaking. The forcefulness of the word drew surprised looks from everyone. "I mean…"

Henrik cleared his throat and said to Karl, "You say you've been living in Brennan since…" When Karl nodded, Henrik said, "It would be helpful to have someone who knows the *Alle'oss* underground in Brennan. For our cause, I mean."

Nia's gaze left Harold, and she said, "That's true. We've made some inroads through Torsten, but…" she glanced around as if she thought he might be listening to their conversation. "That man has a darkness about him. He doesn't seem very well connected."

"Torsten has demons," Karl said slowly. "Demons he's reluctant to talk about." The gaze he turned on Harold was speculative. "Okay, I'll stay and do what I can. We'll find someone else to investigate this monastery."

Still feeling the flush that ran down his neck onto his back, Harold tried for indifference as he said, "Good."

"Now, let's get out of here," Nia said, rising from her seat.

Chapter 13

The 34th Day of the Month of Ungemon

Hoerst

Hoerst glanced to his left as he mounted the steps to the palace and came to a stop.

"Was that…" Stefan, who was a step below Hoerst, asked.

"I believe it was," Hoerst replied and changed course toward the entrance to the Imperial Gardens.

"We'll be late," Stefan said.

"Ludweig always keeps us waiting," Hoerst said, peering through the gate into the gardens. He arrived in time to see Sera and Nicola, accompanied by one of Nicola's maids in waiting, disappearing into the gardens. The reports he was getting suggested their relationship was progressing beyond simple teenage infatuation. While there were no reports of intimacy, it was difficult to keep them under constant observation.

"You think the emperor knows about that?"

Hoerst glanced at Stefan. "I think not. If he knew, I suspect his reaction would be swift and violent."

"If it's not them," Stefan gestured toward the gardens, "what is the reason for the emperor's…"

"Unstable behavior?" Hoerst offered.

"I was going to say unhinged," Stefan said.

"Breeding, in part." Hoerst turned and walked toward the entrance to the palace. "His father was a troubled man toward the end, and Ludweig is nearly the same age as his father when his erratic behavior became too difficult to hide." Hoerst glanced up at the portrait of Emperor Waldemar, Ludweig's father, which hung in the entrance hall. "Weak men eventually fold when the pressure is too great. I suspect his obsession with his daughter and the vision only provides a focus for his many anxieties." As they mounted the stairs to the upper levels, he asked, "What news on Inquisitor Wolfe?"

"He and Sergeant Henrik have disappeared," Stefan said. "There are rumors they left on a barge for Maintz."

Hoerst ignored the hint of reproach in his voice. It was Hoerst's idea to allow Harold and Henrik to remain free in hopes of gleaning information on the *Alle'oss's* plans. The oafs that were following Harold were obviously careless, underestimated him, and now he was on the run. Still, even if he were a spy for the *Alle'oss*, there wasn't much he could do to interfere with Hoerst's plans now. The Ninth Legion and the Union mercenaries would soon be in position to spring their trap. With any luck, that would mean the end of Minna and Alyn Hunter. If his witches killed Sister Keelia as well, so much the better. With them out of the way, he could leave the subjugation of Argren to others and get on to more important matters.

"What about this business in the Fallows?" he asked.

"A new player in the underground. A woman. She's apparently subsuming some of the smaller gangs," Stefan said. "The larger Sefiliad are taking notice."

"A woman?" Hoerst asked. "Who is she, and where did she come from?"

"We're investigating."

It was probably nothing. The web of criminal organizations and their gangs were constantly in flux, but any uncertainty was worrying, with his plans reaching a critical crossroads. "Find out who she is." Ludweig's assistant was waiting for them in the anteroom to the emperor's office, his brow creased in worry.

"I'm not sure what's happened, but the emperor was raging," the man said in a low voice. "He's calmer now, but he's still troubled."

Hoerst thought the office was empty when he entered until he noticed Ludweig standing on the balcony overlooking the gardens. Had he seen? He and Stefan glanced at one another as they stepped out onto the balcony. "Your Eminence?" he asked, approaching the railing and looking down to see what the emperor was looking at.

"She was with the Volbroch," Ludweig snarled. "That's the reason your witch had that vision. The half-breed is whispering poison into her ear. She and her father, Marshal Storm, they planned it together." The emperor let his head drop. When he spoke again, his voice lost its vehemence. "She was always so... fanciful. Nicola. Reading books. Talking about the places she read about. She's impressionable. I hoped the Seidi would instill some discipline in her." He gestured vaguely with a hand. "I thought, after her sister, Kari..."

Hoerst was alarmed to see the glint of tears on the emperor's cheeks. He never saw the man weep before. The Malleus hoped Macha's vision would lead to Ludweig's deterioration, but not so soon. There were still many things to put into place. He gave Stefan a worried glance, then said to Ludweig, "Your Eminence, we discussed what to do about Nicola." He waited to see if Ludweig remembered. When the emperor raised his head, Hoerst continued, "This marriage to Lord Brucker is just what she needs. Brucker will take her in hand, and she will be far away from Brennan. It will be impossible for the prophecy to come true."

Hope animated Ludweig's expression. "Yes," he said. "Brucker was furious about that situation with Kari." He gazed out over the gardens, nodding. "Yes, that is good. We will placate Brucker, buy his loyalty and, as you say, Nicola will be safe and far away."

Hoerst let his held breath sigh out. That the emperor mentioned his oldest daughter, Kari, without flying into a rage, was a good sign. When she fled rather than submit to a marriage to Brucker, it nearly broke her father.

Ludweig turned away from the rail, suddenly the image of the forceful, charismatic leader most of the Empire knew. Other than the tears on his cheeks. "We'll tell her in the morning." He clapped Hoerst on the shoulder and strode toward his office.

"Your Eminence," Hoerst said more abruptly than he should have. When Ludweig stopped and turned around, a dangerous scowl on his face, Hoerst said, "Perhaps I can be present when you tell her?" Ludweig's scowl deepened. "After all, I arranged the details with Malefica Briana." The emperor's face cleared and Hoerst continued, "Your daughter may have questions."

"Good idea," Ludweig boomed. "Join us at breakfast and we will tell her together."

"You think Lord Brucker can take Nicola in hand?" Stefan murmured when they were alone on the balcony. "I mean, Brucker is a violent man, but... a Seidi novice?"

"Of course not," Hoerst answered. "But it will never get to that. Nicola will never submit to this marriage."

"You have a plan."

Hoerst smiled and followed the emperor into his office.

· · ·

The mood in the royal family's private dining room was light as Hoerst took his seat the following morning. The emperor must have warned his family he would be there, as his appearance went largely unremarked. Empress Crysta and the heir apparent, Roderik, sitting at one end of the long table, couldn't be bothered to interrupt their conversation long enough to greet him. At the other end of the table, Ludweig barely glanced his way, too busy telling his younger sons a story they all obviously found amusing. Hoerst smiled at the scene, reassured to see the emperor so jovial.

The chilly reception was intended to remind Hoerst he was beneath their notice. A familiar slight, but one Hoerst would remember. Only Nicola, as usual, revealed what she really thought. The princess watched him from across the table, her opinion of his presence plain on her face. When he smiled, her eyes narrowed, but she held his gaze until her father burst into loud laughter. When her eyes flicked toward her father, Hoerst was sure he saw something like disgust ripple through her expression. If she were actually involved in a conspiracy to murder her father, she wasn't hiding her intentions very well.

An army of servants appeared, bearing enough food to feed a significant portion of the Brochen in the Fallows. After the servants withdrew, Ludweig spread his arms and said, "Begin!"

As Crysta and Roderik on one end of the long table and Ludweig and his younger sons on the other resumed their conversations, Hoerst found himself alone with Nicola. She eyed him, an enigmatic expression on her face, but when he offered a plate of sliced melon, she returned his smile. Knowing the confrontation that was coming at the end of the meal, Hoerst rather enjoyed himself. Despite her earlier reticence, the princess was a captivating conversationalist; well read, insightful, funny and very nearly able to hide the fact she loathed him.

When the emperor finally set his knife and fork down, signaling the meal was ended, Hoerst gave Nicola a cold smile. Her face froze.

"Nicola," Ludweig said.

Nicola turned to face her father, her body so tense, Hoerst thought for a moment she might sprint from the room. Instead, she forced her face into a regal mask and asked, "Yes, Father?"

Without preamble, Ludweig said, "A suitable match for you has been on my mind for some time."

Her mask dissolved in an instant. She glanced at Hoerst, then she said to her father, "I'm a novice of Seidi. You can't *force* me to marry."

Normally, that was true. It was one freedom granted to the sisters of the Seidi. The Seidi, however, was not immune to the strictures of Volloch society. Though the sisters had more say in their fate than most Volloch women, in the Seidi, the Malefica was the ultimate authority.

At a gesture from Ludweig, Hoerst said, "Malefica Briana has agreed to grant a special dispensation for you, Nicola, in deference to your unique position." He made it sound as if he thought she should be happy about the news, but the truth was, if the Malefica decreed it, there was little Nicola could do to refuse.

"It would be one thing if your sister was still —" Ludweig stopped speaking, a familiar anger flickering around the edges of his expression. Afraid he would lose the initiative, Hoerst was about to speak, when the emperor's wife spoke for the first time.

"If you want to blame anyone, Nicola, blame your sister. Lord Brucker is a powerful man. This match is important for your father and for the Empire. If your sister had not run away, you could continue to pretend to be a Seidi sister. But as your sister abandoned her family, her responsibility falls to you. You will do your duty as we all must."

"Right," Nicola said coldly. "You would know about odious duties, wouldn't you, Mother? I've heard you wept for days when you were sold to father." She waved a hand to encompass her siblings. "And you've made no secret how distasteful you find procreating."

"Nicola!" Ludweig said, pounding the table with his fist.

Nicola stood abruptly. Hoerst was alarmed to feel her opening herself to Daga's essence. "Nicola," Hoerst said. His voice wasn't loud, but it caught her attention. "Don't do anything you will regret."

Nicola stared at him, panting, her face flushed. For a moment, Hoerst thought she would ignore him, but then her presence dimmed.

She turned to her father, having regained some of her composure, but her quavering voice revealed her anger. "You will not sell me off like some brood mare like you tried to do with Kari." She turned a cold expression on Hoerst. "I will burn this place down before that happens." She glared around at everyone for another moment, then gathered herself, turned and walked slowly to the door.

As soon as the door closed, Roderik said, "Well, that didn't go well." He plucked a pastry from a tray piled high with a variety of confections and slouched back in his chair.

Ludweig leapt up, throwing his chair across the room. "We should never have allowed her to enter the Seidi."

"It was you who let her do it," Crysta sniffed. "I told you to send her to that place in the mountains where you sent Kari. After a winter there, she would sing a different tune."

"I've already promised Lord Brucker Nicola's hand, and after the fiasco with Kari, there's no telling how he'll react if —"

"Oh, I think we know how he'll react," Roderik said. He took a bite and said through a mouthful of pastry, "Kari was willful too, and she didn't even want to be a sister." Wrinkling his nose, he dropped the remainder of the danish onto the platter and took another. "It's the women in the family," he said, emphasizing the words with the pastry. "They don't know their place." Bowing his head to his mother, he said, "Present company excepted, of course, Mother."

His mother held his gaze for a dangerous moment, then her eyes followed Ludweig, who was pacing. "You will just have to make her go. Lord Brucker will bring her to heel."

That advice might have worked with most disobedient daughters, but Nicola was a novice of the Seidi. Briana told Hoerst what Nicola's gifts were. Lord Brucker would meet an unhappy end if he were to abuse Nicola like he did his other wives. But Hoerst expected Nicola's reaction, had counted on it, and was ready to offer a solution. "Your Eminence," he said. "If I may." Ludweig stopped pacing and nodded impatiently. "I have a suggestion."

"Yes?"

"If I could speak to you in private."

Ludweig waved his arms and shouted, "Out, everyone!"

The two younger sons fled. Ludweig glared at Roderik, until he rose slowly, gave his mother a peck on the cheek and sauntered from the room.

"Really, Ludweig," his wife said, dabbing at her cheek with a napkin. "At breakfast? Can't you take your business somewhere else?"

"Have you not been paying attention?" Ludweig asked. "We are discussing your daughter's disobedience."

Crysta blinked. "Yes, of course. Which means you should not keep whatever you are going to discuss from me."

Ludweig came over to where his chair would normally be at the end of the table. Noticing it laying on the floor, he pulled out a chair formerly occupied by one of his sons and fell into it. "Hoerst," he said and waved his hand at his wife.

Hoerst glanced at the emperor's wife, then spoke to Ludweig. "As you know, we've developed methods for ensuring… compliance among the Brochen witches we capture." At a sharp intake of breath, he looked back at Crysta.

"Did I hear right?" she asked. "You're trying to *tame* Brochen witches?"

"Yes," Hoerst said. "Quite successfully."

She stared at him, then her nose wrinkled and she turned to her husband for confirmation. When he nodded, she asked, "Does the High Priest know about this?"

"No," Ludweig said. "The less that old fraud knows about anything, the better."

Before Hoerst could continue, the emperor's wife asked, "And what do you do with these… witches?"

"That's not your concern," Ludweig said. "I *would* suggest you confine yourself to managing your offspring, but clearly that is a task beyond your abilities."

She glared at her husband. "Well, I will leave you men to your important business." She rose from her chair. Giving Hoerst a nod, she said, "Malleus, good luck with your blasphemies. Your Eminence," she said to her husband, then turned slowly, glided to the door and let herself out.

Hoerst stared at the door, feeling a smile growing on his face. When he looked back at the emperor, Ludweig was glaring at him expectantly.

"Yes," Hoerst said, "as I was saying, with our techniques, even the most willful witches can be tamed."

Ludweig's face went blank for a moment, then comprehension appeared in his expression. He gazed at Hoerst and said, "But you've told me your methods weren't always successful."

"We've made a great deal of progress recently," Hoerst said. "And of course, all of our subjects have been Brochen witches. It's necessary to break their will before we can instill in them the proper attitude. Such extensive conditioning will not be necessary with Nicola. We only need to teach her obedience."

Ludweig covered his mouth with his hand and gazed into the corner of the room. After a few moments, he leaned forward and rested his elbows on the table. "Let us be clear on what you are proposing," he said. "You're suggesting I give you Nicola so you can use your techniques on her."

Hoerst nodded.

"And you can make her more compliant?"

Hoerst nodded again.

"Will she remember who she is, who her parents are? Will she be the same person?"

"Yes, of course," Hoerst said with a smile. "The only difference is that she will obey *you* above all others."

Ludweig stood and took a step away from the table before stopping and turning toward Hoerst. "She will not want to go."

"No, but we have experience handling dangerous women."

"She won't be hurt."

"No, nothing permanent," Hoerst said. "We will treat her with the utmost care."

Ludweig walked away from the table, then returned to stand across from Hoerst, his hand on the back of the chair Nicola vacated. "How long will this take?"

Hoerst shrugged. "A matter of months. Three, four. It's hard to tell." He smiled. "No longer than it takes to plan a wedding. Lord Brucker need never know, and Nicola will be the perfect, compliant wife when she returns." Hoerst suppressed a smile. He could see in the emperor's eyes, he had him.

"Nicola is popular. She will be missed."

"It is well known the princess has always wanted to venture beyond the walls of the Imperial District. We will simply say Malefica Briana finally granted her wish."

"What about the half-breed?"

"Leave that to me."

Ludweig's hand went to his mouth again. When he dropped it, he gave Hoerst a quick nod and said, "Yes, see that it's done." When Hoerst stood, Ludweig said, "Make sure it's done quietly. The fewer people who know, the better."

"Of course, your Eminence." Hoerst bowed his head and turned to go. He maintained his composure until he was out of sight of the emperor, then allowed himself a chuckle. That couldn't have gone any better. With Nicola gone, the emperor's mental condition would stabilize, allowing Hoerst to complete his preparations. When he was ready, Nicola would return a broken shell of herself. It would send Ludweig over the edge, providing the perfect excuse they needed to replace him with Roderik.

Hoerst walked through the doors into a warm day, paused and smiled up at a blue sky, a rare sight in the capital which was usually cloaked by a smoky haze. It was the intricate maneuvering of the pieces on the game board that was so satisfying. It was true, when all his plans came to fruition, he would have power and wealth beyond imagining, but he suspected he would be rather bored when it was all over.

Catching motion out of the corner of his eye, he looked to his right in time to see Sera Storm entering the gardens. Nicola would tell Sera about the marriage. The half-breed would know the story they concocted to explain Nicola's absence was a lie. While no one in Brennan would listen to her, the problem was Victor Storm. The marshal's reports from the front were more than alarming. It wouldn't do to distract him at this critical moment. They would have to take the couple and the half-breed's mother at the same time. If they did it quietly, Sera and her mother would disappear into the Inquisition's dungeons, and no one would ever hear from them again. Victor would discover what happened eventually, but not until it was too late.

Chapter 14

The 34th Day of the Month of Ungemon

Sera

Sera came to a stop as soon as she passed through the gate into the gardens. Nicola stood with her face in her hands, her shoulders shaking. Maeve stood next to her, a hand on her back. Her tingly anticipation at seeing the princess gone in a second, Sera glanced warily around. Seeing no one else in the gardens, she crossed the space between them. Maeve saw her coming and stepped aside to allow Sera to take Nicola into her arms.

Nicola startled and raised a tear-streaked face. Before Sera could speak, the princess glanced back at the palace, then took Sera's hand and led her into the gardens. Sera tried to speak again, but Nicola hushed her. They walked in silence until they emerged onto the small balcony where they shared magical moments.

"Now, will you tell me what's wrong?" Sera asked.

A spasm of anger rippled across Nicola's face, arresting her explanation. She clamped her mouth shut, turned away and stepped up to the rail overlooking the city. Sera watched, fascinated. She never saw Nicola so much as flustered, let alone so angry she couldn't speak. She remained quiet, watching the princess struggling with emotions that brought pink splotches to her cheeks, her chest rising and falling with agitated breaths. Finally, Nicola closed her eyes, took a deep breath, and let it out. When her eyes opened again, instead of offering the explanation Sera desperately needed, she said, "It must be Hoerst." Her voice was rough from suppressed anger. "A spider, spinning his webs. I wondered why he was there this morning. But why? What does he have to gain?"

Her patience finally spent, Sera took Nicola's arm and pulled her around. "Tell me what's happened," she said firmly.

Fear replaced the anger in Nicola's expression. "They're trying to do to me what they tried to do to Kari."

"Kari?" Sera asked, having trouble making the connection. "The princess? Your sister?"

"Yes," Nicola said. "They tried to sell her to Lord Brucker." She spat the name, anger once again rising to the surface. "To marry her off like she was a prize heifer."

Nicola returned to the rail, leaving Sera at sea. "Wait," she said and joined Nicola. "Kari never married Brucker."

"No," Nicola said, impatience edging her voice.

"So, they want *you* to marry that ogre?"

"As if I would ever marry that… man," Nicola said. Arms rigid by her side, she took a deep breath and held it. After a moment, she let the breath escape through parted lips and gathered herself, once again the poised princess. "I'm sorry. I'm just so angry, I could spit. You, of all people, don't deserve to be in the way of it."

Sera took her into her arms, thrilling, despite the circumstances, as the princess molded herself to Sera's body. "What happened to Kari?" she asked. "She just disappeared. No explanation."

"She ran away," Nicola said, nuzzling against Sera's chest. "She came to my room the night she left to tell me she was running away. Wouldn't tell me where. In the morning…" Sera felt her shoulders rise and fall. "She was gone." Nicola disentangled herself from Sera's arms and gazed east toward Argren. "I didn't see her again until years later when the Inquisition dragged her back. They found her in Argren."

"The Inquisition?" Sera asked, with a sinking sensation. "What happened to her?"

"I don't know," Nicola said. She lifted a hand and tapped the railing with her palm. "I only saw glimpses of her before she disappeared again. The only thing I know for sure was she was pregnant."

"Pregnant?"

"Yes."

"Who was the father?"

"I don't know," Nicola said. "I never got a chance to ask her."

"And your parents… what… they never told you what happened to her or the baby?"

Nicola gave the throaty chuckle Sera found so distracting at other times. "My parents?" A ripple went through her body as her anger reemerged. "Those monsters?"

"Is… are you sure she's still alive?"

When Nicola didn't answer, Sera leaned on the railing and waited. When she felt the princess relax, Sera said, "I don't know Brucker well. He's been to our house a few times, at parties my parents throw. He's one of the few elites who come. I've only spent a little time with him, but I can tell he's a pig. The way he talks… he doesn't seem the type who would marry your sister if he knew she had a baby."

"I know," Nicola said.

"So, they shipped her off somewhere to have the baby in secret," Sera said. "Maybe, they were hoping, once she had it, Brucker wouldn't know the difference."

Nicola snorted. "Not likely. He would have her examined before he would have her." Nicola peeked at Sera and said more calmly, "But I agree, they sent her off somewhere to have the baby. I have to believe she's still alive."

"Where?"

"I don't know."

"Some lord's estate?"

"You know how they gossip," Nicola said.

"One of the emperor's estates?" Sera asked, straightening and resting her hands on the rail.

"Maybe," Nicola said with a shrug. She glanced up at Sera, brow furrowed. "Why are you so interested?"

"Because we're leaving," Sera said. "The only question is where we go." Sera gestured toward the east, where Argen rested beyond the horizon. "Since your sister ran away, maybe she knows where we could go. How to hide. It's a place to start. An ally outside the capital."

Nicola gaped at her, then gave her head a small shake. "What are you talking about?"

"We're leaving," Sera said.

Nicola stared at her, then her mouth snapped shut. She crossed her arms over her chest and shook her head again. "I can't leave."

"Why not?"

Nicola started to speak, stopped, then gazed out over the city, her mouth working soundlessly. Finally, her head tilted in a way Sera knew meant she was explaining what she thought was obvious. She made a short cutting gesture with one hand. "I'm a novice of the Seidi." She tossed the hand toward the city. "I'm a princess of the Empire, for Daga's sake. I have friends... Maeve... I..." She fell silent, wide eyes gazing at the horizon.

"You have a family who would marry you off to a monster," Sera said softly.

"Oh, they won't marry me off," Nicola said with an affronted chuckle.

The song in Sera's mind swelled as Nicola lifted a hand and produced a small flame above her palm. She gave Sera a firm nod, then extinguished the flame, muting Sera's song. What was the connection between her song and Nicola's magic? Determined to convince the princess to leave with her, Sera filed that riddle away for later.

"Does the Malefica know?" Sera asked.

Nicola paled. "She gave the marriage her blessing."

"Listen," Sera said. "We haven't talked about you being a novice and all. I don't know what your gifts are, but there are a lot of sisters in the

Seidi." When Nicola looked up at her, she asked, "Whose side will they take?"

"Mine."

"Are you sure? All of them?"

Nicola didn't answer. After a moment, her lips twisted, she turned away and pressed her side against Sera. They stood in silence, looking out over the city. Nicola peeked up at her again and asked, "So, you want to steal me away?"

Sera was suddenly aware of Nicola's body pressed against her side. Heart fluttering, she slipped an arm around Nicola's waist and pulled her close. "Yes, my damsel. I'll whisk you away."

"They'll come after us."

"They'll have to find us."

"You'll protect me?"

Sera chuckled. "Not sure who will be protecting who. But yes," she said. She offered her mouth, and Nicola surrendered to her kiss. They separated, their lips brushing and Sera murmured, "I would do anything for you. Lay down my life to keep you safe."

Nicola sagged against her. Sensing the crisis passed, Sera's hands began to wander, and Nicola's body responded. She rose on her toes, reaching for Sera's kiss. Suddenly, the princess went rigid and fought free of Sera's embrace.

"Wait!" Nicola said.

"What?" Sera asked, alarmed.

"Maeve," Nicola said and plunged through the hedge.

"Maeve?" Sera asked, hesitating with her arms still extended, before following.

When she emerged, Nicola had her alarmed maidservant by the arms. "You were Kari's maidservant before me," Nicola said.

"Yes, mistress."

"Did you see her when they brought her back? When she was pregnant?"

Maeve looked as if she wanted to pull herself free, but Nicola held her firmly. She glanced at Sera, then leaned toward Nicola and whispered. "They told me to never tell."

Nicola frowned at her, then startled and look past Maeve toward the corner where the lane turned to follow the back of the gardens. Letting her maidservant go, she spun around, took Sera's arm, and led her in the opposite direction. Mystified, Sera glanced back at Maeve, who looked as confused as she was. When Sera tried to speak, Nicola spoke over her.

"The gardens are really quite lovely this time of year," she said. "The winter has its charms, with the snow and ice, but summer is my favorite time of year."

"Uh… yes," Sera said. "Though spring has its charms as well." She winced. *Charms?*

When they turned a corner, Nicola glanced over her shoulder, leaned in, and whispered. "We're being watched. If we leave, your mother will be in danger. Can you get her to leave?"

Sera nodded. "Probably." How was she going to do that?

"How long do you need?"

"A week?"

Nicola's brow furrowed. "Too long."

"Three days," Sera said. Not nearly long enough.

"Oh, that would be lovely," Nicola said with twittering laughter. "You must introduce me to him." Her fingers dug into Sera's biceps.

When they turned the corner into the lane that led to the entrance to the gardens, Sera whispered, "Can you get to my house?"

Nicola gave her head a small shake. "No. Let's meet at the training yard where I watch you train," Nicola said, gracing Sera with a mischievous grin. "Midnight, three days from tonight. How do we get out of the city?"

"Leave that to me," Sera said.

"I think I know where Kari is. I just need to check something with Maeve," Nicola whispered. She let go of Sera's arm and walked away without a backward glance. Maeve hurried to keep up. When the princess disappeared into the palace, Sera headed toward the exit, resisting the urge to search for their observer.

As she made her way through the streets of the Imperial District, she considered what to do about her mother. She would have to leave, in secret, and soon. Sera shoved her hands into her pockets and hunched her shoulders. The thought of telling her mother about Nicola filled her with shame. Her mother would explode, and she would be right to.

How foolish it seemed now. Of course, they were being watched. The only questions were why they waited so long to intervene, and how long did Sera and Nicola have? The usual scrutiny the residents of the Imperial District gave her suddenly took on a sinister aspect. Catching a woman pushing a cart full of flowers peering suspiciously at her, Sera turned down a side street. There were others on the narrow street, none of them obviously paying attention to her, but they wouldn't if they were Inquisition agents.

She rounded a corner onto a deserted street, stopped and peered back the way she came. She couldn't blame Nicola. The princess had never walked the tightrope Sera had her whole life. She probably thought the worst they would receive was a firm scolding. But Sera should have known better. If the emperor thought a half-breed was defiling his daughter, Sera would disappear. It wouldn't surprise her if this marriage was a means to get Nicola away from her. They would wait until Nicola was gone, then they would come for Sera and her mother.

Of course, she might not have to wait for the Inquisition to come for her. Her mother would kill her first. The precariousness of their position among the Volloch in the Imperial District was one of her favorite lectures since Sera was a little girl. Of all the people Sera could fall in love with, why did it have to be the daughter of the emperor?

Sera put her back to the wall and stared at the cobbles at her feet. But they *were* in love, and Sera wouldn't abandon her. She would get Nicola and go to Harold Wolfe. That's what her father told her to do. He would know how they could get out of the city. Could she take her mother? No, they would come after Nicola. She didn't know where they were going, but she knew it would be dangerous. Her mother needed to be with her father.

Pushing herself off the wall, she forced herself to walk at a normal pace, expecting brothers of the Inquisition to appear at any moment. Instead of returning home, she headed to the training yard.

· · ·

"Werner," Sera said as she breezed into his office.

Werner, engrossed in paperwork, startled and looked up. When he saw who it was, his eyes narrowed. "What are you up to?"

Sera flopped into her usual chair and feigned outrage. "That's nice. Can't a girl be friendly?"

Werner hesitated, then set his quill down and settled back in his chair, gazing at Sera over steepled fingers. "Out with it," he said.

Sera sighed, sat forward and rested her elbows on her knees. When she looked up, Werner was watching her with concern. Deciding to abandon the carefully worded stratagems she concocted to gain his assistance, she said, "I've got a problem."

Werner stood, closed his office door, and returned to his seat. "Tell me," he said.

Sera spilled, telling him about her and Nicola's first meeting, their semi-clandestine walks in the garden, and ending with the arranged marriage. She left out the most intimate details, but Werner could guess some of that from her blush. When she was done, she hesitated, then said, "We're leaving. Nicola and I. Three days from now." She expected a strong condemnation, but Werner simply watched her for a few moments, then lifted his gaze to the ceiling. She let him think, mentally rehearsing counters to the objections he might raise.

"Has anyone seen the two of you together?" he asked finally.

"I think we were being watched. At least, I'm pretty sure we were being watched today." She sat back and sighed. "I'd be surprised if we haven't been watched since the beginning."

"Sera." The disappointment in his voice was almost too much for her to bear. "You know what they'll make of a dalliance between a half-breed and the princess."

Dalliance? Even though she had the same thought, the use of the half-breed slur spiked Sera's anger, but before she could retort, he spoke again.

"If you do this, if you leave with Nicola, you can never come back."

She deflated. "I know."

"They'll come after you. They'll never quit. I'm not sure what they'll do to Nicola if they catch the two of you, but they'll execute you."

Sera swallowed and nodded. "I know."

"You could leave without her. They might come after you, but they would eventually give up."

"No!"

Werner lifted his gaze to the wall over her head with a troubled expression. When he looked at her again, he asked, "What about your mother?"

"That's why I came to you, first," Sera said, sitting up, relieved to have an answer to this question, at least. "You're leaving for the front tomorrow with the new recruits. You can smuggle mom out of the city." Werner stared at her. "Bring her to my father, then she and dad can figure out what to do."

"Your mother will never be able to return, either."

"She hates it here."

"You're taking away her right to decide for herself."

"She stays here for me and my father," Sera snapped. Why didn't he see the brilliance of her plan? She took a moment to calm herself. "She won't need to stay here for me anymore. I'll be gone." Before Werner could reply, she said, "And my father…" She gestured vaguely. "He's the only thing keeping the army together. You told me that. They wouldn't do anything to him." It was all she could do to meet his eyes.

"Where will you go?"

"I can't tell you that," Sera said, slumping in the chair again. "But we have a plan." She hoped it wasn't a lie, that Nicola really knew where Kari was, but she could sense Werner's doubts and didn't want to give him ammunition.

"At least tell me how you plan to get out of the city," Werner said. "The princess can't simply waltz out one of the city gates."

Relieved, once again, at being asked a question she had an answer to, she sat up. "My father told me, if I got into trouble, to go to Harold Wolfe. He's an inquisitor. He can help us get out of the city. "

"That's the plan?"

"Well… yes, that's the plan."

Werner sat forward and rested his elbows on his desk. "You'll need a contingency. Harold's a good man, but there's no guarantee he'll help you kidnap the princess."

"It's not —"

Werner held up a hand. "That's what they'll accuse you of and anyone who helps you." He sat back, steepled his fingers again, and let his head fall back. "Have you thought about how you'll get out of the Imperial District?"

Sera gaped at him.

When she didn't answer, Werner lowered his gaze. When he saw her face, he chuckled. "That one I can help you with."

"You mean… you'll help?" Sera asked, trying not to sound too surprised.

"Yes," Werner said. "I don't like it, but the moment you let someone see you with the princess, this became inevitable. I have no idea why we haven't had the Inquisition at our door already." He gazed at her, considering. "I shouldn't tell you this, but as we're both about to become outlaws, I don't suppose it matters. The war is not going well. Your father thinks it's only a matter of time before the army collapses. He's making contingency plans for that event." He glanced at the door behind Sera. "He has to be careful, but his last message made veiled references to you and your mother leaving Brennan. I think it was a hint." He hesitated. "You *could* come with your mother and I."

Sera shook her head. "We have a plan. Besides, it's like you said, they'll never stop looking for us. They won't do anything to dad, so mom will be safe there. But if he were helping hide Nicola…"

"You have money, clothes, transportation…?"

"Yes." Another lie. "I've saved some and Nicola, well, she's a princess. She has enough for both of us." *Does a princess even need money?*

Werner nodded. "Wherever you're going, make sure it's out of the Empire."

Sera nodded. "I don't know how to thank you, Werner."

"Thank me by not getting caught," he said. "Now let's go break the news to your mother."

• • •

"What has happened?" Sera's mother said as soon as Sera and Werner entered the kitchen. When they didn't answer immediately, she returned her teacup to its saucer and gave Sera an expectant look.

Sera glanced at Werner but found no help there.

"Don't look at me," he said. "This is your mess."

"Mess? What did you do, Sera Storm?" her mother asked.

Sera glowered at Werner and fell into a chair at the table. "I wouldn't characterize it as a me —" She paused, mouth open, then shook her head and said, "Let's not exaggerate. It's a *bit* of a mess, but it might turn out for the best." She waved a hand at Werner. "Isn't that what you said? It's a good time to leave the city?"

"Leave the city?" her mother asked. She looked from Sera to Werner. When he nodded, she sipped her tea, returned the cup to the saucer, then settled herself. "Tell me, Sera."

Having rehearsed the story with Werner, Sera recited it with fewer pauses, though she kept her eyes on the table and she could feel a flush warming her cheeks. She didn't look up until she finished.

Her mother looked to Werner for confirmation. Then she took another sip of her tea and gazed around the kitchen. "I do love this house," she said. "We've had many happy memories here."

Watching her mother's shining eyes, Sera had to look away, a hollowness opening in her chest.

"But I have felt like a prisoner here since the day we arrived," her mother said.

Sera looked up. Seeing a wistful smile on her mother's face, she jumped up, ran around the table, and threw her arms around her mother's neck. When she let go, she threw a smug smile at Werner, then asked her mother, "So, you'll leave?"

"I don't see that you've left us any other choice," her mother said. "I will not remind you, I have warned you about this sort of thing since you were a little girl."

"I know, Mo —"

"But… I'm only surprised it took so long."

Sera stared at her.

"You have always bridled at injustice," her mother said. "When you were a child, you would come home bruised and bloodied. Despite your father and my admonishments, you just couldn't turn away when the Volloch children teased you." She sipped her tea and sighed. "I worried for you, of course, though I knew bloody noses would be the extent of it. But you've grown into a strong, capable woman. Every day, I fear you will encounter some arrogant lordling abusing a servant or, Daga forbid, a brother of the Inquisition bringing one of those poor girls to the prison. It will be a relief to know you are away from here."

Before Sera could respond, her mother looked to Werner and asked, "When do we leave?"

"I leave to bring the new recruits to the front tomorrow," Werner said. "We'll smuggle you in one of the wagons."

"Me and Sera," her mother said.

"No, mother, I'm not coming with you," Sera said, knowing it was inadequate. She was so surprised to have gotten this far without a major row, she wasn't prepared to soften the blow.

Her mother checked with Werner once again for confirmation, then frowned up at her daughter. "Where will you go?"

"Werner is going to take you to dad," Sera said. "Dad will know what to do, and it will be easier for you to go somewhere safe once you're out of the capital."

"You're avoiding my question. Where will you go?"

"I can't tell you that," Sera said. "Nicola and I have a plan."

"You and Nicola have a plan." Her mother sat quietly, hands folded in her lap. After a moment, she looked up at Sera and asked, "Will I never see you again?"

"Of course, we'll see each other again," Sera said, suddenly aware that might not be true.

"How will I find you if you won't tell me where you're going?"

"Dad will know where you are," Sera said. "I'll always be able to find dad. As soon as we're safe, we'll get in touch with him."

"Sera," her mother said. She gazed at her daughter, eyes shining in the candlelight. "Do you love this girl?"

"Yes, Mom," Sera said. She knelt beside her mother's chair. "More than... I never thought... I mean, it never occurred to me I could love anyone so much." She took her mother's hand. "It's like the stories you used to read to me, Mom." A tremulous smile touched the corners of her mother's mouth. "Complete with princess."

Her mother sighed, glanced at Werner, then said to Sera, "Well, you best come help me pack. You can tell me all about your princess."

Chapter 15

The 34th Day of the Month of Ungemon

Sera

Sera dropped her pack onto the kitchen table, stood completely still and listened to the silent house. It was never this quiet, even deep in the night. She glanced down at her sword, sheathed at her side, the ramifications of what was about to happen sweeping over her once again.

That morning, she and Werner successfully secreted her mother into one of the supply wagons accompanying the recruits to the front. Sera watched the wagon roll onto a barge that ferried it across the river, turning away only after it was safely docked on the far shore. Their parting was more difficult than she expected. There were tears shed. Sera didn't know if she would see her parents again, and she could tell her mother thought the same thing. Both pretended it wasn't so.

After leaving the harbor, she stopped at the training yard. With Werner and the most recent batch of recruits gone, it was deserted, so she threw herself into solo forms to burn off her anxiety. She experimented with the song in her head until it answered when she called, swelling when she needed it and retreating into the background when she didn't. She practiced her forms relentlessly, thrilling at how her body flowed, dancing the steps, seemingly of its own accord. Her strokes were impossibly fast and precise, as if time itself, awed by her virtuosity, slowed. As exhilarating as it was, she sensed there was something more, that she was barely scratching the surface of what was possible.

It was magic, she was sure of it, though she never heard of anything like it. She meant to ask Nicola when they met, but the heady presence of the princess swept away all thoughts that were not about her. Soon, they would have all the time in the world together, time enough for her racing heart to slow and her mind to turn to less urgent matters. At least she hoped so.

After practice, when she was pleasantly tired and dripping sweat, she paused, sword dangling from her hand, gazing around the training yard. Although she knew she would be returning the next night to meet Nicola, this was a goodbye to a place that saved her life. Had she not found Werner and the sword, she was sure her childhood dust-ups with the Volloch children would have escalated into something more serious. Though she was far from what her mother would call disciplined, Werner's steady hand tamed the worst of her impulsiveness. She left the training yard, still in her training leathers and carrying her sword, which she normally stowed in the armory.

Arriving in the deserted house, she bathed, donned fresh leathers, and packed. She expected to feel anxious about leaving the only home she ever knew, but now that her mother was safely away, she felt a buzzy sense of anticipation. Gazing around the familiar kitchen, she realized her mother was right, the house was a prison. Far more comfortable than the cells in the nearby Inquisition fortress, but a prison all the same.

"Sera?"

Sera whirled around, drawing her sword and sweeping her mother's favorite teapot off the counter to crash onto the floor.

Nicola stood in the doorway that led to the mudroom. Even in the dim candlelight, Sera could see Nicola's worried expression and it froze her blood. "Nicola! What's wrong?"

Nicola stepped further into the kitchen. "Sorry. Your door was unlocked."

The princess wore boots, black pants, and a tight black blouse. It was the first time Sera saw her out of a dress. Dragging her eyes back to Nicola's face, she asked again, "What's wrong, Nicola?"

"Maeve has disappeared."

A thrill of fear went through Sera. "Are you sure?"

"Yes," Nicola said. She took another step. "I'm so worried about her. I don't know what to do."

"Does she know we're meeting at the training yard tomorrow night?"

"Yes. I needed her to help me get out of the palace."

Sera sheathed her sword, swept her pack off the table and headed toward the door, taking Nicola by the arm as she passed. "We have to go. Now!"

"You think they got Maeve?"

Sera cracked the door and peeked into the walled courtyard behind their house. "Yes. Even if they didn't, we have to assume they did." She glanced down at Nicola's boots. "You dressed to travel."

"Tonight is my night to go to the Seidi. That's where they think I went. This is what the novices are wearing now."

"We… we can't do anything for Maeve," Sera said.

"I know."

"Maybe they'll let her go."

"Maybe," Nicola said, though her tone suggested she didn't think it was true.

"Do you have any money?"

"Money? No, I never need money. I was going to steal some from my brother tomorrow. He's allowed a social life outside the palace."

"It's okay," Sera said. "I have some." Her mother gave her all she had on hand to add to what Sera saved on her own. It wasn't much, but it would get them far from Brennan. Peeking once more into the courtyard and finding it deserted, she pulled the door open and stepped through. They crossed to the gate in the center of the opposite wall. Sera opened it and peered into the street. Nothing moved. "Come on," she whispered and pulled the gate open.

"Where are we going?"

"We have to get out of the Imperial District," Sera said.

They only made it a few steps when she heard it. It was only the click of a hobnail boot on the cobbles behind them, but on the quiet street, it might as well have been a thunderclap.

Sera whirled around. Men, silhouetted against the streetlight at the end of the block, approached and spread out across the street. They didn't speak, but raised their arms as if pointing. Sera called on her song, just as she heard the unmistakable thunk of crossbows firing.

"No!" she screamed. Lunging sideways to put herself between Nicola and the crossbow bolts, she squeezed her eyes shut, anticipating the agony of the bolts piercing her body.

There was an uncomfortable twisting sensation in the center of her head, but nothing else happened. No crossbow bolts pierced her body. In fact, though the street was quiet before the men appeared, now it was as silent as a tomb. No screams, no triumphant exclamations. No sound, save her song, which had become an ethereal note so beautiful, it prickled her eyes.

She cracked her eyelids open. The men weren't moving. It wasn't just that they weren't walking or reloading their crossbows. They were as still as statues. She whirled around and found Nicola frozen as well, her face locked in a terrified mask. Sera waved her hand in front of the princess's face and got no response. She turned and peered past the men to the streetlight at the end of the block. It was dimmer, its light wavering, as if someone pulled a breeze-tossed veil across it.

She straightened and gazed around at the scene. Was this the *more* she suspected her song could give her? The change in her song suggested it was. If so, what was it, or where was it? Leaving the princess, she walked cautiously toward the men. Brothers of the Inquisition. She didn't know them. The inquisitor was familiar, but she couldn't place his name.

Now what? Returning to Nicola, lost in thought, she almost missed the crossbow bolts in the dark. They hung motionless in the air, two paces from Nicola. Three of them were converging on the princess, low so they would hit her legs. The other two converged on the space Sera had occupied.

Sera swiped her blade at the nearest bolt and gaped as her sword passed through it. She looked at her blade and then returned her gaze to the bolt. On closer inspection, she realized they weren't completely frozen. Though it was slow, they made their inexorable way toward Nicola. So, wherever she was, what was happening before she arrived was still happening. If Sera didn't do something to stop them, the bolts would strike Nicola.

She held her hand above a bolt and let it hover before swatting down at the bolt. Her hand passed through the bolt and went instantly numb, as if it had fallen asleep. She yelped and held her hand to her chest. The bolt was unaffected.

It crossed her mind, she might be dead, but decided it wasn't likely. The bolts intended for her still hung in the air. They didn't strike her. She looked down at herself to be sure and confirmed there was no blood or other evidence of a wound. But wherever she was, she had to figure out how to help Nicola.

Shaking fiery tingles from her hand, she watched the bolts closing in on the princess, trying to remember how she got here. She called on her song when she saw the brothers. When she heard the crossbow fire, she panicked. There was that uncomfortable, twisting sensation in her head, then she was here. So, if her panicky need to escape got her here, maybe the same panicky need to return to rescue Nicola would bring her back.

But what to do about the bolts? She waved her sword up and down through them. She eyed the princess. If she could shove her out of the way… No. The thought of her hands sinking into Nicola's body made her shudder. And even if she could return to where she was before, she wouldn't have time to push her out of the way. The only option left was to block the bolts, and preferably with something other than her body. Her sword was too narrow, but she still had her pack.

Pulling the strap from her shoulder, she stepped into the shrinking space between the bolts and Nicola. After studying the angles, she sheathed her sword and angled the pack so that it would catch the bolts converging on Nicola.

Now what? She glared at the bolts, then squeezed her eyes shut, trying to work up a good panic. Nothing happened. When she opened her eyes, the bolts were nearly at the pack. She shook the pack, growling through clenched teeth. Nothing. She thrust the pack forward, but the bolts simply sank into it without effecting their flight. If she didn't figure this out soon, it would be too late. Her back was almost against the princess.

Staring at the bolts, she pictured them tearing into Nicola's body and began to pant. "Come on!" she screamed and focused on her song.

Her mind twisted, and the veil lifted. The sound of bolts thudding into the pack was nearly drowned by Nicola's scream. Startled, Sera dropped the pack and looked up. The brothers recovered first. Two of them drew swords, and two of them worked at reloading their crossbows. The inquisitor took a step backward.

Sera sprinted toward them, drawing her sword and calling her song. Moving faster than any normal human, she was on them before they were ready. She swept the first man's sword aside, flicked her wrists, to draw the tip of her blade across his throat. The inquisitor turned and fled. Sera let him go and turned her attention to the other three.

Three efficient strokes was all it took. It happened so fast, they had no time to scream.

Though it hadn't taxed her physically, she panted, heart heaving, as she gazed down at the bodies, bloody sword hanging from her hand. Lifting her boot out of the way of a rivulet of blood, she stepped back. They were brothers of the Inquisition, and they came to take Nicola. What was she supposed to do?

"Sera?"

Sera startled when Nicola touched her arm. Nicola's panicked expression and men's shouts, coming from the front of the house, penetrated her shock. "We need to go," she said. Nicola had the pack slung over her shoulder, so Sera took her hand, fled from the approaching sounds of pursuit, and turned left at the next intersection.

As they neared the eastern wall of the Imperial District, they slowed, then came to a stop beside a small garden. Sera could still hear the shouts, but they weren't coming nearer. Yet. Noticing her bloody sword, she relinquished Nicola's hand and wiped the blade with the leaf of a hosta. She fumbled twice, trying to return it to its sheath with trembling hands before slamming it home.

When she reached for Nicola's hand, the princess flinched. Her arm still extended, Sera looked into Nicola's wide eyes.

"I'm sorry," Nicola said. "It's just…" She gestured back toward the bloody scene.

"We have to go," Sera said. She hesitated, then started walking. The relief at hearing Nicola's footsteps behind her almost brought her to tears.

"Where are we going?" Nicola asked after a few moments.

"Up here," Sera said, pointing to a low octagonal building nestled up against the wall. She reached for the door, praying Werner did his job. At first she thought the heavy iron door was locked, but when she put her foot on the wall beside the door and pulled with all her strength, it opened with a metallic groan.

She glanced back at Nicola and slipped through the gap. Beyond the dim wedge of light allowed through the narrow opening, it was pitch black. When Nicola followed her, she yanked the door shut and asked, "Can you do that fire thing? The one you did the other day?"

Suddenly, Nicola stood next to her, a small flame hovering over her upraised palm. Awash in flickering golden light, Nicola's wretched expression sliced through Sera's remaining shock. She reached for the princess, heedless of the flame. As her arm went around Nicola's waist, they were plunged into darkness.

"I'm sorr —" Nicola got out before Sera's mouth covered her lips.

The lingering adrenaline of their narrow escape and the tension between them lent them an urgency that momentarily eclipsed their danger. When Sera finally relinquished her kiss, Nicola pulled away, but Sera held her tight.

"It's okay. I've… I never saw anything, or did anything like that, before. I've never kill —"

"What happened?" Nicola asked when Sera didn't continue. "You… It all happened so fast, then you were…"

"I don't know what happened back there," Sera said. "Or, at least —
" She let Nicola go. "We'll talk about it later. We have to go now."

Nicola produced the flame again and peered around. "What is this
place?"

"Entrance to the storm drains," Sera said. She stepped up to a wall
that encircled the center of the room. Beyond the low wall, a four foot
opening plunged downward into blackness. The rungs of a ladder were
chiseled into the stone.

"Is it safe?" Nicola asked.

Instead of answering, Sera retrieved the pack from Nicola and dug out
a small lantern. Once she had it lit, Nicola extinguished her flame. Sera
lifted the strap of the pack over her head and slung it over her shoulder.

"Not sure how safe it is, but I don't think we have much choice," Sera
said.

"So, we go down there, then what?"

"Come on," Sera said. "I only need to explain *if* we make it to the
bottom." She was holding the lantern over the tunnel, peering into the
darkness, when she heard Nicola make a soft sound. It took her a moment
to recognize it as a huff. Swiveling her head toward the princess, she found
her staring across the room, brow furrowed, lips twisted in indignation.
"Princess?"

Nicola blinked, then indignation gave way to outrage. "Those men
shot at me!"

Sera held her grin in check. "I think they shot at both of us."

Nicola's eyes flicked to Sera. She threw out a hand and said, "Yes, but
I'm —"

Sera waited, but Nicola merely stood still with her hand extended.
"You're a princess of the Empire."

"Well… yes," Nicola said, her blush visible even in the dim light. Her
arm fell to her side. She pulled her shoulders back, lifted her chin, but the
tremble in her lower lip ruined the effect.

Sera couldn't hold back her laughter.

"Hush!" Nicola said, squeezing Sera's arm and glancing over her
shoulder to the door. "It's not funny." When Sera had control of herself,

Nicola said, "They were trying to kill me. Which means either Hoerst is acting without my father's knowledge, or... my father wishes... me... dead."

Her crumpled expression chased all humor from the situation. Sera reached for and turned her so she was forced to meet Sera's eyes. "They were aiming for your legs."

Nicola blinked, a furrow appearing between her brows. "Were they?"

"Yes," Sera said. She let a small smile curl her lips. "They only wanted to *wound* you, then drag you away and give you to a monster named Lord Brucker."

Nicola peered up at Sera, her troubled expression showing she wasn't sure if she was being teased, then her lips twisted and a ghost of the smirk Sera loved appeared. "Yes, well, quite right," she said, an echo of the haughty princess. She leaned forward, resting her forehead on Sera's breastbone, arms hanging limp.

Sera rested her hands on Nicola's shoulders and waited. After a moment, Nicola murmured. "I can't do this."

Sera pulled her close. "*You* don't have to," she said, burying her face in Nicola's hair, breathing her scent. "*We're* doing this. Together."

When Nicola's arms came around Sera's waist, returning Sera's hug, Sera said, "Now, come on, we have to get moving."

Nicola stepped back, wiping at the moisture on her cheeks. "Right." She stepped up to the wall, peered down into the dark pit, and gave Sera a quick nod. "You first."

The hardest part was getting onto the top of the ladder. An opening in the wall provided access. They had to sit on the edge, then turn and feel for a rung with their feet, holding onto the edge of the wall. The rungs were carved to provide an easily gripped ridge, and the stone was dry. Still, they were descending a narrow tunnel into darkness, lit only by a small lantern that hung from the pack on Sera's back.

Sera stumbled on wobbly legs when she put her foot into the warm ankle deep water flowing through the tunnel at the bottom of the shaft. She helped Nicola down and they both stood, catching their breath and working stiff fingers.

"Now what?" Nicola asked.

Sera unhooked the lantern from her pack and handed it to Nicola, then dug into her pack and pulled out the map she and Werner drew from documents they found in the City Planning Office. It showed only the part of the city's storm drain system that led from the Imperial District to the access point nearest Harold Wolfe's apartment.

She held it out so Nicola could see it. "This will take us to the neighborhood where Harold Wolfe lives."

"Wait," Nicola said. "Isn't he an inquisitor?"

"Yes," Sera said. "But he's a good man. My father told me to go to him if I was ever in trouble." Noting Nicola's skeptical expression, she said, "I'd call this trouble."

"And what do we do when we get there?"

"He'll help us get out of the city."

"Does he know we're coming?"

Sera looked at the map, then peered down the dark tunnel. "No." She started walking.

"Do you know him?" Nicola asked.

"Yes," Sera said. She stopped, held the map up to the lantern Nicola held. "It looks like we turn right here." Glancing at Nicola's face and seeing her worry, she said, "Trust me. This will get us out of the Imperial District. They won't expect that, so it will give us time. If Harold can't, or won't, help, we go to the harbor and take the ferry across the river. Once we're away from the city, we can come up with a plan to find your sister." Nicola's face smoothed, and she gave Sera a small nod. "Did you find out where Kari is?"

"Yes. Maeve —"

"Maeve knew where she went," Sera prompted when Nicola couldn't finish.

"No, but we figured it out. Together." Nicola looked up at Sera.

"The hardest part is over," Sera said and took Nicola's hand. "Come on."

Chapter 16

The 34th Day of the Month of Ungemon

Sera

Nicola held the lantern up to illuminate the map Sera held to her nose, trying to decipher Werner's cramped script.

"This doesn't look right," Sera mumbled.

"That was apparent some time ago," Nicola said.

Sera let her arms fall to her side, the map dangling from her hand, and turned to look back the way they came. "Maybe we took a wrong turn."

"I don't think so," Nicola said, holding the lantern up so they could see farther down the tunnel. The light extended several paces, then it was as if the dark absorbed it. Only occasional glints on the water burbling down the center of the sloped floor penetrated the gloom. "We were careful."

"And Werner and I were very careful when we drew the map," Sera said. "So, the maps are wrong." She and Nicola looked at one another. "We're lost."

"Yes, we are."

"We could just get out at the next exit we see," Sera said. She almost dropped the map into the water, then folded it and tucked it into her pack.

"I don't remember seeing any exits," Nicola said.

"We could always go back."

"No!" Nicola said emphatically. "I would rather die down here with you than go back."

"That's… cheery," Sera said with a grin.

"I'm a cheery girl," Nicola said. She returned Sera's grin, then peered down the tunnel. "Besides, there have to be other exits. We just haven't seen one."

The water took up the middle third of the floor, leaving narrow strips of damp bricks against each wall. While they gazed down the tunnel, trying to decide which way to go, a sound with the regular cadence of footsteps rose above the drips and gurgles.

"Should we run?" Nicola whispered, pressing herself against Sera's arm.

"Not fond of the idea of running blindly down these tunnels," Sera said, pulling Nicola behind her and drawing her sword.

A high-pitched giggle echoed eerily off the stone walls.

"Oh, Daga," Nicola breathed, peering around Sera's shoulder and pressing up against her back.

Sera lifted her sword, stepped forward to give herself room, and lowered herself into a ready stance.

The footsteps drew near, then a hint of motion in the shadows coalesced into a boy. A filthy boy, wearing what looked like a ragged burlap bag for a shirt and pants that extended only to his ankles, exposing bare feet. He stopped in the lantern's penumbral light. He was visible, but shadows shrouded his face. A small girl's head, surrounded by a wild mane of blond hair, appeared from behind him and peered curiously at them.

Sera glanced back at a nonplussed Nicola, then looked down at her sword and sheathed it, feeling slightly foolish.

"Hello," Nicola said, leaning out so the children could see her.

"Hello," the boy said. They gazed at one another until the boy said, "You're lost."

"Yes," Nicola said. "Very observant of you. Can you… um… do you know where we are?"

The boy nodded, but remained silent.

"This is weird," Sera muttered.

"Do you have anything to eat?" the boy asked.

Nicola jabbed Sera in the back. "Oh, right," Sera said and fished inside her pack for a strip of dried beef. She held it out and took a couple of steps toward the children. The boy met her halfway, took the offering, then retreated and handed it to the girl. She took a bite and chewed, peering at them out of owlish eyes.

"Now," Nicola said graciously. "Can you help us?"

The boy's gaze shifted from Sera to Nicola. "Where do you want to go?"

Nicola poked Sera in the back again. "Oh, um, where did Werner say Harold lived?" She started to dig the map out of her pack when the boy spoke again.

"Harold Wolfe?"

Sera froze, gaping at the children, one arm deep in her pack.

"So weird," Nicola whispered.

"Yes, we're trying to find Harold Wolfe," Sera said.

"Follow me," the boy said. He turned, took the little girl's hand and disappeared into the darkness.

Nicola pushed Sera. "Hurry, don't let him get away."

They scrambled after them, jostling one another and splashing in the ankle-deep water. The lantern swung wildly, leaving the children momentarily in pitch black, then swinging around in time to illuminate them as they turned into another tunnel.

Nicola stopped at the intersection, held the light out, and peered around the corner. She glanced over her shoulder at Sera, and said, "There's something weirdly familiar about him. Are they ghosts?"

"Whatever they are, he knows where Harold Wolfe is," Sera said, prodding Nicola forward. "That's good enough for me."

The boy led them through a confusing series of tunnels, then stopped below an opening in the ceiling identical to the one they used to descend into the storm drains.

Sera came up behind the boy, who peered up into the opening.

"You go up there," the boy said.

"Where will we come out?" Nicola asked.

He glanced over his shoulder and said, "We'll show you." He looked down at the little girl and said, "Climb up, okay?"

The girl nodded, sending her hair drifting around her head. She stuffed the last bit of beef jerky into a pocket, then shot up the ladder cut into the walls.

"Whoa," Sera mumbled. She smirked at Nicola's startled expression, leaned close and whispered, "Sooo weird."

The boy followed without any indication he heard her or cared.

They emerged into a building similar to the one in the Imperial District. While Sera helped Nicola to her feet, the children went to the door.

"It's not locked?" Sera asked.

The boy shook his head, put both hands on the door, and leaned into it. The girl did the same with a high-pitched grunt. Before Sera could render assistance, the door ground slowly open.

Though it felt like they were in the tunnels for hours, it was still night. The neighborhood they emerged into looked like the slums in Sera's mother's stories. Debris littered the vacant log that surrounded the entrance to the storm drains. The building directly across a dirt street leaned precariously out over the street, dark gaping windows watching them emerge.

Nicola pressed close to Sera, the fingers of one hand digging into Sera's arm. Sera looked up at the stars. Sunrise was only an hour away.

The boy waited for them to take in their surroundings, his face lost in shadow, then he said, "This way." He turned and walked away, with the girl skipping along beside him.

Sera pulled Nicola into motion.

"This is the Fallows!" Nicola whispered. She looked up at Sera with wide eyes. "It's really dangerous here."

Sera peeled Nicola's fingers off her arm and took her hand. She gestured to the little girl, stealing glances at them over her shoulder, chewing the last of the beef jerky. "She doesn't look worried." Privately, Sera agreed with Nicola. She had never been in the Fallows, but she heard stories and had often gazed at the ramshackle neighborhood from the top of the wall that shielded the Imperial District from the rest of the city. From that distance, it looked peaceful, but she imagined a seething cauldron of iniquity from her mother's stories.

"She's a ghost. What does she have to fear?" Nicola said, returning her grip to Sera's arm. "You'll protect me, right?"

Sera nodded reflexively, then remembered who the princess was. "Hold on a minute. You're a novice of the Seidi, able to bring forth fire, and whatever other terrifying magics."

Fear's marks fell from Nicola's face. She stared blankly at Sera for a moment, then her brow furrowed and her head bobbed. "Right, right." She clenched a fist in front of her. "I *am* a novice of the Seidi, for Daga's sake." The fist opened, and her fingertips caressed the tattoo at her left temple. Sera's song swelled for a moment in response to Nicola opening herself to her magic, as if she needed to reassure herself of the truth of her words. She glanced up at Sera with a determined frown. When she saw Sera's smile, the frown fell away. "What? It's just… I never had to, you know…"

"I know exactly what you mean," Sera said with a grin. The princess drew in a breath and pulled Sera to a stop. Sera tensed, her hand going to the hilt of her sword. The boy and girl were approaching a group of rough-looking men and women gathered in front of a building. Oblivious to the fact they stopped, the children wove their way through the group, climbed the few steps to the stoop and disappeared through the double doors.

Nicola slipped behind Sera and nudged her forward. "Quick," she said. "Don't let them get away."

The men and women, who barely acknowledged the boy and girl, turned as one when they heard Nicola.

"Uh oh," Nicola whispered.

"Well, what have we here?" a tall, thin woman said. They approached, spreading out, a few of them producing truncheons. "A couple of tourists, looks like."

"The big one's Volbroch," an enormous man rumbled. "But the other one's Volloch."

"Careful, she's one of them Seidi witches."

That caused them to slow as they squinted at Nicola's face. Sera drew her sword and moved to put Nicola against the building at her back. The faces of the men and women surrounding them on three sides hardened at the sight of her steel. Could she reproduce what she did earlier that night against so many?

"Pasha!"

Heads swiveled toward the voice.

"They're okay." A man's voice.

Sera risked dragging her eyes from her opponents to glance toward the sound of the voice. Though he wasn't wearing his uniform, and he had a beard, it was unmistakably Harold Wolfe.

Nicola jabbed her back. "That's the inquisitor," she said urgently.

"Just looked lost, is all," the woman named Pasha said. "We were offering *assistance*." She took a step back, bowed and swept an arm in invitation.

Sera sheathed her sword, took Nicola's hand and made her way through the crowd, forcing herself to meet the smirking faces of the people parting to allow them to pass.

Harold and a woman with the tattoo of a sister stood on the stoop next to the boy and the little girl.

"That's Sister Nia," Nicola whispered as they mounted the steps. "Everyone thought she ran away with Malefica Deirdre. Can this get any stranger?"

When they arrived at the top of the steps, Harold looked down at the boy and said, "Thank you, Lika."

The boy offered a two-finger salute, took the girl's hand and descended the steps without a word.

"Sera Storm," Harold said.

"Inquisitor Wolfe," Sera said.

"It's no longer inquisitor," he said with a smile. He looked at Nicola, squinted, and bent forward to peer at her face.

"Novice Nicola?" the woman Nicola called Sister Nia said.

"*Princess* Nicola?" Harold asked. He looked from Nicola to Sera. "What in Daga's name is going on here?"

Sera felt her face heat. Something about the tone in his voice. Suddenly, she was a little girl in her father's study, listening to one of his lectures on the importance of turning the other cheek. She lowered her eyes and glanced at Nicola. The princess stood, back straight, chin lifted, no embarrassment in her expression.

"Harold Wolfe," she said in her princess voice. She looked at Nia and said, "Am I to presume I no longer address you as *Sister* Nia?"

"No, just Nia is fine," the woman said with a smile. "And how are we to address you?"

Sera watched the princess, curious about her response. Nicola blinked, gave her head a small shake, then ignored the question.

She took Sera's hand and said, "We wish to leave the city and require your assistance."

Harold exchanged a look with Nia. "And why do you need to leave the city?"

"My father has offered my hand to Lord Brucker," Nicola said. Anger broke through her princess demeanor when she said, "And I refuse to be sold off like a farm animal."

Harold glanced at their joined hands and said, "I see."

Nia looked past them at the men and women watching the exchange and said, "Perhaps we should discuss this privately."

"Yes," Nicola said. "That would be for the best."

Harold turned with a grin and led the way into the building. They climbed to the third floor and entered a small apartment at the end of the hall. An old woman sitting on a sagging sofa looked up as they entered.

"Now, who's this?" she said, squinting at them in the low light. When she saw Nicola's tattoo, she startled. "Gimlet!" she called.

An enormous man emerged from another room at a run. "What's got you excited, Di?" he asked, before he noticed the newcomers. The old woman pointed at Nicola. "Well, hello, who's this then?"

"That's the *princess*," the old woman said. "Princess Nicola. I saw her at the winter festival last year."

Gimlet stared at the old woman, then turned toward Nicola. He leaned in close, peering down at her, causing Nicola to bend backwards until she pressed up against Sera.

"Well, how about that?" the man said. "We got inquisitors, sisters and now a princess in our humble home. Nice to meet you, Nicola." He stuck out a massive hand. When Nicola ignored his hand, he let it drop without showing any sign of insult, turned to Nia and asked, "They part of all this?"

Before Nia could answer, the old woman spoke. "Gimlet, where are your manners? She's Her Royal Highness to us common folk."

Gimlet waved a hand, "She may be Her Royal Highness up in the palace, but this is the Fallows. S'long as she's in our house, she's just Nicola." He looked down at the princess. "Right?"

Nicola's bobbing head bumped Sera's breastbone. "Yes," she said. "Nicola will do." She gathered herself and muttered, "As long as we're…" She glanced around. "In your house."

Sera caught Harold grinning at the princess and nudged him with her elbow. When he looked at her, she nodded toward one of the doors. "We were looking for privacy," she said.

"Right," he said. "We were." He gestured toward a door and led them through it into a small bedroom.

It was crowded with the four of them in the room. Sera sat on the edge of the small bed, pulling Nicola down next to her. Nia sat in the only chair, leaving Harold to stand next to the door.

"Now, what is this about leaving the city?" he asked.

"We are running away, because I refuse to be sold to Lord Brucker," Nicola said.

"But not even the emperor can force a novice to marry," Nia said.

"Malefica Briana has given the marriage her blessing," Nicola said. Her lips pursed for a moment, then she said, "I suspect that is Hoerst's doing."

Nia and Harold looked at one another.

"There is another problem," Sera said. "Nicola and I have been… meeting." When she looked up and saw Harold's raised brows, she rushed to say, "Just walks in the garden. Nothing…" She flushed and glanced at Nicola, who took her hand.

"And the emperor knows about this?" Harold asked.

"Yes," Sera said.

"We were being watched," Nicola said, her normal assurance faltering.

"So, you're leaving to prevent this marriage to Brucker," Nia said. "But you also have to leave to keep Sera out of prison."

Sera and Nicola nodded.

"Do they know you left yet?" Harold asked.

"Yes," Sera said. "I think they must have followed Nicola. They were waiting outside my house."

"How did you escape?" Nia asked. "Nicola, did you —"

"No!" Nicola said. "It was Sera. You should have seen her. I've never seen anyone move so fast."

Sera caught Harold giving Nia a significant look, but before she could ask what it was about, Harold asked, "Where do you plan to go? They'll come after you."

Nicola caught Sera's eye and gave her head a small shake.

"We need their help," Sera said. Nicola hesitated, glanced at Harold and Nia, then nodded. "We're going to find Nicola's sister, Kari," Sera said. "She ran away before. We hope she can help us decide what to do."

"But I thought they captured Kari," Harold said.

"Yes, they found her in Argren," Nia said. "The rumor was she was pregnant, and they shipped her off to have the baby."

"But she never came back?" Harold asked. "After she had the baby?"

"No," Nia said.

"What happened to the baby?"

Nia shook her head and looked at Nicola.

"I never found out," Nicola said.

"But even if Kari is alive," Harold said. "She's likely being held prisoner... no telling where."

"I think I know where she is," Nicola said. "When she was a girl, Kari used to spend summers at a monastery in the Northern Mountains," Nicola said. "I never went, but she used to tell me how beautiful it was. She loved being there, away from..." She gestured vaguely around. "Everything."

Watching Nicola, entranced by the sad smile on her face, Sera didn't notice Harold's and Nia's reactions until the room grew silent. When she looked at them, they had stunned expressions on their faces.

"What?" Sera asked.

"Was this an Eidolon monastery?" Harold asked, his calm voice at odds with his expression.

"Yes," Nicola said. "Why?"

"The woman Ragan met," Harold said to Nia. "Could it be Kari? Karl did say she was Volloch."

"What are you talking about?" Nicola asked. "Did someone see my sister?"

Ignoring her question, Nia said, "And if Karl saw her, it would have to be after the baby was born."

"We *were* looking for someone to investigate this monastery," Harold said.

"Tell me what you are talking about," Nicola said in her princess voice.

"We were and here they are," Nia said to Harold. "Another coincidence?"

"What are you talking about?" Sera asked, frustration edging her voice.

Harold looked from Nicola to Sera. "We'll help you get out of the city," he said. "If you do something for us."

Part II
Argren

The tales of Minna Hunter are full of fire, lightning and wind. That's why the *Alle'oss* came to defend Argren when the Empire's legions gathered at the Cut. They believed she and the spirits would lead them to victory. But I know what makes my sister great has nothing to do with the spirits. No one should be expected to shoulder the expectations of an entire people. Let alone a girl of fourteen summers. Had anyone known how little she knew of our mother's plan, they would have despaired. But Minna did not.

From Alyn Hunter's commentary on The Book of the Witch by Ragan Hunter

Chapter 17

The 29th Day of the Month of Annenmon
Year 1143 of the Imperial Era

Minna

Minna sat comfortably on Edda, watching Linea swoop up a steep hill on which spring's green shoots nudged aside soot left behind by a forest fire. She turned toward Ulf and found him returning her grin. It was the spot where they careened down the slope, landing in a cloud of ash at the bottom. Only moments later, they encountered the brother with the white stripe in his hair, the man who pursued her through Brennan. She glanced across the highway to the spot she and Ulf entered the forest as they fled the brothers. They barely escaped, and wouldn't have without Aron's and Zaina's timely intervention.

But that wasn't what she remembered most about that day. It wasn't what her mind returned to time and again the past two months. No, what would forever hold a special place in her heart was the moments before the brothers found them. It was when she and Ulf truly became friends. After days of danger and tension, holding it together for one another, the ridiculous situation left them giggling like children. Something about showing each other their silly selves bonded them in a way none of the dangers they faced could.

She reached out and took Ulf's offered hand for a moment, then let it fall and looked back at her parents. They insisted on accompanying her to defend Argren from the Empire, despite her protests.

"Alyn is off to *Helala*," her mother argued before they left Fennig. "What reason do we have to stay in this empty house?"

"What are you going to do if you come?" Minna asked. "There will be fighting. People will die." What she didn't say was she didn't want her parents to see her doing what she knew she would have to. Her nightmares featured the men she killed the previous winter. She wasn't looking forward to killing again. "Why don't you go to *Helala* to be with Alyn?"

Her father only grinned and said, "An army must eat. They will welcome an experienced hunter."

"There will always be the odd job needs tending to," her mother said.

"Alyn will be safe in *Helala*," her father said. "We know we can't protect you, but we want to do our part."

So, they came when she and Ulf left Fennig, and Minna had to admit their familiar presence eased the anxiety she felt at what was to come. She enjoyed spending time with her mother, now that she could be in Minna's presence without pain. Besides, it gave her parents more time to get to know Ulf.

She was less sure what she thought of their other companion. When the man riding behind her father saw her looking at him, the red tangle of his beard split, revealing rows of white teeth. Agmar showed up at the stables the morning they left. "Coming with," was all he said. He rode the old draft horse Minna saw many times pulling the wagon that brought his farm's produce to town on market days. With no saddle, his long legs dangled on either side of the horse, an old woodman's axe balanced across the horse's back. Though she wasn't sure how much help he would be to the army, she supposed they couldn't afford to turn anyone away. She turned away without returning his smile. To her surprise, she found she wasn't as angry with the big farmer as Ulf and her father were, but she wasn't ready to let him off the hook entirely.

"Minna," Ulf said, pulling her out of her thoughts. He pointed ahead, where the Imperial Highway emerged from the Wollen Cut. The spot they first saw the brothers who chased them was blocked by a wooden barrier. One of the *Alle'oss* archers standing on a parapet near the top looked back and caught sight of her.

The man shoved the woman next to him, and as she turned angrily on him, he pointed at Minna and shouted, "It's her!"

The woman whirled around, stared at Minna for a moment, then said, "Thank the Mother! It's Minna!"

Others turned to see what got their attention, and soon, they were all staring at Minna. Not sure how to respond, Minna focused on a familiar figure standing at the side of the highway.

"*Ertsu atlessa ara lessat aka atukar esota* (You're just in time for the fun to start)," Zaina said. She waited for them to dismount, then turned and walked along the northern rim.

Glancing back at her parents, Minna debated whether to tell them to remain behind, but Ulf took her arm and pulled her into motion. Scrubby pine trees, stunted by thin topsoil, edged up to the rim of the Cut, leaving a narrow strip of open ground at the edge. The archers occupying the open ground watched her pass, forcing her and Ulf to pick their way carefully over the uneven ground among the trees.

One man, someone she didn't know, smiled and said, "Hello, Minna."

When Minna gave him a nod, it seemed to break down some sort of barrier, and soon everyone was greeting her.

"This is weird," Ulf murmured.

"Someone has been telling stories," Minna said. They broke out of the trees, and she pointed to a familiar group of people standing where the wall of the Cut met the face of the escarpment. "And I can guess who it is."

Almost as if he knew she was thinking of him, Aron turned, his face splitting into a wide smile when he saw her.

"Minna," he said when she came close. "Your timing is impeccable, as always."

Minna stepped up beside Zaina and asked, "What are we just in time for?"

Zaina pointed to the west.

From the top of the cliff, the Imperial city of Hast was visible on the western bank of the Odun River. But it wasn't the city that drew gasps from Minna and Ulf. It was the immense camp on the relatively flat land east of the river. Thousands of small white tents, arranged according to the Imperials' mania for structure, extended north of the highway. At the center of the tents, several larger tents surrounded a large open space where Minna could see what looked like men fighting with swords and shields.

"Oh, Mother," Ulf breathed beside her.

"It must be the entire Imp army," Minna said, looking hopefully at Aron for confirmation.

Aron chuckled. "Not even close. This is just the Ninth Legion."

Minna's head swam. She reached out and rested her hand on Ulf's arm, afraid of losing her balance so close to the edge of the cliff. "How…" She started to ask how they could ever defeat the Empire, but the question was too enormous, the answer too frightening.

For a moment, she felt the weight of the task her mother, Ragan, left her. She looked back at the thin line of archers watching her. How could the *Alle'oss* ever hope to win their freedom against these odds? Ulf caught her eye and gave her an encouraging smile. She pressed her lips tight and gave her head a shake. Her mother saw a future in which the *Alle'oss* were free. She must have had a plan. Minna just needed to discover what it was. One step, then another.

"Don't worry," Zaina said. Her hand swept across the vast camp. "Those aren't our immediate problem." When Minna looked at her, she pointed down.

On the highway, a group of Imp soldiers marched slowly toward the entrance to the Cut.

"They look different," Ulf said. "I mean, from other Imps."

"These are heavy infantry."

"Heavy infantry?" Ulf asked.

"They're meant for heavy, close quarters fighting." Zaina pointed again. "They wear armor. Cuirass, helms, greaves." Missing Ulf's and Minna's confused expressions, she continued. "When they go into battle, they stand side by side, lock those big shields together. It's like a wall. The second row of men reach over the wall with those spears." She mimed stabbing overhand with a spear. "I imagine it's pretty scary if you're on the wrong side of it."

Minna looked west toward the camp. "Looks like they have a lot more of them out there. Wonder why they're only sending this bunch."

"Reconnaissance," Aron said. "They're just trying to find out if we're really up here. They don't mind sacrificing this lot to find out what we're up to. These are probably Styrian or some other expendables." He pointed to a group of men on horseback, gathered on a hill a league behind the marching soldiers. "My guess is one of those is General Prather. The Ninth Legion is his. He's testing our response."

"So, what do we do?" Minna asked.

"We kick their asses and send them home," Zaina said. "Preferably in a fashion that gives them pause."

"But… they're slaves," Ulf said before Minna could.

Zaina gave him a blank look. "Slaves don't become heavy infantry. These men might be the Brochen caste and considered expendable by the Empire, but they'll happily kill *Alle'oss* to better their own lot. What's our alternative? Invite them in and offer them tea?" She looked at the men, who would be within bow range soon. "This is war," she said, almost to herself. "People die, and not always the right people."

"Bit of a relief, actually," Aron said. "I thought they were just going to camp out there until winter."

"You wanted them to attack?" Minna asked.

"No," he said. "But they've been sitting out there so long, I was beginning to worry they were up to something." He glanced at Minna. "You should be able to handle this, no problem. Right?"

Minna gestured to the *Alle'oss* archers lining the rim of the escarpment. "What about them?"

Zaina shook her head. "Watch," she said, and pointed at the soldiers.

The shields the men carried bore a gold eagle against a red background. Nearly two paces high, they would protect most of a man's body. As they came into bow range, Minna heard a man shout an order, and as one, the Imps lifted their shields above their heads, interlocking them to form a roof. The men in the front row held their shields in front, protecting them from the archers behind the barrier at the top of the Cut.

"Might get a lucky shot in, but not enough to stop them." As Zaina spoke, an archer loosed an arrow that struck a shield, barely penetrating the hardwood.

They watched the men, weighed down by their shields and armor, enter the Cut and make their slow way up the slope.

"Fire?" Ulf asked.

"No," Minna said. She closed her eyes and sighed as she let her center expand. Welcoming Linea into her center, she gave herself a moment to enjoy her spirit guide's joyful presence. Then, sinking into her center, she reached out to the *luft'and,* the ethereal spirits of the air realm, and sensed a multitude of the delicate spirits responding. As she stretched her center into the physical realm, her mother's soft grunt startled her. She hadn't noticed her parents following them. For a moment, the presence of her parents distracted her, but then she heard it, soft and pure. Her spirit song.

Linea swooped joyfully, a glittering presence in her mind. Lifting her arms, Minna channeled the *luft'and* into the physical realm, smiling at their delighted response to the westerly wind carrying a promise of summer. She opened her eyes and swept her arms up and to the right, sending the spirits gusting above and behind the marching men. Her song rose, reaching up through octaves, Linea's lower harmony weaving around it. Out of the corner of her eye, she caught a glimpse of Aron's worried expression as he watched the men nearing the top of the Cut. She thrust her hands towards the highway. The spirits' plunged with a roar that reverberated off the walls in the narrow Cut. Just before they struck the ground, Minna pivoted, sending the hurricane into the back of the marching formation. Then she lifted up on her toes and thrust her arms over her head.

The large rectangular shields were instantly kites. Men, their arms attached to the shields by leather straps, were lifted from their feet and scattered like leaves in autumn, tumbling through the air, smashing into the walls and falling in heaps. Taken by surprise, the waiting *Alle'oss* archers gawked at the spectacle.

"Loose," Zaina and Aron shouted together, and arrows rained down on the disorganized soldiers.

Minna's lightning arced down, crawling across the sheer granite walls, and finding the soldiers' steel armor, the buzz deafening in the narrow canyon.

And then it was over. The few Imps who were able ran, leaving the dead and grievously wounded lying scattered across the highway.

Cheers arose from the *Alle'oss* archers, but the group around Minna stared at the bodies in silence.

"That was cleverly done," Aron said quietly.

Minna looked up to find him and Zaina grinning at her. She nodded and looked down into the Cut. "What do we do? Just leave them down there?"

"They'll come gather the bodies and tend to the wounded," Aron said. When Minna and Ulf gave him uncertain looks, he explained. "Rules of war. Even the Kaileuk allow the other side to collect the bodies after a battle." He pointed to wagons approaching on the highway.

"There are rules?" Ulf asked.

"All very civilized," Zaina said.

Minna watched the wagons approaching. "That was too easy," she said. "Is that all it will be?"

"No," Aron said. "Unfortunately, this is the least of our problems." As he turned away, he said, "War council in headquarters in an hour."

Minna turned to watch Aron and Zaina walk away. When she saw her parents looking down at the carnage she created, a hot, shameful flush warmed her skin. While they were in Fennig, she told her parents about her and Ulf's efforts to rescue Alyn. Though she made sure those stories had the gauzy unreality of all stories told around the fire at night, she was sure they couldn't help filling in the shadowy parts on their own. They must have known she had to kill people. She watched her parent's grim expressions as they looked into the Cut. When her mother looked at her, Minna couldn't meet her eyes.

"What do you think he meant by that?" Ulf asked.

"Hmmm? What?" Minna asked.

A small furrow appeared between his brows when he saw her face, and he reached a hand toward her.

Minna gave him a reassuring smile and said, "Oh, what Aron said. Not sure I want to know."

Chapter 16

The 29th Day of the Month of Annenmon

Minna

The small hut was typical of those the *Alle'oss* built for temporary shelter. The walls enclosing the round space were clay and straw laid down over a base of interwoven sticks. The thatched roof rose to a peak where a small hole allowed smoke from the fire in the center of the floor to escape. Linea drifted slowly in the space, adding her light to the sunlight coming through the open door. Minna pressed her finger into the still wet clay. The clay and the thatch gave the space a musty odor.

"Cozy," Ulf said, peering over her shoulder.

"There's only one bed," Minna said. She turned, and they looked at one another. During their flight to Brennan the previous winter, they often slept together under their cloaks, sharing their warmth. On the one occasion they were inside a hut like this one, they slept in separate bedrolls in the same room. Minna assumed they would share their temporary home once they arrived.

Ulf shrugged. "I'm not sure your parents would be happy with us sharing a hut." One corner of his mouth twitched up. "We're not promised, yet."

The simple word hit them both like a thunderclap. Yet. They held each other's gaze. "The bed's small, but the ground is soft. We've slept in worse places," Minna said.

Ulf gave her the smile she first saw under the overpass the night before they arrived in Brennan. She took a step toward him and felt his arms circling her waist.

"Minna."

They jerked apart as Zaina poked her head through the open door. She started to speak, then hesitated, looking from Minna to Ulf. A sly grin slid onto her face and she said, "War council, now." Before she disappeared, she said, "Only Minna. Sorry Ulf."

"It's okay…" Ulf's voice trailed off. Then they were alone again. "It's great that your parents came with us," he said, his tone suggesting otherwise.

"Yeah," Minna said. "Well, I have to…" She gestured toward the door.

"Sure, you go ahead," Ulf said. "I'll… take care of the horses, make sure they're fed and watered."

"Right," Minna said. "Good idea. I'll look for you after the… war council."

They stepped from the dim hut into the late afternoon light. The hut was situated near the center of a bustling encampment. Minna hadn't really thought about what an army entailed, but her mother was apparently right about the need for all manner of people. There were men and women carrying weapons of various sorts, but there were a lot more who didn't look like the fighting type. A village had sprung up among the widely spaced trees on the edge of the escarpment. Linea zoomed over to investigate a group who were preparing the evening meal in a large open-air kitchen. Minna's mother was among them. She smiled and waved when she saw Minna.

Minna returned her wave, but her mother's attention was drawn away before she saw.

"Well, I'll see you," Ulf said, and headed toward the makeshift stables.

"Bye," Minna called. People noticed her as soon as she started walking, waving and calling out. It was hard to hide when you were the only person with black hair. She returned their greetings, but anxious to escape their attention, her steps quickened.

Zaina gave them a quick tour of the camp earlier, pointing out Aron's headquarters. It was one of the few timber-framed buildings in the camp. The planks looked as if they were just cleaved from the tree. A familiar figure slouched on a bench on the wide porch, watching her approach. "You're late," Jason said, but his grin took the sting from the rebuke.

Minna stepped onto the porch and waited for Jason to rise. "You're still here," she said to the man who was her only friend for most of her childhood. Returning his grin, she said, "I thought you would go with Keelia."

"Leaving tomorrow. Wanted to see you before I left," he said, then his grin fell away. "You ready?"

Minna shook her head.

Jason nodded, his eyes following a group of archers who were pointing at them as they passed. "Don't define yourself by their expectations. You can't win this war all by yourself. Just do what you can, that's all you can do." After Minna nodded, Jason pulled the door open and stepped aside to let Minna enter.

A single room took up the entire building. The only furnishings in the room were two small beds and side tables in opposite corners and a large table around which Aron, Zaina and other people Minna never met gathered. When she entered, Aron looked up. The conversation died and everyone turned to look at her. She stopped, returning their stares, until Jason put his hand in the middle of her back and nudged her forward.

She stepped up to the table, focusing on Zaina's smile to avoid the others' attention, until she noticed the red-headed man standing beside Zaina. The beads in his braid showed he was from Richeleau. He regarded her with an expression that managed to be placid and intense at once. When she met his eyes, there was recognition in the small smile he gave her.

Minna dropped her gaze to the table. At first, she wasn't sure what she was looking at. Though she still read only haltingly after lessons with Deirdre and Ulf, she could decipher most words. When she saw the name of the city of Hast, she realized she was looking at a map. She knew what a map was, of course, but she never saw one before, beyond the rough sketches she and her father drew in the dirt while they hunted. Forgetting the others, she put her finger on Hast and traced the Imperial Highway until it jogged north and entered the Wollen Cut. She followed the line that must be the escarpment north until it ended halfway to Richeleau, the Imperial capital in Argren.

Putting her finger on the northern extremis of the cliff, she looked up at Aron and said, "It stops. The cliff."

The man next to her chuckled. "Put her finger on the nub of the problem, just like that."

Minna felt her face heat as the others laughed and smiled indulgently. All except the man standing next to Zaina, who was still watching her with the same placid intensity. She was relieved when Aron spoke.

"Yes, that *is* the nub of the problem," he said. "The cliffs are easily defended. Once we fortify the Cut," he tapped the map where the Cut divided the escarpment, "it will be nearly impregnable." He swept his hand across the map. "Our problem is the land north and, especially, south of the escarpment."

"Why are the soldiers camped near Hast? The Imps?" Minna asked.

"We think there here to ensure you stay put," Zaina said. "You and most of the army."

"So, we just have to stop them here?" Minna asked.

"No, unfortunately," Aron said. He waved his hand toward Hast. "Right now, the legion is a sideshow. The Empire will try to do to us what they eventually did to Styria."

"The Imps have been sending small groups of rangers into Argren from Richeleau," Zaina said. "They're trained to operate in the mountains. They're raiding villages, burning crops, killing indiscriminately."

"Why don't we stop them?" Minna asked.

"We're trying," Aron said. He looked at the red-headed man beside Zaina and said, "This is Lief Admundson. He is our liaison to *Oss'stera*."

Minna frowned. "Our struggle?"

Lief smiled. "Very good."

"*Oss'stera* has been fighting the Empire in northern Argren for a long time," Zaina said.

Lief's eyes finally left Minna and dropped to the map. "We try to intercept the rangers before they can get too far into Argren, and we've had some success. The problem is there is a lot of territory to cover and the rangers are formidable. Well trained, quick and stealthy. Unfortunately, they can replace their losses much faster than we can, so we have to make sure the conditions are to our advantage before we fight. They aren't trying to defeat our army. They're trying to bleed us. Attacking villages, destroying our ability to feed ourselves and creating large numbers of refugees we have to care for."

"We're evacuating the villages near the border to the interior, but that creates its own problems," Aron said. "Refugees have to be fed, housed, and winter will be here before we know it."

"It is as Ragan always said," Zaina said in the silent room. "We are too few, too scattered."

Minna asked the question she'd been waiting to ask Aron and Zaina since she left *Helala*. "What did Ragan say we should do?" Doubt, fear or something like it, flickered across Aron's face, gone before she was sure what she saw. She stared at him, clinging to his words when he spoke, unwilling to give up her hopes.

"She didn't say," he said. He looked across the faces turned toward him. "I know she saw a way through. She just wanted us to make our own decisions. It will do no good to try to guess what she wanted us to do. We have to trust she knew we would make the right choices."

Minna let her gaze fall to the map, barely hearing the conversations that broke out. She thought she would have more time with Ragan, time to find out what her mother wanted of her. But Aife cut her down before Minna could ask her. She always assumed Ragan would have told Aron, her adopted son, what to do. That she didn't was a crushing disappointment. If she had a plan, why didn't she tell anyone?

Aron's hand pressed to the map where Minna's eyes focused, bringing her back to the present.

"So far, they are only attacking in the north," Aron said. He tapped a spot on the coast where Argren bordered the Southern Sea.

Minna stared at the runes beside his finger. *Helala.* The shelter. The refuge where Alyn and Beadu were.

"Our biggest worry is that they will infiltrate the south and find *Helela.* That cannot happen. Keelia is in command of a force that will prevent that."

"What about me?" Minna asked.

"As long as the Ninth Legion is camped outside Hast, we need you here," Aron said.

"But didn't you say the Cut will be impregnable?" Minna asked.

"Aron is being optimistic," Zaina said. "Keelia told us one of the Ninth's specialties is siege warfare. They will try to find a way through."

"*Oss'stera* will continue to cover our right flank," Aron said. "Lief is here, so we can coordinate our efforts. Keelia will cover the left."

"But how do we win?" Minna asked.

The room fell silent again. When Aron spoke, it had the determined cadence of someone trying to convince himself. "Ragan would not have left us with a hopeless cause. We only need to find what she had in mind. I know you wish she left me with the plan." He shook his head. "As do I. But she earned my trust. She would not have sacrificed herself in vain." His eyes lost focus for a moment, then he said mulishly, "Ragan saw a way forward."

The thought crossed Minna's mind that her mother no longer had to worry about it.

Aron looked at each of the people gathered around the table. "It goes without saying anything we say in this room stays in this room. Until we see the way forward, our people must believe there is a plan." He looked at Minna. "It's one of the reasons why you must remain here. If people see you, they'll believe we can win."

Minna gaped at him. She understood why she got so much attention. The stories of how she battled the Inquisition, the Seidi and Aife preceded her. But how was she supposed to carry out her mother's wishes if she was stuck here? This couldn't be what her mother wanted. Before she could protest, Jason took her hand below the rim of the table and squeezed. Minna's mouth snapped shut. She glanced at Zaina, who was giving her a sympathetic smile, then nodded and lowered her eyes.

"Good," Aron said.

Minna's attention wandered as he moved onto other topics. After a time, Jason took her arm. When she looked up, the others were leaving. Jason nodded toward the door, then pulled her into motion. They stopped on the porch. Once the door was closed, Minna said, "This isn't what my mother wanted me to do."

"Are you sure?" Jason asked.

"Yes. No. I don't know, but I can't believe I'm just supposed to stand around, smile and wave to make everyone feel better." She threw her hand out toward the camp and noticed a small group of people watching the exchange closely.

"You *don't* know what your mother wanted," Jason said. "Aron's right. We have to trust she had a plan and it will become clear."

Minna looked away from the gathering audience.

"Because the alternative is too frightening to consider," Jason murmured.

Minna gazed at him, then turned back to the spectators. She swallowed, lifted her hand and waved.

"Keep your eyes open," Jason said. "I think you'll know the correct path when you see it." He pulled her into a tight hug.

"Be safe," Minna murmured into his broad chest. Jason let her go, then with a grin, he turned and walked away.

The door opened behind her, then someone stepped beside her. She glanced up and found Lief standing there, looking out at the camp.

"I knew your mother," he said. "You look just like her."

"My... Ragan?" Minna asked and turned to face him.

The smallest of smiles curved his lips for a moment before fleeing. "Met her... must be ten years ago."

"Where?"

"In Richeleau, or near Richeleau."

"How... what... did you talk to her?"

"Oh, yes," Lief said. "She came to *Oss'stera*, back when we were just a small band of hooligans, and asked us for a favor."

"A favor?"

"It's a long story. Perhaps when we have more time."

"Yes, I would like that," Minna said and watched him walk away. Was that the hint she was looking for? She scowled and gave her head a shake before she remembered people were watching. She couldn't start looking for her mother's hints everywhere. Aron was right about one thing. She had to make her own decisions and trust they were the right ones. She returned a passing woman's wave and set off in search of Ulf.

Karl

Karl spotted the young woman on the porch before he emerged from the trees. It was Minna. It had to be. He never met her, but she looked so much like Ragan, his heart lurched when he saw her. The emotions swirling around his memories of that woman were too treacherous to wade into. So, instead of approaching her daughter, he hid in the shadows beneath a rangy oak and watched her. When the man she was talking to left, she scowled, shook her head and headed off in another direction.

Karl put his back to the tree and looked up into its leafy canopy. When he left Harold Wolfe's apartment that night not so long ago, his betrayal chasing him into the night, he had no plans. In all the years he spent with the inquisitor, he hadn't thought about what would come after. His energy had gone into resisting his growing love for the man responsible for his sister's death. In the end, it required a monumental effort to thrust the knife into his lover's heart, to endure the hurt in his eyes and to leave, knowing he would never see him again.

But he did it. He fulfilled his promise to the Seidi novice, Ragan. And it had apparently been worth the sacrifice. Though they tried to cover it up, there were too many witnesses for them to hide the truth. Someone invaded the Inquisition fortress and rescued the *Alle'oss* witches held there. The day he discovered the truth, he fell to his knees and wept for the ones who survived and for the sister he couldn't save.

After leaving Harold, Karl lived on the fringes in Brennan. He couldn't bring himself to return home and explain where he was since he disappeared. He dyed his hair black to blend in with the Volloch, took odd jobs and found a small community of fellow *Alle'oss,* each of them with their own reasons for living in the shadow of their oppressors. It was a small life, and he told himself, it was enough. But when he heard through the network of his countrymen in Brennan, the *Alle'oss* were looking for someone who could navigate the Imperial capital, he jumped at the opportunity.

How odd that, after a perilous trek across the eastern Empire, he would encounter Ragan's daughter. Black hair, like the wings of ravens which always presaged disaster in old *Alle'oss* folk tales. With a disorienting sense of foreboding, he pushed himself upright, glanced furtively around, approached the building, and knocked. There was no answer. He lifted his hand to knock again when the door opened and a woman with the bluest eyes Karl ever saw looked out at him.

"Yes?" she asked, her eyes flicking up to his black hair, then searching his face.

"My name is Karl Siegling," Karl said. "I heard you were looking for a contact in Brennan."

Her gaze returned to his black hair and lingered, then she stepped back and waved him in. "Aron." A man bent over a table in the center of the room looked up. "We have a volunteer to be our spy."

Karl started at the word spy. But of course, what else could they be looking for? And besides, what exactly was he during his long years with Harold, if not a spy?

The man came around the table and extended his hand. "I'm Aron Hunter," he said with a disarming grin. "This is Zaina."

Karl grasped his forearm. "Karl Siegling," he said, noting the flicker of recognition that crossed the man's face. "Hunter?" he asked. "As in Ragan Hunter?"

"My mother," he said.

Karl kept his gaze steady, resisting the urge to turn and flee. That's why this man recognized him. His mother undoubtedly told him everything about him and Harold.

"How did you hear we were looking for someone?" Zaina asked.

"Oh, um," Karl stammered, dropped his head for a moment, then looked at the woman and said, "Heard about it through contacts in Brennan."

"What sorts of contacts?" she asked.

"There are some *Alle'oss* living on the fringes in the capital," he said. "It isn't easy, after …" He gestured vaguely. "But we get by."

"Why —" Zaina started, before Aron cut her off.

"You're *Alle'oss*," he said. It wasn't a question.

Karl nodded. "I'm from Lara'tan, but I've been living in Brennan for ten years." When Aron and Zaina said nothing, he continued. "Most people know me as a lower level Volloch." He met Aron's gaze. "I've been *trained* to mix with the elite." No reaction from Ragan's son. Karl looked away. "I can go anywhere in the city. Anywhere my financial situation allows me, anyway. I work odd jobs. It's enough to get by." Aron's lips pursed. When he started to shake his head, Karl realized just how badly he wanted this. "You won't find anyone else who can do what you're asking," he said. "What can I do to prove my loyalty?"

"I have no reason to doubt your loyalty. No, my doubts have more to do with whether you are suitable for this task."

"Maybe you can tell me what that is so I can ease your mind."

"We have a mole in the Inquisition," Aron said and paused, watching Karl's face.

The room seemed to blur, leaving only Aron's face in focus.

"We need someone who can serve as a conduit to this man," Aron said. "It will be very dangerous."

Though he knew the answer already, Karl asked, "Who is it?"

"Harold Wolfe."

Aron

At first, Aron wasn't sure it was *the* Karl, the one his mother used to goad Harold into enacting her plans. He never heard Karl's last name, not even from Harold. But when he said Harold's name, the man's face revealed the truth. He waited for Karl to duck his head, mumble some excuse and slink away, but his gaze held steady. After a moment, he gave Aron a nod.

"Can you step outside while we discuss it?" Aron said.

"Of course," Karl said. He nodded to Zaina and exited.

Aron stared at the door after Karl closed it.

"You know him," Zaina said.

"I've never met him, but I know who he is." Aron let his eyes drop.

"Who is it?" Zaina asked.

"Karl Siegling."

"Yes, I heard that," Zaina said impatiently.

When Aron gazed bleakly at her, she frowned, then her eyes unfocused for a moment. "Karl?" she asked. "That Karl. Ragan's Karl?"

Aron nodded. "One and the same," he said. "What are the odds, do you think? If I didn't know better, I'd think this was Ragan's joke on me?"

Zaina didn't answer, rarely did when he let his despair bubble to the surface. She gave him a moment, then put some steel in her voice. "It's been weeks since we started looking for someone to make contact with Harold. He's perfect. He knows Brennan. He knows Harold." She waved a hand and shook her head. "You're just going to have to put your personal feelings aside. We need to find out what's going on in Brennan."

Aron chuckled. "What would I do without you, Zaina?" he asked. "Of course, you're right."

Zaina rested a hand on his shoulder. "Besides, Harold probably hates that man."

"Right!" Aron said, pasting a grin on his face. "Bring him in." When Zaina turned away, Aron let the grin fade away. He remembered how Harold talked about Karl the night they drank together in the tavern in Fennig. Ironically, it was the way he talked about Karl that unlocked the door to Aron's heart. He had noticed how Harold watched him, felt the flicker of attraction. The idea that another man would talk about Aron the way Harold talked about Karl had been in his mind often since that night.

Coming back from his memories, he looked up at Karl. The man watched him guardedly. The truth was, Aron was unlikely to see Harold again. Perhaps Karl returning to his life would allow Harold to find some peace.

"Okay," Aron said. "You leave tomorrow. Zaina will fill you in on the details."

Chapter 17

The 29th Day of the Month of Annenmon

Minna

With the need to feed so many people, the army was forced to impose some organization on how they served meals. Anyone who ate the communal meals was assigned a time slot during which they had to arrive, eat, wash their dishes and utensils, and leave. When Zaina asked Minna and Ulf when they wanted to eat, Ulf suggested there might be fewer people to gawk at her in the last group.

By the time she and Ulf sat at one of the long tables, Minna was so hungry, she felt faint. But Ulf was right. There were few people, and they found a spot at one of the outer tables where they could be alone.

"How were the stables?" Minna asked, trying to keep her voice casual. If Ulf found he could be useful there, he might forget about fighting.

"Still coming together," he said, peering doubtfully at the stew in his bowl.

The only problem with the later time slots was the stew had been simmering for hours. The dregs remaining in the massive kettles had the consistency of her mother's wild strawberry jam. Minna didn't care. She shoveled a spoonful in her mouth, forcing Ulf to wait while she chewed.

Swallowing too soon, she coughed and gulped some water to wash it down. When she could speak again, she asked, "So, a lot of work to do?"

Ulf held up a spoonful of stew and sniffed it before putting it into his mouth. He frowned while he chewed, then swallowed and shrugged. "Not terrible." He grinned and said, "You remember Raif and Fenton? They're training new recruits."

Minna gazed into her bowl to hide her frown. Raif and Fenton were two brothers on Harold Wolfe's escort. Unlike most Inquisition brothers, they were Brochen and joined the *Alle'oss* after helping to rescue Alyn and the other girls.

"What happened in the war council?" Ulf asked, apparently unaware of her disappointment.

She considered telling him everything was fine so he would forget about joining the army, but she couldn't lie to him. Besides, it would become obvious everything wasn't fine soon enough. Still, it was a long way from talking about training and actually fighting. Maybe Ulf's love of horses would win out. With that happy thought in mind, she took another bite and said, "It doesn't look good."

Ulf paused, his spoon suspended above his bowl. "What doesn't look good?"

"There are too many Imps, not enough of us, and we have too much to protect." Glancing at a group at the other end of the table whispering and throwing her looks, Minna leaned forward, lowered her voice and told Ulf what she remembered about the meeting.

"So, Aron wants you to walk around, smile and make everyone feel better?" Ulf asked, tapping the rim of his bowl with his spoon.

Minna waggled her head. "That's the gist of it. There's not much else for me to do." She scooped up another spoonful and shrugged. "That and be ready in case they attack again."

"That doesn't sound like you." When she scowled, he lifted a placating hand. "Not the be ready part. The smile and make everyone feel better part. Not that you *can't* do it. It's just, it's not like you to sit around doing nothing."

Minna swallowed, sighed and gazed into her nearly empty bowl.

"You've been talking about finding out what your mother's plan was since we came back from *Helala*," Ulf said carefully. "And it doesn't sound like Aron and Zaina know any more than you do. I doubt they would keep it from you." He waited until Minna looked up at him. "Are you going to be able to sit around here, being the mascot, for long?"

Minna was so focused on an image of herself, smiling and waving while the rest of Argren burned around her, she didn't notice her father approaching until he dropped onto the bench beside Ulf. Before she could think of an excuse to leave, her mother sat next to her.

"You've been avoiding us," her father said.

"No… I've been busy," Minna said. "Aron wants me to…" She gestured vaguely.

"She's supposed to make everyone feel like everything's under control. Walk around, smiling, saying hello, looking confident," Ulf said, waving a spoonful of stew in time with his words.

"That doesn't sound like Minna," her father said, leaning away from Ulf's spoon.

"Why does everyone say that?" Minna asked.

"I take it everything isn't under control," her mother said.

"No," Ulf said. "We're safe here, as long as Minna is here. But things aren't so good up north."

As long as Minna is here. Normally, Ulf's confidence in her would warm her heart, but it only brought up the image of her parents staring at the men she killed that morning. When she saw her thoughts reflected in her father's expression, she dropped her gaze and scraped at the remains of the stew in her bowl.

"It's war," her father said. When she looked up, he said, "We've lived with the Empire long enough to know what those men camped out there have in mind. If we don't stop them here, they will do to Argren what they did to others before us. They know what you can do now. If they want to leave us alone, we're not stopping them."

"We're more worried about *you*," her mother said.

"You don't think I'm a monster?" Minna caught her breath, blinking away the tears that suddenly pooled in her eyes. *Where did that come from?*

A small choked sound escaped her mother's throat, and her arm wrapped around Minna's shoulders and pulled her close.

"Absolutely not," her father said. "We worry about what it will do to you. When it's over, when we've won, will our daughter be able to have a happy life?"

"She will if I have anything to do with it," Ulf said.

Minna looked up to find him grinning at her.

Her father clapped Ulf on the back and laughed, then he grew serious and said to Minna, "You don't have to worry about what we think." He gave her a small smile. "We know who you are. We trust you'll do what's right."

"You won't get any judgment from us," her mother said. "And we'll always be here if you need us."

With that wall removed, Minna relaxed as her parents and Ulf talked about their first day in the camp. Minna listened, wondering if she could ask for more stew, but when her parents started to leave, she said, "Papa? Can we talk? Maybe take a walk?"

"Sure, Minnow," he said.

Minna stood, taking her bowl and spoon.

"I'll get that," Ulf said. "You go ahead. Meet you at ou — *Your!* Your hut later." His cheeks turned pink as he scooped up the bowls, gave Minna's parents a nod and hurried off.

"Yes, well," her father said, rising from the bench. "Let's walk before it gets dark."

Minna rose, gave her mother a hug and said, "*Tok*, Mama." She joined her father as they made their way to the edge of the escarpment, far enough from the Cut that they could be alone. Standing near the rim, they watched the sun nearing the horizon, enjoying a cool breeze rich with the scent of prairie grasses.

"You want to ask about your mother," her father said.

Minna started and studied his profile. He looked sad, resigned. That explained the furtive look he gave his wife when Minna asked to talk to him. "How did you know?"

"The stories are all over the place," he said and met her eyes briefly. "You didn't tell me you met Ragan."

"I wasn't ready," Minna said. "It was so nice being home. Especially since Mama and I…" She fell silent for a moment, then said, "I didn't want to spoil it."

"I understand that," he said. "I imagine it must have been a shock. To discover everyone has been lying to you your whole life."

"Why didn't you tell me?"

"She told me not to," he said and shifted uncomfortably. "There were many times I felt that was not a good enough reason. Especially after you saw the spirits. I almost told you that day. I knew what was going to happen to you." He hesitated, his gaze on his feet. When he looked up, he said, "I hated Ragan that day, but I honored my promise."

She finally understood her father's tears. She looked toward the western horizon, wondering what stories he heard in the camp, and whether he knew Ragan died.

"I was going to tell you when I came back from the wilderness. Too late, unfortunately." He sat on the rim of the cliff, his feet dangling over a ledge a few feet below, then looked up and beckoned for her to sit beside him.

She lowered herself to sit beside him. They sat quietly while she considered how she felt about his revelation. Her father allowed her and Alyn to suffer because of their spirit sight. But so had Ragan, and she already confronted her anger at her mother when she met her the previous winter. She understood Ragan's explanation, accepted that she felt she was doing what was right for all the *Alle'oss*. She even admired her mother and adopted Ragan's quest as her own. The anger was still there, but it was for the Empire rather than for Ragan. If she forgave her mother, did her father, who was there for her when Ragan wasn't, deserve any less?

No. Maybe. She needed time to decide. But there were more important things she needed to know, so she put it aside. "What did Ragan do when she had the vision of the inquisitor? The one who let us live."

"It changed her. We were so happy." A smile flashed across his face, then faded. "Before. She was thrilled to have escaped the Empire, and we were deeply in love." He gazed into the distance and spoke in a low voice. "After the vision, she was often so distracted, it was like she wasn't really there. Then she started to leave, sometimes for weeks at a time. At first, she tried to explain what she was doing when she was away, but as time passed, she became very secretive." He came back from his memories and sighed. "When she said she was leaving for good, I told her you and Alyn wouldn't know she was your mother. I said it to hurt her. To try to make her stay. Now I know that was selfish of me."

"Selfish to want your wife to stay with you?"

"I suppose it depends on whether you believe her vision would come true. She assured me we would all die unless she intervened to change the future. We argued often toward the end, but she always asked, 'Could we be happy knowing what was coming?' I had no answer to that. If you believe her vision would come true, then yes, it was selfish of me to ask her to stay." The golden light of the sinking sun illuminated his face. "After all, she accomplished her goal. You, Alyn, and I are living proof."

"If you believe."

"Yes."

They sat quietly for a time, then Minna prompted him. "But you didn't tell Alyn or me. Even after you knew the vision didn't come true."

"When she left, she emphasized that I not tell anyone what she was doing. Never. No matter what." He swallowed, licked his lips, and wiped his palms on his thighs. After trying and failing to speak twice, he finally managed to say, "The fact we lived past the time the vision was supposed to occur... Well, I decided to honor her wishes. I knew she had bigger goals by then. I didn't want to damage her chances. The fate of all of Argren was at stake."

"Do you... do you still hate her?"

"No, of course not. I will forever love your mother. Even when I thought I hated her, it was only because I was angry and I missed her."

They sat quietly until Minna said, "I saw her die."

"I didn't know she died until earlier today," he said, his voice thick. "I'm sorry that she is dead, but the truth is, I haven't seen her for years and my heart has moved on. I'm more sorry you had to see it."

Minna leaned her head on her father's shoulder, allowing him a moment before she asked what she needed to. "Did she tell you how she wanted to do it? Defeat the Empire."

"No," he said, sounding relieved at the change in subject. "At first, she wasn't trying to save the world. She was only trying to save her family, and as I said, she didn't share much about what she was doing. It was only after she came home with a newborn Alyn in her arms, she started to talk about ending the Empire. That was right before she left for good. She didn't say much, but I don't think she really knew what she was going to do."

Disappointed, Minna watched the sun touch the horizon.

"All the people here." He waved back toward the camp. "They all think your mother had a plan. I've heard people talking about it. They say Aron, Zaina… and you know what that plan is."

"No one knows what she wanted us to do," Minna said, letting bitterness color her words. "I think she didn't tell anyone because she didn't *know* what to do. But she's dead, so what does she care?"

"I think she did know," her father said.

Minna's head snapped around. Gone was the regret she'd seen in her father's expression. Instead, she saw the man who lifted her up all the times she needed him as she grew up. "Why do you think that?"

"I often asked her why she never told anyone what she was doing when she left us," he said. "Why not go find this novice, Harold Wolfe, tell him she had a vision of him letting you live? He obviously had it in him to do the right thing. I told her to explain it to him and she could avoid all this…" He waved a hand, but didn't finish the thought.

"What did she say?"

"Her answer changed over time. I think she was learning, becoming more sure of herself. Shortly before she left for good, when she was trying to justify herself, she said it was a near thing, the inquisitor letting us live. He fully intended to take you. Otherwise, he wouldn't have come all the way to Fennig. But in the end, he made the right choice."

Minna remembered talking to Harold about that moment while they waited for Ragan and Deirdre in the garden of the shrine of Eidolon. His halting explanation told her how conflicted he was in that moment.

"Ragan said the moral calculation that concluded in that moment started long before, and it was a delicate thing. It hung on a thread. One change along the way and his decision may have fallen the other way."

"But it was Ragan who manipulated him. She was the one who started that…" She waved a hand. "Moral calculation."

"Yes, but she knew he would be receptive because she'd seen the result. And this is important — she was the only one who knew about it."

Minna frowned at him.

"Suppose other people, who Harold knew, were aware of what was happening," he said. "They would treat him differently. Harold would sense something was wrong, and it would arouse his suspicions, change his path to the critical moment. Events might have led another inquisitor to Fennig instead of Harold. Too many things might have changed. Ragan wasn't willing to risk it."

"But if that was so hard to do, how could she possibly have seen how we can win this war?"

"When I took Beadu into hiding, I asked her about what Ragan was trying to do. She said it was impossible, that the cause and effect, the sheh…"

"*Shehdi'enun.*"

"Right. The *shehdi'enun* for humans was too complex. People are just too volatile."

"That's what Beadu told Alyn and me," Minna said. She didn't mention that Beadu believed the gods guided Ragan. It wasn't relevant. The gods weren't going to tell Minna what her mother's plan was.

"She learned the hard way, trying to manipulate events when humans are involved is nearly impossible. As soon as she tells anyone what she saw, she changes the future," her father said.

"So, it's hopeless? Even if she had a plan, she couldn't tell anyone, so what good is it?"

"I don't think that's true," he said. When Minna started to protest, he rested a hand on her shoulder and made her turn to face him. "She told me certain people could be relied on to make predictable choices. Maybe because they have strong moral convictions, religious principles, they're hungry for power, or maybe because they are just plain obstinate. Whatever the reason, she said, if she could nudge — that's the word she used — these people into the right situation, she could be sure, or reasonably sure, what they would do."

"So, you think she… what?"

"She believed certain paths are nearly inevitable, that history is made by a few people with the grit, the determination, the conviction to wrest events to their will. I'm just guessing, but I think she searched for these people, she put them where she wanted them, and she hoped they would pull events in the right direction. Toward the future she wanted."

Minna gaped at him. It all sounded so vague and uncertain. If just telling anyone what she wanted them to do would change the future, how many other things might do the same thing? How many things had to go right? How many people did she *nudge* into the *right* situation and would they *all* have to make the *right* choices for the *Alle'oss* to win?

"I can see you're disappointed," her father said.

"I don't know what to do," Minna said. "And everyone expects me to."

"You only need to be yourself," he said.

"So, I shouldn't try to understand what she wanted?"

"Oh, no. She would have expected you to do that. Learn as much as you can about what she wanted. Just… don't try to *guess* what she wanted you to do. Make your own decisions. Your mother obviously believed you, and others, would make the right choices when the time comes."

"When? What choices?"

"You didn't get a chance to know her like I did. Ragan was not a woman who would leave things at odd ends. I trust she put us in the best possible situation. At least as she saw it."

Minna threw up her hands, opened her mouth, then realized she had nothing to say.

"Ask yourself," her father said. "What could Aron, Zaina, or you, as powerful as you are… What could you do, by yourselves, to defeat the Empire?" When Minna didn't answer, he said, "Winning is not sure." He waved a hand toward the Imp camp. "Maybe not even likely. But if there is any chance we can survive this war, Ragan would have made sure it's within our grasp. I believe — we all have to believe — your mother left the answers we need where we could find them."

"It would have been nice if she just told us where to look for the answers."

"I know. But if she did, we would be making her choices, not our own, and that would change the future she saw. We have to trust her. Just like Harold didn't know he was being guided to make the right choice, we have to believe Ragan's hand is at work guiding us. No one knew more about prophesy and steering the future than she did. Besides, what choice do we have? All we can do is our best, and that is what Ragan would want us to do."

Minna knew her father was trying to reassure her, but all she felt was the first fluttering wings of despair. When she was in Fennig, she allowed herself to imagine her mother hid a secret scroll on which she spelled out what she wanted Minna to do. All Minna needed to do was find it. Now, she was expected to just make her own decisions. What if she decided to return to Fennig and forget the whole thing? Take Ulf to the falls and hide until the war was over. The Imps would never find them there. It was, after all, a choice she *could* make.

But it wasn't. Not really. She could no more abandon her people than Ragan could come back from the dead and tell Minna what she needed to know.

"Come on," her father said, rising and offering her a hand. "It's getting chilly."

As they neared the center of camp, people noticed her and waved. Suddenly, their attention, which was only annoying before, seemed grasping and hostile. Her father told her they expected her to know her mother's plan. What would they think if they knew the truth, that Ragan abandoned her and left her with nothing to guide her? How quickly would they turn on her?

A pair of archers shifted out of their way as she and her father approached on the narrow path. Their smiles faltered when they saw her face, but their reaction only deepened her scowl. She would smile for everyone tomorrow. For now, she only wanted to find Ulf and forget she was supposed to be her people's savior.

When they arrived at Minna's hut, her father pulled her into a hug and whispered into her hair, "Ragan loved you and Alyn. It's a terrible thing to see the future. To know a catastrophe is coming. I would not wish that burden on anyone. I admire your mother for trying to save the people she loved. For trying to save the *Alle'oss*. I just wish…"

When he fell silent, Minna pushed her frustration aside, stepped back and smiled up at him. "*Tok*, Papa."

"Don't lose hope, Minnow," he said. "Your mother was busy doing something all those years. Someone must know something. Something that will help you understand."

"You're right. We just have to keep looking."

"Right. Now, I see Ulf lurking, so I'll let you go. Remember, you can come to your mother and I whenever it gets to be too much."

Minna watched him walk away, sensing Ulf coming up behind her.

"Everything good?" he asked.

No, everything was not good. But she didn't want to spoil their time together. Nodding, she turned, glanced around, and gave him a quick kiss. "Let's go inside and build a fire," she said. "It's getting cold."

Chapter 18

The 29th Day of the Month of Annenmon

Keelia

Keelia looked down at the body of the Imp ranger. "Strip him. Keep everything useful," she said. Bjorn, the man she chose as her second in command, passed the order along, while Keelia turned and climbed the hill on which they encountered the ranger patrol. All around her, the *Alle'oss* tended to their wounded, collected arrows and got themselves organized after the chaotic engagement. Fortunately, no one died. They had been patrolling the foothills of southern Argen for two weeks and seen only glimpses of Imps until today. She had the impression today's brief encounter was more accident than design on the Imps' part. They broke off the fight even though the odds were slightly in their favor.

There were few among the men and women she picked to accompany her to southern Argen with military experience, but Keelia set about instilling the professionalism she grew accustomed to while fighting the Kaileuk. It would take a long time for the *Alle'oss* to get used to the organization and discipline she expected, but they seemed to welcome the change. The rigidity of military life was difficult for people not accustomed to it, but it engendered confidence and removed the barriers of indecision in chaotic and dangerous situations. People wanted to be led if they felt the person in charge was competent and had their best interests at heart. It helped that they were eager to defend their land, and they looked on her with an awe she felt she didn't deserve. She would use it to her advantage while she could.

When she reached the top of the hill, she turned and looked west, toward the flat plains between the hills and the Odun River. She should have been reassured they were accomplishing the objective Aron gave them. No Imp had come close to *Helala* as far as she knew, though it was impossible to be sure. The *Alle'oss* were few and the ground they patrolled was vast and forested. But her scouts and spies assured her the few rangers they saw were all that were roaming the territory.

"You look worried," Bjorn said, as he joined her.

She glanced at him. "Why are they avoiding us?" she asked.

"Afraid of dying?"

She nodded. "The men might be, but Imp officers don't think that way. They know we can't replace our losses." She gestured down the hill. "That was a fair fight. They should have pressed us. That's what Imp military doctrine would dictate." They fell silent, looking to the west. "It's like they're showing just enough of themselves to keep us interested," Keelia said. She held out her hand. "Map."

Bjorn retrieved a map of southern Argen from Siv, Keelia's adjutant, knelt in the grass and rolled the map out.

Keelia helped him weigh down the corners with stones. They studied the map for a few minutes, then Keelia pointed to the foothills south of the escarpment, the area they patrolled since their arrival. "Assuming they *are* trying to keep us here, what are they hoping to accomplish?"

Bjorn didn't answer, but the adjutant, looking over his shoulder, said, "To keep us from noticing something else."

"Right," Keelia said. "But what?"

The woman knelt beside Keelia and pointed to the coast near *Helala*. "What happens if they land here?"

Keelia felt a disorienting sense of the world shifting. It was so obvious, she, Aron or Zaina should have seen it. She could say she was too overwhelmed by the responsibilities and minutiae of command to see the bigger picture, but that was an excuse the *Alle'oss* couldn't afford. She had always been given orders to follow, objectives to achieve. She understood small unit actions, battlefield tactics, following orders. If she was to command, she needed to think strategically. Giving her head a hard shake, she pressed her lips tight. Self-flagellation would do no one any good. She looked at the map and ran her finger along the coastline.

"Why would they land on the coast?" Bjorn said. "They don't know about *Helala*, do they?"

"Probably not. But..." Keelia pointed to Hast. "While the Ninth Legion demonstrates in front of the Wollen Cut, the *Alle'oss* are forced to keep the bulk of their forces there. The Imps might eventually break through the Cut, but with Minna there, it will be costly. But even a small force attacking from the east would unhinge the *Alle'oss* defense." She pointed to a part of the coast east of *Helala* which was less rugged. "They would have to land east of *Helala* to avoid having to go around the Kalana Valley. They travel north to the highway, then turn west." She traced the route with her finger, then tapped the spot where the main *Alle'oss* force camped. "A small force that could move fast. No logistics train to drag up into the mountains. It wouldn't take much. If they attacked at the same time as the Ninth..."

She stood abruptly. "Bjorn, organize a mounted patrol of the coast east of *Helala*."

"Sir," Siv said.

"Yes?" Keelia asked.

"How about sending the new people?"

"Why?" Bjorn asked.

"It's just, they've been operating on their own for a long time, they're good on their horses," Siv said. "Plus, they look like they can handle themselves." She looked from Bjorn to Keelia. "They're scary."

Keelia glanced at Bjorn, who shook his head. "What's the name of their leader?" she asked Siv.

"Willa."

"Go get her."

When they were alone, Bjorn asked, "Do you trust them for something like this?"

"Do you trust them enough to fight alongside them?" Keelia asked. "Besides, Siv is right. If they're reliable, they would be ideal scouts." She looked down the hill and watched Siv returning with Willa. The woman did look dangerous.

Willa nodded a greeting to Bjorn. When she looked at Keelia, her eyes flicked to the tattoo on the left side of Keelia's face. She hesitated for a moment before giving Keelia a shallow nod.

"Willa, isn't it?" Keelia asked.

"That's right."

"You arrived two days ago and haven't come to pay your respects."

"We've been busy." Willa shrugged. "I heard there was an Imp in charge here. I didn't believe it, but…" She gestured at Keelia and stared pointedly at her tattoo. "Here you are."

"Show some respect!" Bjorn said.

Keelia held up a hand and gazed at the older woman. It wasn't the first time she received a hostile reaction from an *Alle'oss*. She used to respond meekly because she thought she deserved it. Not anymore. There was too much at stake. She glanced down at the bow Willa carried, and said, "That's an unusual bow."

Surprise softened Willa's expression slightly. "It's a compound bow," she said carefully. "We've been operating out on the plains. They're shorter, easier to handle on a horse."

Keelia eyed the ragged clothes the woman wore. Like the rest of her people, she looked like she lived hand to mouth. The bows didn't fit the picture. The only people she ever saw using compound bows were the Kaileuk. "Where did you get them?"

"They were donated."

"Not by the Empire. The Imps don't use bows like that."

"Why does it matter where we got them? They kill Imps as well as those." She gestured to Bjorn's long bow.

"Answer the question," Bjorn said.

When Willa didn't respond immediately, Keelia said, "We don't know you. You show up saying you want to join us, but you don't do me the courtesy of a visit. I don't trust you. You didn't get the bows from the Imps or the *Alle'oss*. I want to know who you've been dealing with. Where did you get the bows?"

The two women stared at one another. Willa's eyes flicked to Keelia's tattoo again. "Came by this one by chance. When we found out how well they work, we had friends make copies."

"Friends?"

"*Oss'stera.*"

Keelia and Bjorn looked at one another.

"In Richeleau?" Siv blurted.

For the first time since she arrived, Willa's expression revealed something other than defensiveness. She turned to the young adjutant. "You know of *Oss'stera?*"

The young woman looked to Keelia, who nodded. "We met some of them before we came down here," Siv said. "Leif Admundson was their leader."

Recognition flickered across Willa's face. She looked at Keelia, still guarded, but her demeanor shifted subtly. "I heard *Oss'stera* started near Richeleau, but they're all over now. We first encountered them in Lubern. They own ships that work the trade routes in the Southern Sea. They help us out from time to time." She lifted the bow and said, "The bows were just part of it."

Keelia glanced at Bjorn, then knelt beside the map and looked up to invite Willa to join her. When they were all gathered around the map, Keelia pointed to the coast. "We have reason to believe the Imps might land a force on the coast somewhere along here."

Willa studied the map. "You need someone to keep an eye on it."

"Yes," Keelia said. "How soon can you leave?"

"First thing tomorrow," Willa said. "Any chance I can get a copy of the map?"

Keelia nodded to Siv, who said, "I'll have a copy made before the morning."

"If the Imps land, it will be a small, but powerful force. Most likely they will move north to get arou —"

"The Kalana Valley," Willa finished.

"Right," Keelia said. "We'll send word to Aron to put a blocking force here at the choke point east of the valley. If the Imps land, keep us informed of their movements. Let us know the number, composition. Anything relevant." She paused until Willa met her eyes. "Don't engage unless you have to. If we're lucky, we can catch them from two sides at the choke point."

Willa nodded.

Keelia pointed to where *Helala* would be and said. "There is a village here called *Helala*. Whatever happens, you must make sure the Imps don't find it. Even if you have to sacrifice your entire command. Is that clear?"

Willa gazed at her for a moment, glanced down at the map and looked at Keelia again. "It's not on the map."

"No, and it will never be on a map the Imps might find," Keelia said.

"Why? What is it?"

Keelia hesitated, until Bjorn said, "You'll have to warn Deirdre, and the fastest way to where they're going is through *Helala*. You might as well tell her. She'll figure it out when she gets there."

"Deirdre?" Willa asked. "As in Malefica Deirdre?"

"One and the same." Keelia stood. "*Helala* is a sanctuary for the children that would be taken by the Inquisition. They'll grow up to be *saa'myn*." When Willa stared at her blankly, she said, "Witches."

"Like Minna?" Willa asked.

"You know Minna?" Siv asked before Keelia could.

"Know of her," Willa said. "Who doesn't?"

"Maybe not exactly like Minna," Keelia said. "But you have the right idea. Any questions?" When the woman shook her head, Keelia offered Willa her hand.

Willa hesitated, then grasped Keelia's forearm.

"*Andsutra*," Keelia said.

Keelia and Bjorn watched Siv leading Willa away. "What do you think?" Keelia asked.

"Feel better than I did a few minutes ago," Bjorn said. "Do you trust her? It's a big assignment."

Keelia considered. "Send a couple of people with them. Tell Willa we're sending them as couriers, so she doesn't have to use her own people. Make sure they know to keep an eye on things."

"Right."

Chapter 19

The 2nd Day of the Month of Ungemon

Macha

The ship lurched upward as it passed the breakwater of the harbor of Ulm and encountered the swells in the open sea. Macha gripped the rail and leaned out as the bow plunged, throwing up a sparkling fan of water that left her drenched and spluttering. Hands locked to the rail, she closed her eyes and gave voice to her joy as the sea thrust the ship's bow upward. Sailing was a new experience for her, one she found much to her liking.

After weeks caged up in the barren stone buildings in Brennan, being outdoors on a warm, sunny day was a luxury she wouldn't waste. Even in the depths of summer, the cramped stone fortress in Narvik never lost its chill. Though she had few episodic memories of her childhood, the light sweat glistening her skin and rinsing the capital's stink from her pores, teased at long buried emotional memories.

Manfrid insisted they were not prisoners in Brennan, but Macha recognized their confinement for what it was. She and her sisters were dangerous. The Father and Manfrid were terrified of what might happen were they released into the teeming city. They were right to be.

She opened her eyes and looked up at the seagulls swooping around the ship. They were new to her. She peered into their minds when she arrived at the harbor and found them too simple and grasping to be interesting. Their world was about what could be eaten and what could not. She wasn't sure how they managed to procreate, but wasn't interested enough to pursue the topic. Even the gregarious, gossipy flocks of sparrows in Brennan, as simple as they were, were more interesting.

She turned her head and found the raven still pacing the ship. She reached out to the big bird when she noticed him loitering around the harbor, more to say hello to a creature that wanted nothing from her than any other reason. Curious, he followed her, clambering awkwardly through the rigging until the crew shooed him into the sky when they set the sails. Of all the birds she knew, the corvidae were the most interesting. Crows, ravens, even magpies. They were inquisitive creatures, for whom life wasn't merely a question of survival. They always responded to her probes in their avian way.

Macha and her sisters knew the Seidi sisters no longer believed in spirits. But they once had, and they wrote extensively about what they knew. The library in Narvik was filled with the texts the Inquisition purged from the Seidi's libraries hundreds of years ago. That was how she and her sisters learned about the spirits. It was Neiman, who read every volume in the library, who told her about the spirit which allowed her to communicate with animals.

She looked down at her spirit guide weaving back and forth in front of the ship, his luminescence nearly lost in sunlight glinting on the water's surface. Everyone in Narvik knew the girls who survived their childhood with their sanity intact had a limited time to find a spirit guide and make themselves useful. For those who didn't… well, it didn't pay to become too attached in Narvik. She would have to send him away to be with his own kind soon, but she wanted him nearby until they were out to sea. He would find her when they arrived in Argren.

Turning her attention to the raven, she called the spirit that would give her access to its mind. She allowed herself a moment to enjoy its comforting presence before extending her perception. Suddenly, the world was alive with life forces other than her own. She looked down, surprised at the intelligence she sensed in the creatures that dipped in and out of the water, riding the wave tossed up by the ship's bow. Though her insight into their minds didn't allow her to understand their vocalizations, she could tell her probe was being discussed. She would have to ask the crew what they were called.

The raven settled onto the rail beside her, rustling its wings and cocking its head, one beady eye peering up at her. Macha reached into a pouch at her belt and retrieved a strip of dried venison. The raven watched her hand as she lifted the morsel. "Go home," Macha whispered. She didn't need to speak out loud, and in any case, the bird didn't understand her words. But she found it easier to form the thought they would understand if she spoke it. The bird regarded her, then returned its attention to the meat she dangled. Not until she sensed his assent did she allow him to take the treat. She detected a primitive gratitude as he took to the skies and headed to shore. Ignoring the affronted seagulls, Macha let the spirit go, and the world contracted once again to her own mind.

"TAKE THEM OFF!"

Macha grinned. Manfrid allowed Eriu her freedom while she was confined in Brennan, but insisted she don the iron mittens before they left the Inquisition fortress. Her sister's incessant complaints on the trip from Brennan to the seaport at Ulm wore on everyone's patience. The hustle and bustle of Ulm distracted her for a time, and once they boarded the ship, she occupied herself with terrorizing the crew, shaking her chain at them and giggling at their frightened reactions. From Eriu's tone, Macha guessed the novelty wore off.

Arms out, to maintain her balance, Macha made her way to the rail at the back of the forecastle and looked down at the main deck. There was no sign of Neiman. She disappeared below deck as soon as they boarded. Though she was as inscrutable as ever, Macha could tell the vastness of the open sea terrified her. Macha would check on her later, but it was likely she preferred being alone.

Eriu stood next to the mast, blond ponytail swaying with the rise and fall of the ship. She let her head fall back and wailed, "OOOTTOOOO."

Otto, the man Manfrid tasked with riding herd on them, joined Macha at the rail. He was taller than Macha by a good foot, but so painfully thin that Macha probably outweighed him. Of all the staff at Narvik, Otto was Manfrid's closest confidant. That was why Manfrid chose him. It was a choice he would likely regret. Otto was terrified of her and her sisters. His fear aroused a predatory instinct in all of them, but the real problem was that Eriu hated him for reasons known only to her. And Otto knew it.

He returned Macha's gaze, swallowed, sending his prominent Adam's apple bobbing, and said, "Manfrid said to leave them on until we get to Argren?"

Macha grinned. It was a statement of fact, but he made it a question. When she didn't answer, he grew nervous under her gaze.

"OTTOOooOOoo."

"I… should remove them," he said. "Right?"

"Yes."

He hesitated, looking down at Eriu, jaw muscles working. Then he gave Macha a determined nod and headed to the stairs that led to the main deck. He stumbled down the steep steps, then braced himself against the rail while he fished the keys from a pocket. When he had them in his hand, he lifted them and shook them as if he were trying to distract a wild animal. The jangle of the keys was lost in the wind, but Eriu, sensing his presence, whirled and crouched, focusing her unsettling gaze on the keys. Their minder eased toward her, swaying on his feet and speaking soothing words, no doubt, though Macha couldn't hear what he was saying.

Eriu straightened, suddenly the picture of innocence, her head at a coquettish angle, her hands offered up. Otto watched her warily. When she didn't move, he took her hands one by one and removed the mittens. As soon as the second fell away, she lifted her hands, fingers spread, and shouted, "BOO!"

He stumbled backward, landing on his backside when the ship lurched upward.

Then, as if losing interest, Eriu spun away and waltzed gracefully toward the windward side of the ship, arms up, fingers waggling. When she got to the rail, she thrust her palms out and sent twin gouts of flame into the cloudless blue sky.

"Whooo hooo hooo, that's good," she sang, her trilling voice cutting through the wind.

The captain of the ship, who had been watching the interaction, appeared beside Macha. "Fire. It's no good on a ship," he said, tapping the railing with a finger hardened by callouses. "She catches fire, we all die."

He had the leathery skin of his kind, a knit cap despite the heat and a beard that grew down his neck and joined the forest on his chest. She took his perpetually furrowed brow as a sign he wasn't pleased with his cargo. "Just sail the ship," she said. "I'll take care of my sisters."

He looked as if he wanted to argue, but decided against it and turned away.

It was a good point, though. Eriu wasn't stupid, but she could be dangerously careless, especially with other people's lives. Hence the mittens. Macha watched her prancing across the deck, laughing when the crew shied away from her. "Eriu," she called.

Her sister whirled drunkenly around and looked up at Macha. "That's meeee."

Macha knocked on the rail with a knuckle. "Wood burns," she shouted over the wind.

Eriu's lips formed an o. She covered her mouth with the fingers of one hand, then extended the other arm, palm up. Sleet cascaded onto the deck, sending the crew running for cover. Caught in her own joke, Eriu shrieked and threw her arms over her head. When the deluge ended, she peeked up at Macha, suddenly the worried little girl Macha remembered from the day Eriu arrived at Narvik. But Macha always knew what her troubled little sister needed. She laughed. A full-throated expression of joy she didn't feel.

Eriu's face cleared. A small grin sprouted and flourished into a toothy smile. She extended her arms, letting her tinkling twitter mingle with Macha's deeper laughter. The storm passed, she sketched an elaborate bow, then resumed prowling the deck.

Macha watched her for a moment. She wasn't worried about Eriu. She could be naughty, but she listened to Macha. Most of the time. Macha descended to the main deck, gave Eriu one more glance, then headed below. It was time to check on Neiman.

Chapter 20

∽✲૭

The 2nd Day of the Month of Ungemon

Minna

Minna stood on the edge of the escarpment, enjoying the contrast between a chill westerly wind on her face and the warm spring sun on her back. Far below, at the base of the cliff, Linea, communing with other *lan'and*, glittered in the escarpment's deep shadow. Farther away, the shadow retreated as the sun rose, revealing spring's exuberant greens glittering with morning dew. Dark clouds gathered on the western horizon, harbingers of the spring rainy season. Tonight, she and Ulf would find out how well they applied the thatch to her roof.

Lowering her gaze, she focused on the Imperial encampment. Small white tents dotted the plain made brown by the passage of many feet, a miniature version of the grid-like streets of Imperial cities. Muffled by distance, men drilled with a variety of weapons from dawn to dusk in the open space in the middle of the camp. Smoke rose from what she guessed was the kitchen. It all looked rather harmless from a distance, and there had been no more attacks after their first disastrous foray. What were they waiting for?

In the week since she arrived, she did what Aron wanted. She let people see her, smiled, and answered an endless stream of questions. She hid her impatience. But behind her smile, she ruminated on what her father told her. He said her mother left the answers Minna needed, and it was up to her to find them. Now she examined every interaction, twisting herself into knots, searching for hidden meanings. Everyone was under suspicion. How would she know whether Ragan planted someone to nudge her like she did with Karl and Harold?

It was exhausting.

She started coming to this spot every day because Aron told her people would feel more secure if they thought she was keeping an eye on the Imps. The first few days, a crowd accompanied her. Seeing Minna at the scene where she saw the Imperials off in such spectacular fashion spawned a festive atmosphere. Minna was amused the first time she heard someone recount the tale, but as the retellings became ever more lurid, it grew tiresome.

Much to their disappointment, she ignored it all. Despite their requests, she refused to give her own account of the tale, claiming she was just here to study the Imp camp. And to her delight, the novelty of watching her gazing resolutely toward the west wore off after the first few days. The crowds diminished until only the sentries on duty remained. She could drop the facade. The sentries expected it. After all, she was keeping watch. That thought brought a genuine smile to her face.

She gave herself a shake and concentrated on the Imp army. There was something different today. It appeared as if they were building more permanent structures. Freshly cut logs were stacked near the highway, and she could just make out the pits where men used long two-person saws to cut the logs into planks. Other men swarmed over what appeared to be long timber-framed buildings next to the highway. When the wind was just right, she heard their hammers.

"What do you think is going on there?"

Minna jumped. She was so focused, she hadn't noticed anyone joining her. Suppressing a sigh, she fixed a smile on her face and turned to face the newcomer. He was a few years older than her. The ornaments in the braid by his left ear showed he was from near Richeleau, like Lief. The dusky blond hair on the right side of his head was shaved to soft fuzz. She saw younger men and women around the camp wearing their hair the same way. His buckskins and moccasin boots had seen hard wear, and he had the lean, hard look of an experienced fighter. He stood casually, almost slouching, half-turned toward her, his hands propped on an unstrung long bow. He was gazing at the camp, but when she looked at him, he glanced at her. She was used to a variety of reactions to her, but the disappointment on his face froze her smile.

"Don't do that," he said with a scowl.

"What?" Minna asked, too surprised to be offended.

He waved his hand back toward the *Alle'oss* camp. "That thing you do," he said. He pasted a smile on his face, lifted a hand and affected a stiff, formal wave. "Smile, wave, show everyone your happy face."

Suddenly, the sun on her back was much warmer. "What are you talking about?" she asked, some of the frustration she bottled up leaking into her voice.

"*There* you go," he said, his face transformed by a smile that brought a dimple to one of his cheeks. "That's more like it."

Still off balance, she gave him a sweet smile and said, "You don't know. Maybe I'm just naturally cheerful."

"I'm sure you are," he said, one shoulder shrugging. He pointed to the Imp encampment. "But even the sunniest person has to be a little worried about that." He let his hand return to his bow, a sly smirk sliding onto his face. "Even a legendary witch."

Realizing her mouth was hanging open, Minna snapped it shut, eliciting an irritating chuckle from him. "What are you talking about?"

"Surely, you've heard the tales of the Battle of Minna and Aife."

Minna studied his face, trying to decide if he was just teasing, or he was mocking her. Her eyes narrowed, and she looked west, toward Brennan, where she fought that insane witch the previous winter. "I don't have to hear it. I was there." When he didn't reply, she looked at him again and found him gazing at her, a distracting smile on his face.

"Now see," he said. "That's real."

Minna looked away, a flush climbing the back of her neck.

"Name's Sigurn," he said.

"Minna," she said.

"I've heard."

She wasn't looking at him, but she could hear the smirk in his voice. She turned away from the rim of the cliff. "It's *saa'myn*, Sigurn, by the way," she said. He looked at her, one eyebrow rising. "Not witch."

He nodded, the sly smile back on his face, then he looked toward the Imp camp.

Minna studied his profile, then turned and walked along the top of the Cut, barely noticing the men and women she passed, until she nearly ran into someone. "Excuse me," she mumbled, and slipped past the man. Linea appeared, weaving back and forth ahead of her. With a shake of her head, she put the strange boy out of her mind. She needed to hurry if she was going to watch Ulf training.

Aron gave Raif and Fenton the unenviable task of training the *Alle'oss* to fight with swords. The *Alle'oss* had no tradition with swords before the Empire occupied their homeland, and made the carrying of weapons other than knives and bows illegal. It only took the brothers two days to decide it was a lost cause. Instead, they began teaching them to use spears. When Minna asked Raif why, he said, "No one fights with swords in a battle. Spears are much more versatile and the basics are easier to learn." Then he winked and said, "Besides, you can throw a spear and run away."

Between Ulf's training and the demands on Minna's time, they saw very little of one another. Ulf snuck into her hut each night after most of the camp was quiet, but he was so exhausted from training, they barely had time to say hello before he was asleep.

Knowing how she felt about him joining the army, Ulf asked her to stay away when he trained, and Minna tried to honor his wishes. But while he slept, she examined the bruises on his arms, chest and back. The bruises he tried to hide from her. The past two days, she hid in the forest and watched Ulf practicing with a spear. What she saw confirmed her doubts. It wasn't that he was clumsy. It was just that he was hesitant at the wrong moments. She thought he just didn't have the temperament for it. She didn't say anything, but she hoped he became so discouraged, he quit. In the balance between her guilt against her worry for his safety, worry tipped the scale. So, she kept her mouth shut, shooed her guilt into the back of her mind, and hoped practice went badly each day.

The clack of practice spears and Raif's shouted admonishments became audible before the training yard came into view. Minna approached the clearing from behind a large tree, leaned out and watched. There were nearly forty men and women training. Agmar was instantly recognizable, towering over the others. His spear looked like a toothpick in his hands. He was clumsy, overextending on his thrusts and getting his feet tangled. But for a big man, he was surprisingly fast, and he attacked with a ferocity that overwhelmed his intimidated opponents. The woman he was sparring with today stumbled and landed on her back, her spear flying out of her hands. Agmar smiled congenially down at her, offered his hand, and lifted her clear off the ground before he set her down.

Minna scanned the others weaving back and forth in the yard. Ulf was not among them. Was he like the handful who were injured so badly they were taken to the healers, or did he give up? As she walked along the border of the training yard, searching for him, someone spotted her. She automatically hitched the smile on her face before Sigurn's rebuke intruded into her thoughts. She let her smile widen and returned the waves. Who should she listen to, Aron or that arrogant boy?

Raif came over to meet her. "He's not here," he said.

"He didn't come?" she asked, trying to keep the hope out of her voice.

"Oh, yeah, he came," Raif said with a grimace. "That boy shouldn't be anywhere near a spear."

"What happened?"

"Zaina watched him get whacked a few times. Then she came over, took the spear from his hands and led him off."

"Where?"

"They were headed in the direction of the archery range," he said.

"*Tok,*" Minna said and set off at a jog. She found Ulf and Zaina on the archery range. Ulf held a bow, looking much less awkward than he did with a spear. He listened to Zaina's explanation as she mimed drawing and aiming. When she finished, Ulf nodded and set his feet. Zaina plucked a blunted arrow from several stuck in the ground at their feet and handed it to him. Ulf nocked it, pulled on the string experimentally a few times, then lifted the bow and drew the string to his ear.

"Loose," Minna whispered.

Ulf released the string. The arrow crossed the thirty paces to the target and penetrated the bales of hay to the fletchings. Surprise threw Minna's hands above her head. As Zaina and Ulf celebrated, she let her arms drop. Zaina slapped Ulf on the shoulder, handed him another arrow, and moved off to help others. While she watched Ulf put the second arrow into the target, Minna felt a little guilty for being so surprised. And a little hurt. She could have taught him to shoot, if he asked.

"That's stupid," she admonished herself, and left the cover of the trees.

"Hey," she said with a smile. "Most people can't even draw a bow like that." She gestured to the handful of arrows sticking from the bale of hay. "Much less shoot so accurately so soon."

Ulf turned toward her, revealing a welt near his left temple. His eye was nearly swollen closed, but he was smiling from ear to ear. "Hi, Minna."

"Ulf!" Minna said. "What happened?"

"Got whacked," he said cheerfully.

She rested a hand on his arm, leaned forward, and examined the wound. "That's why you're here."

"Yeah," he said as he nocked another arrow. He glanced over his shoulder, then leaned toward Minna and spoke quietly. "Zaina came over after I got this and jerked the spear out of my hand. You should have seen her face. Scary." He drew the string and let the arrow fly, grinning at her when it hit the target. "She just walked away and Raif said, 'I suggest you follow.' Thought she was going to make me dig latrines or something."

He looked down and found he had no more arrows. "She can be nice when she wants to be."

He started walking toward the target, and Minna reached out and caught his arm. When he looked back at her, she said, "Wait until everyone else is done."

"Oh, right," he said. His face split in a wide smile. "Who knew, right? I'll be able to help."

"Ulf, you could help in the stables. They told me they need people."

His smile wavered, the implications of her asking whether they needed help in the stables sinking in. "I'll be able to help *fight*."

Minna thought of Sigurn. He was only a little older than Ulf. The casual way he held his bow suggested he was accustomed to using it. Ulf had as much right to fight as Sigurn did. But…

"I don't want you to fight." She knew it was the wrong thing to say as soon as she saw his face. "Ulf, I'm sor —"

Ulf looked away. Noticing the other archers retrieving their arrows, he said, "I need to practice. I'll see you later." He turned and walked away.

Minna watched him go, a swirl of emotions locking her in place. When she noticed people watching and whispering, she turned and fled. Slipping into the trees, she kept going until she was out of sight of the path, then stopped and stood motionless, staring at nothing. Ulf was right. He had as much right to fight as anyone. But she couldn't forget the bleak picture painted at the daily war councils. She didn't want him to fight, especially while she was stuck here, where she couldn't protect him. The image of the Imp soldiers lying broken at the bottom of the Cut came into her mind, and the frustration and worry she kept bottled up for days burst forth.

Sagging against the rough bark of a pine tree, she sank to sit on the ground, and pressed her palms to her face, as if she could stanch the tears. Stupid and weak. That's what she was. In the brief time she knew Ragan, Minna glimpsed the hard woman who manipulated and sacrificed people in pursuit of her goals. Was her mother always like that, or did she have to become that woman? Was that what Minna needed to do? Be willing to sacrifice Ulf to save her people?

She wiped her hands down her face, smearing the tears and pressing her knuckles into her cheeks. No one would be safe until the Empire was gone. She needed to be prepared to do whatever her mother wanted her to do. Weakness would only allow the Imps to kill everyone she loved.

She let her head drop back and noticed Linea circling slowly above her. Opening her center, she welcomed her spirit guide in, closed her eyes and let Linea's joyful presence soothe her jangled nerves. Suddenly, she was walking in the forest, laughing as Ulf told her a story about a prank he pulled on his older brother. It was a month before they left Fennig. They both knew it would come to an end, but they wanted to enjoy the time they had together.

"You're right," she whispered. "Let tomorrow be what it will. Ulf is here now."

The truth was, she was lonely. Keelia was patrolling the southern frontier. Alyn and Beadu were in *Helala*. Most people treated her like some mythical figure, tittering at her most mundane utterances. Her parents were busy and, even when they were available, she was distressed to discover they were no longer enough. And now she alienated the one person she could rely on. The person who stuck by her the previous winter, never complaining, always willing to pick her up when she needed it.

Hearing the small group of children who followed her everywhere creeping down the path and whispering, she let Linea go and stood.

"She went this way and didn't come out the other end," one of the older girls said.

"Is she hiding?" a boy speculated.

Minna stepped onto the path, drawing startled gasps from the children. With a guilty satisfaction, she scowled at them, turned, and hurried in the opposite direction. Not that it would do any good. They would follow.

To distract herself from her problems with Ulf, she turned her thoughts to the enigma of her mother's plan. She had long since come to the obvious conclusion the best way to discover Ragan's intent was to read her journal. But the journal was in *Helala* with Alyn, where, they decided, it would be safer. And besides, though Minna read anything she could get her hands on, there was no one here who could continue her lessons in Ancient Vollen.

She was considering how she might approach Aron about contacting her sister when a familiar voice broke through her thoughts. A man's voice. She stopped and listened, trying to place where she heard him. Coming up empty, she followed the sound until she emerged into a small clearing where several *Alle'oss* sat around a fire. Her sudden arrival brought the conversation to a halt as everyone looked at her. Feeling her face warm, she turned to escape back into the brush when the familiar voice called her name.

She looked over her shoulder and found Sigurn beckoning. She hesitated, loneliness and weariness at being the center of attention pulling her in opposite directions. Their earlier conversation was the only normal conversation she had with anyone outside her small circle since she arrived. Even his gentle teasing was refreshing after all the fawning praise. Scanning the other faces warily, she noticed curiosity, but none of the awe she was used to. Lief, the *Oss'stera* leader who knew Ragan, sat next to Sigurn.

"Minna. Come sit," Lief said.

Minna turned back to face them. Sigurn scooted over, making space for her beside Lief, and patted the log.

When Minna sat, Sigurn started to speak, then fell silent and scanned her face. Minna dropped her eyes and wiped at what must be the evidence of tears on her cheeks. "I imagine it must be tiresome, everyone following you around," Sigurn said and nodded to the children peaking through the brush.

Minna scowled.

Sigurn stood, took a step around the fire, waved his arms and shouted, "Hey, this is a private conversation. Run along." When the faces disappeared, he returned to his seat, grinned at her and said, "You're safe here."

Minna thought the children were probably still listening, but she returned his grin, touched by his attempt to shield her. She looked around at the others, who were doing their best to look disinterested. "Are you all *Oss'stera?*" she asked.

"Yep," Sigurn said, tapping a patch on his chest.

Minna noticed the patches before, but never looked closely. She leaned out so she could get a better view. It was a woman, back arched, arms thrown above her head. "What is it?"

"It's Wattana," Lief said.

"Wattana?" Minna asked, surprised. "How — What —"

"From the painting, *Spirit Light*, by a great artist named Valdemar," Sigurn said. "You've never heard of Valdemar?"

"No," Minna said. "I grew up in a remote village."

"Fennig," Sigurn said, and gave her a familiar smirk. He stood and lifted his arms theatrically. "Gather around, all of you. Let me tell you the tale of a young girl. A girl with extraordinary powers from the remote village of Fennig…" He paused, gave her a smile, then bowed to the other's applause. Dropping back into his seat, he said, "Legendary witch, remember? Sorry, *saa'myn.*"

Minna was surprised to find herself laughing along with the others. When the laughter died down, she scanned the others and noticed they all wore the patch. "Why do you wear it? The patch."

"Let's just say the painting was an inspiration when we were learning to fight back," Lief said.

"To us," Sigurn said, "Wattana is a reminder of who we used to be as a people. The *Alle'oss.*"

While Minna was considering this, one of the other men said, "It's a real honor to share a fire with another Wattana."

Minna looked up sharply.

"Now, Sven," Lief said. "She gets plenty of that from everyone else." He paused, looking around to make sure he had everyone's attention. "Let's make this a safe place for her. A place she can come to leave that behind. Agreed?"

There was a round of agreement. Sigurn said, *"Otsuna,"* and was answered by everyone else. He winked at her.

Minna was going to ask about the unfamiliar word, but remembered what Lief told her the day of her first war council. She got his attention and asked, "You knew my mother, Ragan?"

"Yes, I did, though not as well as Alar or Tove did," he said.

"Tove?" Sigurn said. "*The* Tove?"

"The very same," Lief said.

"Why?" Minna asked. "Who is she?"

"Tove is Desulti," Sigurn said. He leaned forward, let his eyes drift across the group, who were now listening intently. "Murtair," he said.

Some of those listening nodded, but others looked impressed. The only thing Minna knew about the Desulti was what she learned while she pretended to be one to escape discovery in Hast the previous winter. But even that left an impression on her. "How did my mother know a Desulti?"

"Well, Tove wasn't in the Order when she met Ragan," Lief said. "She was one of the original members of *Oss'stera*. She made our first bow. Carved it with a hunting knife."

It took a moment for the implication to sink in. "Tove's *Alle'oss*?" When Lief nodded, she said, "But I thought the Desulti were all Volloch."

"They were," Sigurn said proudly. "Until they met Tove." He looked ready to launch into the story, before Minna interrupted him.

"Who is Alar?"

"The leader of *Oss'stera*," a woman sitting on the other side of Sigurn said.

"A great man," a man added.

"Leif, Alar and Tove were the original members of *Oss'stera*," Sigurn said with a note of pride.

"It wasn't just us," Lief said.

Sigurn shrugged.

"How well did they know my mother?" Minna asked.

"Pretty well, I guess," Lief said. "She helped us break Scilla, Alar's wife, out of the Inquisition prison in Kartok. Your sister was born on Alar's bed. Though he wasn't there at the time."

"Alyn was born in Richeleau?" Minna asked, surprised. Her father mentioned Ragan returning home with a newborn Alyn in her arms, but she'd been too distracted to ask about it.

"In the mountains above Richeleau, actually," Sigurn said. "Battle raging outside at the time. House burning down around her. Quite the entrance into the world."

She studied his face. He couldn't be much older than her. "Were you there?"

"No, of course not," he said.

"We all know the stories," the woman beside him said.

Minna felt a surge of excitement she hadn't felt since the first war council. These people knew a lot about her mother. Maybe something in their stories would give her a clue. Before she could ask if they would share their stories, Sigurn stood.

"You're staying for lunch," he said. He dipped a ladle into the pot suspended above the fire, filled a bowl and held it out.

Minna took the bowl, returning his grin. "*Tok.*"

"*Aurina sha,*" he answered and ladled himself a bowl.

Minna cradled the bowl in her lap, watching the others engaged in lighthearted conversation. Ignoring her. Breathing in the enticing aroma of the venison and mushroom stew, she let her breath out, feeling herself relax for the first time since she arrived. She would get them to tell her their stories, and maybe she could meet Alar or Tove. Ragan never did anything without intent. If she spent time with these people, there was a reason.

Chapter 21

The 2nd Day of the Month of Ungemon

Alyn

Keeping the tradition she, Minna and Keelia started when they were all in *Helala* together, Alyn climbed into the mountains behind the village every Lindenlatha, her day off. She sat cross-legged on a prominence overlooking the village, remembering a conversation she had with Minna on this spot. Alyn admonished her sister for taking Ragan's burden as her own. She told her sister her life was her own. Minna responded, "I'm not sure that's true anymore. In fact, I don't think that's been true for a long time." Alyn dismissed it at the time, thinking it only a response to their recent trauma. But as she translated more of Ragan's journal, she returned again and again to Minna's words. How much of their lives was their own? How much control did they have? Ragan obviously believed she could control the future.

From Ragan's journal:

Are we, as the sprites the Alle'oss once believed in, tossed about by events beyond our control? Beadu's admonishments would suggest it is so. My old friend concedes it is possible to change an event here or there, but contends the possibilities are so numerous and tangled that they might as well be entirely random. If that is so, then all is lost. But, I hold out hope, a proper understanding of the shedhi'enun, the cause and effect of events, will allow me to grasp the course of the future and wrest it to my will.

Was it arrogance? Beadu, the wisest woman Alyn knew, wouldn't call her friend arrogant, but she repeatedly counseled Alyn against following Ragan's example. Beadu told her the spirits of *annen'heim*, the soul spirits, were not to be trusted. They would lead her astray. Though they couldn't lie, they would show her futures that would deceive her into wrong choices. Beadu also said the *sjel'and* relished the pain their glimpses into the future caused, and would show her the worst possible outcomes. They did it to Ragan when she began her quest.

Alyn had abided by Beadu's wishes. Until now. She didn't want to deceive her mentor, but she was tired of being stuck in *Helala*, not knowing what was happening, not knowing if her family was safe. Not being able to do anything. The possibility of knowing what was to come, of being able to influence the future, was too enticing. And Alyn had reason to believe her experience with the *sjel'and* would be different.

Beadu couldn't explain the vision the spirit showed Alyn while she was in the Inquisition prison. The vision was of the ship that brought Minna and her to *Helala*. Though the presence of the spirit in her mind repulsed her, Alyn sensed no animosity from it. And there was no deception because the vision came true. The spirit showed her a hopeful moment, at a point when Alyn needed hope.

She closed her eyes and sank into her center, the place behind her eyes where her spirit resided, where the physical realm connected to the spirit realm, *mid'heim*. She allowed her connection to *mid'heim* to expand until she sensed her spirit's joyful presence. It was moments like this that made her wonder who she was. Was she the spirit which animated her, or was she her body which could perceive that spirit? With Beadu's guidance, she decided she was both. She was her spirit, and she was the senses and the mind which could contemplate its own existence.

As she sank into the meditative state that was her center, the sounds and scents of the forest, her awareness of her own body, faded into the background. Though she did not have a spirit guide who would introduce her to the spirits of other realms, she was confident the *sjel'and* would answer if she called. She gave herself a moment to enjoy the stillness, then she readied herself and she and her spirit reached out to the spirits of *annen'heim*.

At first, nothing happened. But then she sensed a presence. Unlike the *lan'and*, who roared into her center with reckless glee, the *sjel'and* oozed into her awareness, a shambling, shuddery sensation that raised goosebumps on her arms even while she was deep in her center. Her instinct was to recoil, to eject it from her mind, but she composed herself. She called the spirit for a reason, and she would not run away.

She encountered these spirits on two occasions before. In both cases, the witch, Aife, forced the *sjel'and* into her mind. The first time, she sensed the *sjel'and's* grasping malevolence just before it lunged at her spirit. Only pure terror gave her the strength to eject it from her mind. The encounter left her nauseated and shaken. She expected the same when Aife returned, so she prepared herself. But, instead of maliciousness, she sensed curiosity from the second spirit. Then, unbidden, it showed her the hopeful vision.

Unwilling to expose her own spirit to harm, she kept her distance, regarding the *sjel'and*, which hovered, motionless, not revealing its intent.

Suddenly, she was in another forest, one she didn't recognize. Unlike her previous vision in which she was above the ship, this time she was viewing the scene as if she were standing on the ground. There were small huts scattered among widely spaced trees. Rain pelted down, smoke swirled through the trees. At first, there was only the sound of the rain, then screams erupted behind her. She wanted to turn, but the spirit controlled her perspective. Men and women came into view as they ran past her, throwing frightened looks over their shoulders. Heart thrumming, Alyn felt the urge to follow them, but as in a nightmare, she was immobile. It wasn't real, she reminded herself, as a woman collapsed at her feet with an arrow in her back.

And then Minna appeared out of the smoke and chaos. She stopped ten paces in front of Alyn, looking at something behind Alyn. Alyn recognized the same calm intensity in her sister's expression she saw before Minna fought Aife. Minna lifted her hands, and Alyn flinched as fire engulfed her. The scene rotated until she was seeing the scene from Minna's perspective. Soldiers, some of them on fire, scrambled to escape Minna's flames. They didn't wear any Imperial uniform Alyn saw before, and they were all as tall and wide as Agmar. As Minna's fire guttered out, three women emerged from the smoldering forest and lifted their hands. Alyn screamed a warning as the vision faded.

She was alone in the dark with the *sjel'and*, too stunned and overwhelmed to defend herself. But the spirit merely vanished from her awareness.

Alyn fought free of her center, letting the world snap back into focus. "Minna!" She leapt to her feet, her heart thudding in her chest, unable to catch her breath.

She needed to warn Minna, but after only a few steps, she stopped. Was it a vision of what *would* happen or what *might* happen? How likely was it? There was no way to know. But one thing she could be sure of was the three women were real. *Sjel'and* couldn't lie. And she didn't have to wonder who they were. They were like Aife. Minna killed Aife, but these three women must be the Malleus's new witches. The thought terrified her. Aife had very nearly killed Minna and Keelia by herself. What could her sister do against three of them? The Malleus must have sent the witches to kill Minna. Even if that vision didn't come to pass, another like it was inevitable.

She needed to talk to someone, but the thought of confessing to Beadu what she did left her flushed with shame. She couldn't do that.

"Deirdre."

Minna

After sharing their lunch with her, the *Oss'stera* soldiers left to patrol the perimeter of the camp. Minna set off in search of Ulf, excited to tell him what she learned about her mother. Then she remembered their fight. Besides, he would be training for hours. Her father was hunting and her mother was busy in the kitchens. So, she wandered the camp alone, returning people's smiles, submerging her worries for Ulf beneath speculation about what she might learn from *Oss'stera*.

As the afternoon wore on, she resisted the urge to hide in her hut, but took to less traveled paths, playing cat and mouse with her entourage. Wanting to be alone and feeling lonely at the same time. When her allotted time to eat approached, she watched the sun, willing it to sink toward the horizon faster. She wanted, needed, to make amends with Ulf, and was desperate to get his opinion on what she learned.

Losing patience, she decided it wouldn't matter if she were a little early. After all, it was nearly deserted when she and Ulf ate. She hurried toward the dining area, anticipation quickening her steps. Ulf wasn't there, but she was early, after all. She exchanged greetings with her mother as she retrieved a bowl of what had become a familiar stew and made her way to their usual table.

She was gazing at the unappetizing meal when a commotion brought her head up. Surprised, she watched a crowd emerging from the trees. When they saw her, they entered the kitchen queue, talking excitedly. News had apparently spread about when she had her meals and people adjusted their schedules accordingly. She had her hands on her bowl, ready to flee without eating, when she remembered Ulf wouldn't know where she went. So, she settled herself, and hoped if she didn't make eye contact, they would leave her alone.

Halfway through her allotted time, Ulf still hadn't appeared. Minna sat, eyes on her mostly uneaten stew, idly tapping the edge of the bowl with her spoon. Though no one was rude enough to join her, they gathered at nearby tables, speaking and laughing loudly and casting furtive glances her way. That was somehow worse.

"So much for being alone."

She looked up at the familiar voice to find Ulf standing on the other side of the table, grinning down at her, a bowl in one hand and a spoon in the other.

"You came," she said.

He came around, dropped onto the bench beside her, leaned in and whispered, "Easier to talk without everyone listening this way." Scooping up a spoonful of stew, he said, "Of course I came. You think you can get rid of me that easily?" He shoved the spoon in his mouth and chewed thoughtfully. "You know, I'm getting used to this stuff."

Minna watched him going in for another scoop, their audience temporarily forgotten. When laughter burbled up out of her, Ulf gave her a sideways grin.

"You okay?" he asked.

"You must be hungry," Minna said, watching him shoveling the stew into his mouth.

"Starved," he said. "Haven't eaten since this morning."

Gently, Minna touched the welt beside his eye, causing him to flinch away. "The swelling is going down," she said.

"Yeah. Funny enough, when I could see out of that eye again, I couldn't hit the center of the target anymore."

Minna sat up straight, half-turned toward him, hands cupped in her lap. Determined to be supportive, she said, "You were just getting tired. You have to work those muscles."

Ulf rotated his shoulder and grimaced. "The whole right side of my body aches."

Minna massaged his shoulder, digging her fingers into the spots she knew from experience would need it most. Encouraged by his satisfied moan, she asked, "Where's your bow?"

Ulf leaned in and whispered, "I left it in our hut."

Minna put her mouth next to his ear and whispered, "It's still our hut?"

"Of course," he said. "As long as your father doesn't find out."

Minna was pretty sure her parents were well aware Ulf slept in her hut. She and Ulf would be promised in another year, and who knew what that year would bring? She guessed her parents knew as well as Minna these might be the last days she and Ulf had together.

His grin fell away. Glancing around at the other tables, which had grown quiet when Minna whispered in his ear, he asked, "Are you finished? Can we take a walk?"

Minna looked past him to people pretending they weren't trying to listen. "Sure."

Scooping up their bowls, they dashed to the kitchen, dropped them into the sink without washing them, then slipped out the back into the forest. They ran, hand in hand, ducking branches, and laughing, arriving breathless near the spot on the edge of the escarpment where Minna talked to her father. Linea zoomed out over the rim and winked out of sight as she plunged toward the forest at the base of the cliff.

They were alone. Stepping apart, arms extended, the fingers of one hand entwined, they spun slowly, grinning at one another. Ulf pulled her close and took her other hand. He gazed down at her, serious, then brushed her lips with his own.

She reached for him, but he pulled back. "Listen… I'm so tired every night… we haven't had a chance to, you know, since we left Fennig."

Minna felt her face warming. They talked around the topic of sex when they returned from *Helala*, but had come to a mutual, unspoken agreement that it could wait until the war was over. It was a sort of talisman, an expression of faith, a commitment to one another that the war would end and they would still be together. But that didn't mean they weren't happily exploring the journey to that tantalizing destination. Sometimes fumbling, sometimes embarrassing, always exciting, but they had only fourteen summers and Minna guessed that's the way it was supposed to be.

"That's okay," she said, giving him her secret smile. She glanced around, even though she knew they were alone, then pressed her body against his and said, "We'll have a lot of time for that." There was only a slight hesitation in Ulf's returned grin, but they both noticed it. Minna rushed on, determined nothing would spoil the moment. "Besides, just having you there helps me sleep."

Ulf chuckled, the moment of doubt banished. "You sleep? I wouldn't know. You're awake when I pass out and awake when I wake up."

"Yes, I sleep." Minna reached up and kissed him. "Because you're keeping the nightmares away."

"Speaking of sleep," Ulf said with an apologetic smile.

"Come on," Minna said.

They strolled, arm in arm, taking advantage of a few more minutes alone. Minna told him what she learned from *Oss'stera*. Ulf was the attentive audience she hoped he'd be. Linea returned, appearing and disappearing again as she chased other *lan'and*.

"Alyn was born in Richeleau?" Ulf asked when she got to that part of the story.

"I know. You'd think it wouldn't surprise me anymore. How many other secrets have they kept from us?"

"They?"

Minna waved a hand. "All of them. Ragan. My father. My mother. Aron. Zaina. All of them."

Missing or ignoring the note of bitterness that crept into Minna's voice, Ulf asked, "So you think they know something that will help? These *Oss'stera* people?"

"I do," she said. "I don't know why. Maybe it's just more wishful thinking."

"I don't think so," he said as they arrived at their hut. He turned her to face him. "Your mother was obviously up to something with them. It had to be important." He grinned his crooked grin. "For all we know, this Lief, Sigurn and the rest of them are here because your mother made sure they would be."

"Yeah, right." Minna returned his grin. It wasn't different from what she concluded on her own, but Ulf had a way of making it feel true. Like when he assured her Alyn was alive the day they left Hast the previous winter.

Ulf glanced around at the few people visible in the dusk. "So, should I come back when it's dark?"

"No," Minna said firmly. "I want you for a few minutes before you fall asleep."

"People will talk."

"You think they aren't already?"

Ulf grinned and gestured to the door. "After you."

Chapter 22

The 8th Day of the Month of Ungemon

Keelia

"Sir?"

Keelia, one hand on her tent flap, sighed, then turned to face Siv, who was climbing the hill on which Keelia situated her headquarters. "Yes, lieutenant?"

"Sorry, sir," Siv said. "The patrol from the Kalana Valley returned."

"And," Keelia said. She caught the younger woman's small smirk when she tried to look past Keelia into her tent.

"Rangers are still probing the exits. Nothing serious, but the guards are requesting more arrows."

"Of course they are." Keelia looked down the hill to the sheds, where their small group of fletchers worked around the clock to keep them supplied. "Check with Bjorn. See what can be spared."

"Yes, sir." Siv saluted, barely stopping a wink before heading back down the hill.

Keelia watched her go. The *Alle'oss* under her command displayed far more military professionalism now than they did when she brought them south, but they retained a cheekiness that would never be tolerated in the emperor's armies. Keelia allowed herself a rare smile. She would hate to see them lose that.

"Captain Keelia."

Keelia's smiled widened. She glanced around, then turned to find Jason peering between the flaps of her tent.

"Captain," Jason said with a smile. "I wish to see you in your quarters."

Keelia eased Jason backward with a hand on his chest. "Soldier," she said, with some steel in her voice. "What have I said about being in uniform?"

Jason gave her a sheepish grin and glanced at the small gap between the tent flaps. "Wasn't sure it was you —"

"Soldier!"

Jason snapped to attention, saluted, then gave her a grin and pulled his shirt over his head and dropped it at his feet.

Keelia swatted the hands that reached for her away, stepped close and pressed her palms to his chest, feeling his heat. She pressed him back until his legs came into contact with her narrow cot and he sat. She gazed down at him, blocking out the sounds of the busy camp at the base of the hill. Those worries could wait for a few minutes.

Jason returned her gaze, his usual grin softened by the rare quiet moment. Keelia straddled his legs and sank, squeezing his hips between her thighs and draping her arms over his broad shoulders. She let her gaze wander the familiar contours of his face, lingering on the small cuts on his cheek, evidence of their recent struggles with the rangers, before finding his blue eyes. His hands found their way under her shirt, his blacksmith's callouses against her soft skin, raising goosebumps on her back. Their grins were gone, saved for more lighthearted moments. He waited, allowing her to approach, brushing his lips with hers, tasting his breath. She groaned as the tip of his tongue —

"Sir?" This was followed by a tapping on the tent post.

"Oh, for Daga's sake," Keelia murmured. She raised her voice and said, "One moment." Rising, she snatched up Jason's shirt and tossed it in his lap. "You're out of uniform, soldier. What have I said about that?" she whispered.

"You like it?" Jason asked, his grin disappearing behind his shirt as he pulled it over his head.

"That's right," Keelia said. She checked her clothing and hair, then pushed the tent flap open and stepped outside. Siv stood outside with a man who looked vaguely familiar. At least the young woman had the grace to look embarrassed. Keelia gave the man a once-over and asked, "Yes?"

Siv gestured toward the man and said, "Sir, this is…"

"Karl Siegling, Sister Keelia." He held out a hand and Keelia grasped his forearm.

"It's captain now, not sister," she said. "Karl Siegling. Why does that sound familiar?"

"I couldn't say," he said, but there was something that passed behind his eyes. Worry, guilt?

Her eyes flicked up to his black hair.

"Dyed," he said. "I've been living in Brennan the past few months. It's not a comfortable place for the *Alle'oss* since the escape."

"Right," Keelia said. "What can I do for you?" The words were for him, but she looked at Siv as she said them.

"Hera Siegling needs to return to Brennan," Siv said.

When the man nodded his confirmation, Keelia asked, "If you've been living in Brennan, how did you get here?"

"I came through here a month ago," he said. "That was before the Imps stepped up their activity along the border and, even then, it wasn't easy." He paused and glanced out over the camp. "I could wait for a ship to take me from *Helala*, but I'm afraid time is of the essence. I've been assigned a task in Brennan by Aron Hunter."

Keelia eyed him. He said all the names guaranteed to win her confidence. Few knew about *Helala*.

"He arrived with an escort and a message from Aron," Siv said.

Keelia took the folded paper. The wax seal looked right, and the message inside confirmed his story. She was to offer any assistance she could reasonably offer to get him to Brennan as soon as possible.

"Okay," she said, returning the message to Siv. "What can we do for you?"

"If you can escort me to the Odun River," he said, "I can make it the rest of the way on my own. The Imps don't patrol the plains west of the river."

Keelia blew a breath out through parted lips. Though they could see the Odun River from the high points in the territory they patrolled, Imp infantry patrolled the open plains between the foothills and the river. Still, it was a large area. A small party, Karl and an escort, should be able to sneak past the patrols at night.

But Aron's message said to offer *any reasonable assistance*, leaving it to her to determine what was reasonable. The rangers still melted away before the *Alle'oss* could come to grips with them. Aron denied multiple requests that she be allowed to take the initiative against the Imps who came and went with impunity outside the borders of Argren. She gazed down at her soldiers. Were they ready? Yes, they were, and she wasn't about to throw away the opportunity the vaguely worded message presented.

"Tell Bjorn I need to see him," she said to Siv. When the young lieutenant left, Keelia said to Karl, "If you're hungry, go to the mess, but be back here in a half hour."

•   •   •

Keelia peered up the slope. The copse of trees that crowned the hill was an irregular smudge against the star filled sky. Wood smoke from the Imps' fires and a nearby tangle of honeysuckle perfumed the night air. She imagined she could feel the tension in the *Alle'oss* hiding in the trees behind her, but she knew from experience, the anxiety slicking her back with sweat was all her own. The Imps wouldn't be expecting an attack. It should be a cakewalk. Still, she was as taut as a drawn bowstring.

"You sure about this?" she whispered. "If you miss the sentry, and he makes a sound, the whole thing's off." That wasn't entirely true. With her there, they should be able to handle a company of rangers, but she couldn't afford to lose any of her soldiers. She didn't want this to get messy.

Instead of answering, Jason inclined his head toward Bjorn.

"He's the best shot we have," Bjorn whispered. "That or he's the luckiest human alive, and I'd prefer that, if I'm honest."

Jason grinned and said to her, "Appreciate your confidence, by the way."

Ignoring the quip, Keelia whispered, "You miss, you get back here fast, no second tries."

Jason lifted the strap of his quiver over his head, lay it on the ground beside him, and withdrew a single arrow. Holding it up, he said, "One shot." Grinning at her scowl, he got to his hands and knees and disappeared into the tall grass.

They waited, the only sounds the breeze, the nervous shuffling of the *Alle'oss* and a lone barn owl.

"The man really does have the spirits' luck," Bjorn whispered, trying to reassure her.

Keelia nodded, watching the *lan'and* flitting across the top of the grass. She hadn't called the spirits to her yet, reluctant to open herself to the spirit realms, lest the sentry sense her. She gazed up the slope, trying to catch movement along the path she and Jason chose for his approach. If it went badly, if she heard anything from Jason that suggested he was in trouble, she could call the spirits and make it to the top of the hill in minutes. She forced herself to take a deep breath and let it out slowly.

She was watching the stars in their slow rotation, sure it had already been too long when they heard the warble of a screech owl. The signal. The familiar thrill of impending violence nearly eclipsed the relief she felt. "Right," she said. "Let's go." As she crouched and started up the slope, she heard her sergeants passing the word. Fifty *Alle'oss* rose up and followed like shades.

Jason's pale, grinning face was just visible within the shadows as they neared the top of the hill. He stood when she slipped into the trees.

"One shot," he whispered. "Silent as the grave."

Ignoring him, she stepped over the sentry's body, noting the arrow protruding from his eye, made her way to the other side of the hill, and crouched inside the treeline. While her soldiers spread out on either side of her, she studied the Imp camp. There were more than she expected. It looked like two companies shared the camp, about a hundred men.

The land just west of Argren descended to the plains that bordered the Odun River, the hills slowly flattening and the forests giving way to grasslands. The Imps made their camp in a hollow between three hills. Sentries posted on the hills had long views to the north, east and south. Keelia would have posted more than one sentry on each hill, but the *Alle'oss* had given the Imps little reason to fear an attack.

Peering down on the unsuspecting camp, a heady mix of emotions welled up from buried memories. Terror, disgust, sorrow, anticipation. Memories of her time fighting the Kaileuk. Her racing heart slowed, her thready breath evened out. *Father, forgive me, but I'm looking forward to this.*

The stars provided enough light that Keelia thought she could see a dark smudge on the western horizon that might be the trees hugging the river. Glancing behind her to where Karl huddled, looking terrified, she said to Bjorn, "Get him moving as soon as possible. There might be other Imp patrols about." When Bjorn nodded, she said, "Don't take chances and get back as quickly as you can."

Before he answered, she glanced left and right, receiving nods from the men and women she could see. They were ready. She nodded to Jason. He cupped his hand over his mouth as whispered warnings were passed down the line on both sides. She heard the creak of bows being drawn. "Now," she said quietly and Jason's screech owl warble released the storm.

As bows twanged around her, she threw her center open, rose to her feet and called the *lan'and* to her.

The first flight took a heavy toll, and though the remaining rangers reacted quickly, waking to a surprise attack left them momentarily disoriented. Keelia walked alone down the slope, the Imps arrows sparking spirit light on the shield in front of her. Another flight of arrows from her soldiers fell on the camp.

The rangers may be the Empire's elite, but they lacked the one advantage the Kaileuk had: numbers. Far from the mindless brutes Imperial propaganda would have them be, the Kaileuk learned the sisters' vulnerability; prolonged exposure to spirits left them insensible. With no magic of their own, and willing to spend lives for victory, the barbarians attempted to swarm sisters as soon as they appeared on the field. It was the job of the Empire's heavy infantry to ensure they weren't successful.

Lacking numbers, and less willing to sacrifice their own lives, the rangers fanned out to both sides, trying to outflank her shield. In a well-choreographed ballet, they loosed arrows and moved, peppering her shield to keep her undercover.

But Keelia was not the callow girl who naively begged Deirdre to send her to the front. She danced these steps before. Slowing as she neared the camp, she pulled her shield close, then pivoted it so that she exposed the lead rangers on her right. A spirit wave suppressed their fire, then a crackling bolt of lightning ensured they wouldn't get back up. Rotating her shield, she swept her hand behind its trailing edge, leaving death in its wake.

Arrows pelted her shield, ringing in her center like the ping of hail on a tin roof. Her head swam, the first tantalizing tendrils of the euphoria she sought. But she needed to push it to the edge, needed to climb the heights of ecstasy until she teetered on the edge.

Dropping her shield, she entered the camp, an angel of Daga bringing vengeance and retribution. Unmindful of arrows loosed by panicked men, she strolled among the survivors, the strobing light of her lightning producing frozen moments of anger, desperation, terror and death. More memories she would need to bury.

•　•　•

It was over too soon. Keelia stood in the center of the camp, alone. Letting her head fall back, she gazed at the milky wash of stars the Imps called the emperor's way and the *Alle'oss* called *mana ti malina* (mother's milk). She let the *fjel'and,* the source of her lightning, return to their realm, silently thanking them for the euphoria they gifted her.

It had been a long time. Lightning was less effective in Argren's dense forests, and in any case, the Imps rarely stuck around long enough for her to get involved in the action. Hearing footsteps, she whirled and crouched. Her soldiers approached, staring warily at her and the carnage she wrought.

"Keelia?" Jason asked. "You okay?"

Keelia sighed and straightened. "Bjorn off with our passenger?" When Jason nodded, she said, "Set a picket line to the west."

Jason turned to assign a squad to watch the western approaches to the camp.

Keelia looked around at the faces of her soldiers, who watched her with something between fear and awe. "Search the camp," she said. "Take everything useful." When they were slow to respond, she raised her voice. "Move! We leave in five minutes."

While they jumped to action, Keelia asked Jason. "Casualties?"

"One of the men assigned to take out the sentry on the south hill was wounded, but he'll make it," he said. "It was a good plan, but —"

"The results speak for themselves," she said, interrupting the argument before he could begin again. "No one died."

"Right," Jason said. "This time. I just don't want you getting used to the idea you can save everyone by putting yourself at risk."

"Argument noted," Keelia said softly. "Now, let's get organized and get out of here."

Chapter 23

The 8th Day of the Month of Ungemon

Minna

Ulf emerged from the roundhouse he ostensibly shared with three other newcomers as Minna approached. Noticing him carrying his pack and bow, Minna asked, "You're leaving?"

Ulf gave her an apologetic smile. "My squad has been assigned to the light infantry. We're going to train along the escarpment to the south."

"Light infantry?"

"That's… I don't know what it means, either." He grinned. "But it means I'm officially in the army now."

"Congratulations," Minna said. She tried to match his enthusiasm, but she saw in his eyes, she failed. After their fight and her determination to make hard choices, she tried to be supportive, pretended to be happy for him. But she was beginning to wonder if she had what it took to be like Ragan. She was terrified for Ulf.

"You coming, Ulf?" an older man, the leader of Ulf's squad, called.

"Yes, sir," Ulf answered. He hefted his pack onto his shoulder and picked up his bow. "It will be really safe," he said. "It's a bunch of us newbies, Raif and some of those *Oss'stera* people. They'll be training us to fight together, small unit tactics or something like that." When Minna only gave him a weak smile, he leaned in, kissed her on the cheek and set off after the other members of his squad.

Minna watched him go, fingers going to her cheek, trying to dismiss the thought this unsatisfying moment might be their last. Linea followed Ulf as he disappeared through the trees.

• • •

Minna made her way, alone, through a drizzle to the headquarters for the afternoon briefing. Only Linea accompanied her, flitting off occasionally to greet other spirits before returning to weave back and forth ahead of her. The sullen rain matched her mood. After watching Ulf leave, she visited the *Oss'stera* camp and found it empty. At least the gaggle of children who normally followed her apparently decided she wasn't interesting enough to brave the rain.

Head down to shield her face from the mist, she didn't notice Sigurn when she stepped onto the porch of the headquarters until he spoke.

"*Lehasa*," he said. He sprawled on the bench, legs extended, one arm draped over the back.

"*Hasa*," she answered, his unexpected presence bringing a grin to her face. She ran her fingers through her damp hair, then flicked droplets at him. "What are you doing here?"

"Lief asked me to attend for him."

"And you're waiting for…"

"You," Sigurn said and stood. "Everyone else is already inside. Probably waiting for you."

"I doubt it," Minna said. "Most of the time, I stand next to that table with nothing to say."

Sigurn pulled the door open. "It's not what you say, it's what you hear that matters."

Face warming at the gentle rebuke, Minna followed him inside.

The headquarters was a hub of activity at all hours. Scouts patrolling the borders of Argren brought news of Imp activity. Spies from Hast turned up occasionally. People arrived with updates on efforts to care for displaced people. Rangers probed the exits from the Kalana Valley and reports of their skirmishes with *Alle'oss* units arrived almost daily. There was an endless, bewildering stream of information. It was all filtered through Aron's growing staff to help him grasp the bigger picture. Minna had little sense of what it all meant, only that Aron, Zaina, and the rest of the leadership were looking increasingly worn.

Meanwhile, the Imps probed the Cut twice more since the first time, with the same disastrous results. If that was the extent of the Empire's efforts, Minna would say the *Alle'oss* were winning the war, but the grim news she heard in the war council everyday put the lie to that notion. The Imps were going to burn the rest of Argren to the ground while she was stuck here. Though Aron's words were optimistic, his obvious worry robbed them of meaning. He had no idea how to win this war.

Neither did Minna. She replayed her one conversation with her mother so many times, she no longer knew what was a real memory. It didn't matter. Even her wishful thinking produced no hint of what Ragan expected Minna to do. She hoped to glean some of her mother's secrets from Sigurn and Lief, but Lief was rarely available and none of the other *Oss'stera* members knew her mother.

As soon as Minna entered the room, she could tell something was different. Aron, Zaina, and the others gathered around the table, silently studying the map. There was none of the usual chatter, and the tension in the room crackled.

She stepped up to the table with Sigurn beside her. "What's happening?" she asked.

"News from Keelia," Zaina said.

Minna glanced up at the rafters near one corner of the room. Though the shadows swallowed its black feathers, she knew the raven that carried Keelia's messages perched there. While she watched, lamplight glinted from one of the bird's black eyes. Aron handed her a wrinkled bit of paper without looking up. It wasn't the first message Keelia sent, but it was the first one that produced such a reaction. Most of the short missive described Imp activity along the southern border and a handful of light skirmishes. The only thing that was out of place was a reference to *Helala* in a line squeezed in against the bottom of the paper.

Detached a patrol to scout the coast east of Helala.

"Why is this important?" she asked.

By now, she was used to being ignored, and she understood why. Most of the time, she had little to contribute on issues she didn't fully understand and, as the atmosphere grew increasingly grim, there was little time for anyone to explain them to her. She tried to engage Aron, Zaina and others outside the war councils, but they were always too busy. Even when she tried to explain to Aron what her father told her about Ragan, he acted as if it was old news. So, she resigned herself to being a mascot and a weapon. No one expected more of her. But Ulf leaving left her feeling fragile, and when no one answered, she let her gaze drop to the map, struggling against a growing sense of isolation.

Sigurn leaned over and whispered, "It's probably nothing. Just a precaution. It makes sense to keep an eye on the coast in case the Imps land."

Minna looked up into his calm face. The gratitude that welled up surprised her and moistened her eyes. "*Tok*," she mumbled.

When Sigurn turned his attention to the others, she studied the map, wondering what the *Alle'oss* could do if the Empire landed a force on the southern coast. Who was left to counter them? Worries about Ulf, Alyn and Beadu crowded out all the military minutiae, so she ignored the conversation and busied herself trying to calculate how long it would take her to ride to *Helala*. When she looked up, she was surprised to find the meeting breaking up. Only Aron, Zaina, and Sigurn remained. They were engrossed in their conversation, so Minna left without saying anything.

The drizzle relented while they were in the meeting. She was absently returning the waves of passersby, smiling reflexively, when the door opened behind her. A moment later, someone touched her arm. She looked up into Sigurn's smiling face.

"You'll be by for supper tonight, right?" he asked. "Everyone will be back from patrol."

Before Minna could answer, a man pounded up the path from the direction of the Cut. Minna and Sigurn stepped out of the way so he could enter the headquarters, then exchanged a worried look. A moment later, the door opened, and the man exited at a run, followed by Aron and Zaina.

"Come with us, Minna," Aron shouted in passing.

Minna and Sigurn emerged from the trees near the top of the Cut, then ran along the cliff's edge toward the spot where the escarpment bent north. As she passed them, the *Alle'oss* stationed on the top of the Cut called her name and cheered. She joined Aron, Zaina and a small group who were looking down at the highway.

"It's one of the tortoises," Aron said.

"Tortoises?" Minna asked.

Over the past few weeks, she watched the Imps making progress on the buildings she noticed the day she met Sigurn. To her surprise, one of the buildings was creeping along the highway toward the opening of the Cut. A company of a cavalry and a long line of heavy infantry followed about a hundred paces behind it. The contraption did look somewhat like a tortoise. Long and low, constructed of wooden planks with only one small window in the front. The walls on the front, back and sides sloped outward and extended nearly to the road surface.

"It's a siege engine. Used to attack fortifications," Zaina said. "Men hide inside so they can get close without being shot. Might be a battering ram inside." She brought the edges of her hands together, then pivoted them outward. "The front opens when they get close to the gate."

"How is it moving?" was the first of Minna's many questions. "Can men push that thing up the slope?" When she encountered blank looks and shrugs, she got Linea's attention. The spirit swooped down and bobbed in front of her. "Linea, I need to see what's inside that thing." She pointed at the tortoise. Linea looped once, then soared toward the contraption.

"Linea?" Sigurn asked.

"Yeah," Minna said.

When Linea returned, Minna closed her eyes and welcomed her into her center. At once, she was inside the nightmarish interior of the tortoise. It was smaller than she would have thought, forcing the four sweating men walking slowly to keep pace with the tortoise to stoop. Two of the men worked at a pair of tillers that steered the front wheels. A small amount of light leaked through the small window and the narrow gap between the sides and the highway, but most of the light came from torches that cast shifting shadows on the walls. With no way to escape, the smoke gathered in a thick layer below the low ceiling. Six oxen yoked to the tortoise near the back drove it slowly up the slope.

"Is there a battering ram?" Zaina asked.

"No. There's a huge crossbow at the front," Minna said.

"Ballista," Zaina said.

"How is it moving?" Sigurn asked.

"There are six oxen at the back."

"How many men?" Sigurn asked.

"Four."

Minna opened her eyes as Linea let the vision fade.

"That doesn't make sense," Aron said. "What do they think they're going to do with a ballista and four men?"

They watched in silence as the tortoise neared the entrance to the Cut. A lone arrow flew from the top of the cliff and thunked into the heavy oak planks. The calvary and heavy infantry stopped outside arrow range and watched it mount the slope.

"They obviously think they can bring down the wall," Sigurn said. "Somehow. The cavalry follow, coming fast to exploit the breach, then the heavy infantry come while we're occupied with the cavalry." When Minna looked at him, he shrugged and said, "Suicide. Still, it's more clever than their previous attempts. They're experimenting."

"Whatever they have in mind," Zaina said. "I suggest we interfere before they can get to it."

"It's made of wood," Aron said as the tortoise entered the Cut. He lifted a hand and wiggled his fingers. "Wood burns."

Minna frowned down at the tortoise. "The animals," she said.

"We'll have a barbecue," Sigurn said.

"Minna," Aron said when she only stared doubtfully down at the tortoise.

The contraption slowed as it mounted the steeper part of the slope, but it was still moving. She took a breath and called the *fjel'and,* who burst into her mind with their usual jangly eagerness. She moved along the top of the cliff until she was standing directly over the tortoise, extended her arms and released the spirits. Flames billowed down the rock face, engulfing the tortoise. Cheers rose from the *Alle'oss* watching the inferno.

After a few moments, Minna called the spirits back. The planks of the tortoise smoldered in spots, and steam rose, but the spirits had done little damage. The creak of the wheels was audible in the silence.

"Uh-Oh," Aron said.

"They must have saturated the wood," Sigurn said. "Might be able to get it burning eventually, but not before they reach the top."

Minna reached out to the *luft'and,* the wind spirits, and swept her arms to the side. The spirits soared toward the entrance of the Cut. She gave them a moment to stretch themselves, then swept her arms down and to the left. The spirits plunged toward the highway and roared toward the back of the tortoise. She expected the powerful gale to lift it from the ground, but the sloped back deflected the wind upwards. The tortoise shuddered as the wind passed over it, but its inexorable progress continued.

"What else you got?" Sigurn asked in the silence that followed.

Minna eyed the iron spikes sticking up from the roof. Lightning rods. They had learned her tricks. She bit her lip. Trying to ignore everyone watching her expectantly, she looked at the wooden barrier near the top of the Cut. The stockade spanned the highway far enough down the slope that the ends were anchored on the granite walls. A tangle of sharpened wooden spikes jutted up before the wall. Zaina called it an abatis. It was designed to prevent attackers from getting to the wall. It would be tight, but she thought she could get through it.

Without a word, she sprinted along the top of the escarpment, racing the tortoise to the top. While she ran, she called to the *lan'and* flitting through the nearby trees. Surprised, the men and women crowding the top of the cliff scrambled out of her way. "Is she running away?" someone asked.

As she neared the top of the Cut, the *lan'and* roared into her mind, swirling and greeting Linea joyfully. She had only a moment to acknowledge their raucous greeting before descending the slope toward the back of the stockade. The wall was two paces deep, supporting a platform on which men and women could stand to shoot over the top. The soldiers standing on the platform watched nervously as she approached. When she stopped two paces from the wall, Sigurn joined her. A tunnel two paces wide in the middle of the wall ended in a double door that was closed and barricaded with two thick oak logs. A man and woman stood next to the tunnel, watching her uncertainly. "Open it," Minna said.

"What?" the man asked, startled.

"Open the door," Minna repeated. "I need to get through."

"We can't open it without orders from Aron or Zaina," the woman said.

"This is Minna Hunter. You know who she is. Open the door," Sigurn said. "Now! Before it's too late."

They looked at one another, but didn't move.

"You sure about this, Minna?" Aron asked, stepping up beside her.

"Yes," she said, surprised at how steady her voice was.

"Open the door," Aron said.

The pair jumped to remove the logs with Sigurn's and Aron's help. They pulled the door open to reveal the tangled abatis.

"Stay here," Minna said, then crouched and crawled through the obstacle. When she emerged into the clear, the tortoise was only twenty paces away. She studied the contraption, lifting her hands, but before she could release the spirit wave, the sloped front of the tortoise split down the middle and pivoted outward to reveal a narrow slice of the interior.

She had a moment to register the giant, flaming bolt pointed at her, before the ballista launched the projectile with a deep kachunk.

Fortunately, she already had her hands in the right position, and only needed to send a thought to the *lan'and* in her center to throw out a shield. Spirit light flashed at the point of impact and spidered across the surface of her shield. The impact produced a deep gong that resonated in her center, sending a ripple through the swirling spirits. Minna nearly swooned and stumbled backward into the sharpened points of the abatis until Linea found the right harmony. Leather bladders lashed to the head of the bolt burst, splashing a viscous liquid against her shield and the highway. When the liquid met the fiery head of the bolt, it erupted into a wall of fire. Minna lifted her hands, angling her shield to protect herself from flaming gobbets which flew over the top of her shield.

She released the shield, dropping the flaming liquid onto the road's surface, and found herself in a small circle amid an inferno. Arms up to shield her face, she peered through the heat shimmer at a man frantically turning a crank on the ballista. Arrows peppered the front of the tortoise while two more Imps loaded another bolt. An arrow made it through the small opening to strike one of the men, but the other managed to finish the job and light the end of the bolt with a torch before he was cut down.

Remembering the focused spirit wave Aife used against her and Keelia, Minna eyed the arm of the ballista and slashed her hand down. There was a snap, then a heartbeat later, the immense energy stored in the ballista exploded with a deafening crack. The entire ballista rocked, jolting the flaming bolt out of its cradle. The bladders strapped to the bolt split when they hit the road's surface and a moment later, the entire front of the tortoise was a conflagration.

"Minna!"

The voice came from behind her. Feeling heat on her back, Minna whirled around to find the abatis in flames. The liquid that splashed over her shield must have fallen on the obstacle. Whatever the liquid was, it burned with an intense heat and the flames ate into the damp wood. There was nowhere to run. She looked up at Sigurn and Aron through the flames.

Fog? No, it would take too long. Wind? No, it might only fan the flames. And then she remembered Beadu mentioning the *luft'and* sometimes manifested as rain. *Linea, rain.* She sensed Linea's looping response among the torrent of *lan'and*. If the spirits didn't respond quickly, she would burn alive.

And then she felt them. They flowed into her center, joining the *lan'and's* swirling dance, but rather than the raw enthusiasm of the *lan'and*, these spirits flowed, leaping and twining together like the playful waters of a mountain stream. She lifted her arms out to her sides, palms up, and implored the spirits into the physical realm. *Rain!* They spiraled into the sky above her.

Nothing happened. The fabric of her shirt, still damp from the earlier drizzle, steamed. Frantically, Minna threw a thought toward the spirits. *Now!*

There was an almost imperceptible snap, an indefinable change in the air. Then a deluge fell from the sky. This was not the spring rains that were their constant companion in recent weeks. Heavy drops drummed onto her head, driving her to her knees. Arms up to protect herself, she huddled amid the roar, wondering what she unleashed and what she was supposed to do to stop it. *Linea?!*

And then it stopped. Afraid to move, she listened to the patter of the last drops. When she heard the startled exclamations from the *Alle'oss* on the wall, she peeked up at the drenched men and women staring down at her. When they saw her looking, a ragged cheer started, then rose in volume. She stood and turned slowly. The rain extinguished the flames. The tortoise was unmoving, but she could hear the panicked lows of the oxen. Lifting her arms, she called the spirits home and was surprised the water pooling on the road's surface and running in rivulets down the hill remained when the spirits returned to their realm.

Someone took hold of her shirt from behind. She spun around to find Sigurn reaching through the abatis. "Come back inside," he said.

"What about the other soldiers? The ones that stopped on the highway."

"They aren't coming," Sigurn said.

Minna glanced back at the remains of the tortoise, then followed Sigurn through the tangle of logs. A crowd of excited *Alle'oss* greeted her. Aron threw his arms around her and whispered in her ear, "That was the craziest thing I've ever seen." He stepped back, gave her arms a squeeze, then turned away and gave orders to retrieve the oxen and dismantle the tortoise.

Minna turned around and found Sigurn gazing solemnly at her. He plucked a sodden lock of hair from her cheek and pushed it behind her ear. "Now, that was legendary." He winked and asked, "You're coming to supper, right?"

Minna returned his smile and nodded. He turned away, giving way to other well-wishers. She watched him walk away, Ulf's blue eyes coming to her mind.

Chapter 24

The 8th Day of the Month of Ungemon

Alyn

After her first vision, Alyn went straight to Deirdre. She expected the former Malefica to be so terrified by the vision, she would help Alyn decide what to do about it. But she was wrong. Alyn hadn't even finished describing the vision before Deirdre cut her off.

"Didn't you see what the soul spirits did to your mother?" she snapped.

Shocked and disappointed, Alyn responded in kind. "She wasn't my mother!"

Deirdre shut the conversation down, leaving no doubts about what she thought of the subject. Alyn left, resigned to exploring the visions on her own. But Deirdre tattled on her to Beadu. Between the two of them, they found ways to keep her busy on her days off, and no matter where she went, she wasn't alone. Even while she was translating Ragan's journal late in the evening, someone loitered in the next room. She was sure it was their doing.

It only made her more determined. It took her a month to give them the slip, but once again, she looked down on *Helala* from her spot in the hills above the village. She settled into a comfortable cross-legged position, took a deep breath, and closed her eyes. She gave herself a moment to enjoy the quiet solitude, a cool breeze ruffling her hair, then she sank into her center and called to the *sjel'and*.

It didn't take long. The spirit appeared at the edge of her perception, as before. Conscious of Beadu's warnings, she was cautious last time, but she had been waiting anxiously for this moment and her last two encounters with the soul spirits left her careless. She opened herself up to the spirit. But this was not the same spirit as before. When she sensed its amusement and malevolence, she tried to pull back. But it was too late.

A whirling maelstrom of *sjel'and* poured into her mind, a putrid mockery of the joyous whirl of the *lan'and*. Her spirit writhed, terrified. She pushed against the swarm, a hurried, feeble effort met by a predatory hunger. A kaleidoscope of horrific images collided in her mind, each spirit grasping for her attention. Her mother and father dying at the hands of Imp soldiers. The giant men she saw in the last vision, marauding through *Helala*. Minna falling from a high cliff. A high-pitched scream emanating from her own spirit joined the cacophony. The torrent of images came at a dizzying rate, eclipsing her own thoughts. For one terrifying moment, she feared she would be trapped inside her own mind with the *sjel'and* forever.

"No!" she shouted. She focused on her spirit, seeking its strength and gathering herself. When she was ready, she shoved outward, a mental spirit wave that expelled the *sjel'and*, but took her consciousness with it.

From Ragan's journal:

Beadu tried to warn me, to explain how horrific the sjel'and were. What happened is not her fault. She did her best to prepare me. But she doesn't know firsthand. She's never encountered the vile spirits. She only knows what others have told her. She told me they were creatures of pure malice, the worst of the humans they once were. Grasping and cruel, they relish inflicting pain on the living. I dismissed her warnings. After all, the spirits' only weapon is their knowledge of the future. I thought I was prepared. I was so sure of myself, of my mental resilience. I was a fool. It was only after my first encounter with a swarm that I understood what the old saa'myn knew. The price of delving into the future is often madness.

Alyn's eyes opened to darkness. She had been unconscious for hours. She rolled onto her side and hugged her knees to her chest, sobbing softly and squeezing her eyes shut against shameful tears. Beadu and Deirdre were right. She sank into her center, soothing her traumatized spirit, careful to leave herself closed to the *sjel'and*. When she was ready, she pushed herself up to sit, wiped her tears away and gazed at a sliver of moon high in the sky. They would know what she did, were probably looking for her. There was no way to explain such a long absence. That would be unpleasant, but more distressing was the fact that she lost her only hope for helping Minna. She looked up at the *lan'and* drifting through the forest, drawn by her distress. What use was she?

Minna

By the time Minna extricated herself from the crowd, the sun was low in the west and her hair and clothes were merely damp. The children weren't allowed near the highway, but they were waiting for her when she made her way to *Oss'stera's* camp, and they had already heard a slightly exaggerated version of the attack. Linea wove through the chattering gaggle as they walked. When they arrived at the hedge that blocked off *Oss'stera's* part of the camp, the children stopped. Sigurn had made it clear they weren't welcome.

"Goodbye," the boy who had taken the role as shepherd to the group, said.

"*Jae lōrna,*" Minna said. When she was met with blank looks, she said, "Until morning. Goodnight."

"*Jae lōrna,*" the children chorused. Walking down the path, their piping voices repeated the new phrase, exaggerating the trilled r and laughing at their pronunciations.

Minna pushed through the hedge to find the usual gathering sitting down to their evening meal. A few of them looked up and greeted her in a nonchalant way. She was used to being treated with less deference here, appreciated it, but this response bordered on unfriendly. Thinking she was missing something, she made her way to her usual spot next to Lief and sat. No one looked at her. Sigurn handed her a bowl of stew. "*Tok*," she said. He only grunted a response. "Okay, what's going on?" she asked.

Someone sitting across from her snickered. Sigurn fought a losing battle to keep the smile off his face. Then the dam broke and laughter filled the clearing.

"That's funny," she said, but couldn't keep the grin off her face.

"Sigurn's idea. Said we need to do what we can to keep you humble," Lief said.

"Sigurn already told us the story," the woman said.

Minna punched Sigurn's shoulder.

"What was that for? Was I supposed to keep it a secret?"

"That's for all the embellishments I know you added. I've heard you tell a story."

Sigurn grinned through a mouthful of stew. "You wouldn't have me tell a boring story, would you?"

"Boring? You think that was boring?" Minna asked. When she found the others watching with knowing smiles, she dropped her eyes, dipped her spoon into her bowl, and stirred the stew. *What's happening?* But she knew what was happening. She liked Sigurn, and it was more than the fact he treated her like she wasn't a legendary *saa'myn*. He was funny, easy to talk to, and had a dangerous swagger she found appealing.

Lief cleared his throat. "Speaking of stories, why don't you tell Minna the story of how *Oss'stera* captured *Spirit Light*, Sigurn?"

Minna's head came up. Because of the many demands on their time, they had little time to tell her stories of her mother, and though the stories they told her so far didn't seem relevant to what she needed to know, she was still hopeful.

Sigurn twirled his spoon in the air. "Can't you see I'm eating?" He dropped the spoon into his bowl, gestured to the group with a flourish, and smirked. "Besides, no one wants to hear that old story again." He was rising to his feet before the round of encouragement even started.

Propping a foot on the log beside Minna, he bent toward her and said, "It may be hard to believe now, sitting among such hardened warriors as these." He swept his hand across the soldiers of *Oss'stera*, acknowledging their cheers. "But the *Alle'oss* were not always so mighty."

One of the women sitting across the fire said to her neighbor, "I love this story."

"As well you should," Sigurn said. He stepped over the log and began a slow stroll around the outside of the circle. "Yes, it's true, the *Alle'oss* were once a peaceful people, content to live peaceful lives in our mountainous land. Lives fulfilled by family, friends and good honest toil." He stopped across from Minna, paused and gave everyone time to set their bowls aside and pick up bits of detritus on the ground. Then he leaned forward and said in a dramatic voice, "That was, until the *Empire* came."

Boos and hisses greeted his statement, followed by a rain of twigs, pebbles, and leaves. He batted theatrically at the missiles, then straightened in an affronted huff. "Would you shoot the messenger?" When the laughter died away, Sigurn continued his stroll. "Yes, the Empire…" He paused, pretending to watch for further abuse, then continued. "The Empire found the peaceful *Alle'oss* easy prey. They came into our mountains, spreading terror across our beautiful land, committing the same depredations they inflicted on other unfortunates before us." He stopped behind Minna, spread his arms and said in a commanding voice, "Tell her. Tell our young *saa'myn* of their crimes."

As if they rehearsed, *Oss'stera* responded, shouting over one another, some of them coming out of their seats in their eagerness. Minna was only able to make out some of what they said.

"They burned our homes."

"They made us slaves."

"They robbed and murdered us."

As the group dissolved once again into laughter, one voice cut through the mirth. "They treated us like animals." As the laughter died away, Minna turned to look at Lief, who said it. Lief gave her a solemn look.

"Yes," Sigurn said, his voice quiet. "They treat us like animals and take our dignity." There were nods and distant gazes, people remembering their personal traumas.

Sigurn began a slow walk again. Minna looked up as he lifted a finger. "But there was one man, a great man, a man who saw more clearly than anyone else what *could* be. When no one else did, he believed the *Alle'oss* could throw the Empire from our land. Alar…" he paused, putting a hand to his ear until the cheers abated. "Alar showed us how to fight."

"How?" several people shouted.

Sigurn plucked up a bow leaning on a log. "With these."

"Where did they get them?" everyone shouted.

"Tove and Ukrit journeyed to the distant Ishien River Valley, where the spark of rebellion had fallen on dry tinder. The bowyers of that valley responded when they put out the call." He raised the bow above his head in one hand. "When they returned, Alar saw what they wrought, and he said, 'Tove, Ukrit, you have saved us.'" Setting the bow down, he continued his walk. "Yes, we are hale and hardy now. We are many and formidable. But it was not so, then."

"No!" people chorused while others shouted, "We don't believe you!"

"Yes, I know, but it is so," Sigurn continued. "We were more rabble than rebels. Vagabonds, begging for scraps. Dirty. Starved. Alone. But while Tove and Ukrit were away, Alar, Scilla and…" He stopped and held a hand toward Lief.

"And Lief!" everyone shouted.

Sigurn continued. "Yes, and Lief were spreading the good news. The *Alle'oss* were flocking to our cause. But winter was coming. Alar needed to feed, house and clothe many. So he came up with a plan. A plan that would allow *Oss'stera* to strike the first blow against the Empire and steal enough to get us through that first critical winter."

"What did he do?"

Sigurn stopped and swept a hand out toward the mountains to the east. "For years, he watched the supply caravan making its way to Ka'tan." He scanned the taut faces watching him. "He scouted the best spot for an ambush and devised a clever plan. Then he led the ragged, barely trained rebels into the mountains." Sigurn started his stroll again, punctuating his words with his hands. "They knew if they were late, they would starve. So they raced the Imps. Day and night, they marched, with little to eat and almost no sleep. And, in the nick of time, they arrived to set their trap."

Cheers!

Sigurn propped a foot on the log, rested an elbow on his knee, leaned forward and spoke directly to Minna. "Now, usually the caravan had only a small escort of Imp cavalry. So, even though they were barely trained, Alar was confident *Oss'stera* would prevail. But when the Imps appeared, it was not the cavalry, but the —"

"Rangers!"

Sigurn straightened and spread his arms. "An entire *company* of rangers, trained killers, the Empire's finest. What should they do? Should they run?"

"No!"

"Should they stay and fight?"

"Yes!"

"Yes! Alar knew there was little choice. Either they die by the rangers' hands or starve in the winter." He resumed walking, lifting a finger again. "Now, Tove, Alar's best and oldest friend, asked, 'What do they have in that caravan that they need a whole company of rangers to guard it?'" He stopped, faced the center of the circle and said, "And Alar said…" He put his hand to his ear.

"Let's find out!" The group dissolved into laughter and excited conversations.

"Now!" Sigurn raised his voice to bring the attention back to himself. When the group grew quiet again, he started walking. "They waited with held breath, hiding in the forest beside the road, waiting for the opportune moment." He stopped and imitated drawing the string of a bow. "Scilla, Alar's beloved, loosed the first arrow and the first Imp fell from his horse."

Cheers!

"Then *Oss'stera* let loose a mighty volley and more Imps fell. But these were Imperial Rangers. Were they frightened when they saw their comrades fall?"

"No!"

"No, they struck back! A shadow fell over *Oss'stera* as the rangers' arrows darkened the sky. We were pinned down, hopelessly outmatched. The Imps advanced, drawing their swords, preparing for bloody work."

"What happened?" Minna snapped her mouth shut when she realized she spoke, then smiled at the good natured-laughter.

"I'll tell you what happened," Sigurn said with a smile. "Alar said to Tove, 'Wait here.' Then he took his bow and…" He stopped and, as if offering an aside, he said, "Now, the story is confused at this point. *Oss'stera* had their heads down and each person could recount mere glimpses of the battle. But by piecing the bits together, we can reconstruct what happened." He paused, slowly stretching his hand out before himself, then suddenly clenching it into a fist. "As a blur, Alar, the great warrior fell on the Imps. As a whirlwind, he moved among them, loosing arrow after arrow. Appearing here, then there, a phantom, impossible to kill. A bringer of death."

When he paused and began walking again, Minna turned to Lief and quirked a brow. Lief shrugged and whispered, "I wasn't there."

"Like quicksilver, he was, so that their arrows could not find him. Ranger after ranger fell. The Imps were terrified, of course. Imperial Rangers they may be, but they were only human. They panicked, and when they turned their full attention to saving themselves…" Sigurn lifted his arms above his head. "*Oss'stera* rose up and brought about their ruin."

The members of *Oss'stera,* sitting tense around the fire, rose to their feet and cheered.

Once it was quiet again, Minna asked, "But what about the painting? *Spirit Light?*"

Sigurn nodded and resumed his walk. "Well, as expected, the wagons were full of the supplies they needed to survive the winter. But in one wagon, they found a chest. A chest unlike anything else they found. Ornate and heavy. Clearly, it contained something valuable. It was locked, of course, but Alar took the lock in his hand and ripped it from the chest." He stopped walking and mimed opening the chest. "They opened the chest and there they were. The paintings."

"Paintings. More than *Spirit Light?*" Minna asked.

"Oh yes. There were many, and they were all by great *Alle'oss* masters, stolen by the Empire, the artists banished or murdered. Ukrit and Scilla, great artists in their own right, recognized what they were immediately." He mimed his actions as he spoke. "With trembling hands, Ukrit opened one of the leather tubes and pulled the canvas out. He rolled it out on top of the chest and there it was. *Spirit Light*. Beautiful. Priceless beyond measure." Then, in what Minna felt was a rushed, disappointing end to the story, he said, "So, *Oss'stera* struck the first blow. We lived through the winter and never looked back. And we recovered the cultural treasures which have inspired us through these long, difficult years." With a flourish, Sigurn sketched a bow to rousing applause and cheers, then he dropped onto his seat next to Minna and retrieved his bowl.

"That's it?" Minna asked.

"That's the story," he said.

"But what happened to the painting? Why do you all wear the patch?"

"There is much more to the story, of course," Lief said with a small, distant smile. "Much of it involves your mother, as a matter of fact. But we can tell it on another night."

Minna watched everyone resume eating, discussing the story as if it was the first time they heard it. Though she couldn't explain why, this was the first story they told her that felt important. She wasn't willing to let it go so easily. "Where is the painting?" she asked Lief.

"Hidden," Sigurn said. "Only a few people know where it is. Our Lief, for one."

Minna looked from Sigurn to Lief. "You know where it is?"

"I do," Lief said.

Minna sat quietly for a moment, sensing something important was happening, but not sure what. There were so few people who could tell her anything about what her mother did in the years after she left her family. "Why was my mother so interested in that painting?"

Lief chewed, gazing up at the trees. "I suppose you would have to ask Alar or Tove about that."

Disappointed, Minna chewed her lip and gazed at the bowl of stew, cupped in her lap, untouched. "Have you seen it?"

Lief nodded.

"What is it like?"

While he considered, Sigurn cleared his throat. Lief glanced at him and said, "Go ahead."

Sigurn set his bowl down again and rose to his feet. "You know, of course, who Wattana is?" he asked Minna. He smirked at her affronted frown and asked, "But do you know the true story of Wattana? Not the story told by the Imps; that Wattana abandoned her family in an insane quest to catch the fairy lights and threw herself from the precipice when she realized what she did."

"Yes."

"The painting depicts the truth. The moment when Wattana, standing on the precipice, first spoke to the spirits." He lifted a hand and stared past it, gazing into the distance. "The painting is so realistic, it is as if you are looking at the real thing, the colors, the depth. Breathtaking." He swept his arms over his head in imitation of Wattana in the painting. "The spirits swirl around her, and in her face, you see ecstasy." He let his arms fall and bent toward her. "Not madness." He gazed into Minna's eyes. The only sounds disturbing the silence in the clearing were birds and distant voices. "The first *saa'myn*." He glanced over his shoulder to the treetops, then looked back at Minna. "Are there spirits here among us now?"

Attracted to the group's happiness while Sigurn told the story, Linea had been joined by a swarm of *lan'and*, swirling above the clearing and flitting in out of the trees. Minna nodded.

"And you have felt Wattana's ecstasy?" Sigurn asked softly.

"Yes," Minna said, feeling her cheeks flush.

He gave her a very private grin, then straightened and spoke to everyone. "You see, we always believed *Spirit Light* contained the truth. We had faith. But we didn't *know*." He looked down at her and said, "Now we do." The clearing was silent again. Then he sat abruptly and retrieved his bowl. "They executed Valdemar, the greatest of all the *Alle'oss* masters, for that painting."

Minna sat quietly for a moment, too flustered to meet anyone's eyes. But she would not be deterred when she was so close to what she was looking for. Forcing her embarrassment aside, she asked, "But why is it so important to you? Why do you wear the patch?"

"The painting represents what we're fighting for and what we're fighting against," Sigurn said. "Wattana is a powerful symbol of who we once were. Valdemar's arrest and execution is a symbol of what the Empire has done to all of us."

"They killed Valdemar, not because his painting was a lie, but because it was the truth," Lief said, a rare note of anger creeping into his voice.

"How did he know the true story?" Minna asked quietly. When Lief looked at her, she said, "Wattana and the spirits. How did Valdemar know the story?"

Lief gazed at her, the war of this thoughts playing out on his face. Finally, he said, "Your mother told him."

Minna stared at him, the clearing fading into the background. When he looked away, she looked up as Linea, communing with other *lan'and,* zoomed through the air above the fire. Why would her mother tell Valdemar that story? She knew how dangerous it was. Could it have been a coincidence her mother inspired the painting they were discussing right now? No. Everything she learned of her mother suggested Ragan never did anything without a purpose. The voice of the woman sitting beside Sigurn broke into her thoughts.

"I heard when Valdemar told the inquisitor who arrested him it was the truth, the inquisitor said, 'Of course, it's the truth, that's why I'm here.'"

"That's right," Lief said.

"Wait… how do you know that?" Minna asked.

Lief looked for a moment as if he wouldn't answer, but when he saw Minna's face, he said, "Because a woman who was there survived."

"She's still alive? Where is she?"

"That's not my place to say," Lief said. "You would have to ask Alar or Tove."

Minna's gaze lingered on Lief for a moment, then she stared at the fire to avoid the eyes watching her. Alar and Tove. Again. All her questions seem to lead to those two. Though she couldn't explain how, she knew this was what she was looking for. She needed to talk to Alar and Tove.

She couldn't wait to get Ulf's opinion — Ulf was gone. The elation drained from her. She gazed down at the bowl cradled in her hands, alone amid the spirited banter going on around her.

Chapter 25

The 8th Day of the Month of Ungemon

Alyn

When Alyn finally made it back to *Helala* after encountering the swarm, she found Deirdre organizing search parties. She endured Deirdre's furious lecture and expressed her contrition. She told Deirdre she fell asleep. Deirdre seemed to accept this story, and when Alyn was finally allowed to retreat to her small room, she assumed she got away with it.

But the next day, she began to suspect she misjudged the situation. It wasn't that Deirdre was still angry. If anything, the former Malefica was overly solicitous. When she chided Alyn for missing her morning lessons with Beadu, Alyn guessed their game. The two women decided to allow the old *saa'myn* to render judgment.

On the morning of the fourth day since she encountered the *sjel'and* swarm, Alyn decided it was time to face the music. However, when she emerged from her room, her grim determination was waylaid by an unfamiliar group of *Alle'oss* in the village's central square. In mien and appearance, they were in direct contrast to the residents of *Helala*. Their clothes were ragged, their hair dirty, and the men's beards were long and unkempt. The residents of *Helala* gathered at the edges of the square, watching in fascination as the newcomers watered their horses at the community well. The riders returned this perusal with weary interest.

She heard Deirdre's voice and turned to find the former Malefica and one of the riders emerging from the community building. The rider carried a familiar-looking bow. When the two women stopped to talk, Alyn studied the other riders and noticed similar bows strapped to the horse's saddles.

"*Andsutra*," Deirdre said as the women parted.

The rider strode across the square. As she passed Alyn, their eyes met for a moment. Alyn turned to watch the woman's retreating back. She stopped, hesitated, spun around and stared at Alyn with narrow eyes.

"You have a sister," she said.

Alyn nodded, "How did you know?"

"When you chew your lip like that, you look just like her," the woman said. "You're Alyn."

Alyn pressed her lips together and gave her a quick nod.

The woman extended a hand. "I'm Willa. I met Minna in Hast last winter."

"Oh," was all Alyn could think of to say. She grasped the woman's forearm, feeling her cheeks warm.

"*Andsutra*," Willa said, turned and shouted, "*Eotok!*" and retrieved the reins of her horse from another woman. As they climbed into their saddles, Willa gave Alyn another nod before turning away.

Alyn watched them leaving the square, headed east. The children waved, shouted and swirled in the riders' wake. A few of the men and women lifted hands in response. As they disappeared, Alyn headed over to stand beside Deirdre. "Who were they?" she asked.

"Hmmm?" Deirdre asked, turning toward Alyn. Just before she managed to control her expression, Alyn saw worry lining her face. "Oh, they're scouts for the *Alle'oss* army."

"Scouts?"

Alyn could see conflicting thoughts play out on Deirdre's face. "Just precautionary," she said lightly, turning her head to watch the last of the riders disappearing into the surrounding forest. "They're keeping an eye on the coast."

It wasn't a lie, but Alyn could see in the flick of Deirdre's eyes that it wasn't the whole truth. Deirdre gave her a tight smile, reminded her Beadu was expecting her, then turned and climbed the steps to the community building. Though she knew Deirdre was only trying to reassure her, her half-truth only had the opposite effect. The appearance of the scouts brought the shadow of the war to *Helala.* If they were watching the coast, they had a reason. A group of children, on their way to school, called her name, but instead of pretending everything was okay, Alyn spun around without answering.

Moments later, she stoked a simmering anger as she trudged up the hill on which Beadu's hut perched. They didn't understand. How could they? Neither of them had the gift of prophecy. They didn't have family in harm's way. They didn't have a sister who everyone knew. And worshiped, apparently. Preparing for the expected rebuke from Beadu, she sifted through the various defenses she constructed since she encountered the swarm. It all fell to tatters when she saw Beadu sitting on the log in front of her hut.

The old *saa'myn* didn't look angry. Not that Alyn could tell. She never saw her angry. But, as Alyn took her customary place next to the fire, she decided Beadu's expression conveyed disappointment, something infinitely worse than anger.

"I finished the book on Styrian herb lore," she said brightly, a pathetic attempt at deflection.

"Tell me of your vision," Beadu said.

Despite her angry self-justifications, Alyn's impulse was to lie. But when she met her mentor's eyes, she could tell Beadu expected it. Alyn sighed, bent forward and rested her elbows on her knees. "Which one?"

"Let us start with the first one."

Alyn sat back, ran her fingers through her hair, pulling it away from her face. Buying time. She was sure Deirdre already told Beadu what she saw. She was giving Alyn a chance to come clean. Suddenly, hot tears prickled Alyn's eyes. She sucked in a deep, shuddery breath and clamped her mouth shut on the sob that wanted release. Squeezing her eyes shut, she clasped her elbows and shook silently.

Beadu waited patiently until Alyn settled enough to take a breath. When she opened her eyes, the old *saa'myn* was smiling at her. "You are more like your mother than you think," she said softly. "I know you don't wish to hear that, but it is so."

"Because we both gave in to temptation?" Alyn asked sharply.

"It is true. The allure of knowing what is to come is hard to resist," Beadu said. "Very few could deny that temptation. But that is not what makes you like your mother."

Alyn wiped roughly at the tears on her cheeks. "Then how am I like Ragan, the mother who abandoned her children?"

Ignoring Alyn's anger, Beadu gazed into the distance. "When your mother began her quest, she did so despite my warnings. She remembered it differently as the years passed, of course. I don't know if she wanted to forget our bitter arguments, or she wished to share whatever blame she believed she deserved." She smiled fondly at Alyn. "I saw the same guilty expression on her face as I've seen in yours lately." Alyn dropped her gaze. "But that is only a superficial similarity," Beadu said. "No, it is because you are willing to risk that terrible realm, not for your own gain, but to save the ones you love." When Alyn looked up again, Beadu asked, "What would you do with your glimpse into the future? To what lengths would you go if you believed Minna was in danger?" She let Alyn consider, then she asked, "Can you judge your mother so harshly?"

Alyn stared at her. After the vision of Minna and the three witches, she was ready to run off on her own to warn Minna. The only reason she didn't was she hoped to draw Deirdre into her betrayal. Maybe it was only a small betrayal, a simple lie, but she guessed Ragan used the same rationalizations when she started. "I'm sorry I lied."

"Just so," Beadu said. She settled herself, cupping her hands in her lap. "Now tell me of your visions."

Alyn told her of the vision in which Minna faced the three witches alone and of the *sjel'and* who delivered it. When she was done, she asked, "Will that vision come true?"

Beadu's lips pursed, then she said, "Your mother undoubtedly knew more about prophecy than any woman who ever lived. She learned to judge how likely the visions were. But she spent long years among the *sjel'and* to gain that knowledge."

Alyn shuddered at the thought of enduring the swarm repeatedly for years. "What about that spirit? The one who seemed almost… friendly? It was so unlike the others."

"Yes, you spoke of the same thing when you received the vision in prison," Beadu said with a frown. "I have never heard of such a thing."

They sat in silence until Alyn asked, "Maybe something in her journal?"

"That is possible," Beadu said. "Though she completed the journal before she left home for good, she had begun to make some progress by then." The wrinkles on her face deepened as she squeezed her eyes closed. "She compared time to a river that finds its path. She said some courses are more likely than others, that some currents are irresistible and that some of these currents swirled around certain people. She said one could learn to recognize these currents and the people at their center." She opened her eyes. "But as I said, your mother spent years gaining that knowledge." When she saw Alyn's reaction, she nodded. "Yes, I see you understand. Now, tell me of the second vision."

Alyn related her experience with the swarm and the passage from her mother's journal that described it. Afterward, they sat in silence, listening to the children emerging from their lessons for their midday meal.

"So, you don't have to worry about me trying to see the future anymore," Alyn said forlornly. She was staring into the fire, but when Beadu didn't answer, she looked up at the old *saa'myn* and was surprised to find a deep frown on her face.

"Alyn, what I'm about to tell you is for you and I alone," she said. "Do you understand?" When Alyn nodded, Beadu said, "Here in *Helala,* we are shielded from events in the wider world. That is by design." She gestured to the village square where the children gathered. "The trauma is too fresh for many of the children. They need to feel safe."

"You know what's happening in the war?" When Beadu nodded, Alyn asked, "You haven't told the adults, not even Deirdre?"

Beadu chuckled. "Adults forget how perceptive children can be. They pick up on even the slightest disquiet from those charged with their care." She shook her head. "No, I have told no one what I know. Until now."

"But how? No one has visited other than the supply ships and those… scouts. Did you talk to any of them?"

"No," Beadu said. "I have ways, but that will have to wait."

"Is Minna okay? What about my parents?"

"My knowledge is incomplete and sometimes weeks old, but as far as I know, Minna is well, and I have no reason to believe anything has happened to your parents." She waited to be sure Alyn was done, then said, "One thing is clear to me. The *Alle'oss* are in a precarious position. Were it not for Ragan's confidence in their success… I would despair."

"But, Minna —"

"Minna and Keelia are powerful women, but they are only two and cannot be everywhere at once. The Empire know they can grind the *Alle'oss* down as they have done before to other peoples." She paused. "And this vision of the three women, women like Aife, is very troubling."

"But didn't Ragan leave a plan? Minna said our mother had a plan."

"That is what we all believed, but she told no one of her plans. I hoped she confided in those closest to her, Aron and Zaina, or that she said something to Minna, but that was not the case."

"She didn't even tell you?"

"No. Your mother believed if she told anyone —"

"It might disrupt the proper flow of events when people made what they thought were her choices instead of making their own," Alyn finished. "I read that in her journal."

"Just so," Beadu said. "It is frustrating, but our only recourse is to trust that your mother saw a path forward, one which we can find without her help."

When Beadu fell silent, Alyn looked at her and was surprised at the expression on her face.

"You want me to keep trying," Alyn said.

Beadu nodded and gave her a sad smile. "It seems unlikely your mother would not know of your affinity for the *sjel'and.*"

"You told my sister and me, both of us, our mother didn't want us to follow in her path," Alyn said. When she saw Beadu blush, her mouth dropped open. "You *lied* to us."

"Not a lie, exactly. Your mother did ask me to warn Minna. I assume she simply didn't know about your gift and that she would want me to warn you as well."

"That sounds like a lie to me," Alyn grumbled.

"A small lie, but it was based on an assumption I thought to be true." Beadu smiled. "I assumed your mother didn't mention your affinity for the *sjel'and* because she knew it would be some time before you heard your spirit song. In retrospect, it seems an unlikely omission, even so. There was very little that got past your mother. You remember what I've told you about spirit song?"

"Yes," Alyn said. "You said you hear your spirit song when you are able to expand your connection to *mid'heim* enough for your spirit to hear the songs of the *lan'and.*"

"Just so. And your sister told you of her spirit song?"

"Yes," Alyn said, leaning forward, elbows propped on her knees, hands clasped.

Beadu must have heard the disappointment in her voice. "You know your spirit more than anyone I've known of your age, but you are still quite young. Some things cannot be rushed."

"Is it that important?"

Beadu looked up at the swarm of *lan'and* who always kept her company. "The spirits are emotional creatures." She dropped her gaze to Alyn. "You know this because you have felt the *lan'ands'* joy, their exuberance." Alyn nodded. "Your song is an expression of this emotion that other spirits understand. Because you have *and'ssyn*, the *lan'and* sense your spirit. They respond to your moods because your spirit calls out to them. When you bring them into your center, your spirit feels their emotions. But you cannot truly communicate with them until your spirit can sing."

"Minna said it was when she understood her song that she was able to control the wind spirits against Aife."

"Just so."

"So, if I hear my spirit song, I can communicate with the *sjel'and*?"

"After a fashion," Beadu said. "Your mother wrote of this in her journal. You have not reached that part?"

Alyn shook her head.

"Then perhaps you should ask Deirdre to show you what she wrote about her spirit song," Beadu said. "After you learn what you can from your mother's journal, return and we will talk."

Alyn jumped up. "*Tok*, Beadu." She turned and sprinted away, returning the waves of the children gathered in the square. She raced up the stairs of the community building, then burst into Deirdre's office. "Deirdre!"

The former Malefica startled and dropped the quill she was holding.

"You read my mother's journal," Alyn said.

Deirdre hesitated, one eyebrow quirking up. Retrieving the quill, she set it in its stand and asked, "Your mother?"

Alyn gaped at her. She hadn't even realized she used that word. When did she start thinking of Ragan as her mother? Waving a hand impatiently, she said, "I guess I know her better now after reading her journal. Or, at least, I understand why she did what she did." She took a step forward. "But I have a ques —"

"Have a seat, Alyn," Deirdre said, gesturing to a chair.

Alyn clamped her mouth shut and hurried to sit.

When she was perched on the edge of the seat, Deirdre asked, "Now what is it that has you so excited?"

"You remember what she wrote about the *sjel'and* swarm, about her spirit song?" Alyn asked.

Deirdre's eyes narrowed.

Alyn could sense the rebuke coming, but before Deirdre could speak, she said, "*Beadu* told me to ask you to show me those parts."

"Beadu did?" Deirdre asked, her brows knitting.

Alyn pointed at the door. "You can go ask her." When Deirdre didn't respond, Alyn let her hand drop and said, "I told her everything. About the first vision and the second, the time with the swarm."

"The second?"

Alyn forced herself not to roll her eyes. "Deirdre, you knew, already. You and Beadu just wanted me to confess." She threw up her hands. "I confessed. All of it." She let her arms drop, took a breath, and blew it out. When she spoke, her eyes wandered the office. "I shouldn't have lied. I'm just so worried about Minna and everyone else, and I feel so useless here." She brought her gaze back to Deirdre and said, "I'm sorry."

"Yes," Deirdre said after a moment. "I can show you those passages. For all the good it will do." Seeing Alyn's frown, she said, "You will see. Let's go look."

When they were sitting close together on stools at Alyn's workbench, Deirdre placed the journal on the desk and withdrew her hands. When she didn't move to open it, Alyn glanced at her face, finding her gazing at the journal, her expression tightly controlled.

"You haven't read this since the first time," Alyn said.

Instead of answering, Deirdre gave her head a small shake and reached for the journal. As she flipped through the pages, she spoke. "When I read it, I was just trying to find out what happened. Why she —" She gestured vaguely with her hand, then lay the hand flat on the open book. "I read it so fast, I don't remember all the details." She scanned the page, then flipped forward a few more pages. "Yes, this is what I was looking for." She paused and caught Alyn's eye. "You already translated the passage that first mentions the swarm." When Alyn nodded, Deirdre said, "There is much more, of course, most of it very pessimistic. I believe she was on the verge of giving up until this passage." She pointed to a paragraph. "This was the first thing she wrote that suggested she was understanding the *sjel'and.*" With a glance at Alyn, she began to read.

It wasn't until I began to understand what motivates the sjel'and that I made real progress. I discovered the secret when contemplating what Beadu told me about the lan'and. The lan'and represent all that is good in humanity: joy, love, curiosity, generosity, community. It is only when they become bound to people that they accumulate the burdens that make the sjel'and such miserable creatures. Avarice, cowardliness, spite, isolation… These are the burdens of their material essence they bring with them into annen'heim.

When she noticed Alyn's expression, Deirdre chuckled. "You've encountered the swarm, so you can imagine what she wrote before this passage. This is the first hint that she is making progress."

"But how? Does she say?"

Deirdre scanned the next few pages. "There is more, but I'm looking for the most relevant passage."

"Beadu said you have to hear your spirit song to communicate with the *sjel'and.*"

Deirdre must have heard the hopeful note in Alyn's voice, because she gave her a sympathetic smile. Instead of answering, she began to read.

Beadu once told me the lan'and were like dogs; if you show them you are in charge, they will be happy. Not having an affinity for the land spirits, I wouldn't know. I hoped her advice applied equally well to the sjel'and swarm. But if the lan'and are like dogs, the sjel'and are like a pack of ravenous wolves. They do not acquiesce so easily. I believed they must be dominated and cowed into subservience.

But that couldn't be further from the truth.

It wasn't until I understood my spirit's song that I quieted the swarm. It's hard to remember that beneath their foulness, at their heart, they are lan'and. Isolated from their own kind by their own sins, they suffer terribly. Their memories torture them. The key for me was Beadu's statement that the spirits don't like to be apart from their own kind for long. I believe my spirit song relieves their loneliness if only for a short time and reminds them what they are, and what they will become. They are not transformed. After all, they cannot deny their essential nature. They remain cruel creatures that revel in misery. But when my spirit sings, I sense their longing, and I can use that longing to coax them into cooperating, if only for a brief time.

Alyn gazed at the runes on the page for long moments, while Deirdre waited. Somehow, she thought the fact Beadu told her to ask Deirdre to show her these passages meant she would find something that would help her. Finally, she said, "Spirit song. Minna hears her spirit song."

"Yes," Deirdre said. "I was skeptical. She is so young." She turned an apologetic smile on Alyn. "When your sister spoke of her spirit song, I wondered if the *Alle'oss* heard their song younger than Seidi sisters. The Seidi teaches that it is Daga's angels that we hear, but that is foolish. Sisters who are blessed enough to hear their song rarely hear it before their mid-teens."

"That's what Beadu teaches us. But if Minna heard hers already, I might hear my song before then."

Deirdre looked down at the book and closed it. "Beadu says it was the same for the old *saa'myn* as the for the sisters. The new *Alle'oss* witches are different in other ways, though. Perhaps they will hear their song at a younger age."

"But Minna had thirteen summers."

Deirdre nodded.

"The *Alle'oss* don't have time for me to get that old." Deirdre didn't reply, so Alyn gazed out the window. "I'm so afraid. All the time," she said. "I thought I could help by looking into the future." Dierdre didn't respond. "Beadu said Ragan told her to tell Minna not to commune with the *sjel'and*, but she didn't mention me."

"Beadu wants you to follow your mother's path?" Deirdre asked.

Though she wasn't looking at the older woman, Alyn heard the surprise in her voice. She thought about telling Deirdre what Beadu told her about the war, but decided it wasn't her place to reveal that. Instead, she looked at Deirdre and asked, "How do you hear your song? What do you have to do?"

Deirdre's lips pursed, then she shook her head. "Beadu says you only hear it when your connection to *mid'heim* extends far enough that your spirit hears the songs of the *lan'and*."

"So, it's nothing you do. You just have to be old enough?"

"I'm afraid so."

Alyn slipped off her stool. She started to turn away, then looked up and met Deirdre's eyes. "*Tok*, Dierdre."

"*Sosengu* (sorry)," Deirdre said.

Alyn nodded, then turned away and made her way to the exit. Beadu was surrounded by a group of children, and would be until the evening meal. Alyn should work on her translation, but the urgency she felt for that task had drained away. It seemed she was destined to remain in *Helala*, being useless, while Minna and most everyone else dear to her risked their lives.

Chapter 26

The 9th Day of the Month of Ungemon

Flynn

"You've been reassigned, Flynn," Marshal Storm said, handing Nara Flynn a sheet of paper.

Flynn took it, grinning at the marshal's use of her nickname. It was the rank-and-file soldiers who started calling her by her last name, and she decided she liked having a man's name. That the elite Volloch officers found it offensive was a bonus.

The document was a direct order from Malefica Briana. She ran her thumb over the Malefica's wax seal and examined the signature, which was spot on.

"This doesn't make sense," she said. "Are they aware how precarious the situation is here?"

"They are quite aware," the marshal said.

When he didn't offer any more information, Flynn stared blankly at the marshal for a moment, then looked down at the document again, to reassure herself it said what she thought it said. "It says here I'm to report to the commander of the Ninth."

"That's right."

"Can you tell me where that would be, or is that still a secret?" The whereabouts of the Ninth Legion was the topic of much speculation and rumor among the troops, for good reason. Since the Ninth disappeared, no unit had been withdrawn from the line for rest.

"Sister!" the marshal said sharply at her disrespectful tone, then he sighed, and glance out the window to give himself time to get control of his temper. After a long moment, he gestured to a chair and said, "Have a seat, Flynn."

Flynn slumped into the chair, grateful to be off her feet, and taking a certain satisfaction at the mud she tracked into the marshal's office. She knew that wasn't fair. Unlike many of the officers in the Imperial Army, Victor Storm suffered along with the men under his command. The dark circles under his eyes, the several days' growth of beard, the hair that looked as if he barely dragged a comb through it after a few hours of sleep; they were all signs the soldiers respected.

Sister Flynn was an impertinent snot. Or that was the opinion of Malefica Briana. Flynn didn't care what that sanctimonious, talentless sister thought. Flynn and her sisters at the front were the reason Briana and her ilk could sit comfortably in their tower, ignoring the world's perils, and the Malefica knew it. One of the bad girls that communed with spirits, Flynn spent the past four years battling the Kaileuk. Unlike Keelia, who returned a war hero, Flynn and the other bad girls labored in obscurity. Only the soldiers and a few officers admitted the only reason the barbarians hadn't swept across the Empire was the few sisters in their midst.

While the marshal crossed his office to a locked filing cabinet, Flynn's mind drifted. When was the last time she had more than a few minutes' sleep? She didn't remember.

"Flynn."

She snapped awake, lifted her chin from her chest, and wiped spit from her cheek. "Sir?"

The marshal didn't seem to take any offense. Instead, he handed her a slim file. "That's all I know about the Ninth," he said. "The emperor withdrew them, against my protests. They are currently camped outside Hast and have been for weeks."

Flynn leafed through the few pages, which provided no more information than the marshal just conveyed. "Hast?" she asked, tossing the file onto his desk. "Argren going to be another Ferol?"

The marshal sat back and nodded. "It appears so."

She frowned when the full implications of the Ninth's disposition occurred to her. "You said they've been camped outside Hast for weeks. What are they waiting for?"

"That is a good question," the marshal said. "The other, more pressing, question for me is why they are asking for you."

Flynn smirked. "Because they've been sitting around doing nothing for weeks. The troops are bored and everyone knows I'm the best storyteller in the Empire."

"I've heard that rumor," the marshal said without returning her smile. "I've also heard you are insubordinate, have a sharp tongue, and aren't afraid to use it." When Flynn started to speak, he held up a hand to forestall her. "I'm perfectly willing to look the other way. Obviously. General Prather, who commands the Ninth, is not as lenient."

Flynn's lips pursed. Prather the prat. This was news. "Prather?" she asked.

The marshal nodded.

"Did he ask for me?"

"Seems so."

They gazed at one another until Flynn said what they were both thinking. "Things aren't going well for the Ninth."

"That would be my guess," Victor said.

"This is all going to end badly, isn't it?" she asked after a pause.

Victor's lips quivered, but instead of answering, he slumped back in his chair and gazed out the window.

It was so long before he spoke again, she was growing fidgety and wondering if she should just excuse herself.

"It is unfortunate we aren't able to choose the people who lead us," he said. "Were there an option, I would choose leaders wiser, more accepting of *all* people. But that would require…"

Flynn resisted the urge to double check that the door to his office was closed. She knew he married a Brochen woman. Everyone did. She always assumed that meant the marshal was a more open-minded man than most Volloch. But what he just said amounted to treason. And from the highest ranking officer in the Imperial military. "Well," she said slowly. "We don't have that option." She fell silent, watching him still gazing out the window. "Do we?"

He settled his gazed on her. "Just a thought," he said. He sat up. "In any case, you are to report in two weeks, so you best get started. There's a ship waiting in Ulm that will take you to Lubern and a barge that will take you up the river to Hast. Report to the quartermaster in both cities."

Flynn popped up, snapped her heels together, and gave the marshal her crispest salute. "Yes, sir, Marshal Storm." She smirked at his startled expression, gave him a jaunty wave, and turned to go. Before she closed the door to his office, she grew serious and said, "Good luck, Victor."

•   •   •

Flynn should have taken advantage of a rare opportunity to sleep in a bed, especially after the harrowing trek from the marshal's headquarters to Ulm. It was alarming to see the Kaileuk patrols moving so freely behind the Imperial lines. She and her escort managed to avoid them, but they decided lingering was not a good idea. The only sleep she had since leaving the marshal was in her saddle.

Yes, she should sleep, but she would have plenty of time to sleep at sea, and she hadn't been in a proper tavern in months.

She descended the stairs slowly to the tavern's common room, allowing the patrons to notice her. It was busy. That was good. She preferred a big audience. The whispers already started as she stepped up to the bar. The bartender, a tall thin man with one eye, peered doubtfully down at her. Flynn couldn't help that she looked sixteen. It was annoying how many barkeeps held it against her. She turned her face, making sure he got a good look at her tattoo. When his face cleared, she said, "Your best ale, sir."

Ale in hand, she turned her back to the bar and scanned the room, gratified to see patrons discussing her presence. Yes, it had been months since she passed through Ulm, but they remembered her. Of course. She took a sip and shuddered in pleasure. The men at the front managed to distill a variety of alcoholic concoctions, but the best you could say about them was they wouldn't kill you. Not outright, anyway.

There was a small stage on which a woman crooned a ballad about Lachlan and Illiana, Abria's parents. It was an old song, one of Flynn's favorites, and the singer's voice lent it a haunting melancholy. She gazed around at the festive crowd. Ulm would be one of the first cities the Kaileuk would reach if the army collapsed. How many more carefree nights would these people have?

She let the song and the ale wash away months of anxiety and fear. For this night, at least, she was safe and she wouldn't need to kill anyone. Not that she had qualms about what she had to do at the front. The Kaileuk would not hesitate to kill her and her entire family, given the chance, and her family was the bedrock on which Flynn's charmed life rested.

Her love of stories came from her father. She remembered him as the empire's second best story teller. She smiled, remembering how he laughed when she told him that shortly before his death. Of her many joyful childhood memories, huddling with her brothers at her father's feet, listening to his tales, were among the most indelible. Even before she showed signs of being sensitive to Daga's essence, her favorite stories were the fairy tales of Seidi sisters dispensing justice and protecting the weak. Her father was a good man, and he chose his stories to instill in his children the values he held dear. On the day she left home for the Seidi, her father told her to remember the stories and always do what was right. She promised him she would.

The world's ugliness had worn away her naïve idealism, but her father had done his job. She always did what she thought was right. The trick was in knowing what was right.

"A story!" someone shouted.

The singer finished while she ruminated, but buzzing from ale and fatigue, she was too slow to answer the call she'd been waiting for. By the time she roused herself, a man was stepping onto the stage to rowdy cheers. He was portly, with long snow white hair. The corners of his eyes crinkled as he smiled, acknowledging the crowd's enthusiasm.

Someone shouted, "The Battle of Minna and Aife!" There were a few moans, but the cheers drowned them out.

Flynn perked up. The Battle of Minna and Aife? This was a story she never heard before, and Flynn made it a point to know all the stories told in the Empire.

The storyteller sipped from a tankard of ale, then gazed out over the crowd, waiting for an expectant hush to fall. He was better than most of the hacks Flynn had seen. When it was so quiet you could hear a pin drop, he waited some more, drawing his audience in. Flynn caught herself leaning toward him. He was really good.

"This story began some years ago." He started quietly, but his deep baritone carried to the far corners of the room. "A babe was born in a remote village in Argren." He paused, lifted a brow, and graced his audience with a small smirk. "And her name was?"

"Minna!" the crowd roared.

Flynn straightened and set her ale down before she dropped it. Argren? A story about an *Alle'oss* girl? While the storyteller took a sip of his ale, letting the crowd settle, she scanned the room. Flynn wasn't lying when she told the marshal she was the best storyteller in the Empire. She was. She was used to the kind of focused attention she saw on these faces, but she rarely saw it with other storytellers. They were anticipating this story, though it was obvious they heard it before. And it was a story about an *Alle'oss* girl.

She picked up her tankard, leaned her back on the bar, and let the storyteller draw her in. Her initial impression was correct. He was good, though he rushed through certain parts and lost momentum just before the climax. But when he turned his face to the ceiling, arms spread, mimicking the hero's swoon after the battle, his audience sat motionless, mesmerized.

Flynn applauded with the rest when he took his bow. It was a hell of a story. The crowd called for more, but, exhausted and deciding she didn't want to try topping this story, Flynn trudged up the stairs to her room, watching the storyteller accepting tips and compliments as he circulated around the room.

While she was isolated at the front the past two years, news of what was going on in the rest of the Empire was rare and fragmentary. That people were openly telling stories that featured an *Alle'oss* witch as the hero was shocking. How the storyteller escaped the notice of the Inquisition was beyond her.

She splurged for a private room and insisted they replace the straw in the mattress. Rolling onto the lumpy mattress, she stared at the ceiling and replayed the story. It was absurd. They obviously mined Seidi myths of powerful sisters like Abria and Ione. It was a common motif. But why an *Alle'oss* hero? If she hadn't seen it for herself, she would never believe an Imperial audience would accept such a thing. Still, it was a hell of a story, and, with some polishing and a few embellishments, Flynn could tell the hell out of it.

Chapter 27

The 20th Day of the Month of Ungemon

Ulf

Ulf and the five other members of his squad stood in a rough circle, shuffling nervously and staring at the ground. He was reminded of the time he and his brothers nearly burned down the stable. He never saw his father so angry. Mikaela looked up and shrugged when she noticed him watching her. All of them had an idea why Raif asked them to stay behind when the other squads headed out for the day's tactical exercise. They just didn't know what the verdict would be.

They left the main *Alle'oss* camp in high spirits, and headed south along the rim of the escarpment, until they came to the point where it bent to the east at the mouth of the Kalana Valley. Since they arrived, they drilled in the thick forest along the northern rim of the valley. Every day followed the same routine. Up before dawn, a cold breakfast, then Raif or one of the *Oss'stera* soldiers lectured them on tactics. Following two hours of archery practice, they ventured into the forest for tactical exercises.

It didn't take long for their squad's deficiencies to become apparent. Their performance had been so dismal, Ulf began privately thinking of them as the misfits. Most of the new trainees had little experience with bows and spears, but the misfits had not a whit of woodcraft among them.

Ulf's flight through Argen with Minna the previous winter qualified him as the most experienced. They started with simple, squad level exercises, and practiced them until most of the squads could execute them smoothly and silently. But no matter how often the misfits practiced, every Imp within a league's radius could have heard them bumbling through the underbrush.

But it was when they advanced to more complex exercises involving multiple squads that things really fell apart. They were supposed to react instantly as a unit in response to signals delivered by a horn, but as they never mastered the squad level exercises, the additional requirement to coordinate with other squads was quite clearly beyond them. In the resulting confusion, they missed or misheard signals. They lost sight of one another and wandered off in the wrong direction, becoming separated and opening gaps an enemy could exploit. Arguments ensued. It was one disastrous exercise after another.

The lectures were all well and good, but in Ulf's opinion, staying organized in the dense forest was impossible. All the new squads were having problems, but the misfits seemed especially inept. Raif just shook his head, but it seemed to Ulf the *Alle'oss* might be better off leaving him and his squad right where they were. In the middle of nowhere.

Today's exercise was a simulation of a meeting engagement with Imp Rangers. The trainees were pretending they were moving through the forest when they stumbled upon a smaller group of rangers, played by hardened *Oss'stera* soldiers. Ulf wasn't looking forward to it. It was a particularly fluid situation, requiring communication and tight coordination. He sighed heavily, thinking about the disaster the previous day's exercise became. Somehow, he and Mikaela wound up alone and lost a league from the rest of their squad.

So, it wasn't a surprise when Raif asked the misfits to hang back while the other squads moved out after archery practice. The only good thing about this morning was the constant rain relented overnight. Now, instead of being soaked through to the skin, he was merely damp.

"Ulf."

Ulf looked up and found Oren approaching. Oren was the unfortunate *Oss'stera* soldier Raif assigned to whip them into shape. "Yes, sir," Ulf said.

"You remember the objective?"

Ulf glanced around at the other blank faces of his squad mates and noticed, for the first time, they were one person short. Bern, their squad leader, was missing. "Where's Bern?" he asked.

Oren's scowl seemed to be a permanent feature of his young face. But Ulf had discovered it was a nuanced thing that revealed the many shades of his annoyance. By ignoring his question, Ulf earned a full on glower. "Bern has been reassigned," he answered curtly. "Now, Ulf, do you remember the objective for today's exercise?"

Ulf stared at him blankly. He assumed Bern would listen during the briefing. "Why?"

Oren's glower sank to as yet unseen depths, but before he could respond, Mikaela came to Ulf's rescue. "We're screening the right flank."

"Right," Ulf said, Mikaela's words jogging his memory. "When the main force makes contact with the rangers, we're supposed to take the high ground over there." He pointed to the west, though the ridge wasn't visible through the trees. "We keep the Imps from taking it," he said. "At all costs." The phrase must have filtered into his inattentive mind without his knowledge, because Oren's scowl moderated into surprised annoyance. Before he could respond, Ulf asked, "Who's the new squad leader?"

"You are." His scowl revealed what he thought of that bit of news.

"Why me?" Ulf blurted.

"Wasn't my idea, so I couldn't tell you," Oren said. "Now, get your squad moving. You'll have to double time it to catch the others." He held up a hand before anyone could start moving. "It was my opinion this squad should be broken up and reassigned. Raif thinks you should get one more chance. Let's hope you prove me wrong." Glower, a quick nod, then he spun on a heel and disappeared into the forest.

Ulf looked around at his squad mates, who were watching where Oren disappeared with glum faces. All except Mikaela.

She slapped Ulf's back and said with a grin, "Congratulations! You're in charge for the last ride of the misfits."

Her use of his private name for their squad brought a smile to his face. "Right," he said. "That makes me emperor of the misfits." That coaxed a few grins from his squad. "Alright, you heard the man. Let's move out." As the others turned to go, Ulf caught Mikaela's sleeve and whispered, "You remember where we're supposed to go?"

She snapped a salute. "Yes, I do, your eminence."

"Good. You take point."

• • •

Ulf peered through the trees, catching a glimpse of Mikaela's deep burgundy curls. She glanced back when he approached and smiled when she saw it was him. Beyond all expectations, they arrived at their assigned position in good order and only slightly late. They spread out in a line at an angle to the main force and kept pace, ostensibly preventing a surprise attack on their flank. It was a difficult maneuver in the dense underbrush. Their previous attempts had seen them wandering all over the forest and losing contact with the force they were supposed to be protecting. Determined to avoid their previous disasters, Ulf roamed back and forth along their line, making sure no one got lost.

He knelt beside Mikaela, who gave him another exaggerated salute. "So far, so good, right?"

"So far," Ulf said. The ridge that was their primary objective was visible through the canopy off to their right. "Um, Mikaela?"

"Yeah?" she asked, peering at their squad mate, Vin, to her left.

"Why do you think Raif made me squad leader?" he asked. Given their obvious deficiencies, it occurred to him, Raif might hope they failed so he could rid himself of the troublesome squad.

She twisted around and stared at him. "You're kidding, right?" she asked.

"No."

"Ulf, we've been in the forest for an hour today and everyone is still where they're supposed to be."

"But —"

"Mother, help me, Ulf," she said, shaking her head. She turned back and made sure she was still in contact with her neighbors.

Ulf stared at the back of her head. He hadn't really done anything special, just made sure everyone followed the plan. Maybe that was all there was to it. When Mikaela glanced back at him, he said, "I expect it will start pretty soon."

As if on cue, shouts rang out from the main force to their left, followed by three short blasts on a horn.

"That's it," Mikaela said. "You better give the order."

The order. What order? Ulf's eyes snapped to the ridge. "Right, the order." He stood and shouted, "Misfits, close spread formation, take the high ground on our right, move out!" The squad repeated the order down the line, then they were moving. Ulf let Mikaela go ahead, keeping an eye on her neighbors to the right and left. He could only hope the two out of sight on the ends of the line were keeping up.

As they neared the ridge, the forest was coming alive behind them. The first isolated shouts multiplied until it was impossible to hear individual voices. Something was wrong. There was an unfamiliar stridency to the usual clamor. He heard Oren shouting orders, but couldn't tell if they were intended for his squad or not. And then he heard something that sent a chill through him; the staccato flicker of arrows cutting through the underbrush. And then someone screamed.

He hurried after his squad and stepped out of the brush beside a small stream that ran along the base of the ridge at the same time as the rest of his squad. He could tell by their expressions, they were as shocked as he was, though he couldn't tell if it was what was happening behind of them or that they managed to complete the maneuver successfully.

"What's happening?" Mikaela asked.

"Sounds like a real attack," Ulf said, his words punctuated by another scream.

"We should go back and help," Vin, standing on the other side of Mikaela, shouted. Vin was from a village near Richeleau. Though he never joined *Oss'stera,* he had taken to shaving the right side of his head like they did.

Ulf looked back toward the shouts, uncertainly.

"Ulf," Mikaela said. "You're squad leader. What do we do?"

"No," he said. "Even if it's a real attack, the plan's the same. We're supposed to hold the high ground to keep the Imps off our flank." When no one moved, he said, "If we don't get up there before the Imps, we'll never take it. String your bows." To his surprise, all of them, even Vin, responded. When they were ready, Ulf shouted, "Spread formation abreast! Stay even, get to the top and find cover!" The six misfits headed up the wooded slope.

Halfway to the top, Ulf remembered to nock an arrow. He drew the arrow from his quiver, but his hands were shaking so badly, he dropped it. When he leaned down to retrieve it, he tripped on wobbly legs and fell to his knees on the steep incline. He managed to get to his feet and catch up to Mikaela, visible on his left, and was relieved it didn't appear she noticed.

When he arrived, puffing, on top of the ridge, he glanced to his left and found only four of the other five misfits looking back at him. "Where's Vin?"

"Turned back."

That was disappointing, but there was nothing to be done about it now. He crossed the ridge and looked down. The ridge faced west, less than a league from the rim of the escarpment. This side of the ridge grew steeper near the top, leaving the rocky upper thirty paces devoid of trees and underbrush. He was scanning the tree line below him when men in the green uniforms of the Imperial Rangers appeared. It was the reason they were there; to stop this kind of attack. Still, he was so surprised, he could only stand and stare. Fortunately, Mikaela reacted.

"Rangers!" she shouted.

The rangers looked up at her shout. Ulf glanced at the misfits and found everyone looking back at him. "Hold the high ground!" he shouted.

He drew the string of his bow, took aim, and loosed. The arrow flew high. The rangers advanced up the slope, returning fire. Ulf knelt, drew another arrow, and dropped it.

Arrows flew over their heads. Though the rangers were far more adept archers, they were climbing a steep slope and the misfits could duck beneath the crown of the ridge. Ulf picked up the arrow with sweat-slicked fingers. *Minna would not drop her arrow.* The thought popped into his head unexpectedly, but the memory of Minna standing resolute under pressure was what he needed. He nocked the arrow with steadier fingers and peered over the edge at the advancing rangers. They were only twenty paces below the top, still coming, pausing occasionally to return fire. Drawing the string, he sighted on the man he guessed was the leader, took a breath and loosed. The man bent over, hands on the arrow protruding from his abdomen, then he tumbled backwards down the slope.

Ulf's hands drew and loosed without his intervention. Draw, aim, loose. Draw, aim, loose. They were going to stop them. He glanced at the rest of his squad and was happy to see four misfits still standing. Six rangers remained, chugging up the steepest part of the slope near the top. He aimed at a man closing in on Mikaela, who was looking elsewhere.

Before he loosed, a big ranger rose up over the rim of the ridge in front of him. Ulf swung his bow around and loosed in one motion. The hasty shot flew over the Imp's shoulder, but forced him to duck away. With no time to retrieve another arrow, Ulf swung his bow like a staff and struck the big ranger in the temple. The man stumbled, one foot slipped over the rim of the slope, then he tumbled out of sight. Ulf nocked another arrow and peered over the edge.

"Help, Ulf!"

Ulf looked to his left and saw Mikaela, her bow held defensively in front of her, backing away from the ranger, who made it to the top of the ridge. Ulf drew and loosed, striking the ranger in the back. The man fell to his knees, reaching back for the arrow, then fell forward and lay still. He and Mikaela stared at one another for a heartbeat, then they drew arrows and looked down the slope. Bodies littered the slope and were strewn along the tree line where the slope became less steep, some of them moving, but there were no more rangers climbing.

He looked along the top of the ridge, seeing in the faces of his remaining misfits the swirl of emotions he was feeling. Horror at their first real taste of combat, relief at having survived and sorrow for their fallen comrade. Jarl, a boy from Ka'tan, was down. "Mikaela, keep watch," Ulf said. "Helga, check on Jarl." He crossed to the other side of the ridge and looked out over the forest, listening for sounds of fighting. Out of the corner of his eye, he caught movement in the dense brush on the face of the ridge. Ducking down, he peered into the tangle and saw men in green uniforms moving stealthily through the trees. More rangers. The undergrowth extended almost to the top on this side, and it wasn't as steep. They would never be able to hold the top of the ridge. Besides, if there were rangers climbing this side of the ridge, the main force they were supposed to be protecting was already in big trouble.

He backed away from the edge until he was out of sight of the rangers, then jumped up and dashed across the spine of the ridge. "Misfits," he shouted. "Rangers, coming up the other side."

Mikaela looked around, panicked. "What do we do?"

"We run," Ulf said and looked down the steep side of the ridge. "Helga, Jarl?" Helga shook her head. "Let's go," Ulf shouted.

As one, they leapt over the edge, sliding down the slope on their seats. Reaching the tree line, they dodged past the wounded rangers and fled.

"*L'oss!*" A ranger's shout from the top of the ridge followed them into the trees.

●　●　●

"Anyone have any arrows?" Ulf leaned his back against a granite outcrop, bent over and caught himself on his knees.

"I've got one," Mikaela said.

Ulf looked to Helga, who shook her head. "I'm empty, too," he said.

"Won't do much with one arrow," Helga said.

Ulf had noticed Helga tended to focus on the negative side of most situations. Unfortunately, she was right this time. After their escape from the ridge, they ran west until they neared the escarpment. Ulf hoped the rangers had better things to do than chase them, but finding their comrades in a pile at the base of the ridge was motivating. The misfits fled north, traveling the thin strip of open space between the forest and the cliff. Every time they tried to turn east to search for what was left of the *Alle'oss,* they encountered small groups of rangers. During one skirmish, the fourth member of their squad was killed and now there were only three misfits left.

"Wonder what happened?" Mikaela asked.

"Ambush," Helga answered. "Everyone else is probably dead."

"Not so sure of that," Ulf said. "Did you notice the Imps we've seen seem as anxious to avoid us as we are to avoid them?"

Helga shrugged.

"And it looks like there's only two or three at a time," Ulf said.

"So, what do you think happened?" Helga asked.

Ulf pushed himself upright and pulled his hair into a tail, letting some air onto the back of his neck. "The Imps found a way out of the valley. They were moving north, meaning to scout the army at the Cut. They stumbled onto our exercise by accident. There was a skirmish, the Imps scattered, separating into small groups in the confusion."

"I don't know," Mikaela said. "It seemed like a coordinated attack. Why else would they attack the ridge?"

Ulf considered, then said, "They were scouting the top of the escarpment. When they heard the horn, they came running." When he saw the doubt on their faces, he shrugged. "It doesn't really matter what happened. All that matters is what we do next."

"And what do we do?" Helga asked.

While Ulf was formulating a response, they heard a voice in the forest behind them.

"Ours or theirs?" Mikaela asked.

"Not sure we can risk finding out," Ulf said. He stood and walked toward the edge of the escarpment. The city of Hast and the camp of the

Ninth Legion were visible to the northwest. He knew where they were. Looking back, he said, "Come on, I have an idea."

They heard more voices, this time with the unmistakable accents of Imperials. Helga caught up to Ulf. "Where are we going?"

"Just up here," Ulf said. He stopped and spun around, examining the nearby terrain. Following a whiff of wood smoke to a small firepit, the embers still smoking, he found six bedrolls, packs and other signs of recent occupation. It appeared the guards he hoped to find left in a hurry. Approaching the cliff's edge, he peered down, then turned and smiled. "This is it. Come on."

Mikaela was the first to step up beside him. "Stairs," she said with some surprise.

"That's right," Ulf said. He pointed to the bedrolls. "Those probably belonged to the squad assigned to guard it." The stairs were chiseled into the face of the cliff by the *Alle'oss* long before the Empire created the Wollen Cut. Forgotten by nearly everyone for years, they were rediscovered by the nascent resistance some years before. Ulf descended the first few steps and looked up. "We only have to go down partway, then wait until the Imps leave."

Helga looked down in horror. "I'm not going down those."

Ulf looked down the stairs. They were about a pace wide, cut into the granite face of the cliff so that the stone arched above them. The arch was just tall enough that Ulf could descend without stooping. He looked up. "It's not so bad. Just… keep your shoulder close to the stone and be ready for wind gusts."

"No way!"

Mikaela looked to the south, then started down the stairs. "Imps coming!" she said and shooed Ulf ahead of her.

They descended the narrow stairs faster than even Ulf thought prudent. He heard Helga muttering to herself behind him. A third of the way down, a tunnel entered the rock face. Inside, stairs led to a lower level, then the stairs cut into the cliff resumed in the opposite direction. Ulf led them into the tunnel and stopped. There was just enough room to accommodate all of them.

They waited, their heavy breaths audible above a howling wind in the small space.

"How long do we wait?" Mikaela asked.

Ulf leaned out and peered up the stairs, then jerked back. "They're coming."

"What?" Helga said. "What do we do? We're trapped."

"No, we're not," Ulf said. He led them to the lower level, then started down the stairs. Helga shouted something behind him, but he couldn't make it out over the wind. As he neared the bottom, he glanced back and was relieved to see no rangers. He stepped onto the piled scree at the base of the cliff on stiff legs, then turned and caught Mikaela and Helga before they could run toward the forest thirty paces away.

"We have to get out of here," Mikaela said.

"If we get too far from the cliff, they'll see us," Ulf said. "Come on." He led them stumbling across the top of the scree parallel to the stone face, until they were a hundred paces from the base of the stairs, then sprinted for the cover of the trees. When he looked back, the rangers, painted in orange by the setting sun, were descending the last few steps, facing in the opposite direction.

"So, we wait until they leave, then we go back up?" Mikaela, crouching next to Ulf, asked.

"That's the plan," Ulf said.

"I can't go up those stairs," Helga said. "That was the worst thing I've ever done."

Ulf chuckled.

"What?" Mikaela asked.

"That's what Minna thought," he said. The rangers apparently decided to take a break on the grass below the scree pile. "We came down those stairs when we were going to Brennan to save her sister." He turned and grinned at Mikaela. "She's so fearless most of the time, but you should have seen her face on those stairs. She was a pale as a spirit." Smiling at the memory, Ulf looked back at the rangers.

"What's she like?"

Ulf glanced at Mikaela, who was looking at him with a strange expression. "Who, Minna?"

"Yeah."

"She's… I don't know. She's like you and me," he said finally. "Except for the fire and lightning and spirit stuff." He sat, putting his back to the trunk of a hickory tree. Glancing over his shoulder to make sure the Imps weren't moving, he said, "What I mean is, she's not always this all mighty *saa'myn*. Sometimes she's unsure of herself and quiet."

"But the stories," Mikaela asked doubtfully. "Did she really do all that stuff?"

"Oh, yeah," Ulf said with a chuckle. "Well, I wasn't there for all of it, but the stories are mostly true. I mean, she's like us *most* of the time, but when it comes time to, you know, fight, she's fearless. I've seen it happen." He drew his hands down in front of his face, trying to imitate Minna's fighting expression. "She gets all calm on the outside, but you can see there's this fire inside." He stopped and looked at Mikaela and Helga, who were watching him with rapt expressions. "Anyway, she's all people think she is and more."

"You really like her," Mikaela said.

"Yeah," Ulf said. He turned and watched the Imps who looked like they were settling in for the night. "Looks like you don't have to worry, Helga. We're not going up those stairs tonight."

"Great," Helga said. "Now, what do we do?"

Ulf was about to point out it was Helga who said she didn't want to go back up the stairs, when Mikaela spoke.

"We can go to my village."

Ulf turned to face her.

"It's in the valley." Her lips pursed. "I'm not exactly sure where we are, but it shouldn't be too far from here."

"That's the wrong direction," Helga said.

Instead of answering Helga, Mikaela looked at Ulf. "We don't have any food. We can't go north. We don't know how long we have to wait before we can go up the stairs, and now that we know the Imps know about the stairs, we don't know what we'll find if we go up." She looked at Helga. "My parents will feed us, then we go east and find an exit out of the valley."

Ulf looked from Mikaela to Helga, who still looked skeptical. "It's either that," he said, "or we wait and climb the stairs."

Helga turned and started walking south. Ulf exchanged a grin with Mikaela and followed.

Raif

Raif was studying the map when Oren appeared. "What's the news?"

"As near as I can tell, we have six dead, ten wounded, and five missing," Oren said. "The initiates are watching the perimeter and *Oss'stera* are chasing down Imp stragglers."

Raif stood. "I suppose we should count ourselves lucky," he said. "What's your assessment of what happened?"

"I think the rangers found a way out of the valley," he said. "Scouts, probably. Whatever they were doing, they weren't expecting us to be here. That and *Oss'stera's* experience are the only reason it wasn't worse."

"I agree," Raif said. "Reorganize the squads to replace losses, then get ready to transport the wounded back to the Cut. We'll let the *Oss'stera* unit find out where the Imps came from and set squads to guard the exits."

"Yes, sir."

"Oren," Raif said as he was turning away.

"Sir?"

"What about our troublesome squad? They were supposed to defend the ridge."

"Looks like they had a scrap. There's a pile of Imp bodies on the far side."

"You sure it was them?" Raif asked, surprised.

"Found Jarl's body on the top of the ridge."

"What about the rest of them?"

"No sign. Those are the missing five."

"Thank you," Raif said. The first thing that went through his mind as Oren turned away was he would have to tell Minna.

Chapter 28

The 20th Day of the Month of Ungemon

Macha

Macha watched, fascinated, as the crew brought the ship in close to shore. The captain, standing close to her on the quarterdeck, conducted the ballet with some urgency. She didn't blame him. No one in the crew ran afoul of her sisters, but the captain took the mysterious disappearance of Otto as an ominous sign. Macha couldn't be sure what happened to their handler, but ever since he failed to appear on deck one morning, Eriu had been almost serene by her standards. As if on cue, her sister's voice rang out.

"Wooohooo!" she sang, leaning precariously out over the rail. "Laaaand Ho!"

Macha was sympathetic. The novelty of being on the ship wore off after the first couple of days. She was used to people's uneasy response to her and her sisters, but in the confined space, the crew's palpable fear was oppressive. After the first week, it became a moment by moment struggle not to lash out. The captain didn't know how much he owed to her spirit guide, who appeared a few days before they reached their destination. It was only his calming influence that got her through.

Neiman coped by hiding in the small cabin they shared. Eriu prowled the deck all day, every day, but she hadn't harmed anyone. It was likely Otto's fate saved the crew. Macha looked down at her sister, leaning out over the rail, both arms extended, hair streaming behind her in the wind. It felt somehow wrong to be proud of her, given their minder's fate, but Macha couldn't help what she felt.

Movement at her elbow drew her eye. Neiman returned her gaze through hooded eyes. It was her first appearance on the ship's deck in daylight since they left Ulm. "Sister," Macha said. "Are you as ready as I am to be on dry land?"

One corner of Neiman's lips twitched. It was the closest thing to a smile that Macha ever saw on her face. She reached out and gave Neiman's arm a squeeze, then let her hand drop and gazed toward the shore.

"Drop anchor," the captain shouted. "Lower the longboat."

Macha watched him gather himself and swallow heavily, then he turned toward her and said, "We'll not be staying longer than we have to. You best collect your things and get yourself on the boat." When she gave him a nod, he glanced at Neiman and turned away.

"Well, sister," Macha said. "You heard the man."

Minutes later, Neiman sat quietly beside Macha, watching the beach coming closer. Eriu sat in the bow, or occupied the bow, at any rate. At the moment, she crouched on her knees, her upper body extended over the front of the boat, fingers trailing in the water. Macha guessed her manic performance was the reason for the crew's prodigious efforts on the oars. She was fine with that. She was so ready to be off the water, she could barely sit still.

As they neared shore, she forgot her sisters for a moment and studied what they were approaching. Between a narrow rocky beach and towering bluffs, a flat plain was occupied by hundreds of white tents. Smoke rose from fires and drifted sullenly above the camp in a light breeze. Men moved about. Snatches of rough voices speaking a guttural tongue reached her ears between the rhythmic creak of the oarlocks. Macha didn't have many examples of humans to draw on, but to her eyes, the men in the camp appeared larger than normal.

"Who are these men?"

Macha looked at Neiman, who was watching the camp with wide eyes. That simple question was the first time Macha heard her quiet sister's voice in days. Manfrid and the Father didn't tell them much, but Macha worked out what was going to happen on her own. "They are going to attack the *Alle'oss*. The witches we seek will come to their defense and we will kill them."

Neiman nodded slowly, her eyes never leaving the camp.

Eriu leapt from the boat into waist deep water and waded through the low surf, hands held delicately clear of the water. When the keel of the boat ground into the rocky bottom, Neiman sprang up, clambered over the bow into ankle deep water and joined Eriu on the stony beach. Macha met the first mate's eye, gave him what she hoped was an unsettling grin, rose gracefully and followed her sister. Almost before her foot touched dry land, the sailors were pushing the longboat back into the low surf.

Her sisters stood shoulder to shoulder, staring at the camp. Macha looked past them to the men who noticed their arrival and were gathering to watch. Now that she was closer, she decided her initial impression was correct. The men were enormous, solidly built and taller than her and her sisters by at least a foot. Some of them wore colorfully decorated leather armor and carried vicious-looking weapons. But what was most unsettling was their expressions. She was used to all kinds of reactions from the few normal people they encountered — curiosity, disgust, fear, lust. Normally, she could care less what people thought of them, but she found these men's flat, emotionless stares disquieting.

Glancing at her sisters, she guessed they felt the same. When no one greeted them, she scanned the men for someone who looked like they were in charge. They all looked the same to her, but spotting a tent on the far side of the camp much larger than the others, she nudged Neiman to get her attention, then took the lead, walking around the perimeter of the camp. The men watched silently. As they walked, her eyes rose to the top of the sheer stone cliffs that loomed behind the camp. Shadows among deep green evergreens, wreathed by misty clouds, gave it an ominous aspect.

Above the low murmur of the surf, a comforting call interrupted her brooding. A flock of crows, perhaps anticipating the carnage that was these men's business, perched in a stand of wind swept pine trees beyond the perimeter of the camp. She let herself open, called the spirit and reached out to the birds.

A flood of images followed her greeting. Coming to a stop, she gazed up at the bluffs again, where unseen eyes looked back at her. She was so involved in deciphering the birds' images, she didn't notice the commotion behind her until Eriu clutched her arm. She spun around and found the massive soldiers transformed. Gone were the flat stares, replaced by angry grimaces. Macha stood frozen as the men approached. The spirit never let her delve into the minds of people, but she could sense these men. Not what she sensed in intelligent animals like crows, but a low buzzy hum that carried only a hint of intent. And what she sensed frightened her.

The closest man lunged toward Neiman. Neiman lifted a hand and the hulking man flew backwards and crumbled to the ground. The rest hesitated, but the buzz in Macha's mind intensified in an instant. They were moments from a bloodbath. She let the spirit go, closing her connection to the men.

Eriu lifted a hand.

"No!" Macha shouted. She stepped in front of her sister and took hold of her wrist. Eriu's frightened eyes snapped to her. Macha, her face close to Eriu's, said, "Shield." For a moment, she was afraid Eriu would ignore her, then the light of sanity flickered behind her blue eyes. She gave Macha a nod and Macha stepped away.

Eriu lifted her hand and raised her invisible shield. Neiman, who was backing away from the men, both hands in front of her, noticed and followed her sister's example. The men pressed up against the shields, glaring at them. It wasn't that Macha was reluctant to kill these men. After their assault on Neiman, she would happily lay waste to the entire camp. It was more a question of tactics. Would she and her sisters survive a violent confrontation unscathed? While she was considering the problem, she prepared to summon the fire spirits.

"Topol!" someone shouted from the back of the throng.

The men reacted instantly, backing away, the stony stares reappearing. A short, round man appeared through the crowd, followed by what appeared to be three *Alle'oss* men. The four men looked like children among the hulking soldiers. The short man said something Macha couldn't understand and one of the men, indistinguishable from the rest, responded and shouted at the others. Slowly, they turned away and returned to the camp.

After a glance at Macha, Eriu and Neiman dropped their shields.

The short man watched some of his men pick up the body, then turned to Macha and studied her with watery eyes. "You killed one of my men."

"Who are you?" Macha asked.

"Chagan Koutman. These are my men," he said, gesturing to the camp.

"Tell your animals to keep their hands to themselves," Macha said.

He gazed at her, then studied Eriu and Neiman appraisingly. "They would not molest you unless they were provoked."

Macha looked over her shoulder at the crows. Something about these men made them susceptible to her spirit and, like most creatures, they noticed her intrusion. Though the connection wasn't sufficient for her to sense their thoughts clearly, they could sense the spirit entering their minds. And they apparently didn't appreciate it. She looked at the short man and said, "You're being watched." She pointed. "From the bluffs."

Chagan glanced to where she pointed, then studied her face. "And you know this, how?"

Macha allowed herself a grin. "A bird told me."

Chagan's wet lips pursed, but before he could respond, one of the *Alle'oss* standing behind him spoke. "It must be a witch thing."

"You can speak to animals?" Chagan asked Macha.

"Yes," Macha said. "It doesn't work on humans, but..." She looked over his shoulder toward the camp, leaving the implication unsaid.

"Don't do it again," Chagan said.

"Might be useful," the *Alle'oss* man said.

"I can see that," Chagan said. "But you saw what happened. It's not worth the risk."

"Why don't you let them go with us," the *Alle'oss* man said. "We'll be scouting a day ahead of you. You told me yourself you didn't like the idea of having 'those witches' along."

The man hesitated, then turned away from Macha and said, "Good, they're your problem. The plan is the same. You head out today. We'll follow tomorrow." Without looking back, he headed back to the camp.

Macha watched him go, then looked at the *Alle'oss* man who was studying her.

"Name's Svend," he said. He introduced his companions, then gestured toward the retreating man. "He's the commander of these mercenaries. And yes, he is as disagreeable when you get to know him as first impressions imply." He looked at her expectantly.

"Macha," she said finally. She gestured to her sisters. "Eriu and Neiman. Who are these men?"

"Mercenaries from the Union," Svend said. When he noticed her incomprehension, he pointed south and said, "The Union is across the Southern Sea. Mercenaries are hired soldiers. I guess the emperor is finally running out of men for his wars."

She gazed at him and said, "You're *Alle'oss*." She was merely curious about why *Alle'oss* men were there, but his response only piqued her curiosity further.

He met her eyes for a moment, then let his head drop. When he looked up again, his expression had hardened. Instead of answering her, he gathered his long blond hair, and tied it into a tail with a leather thong. When he was done, he glanced up at the bluffs and asked, "You say we're being watched?" When Macha nodded, he asked, "How many?"

"I saw three."

He nodded, glanced at her sisters, and said, "We leave in an hour." With that, he turned and headed back to the camp, followed by the other *Alle'oss*.

"I don't like those men," Eriu said in a flat voice.

Macha followed her gaze to the mercenaries who, though they returned to their work in the camp, were watching Macha and her sisters. "I'm not sure they are men," she said. "Not entirely." She walked over to stand in front of Neiman. "Are you okay?"

Neiman nodded, but her glistening eyes told a different story.

"You did the right thing," Macha said. She glanced up at the top of the cliff, smiled, and said, "We'll be heading up into the forest. It will be quiet and we'll be alone. Nearly."

"Except for those traitors," Eriu said, her singsong voice returning.

Not for the first time, Macha wondered if Eriu, an *Alle'oss* herself, had any reservations about the task the Father set for them. She didn't appear to. Eriu lifted her arms out to her sides, let her head fall back and spun slowly, humming softly to herself. When Macha looked at Neiman, her sister looked from Eriu to Macha, her lips twitching again. Macha smiled and said, "Come on, let's go find some food."

Willa

Willa and two of her men, Ogden and Halfdan, watched the three women walking slowly around the perimeter of the camp.

"What do you think happened there?" Halfdan asked.

"No idea," Willa answered. They found the camp earlier in the day, thirty leagues east of *Helala*.

"Who are they?" Halfdan asked.

"Mercenaries from the Union," Willa said.

"Those are the biggest men I've ever seen," Ogden said. "They don't look real."

Noting the worry in his tone, Willa reassured him. "They die like anyone else."

"Not worried about the mercenaries," Halfdan said. "It's the women."

"I'm guessing they're witches," Willa said. "Least that's what it looked like when that merc got a little too familiar." They watched in silence, digesting this revelation.

"What do you think they're doing here?" Halfdan asked.

"I think Keelia was right. The emperor hired them to attack the *Alle'oss* from the rear." She pointed to the ship disappearing to the south. "That was an Imperial ship."

"Why camp here? What are they waiting for?"

"My guess is they were waiting for three witches," Willa said. She pointed to the normal-sized men rolling up bedrolls and stuffing their belongings into packs. "Those three look like *Alle'oss*." She paused and spat over the edge of the cliff. "Scouts, and it looks like they're getting ready to move out."

She retreated from the edge of the cliff, squatted and rolled out the map Keelia gave her. "The question is, which way are they going?" They studied the map in silence.

Ogden traced the route they took from *Helala* in reverse. "Not much we can do if they head this way. We won't be able to stop them, and by the time we let Keelia know, it will be over."

Willa grunted a response.

"Could be the witches are intended to take care of Deirdre," Halfdan said.

"A lot of men for a bunch of children," Willa said. "I make it a thousand, at least. Plus, if they wanted to attack *Helala*, I think they would have landed closer." She tapped the map where a spine of the mountain range neared the coast. "If they are going to *Helala*, they'll have to squeeze through here. That'll take some time. Let's put someone in the heights here to keep watch. If they go that way, they'll have time to warn Deirdre to evacuate everyone." Halfdan and Ogden nodded. "But I'm betting

Keelia is right and they're going north. Ogden, you take ten and range ahead to the north. I doubt they got all the villages on the map here. Let's try to warn anyone in their path. Halfdan, pick four you trust to keep an eye on those scouts, then take ten and keep track of the main body." She eyed the map and pointed to a small village that she guessed would be to the west of the route taken by the mercenaries. "I'll be here," she said, tapping the map. "Keep me abreast of what's going on."

"Right," Halfdan responded. He rose and said, "I better get going if we want to catch the scouts."

Willa nodded, stood and rolled up the map. "Ogden, send a raven to Keelia. Tell her to be ready."

Chapter 29

The 22nd Day of the Month of Ungemon

Minna

Minna stood on the edge of the cliff, looking down on the men and women at work in the Cut. After the confrontation with the turtle, the *Alle'oss* took measures to prevent a repeat attack. Squads of *Alle'oss* archers ranged out from the Cut, playing a deadly game of hide and seek with their Imperial counterparts. This gave the *Alle'oss* space to build another stockade at the bottom of the Cut, where it opened out into the foothills. Behind the stockade, they buried logs at intervals that extended vertically a pace above the surface. No turtle would climb the hill. And behind the original wooden wall at the top of the hill, stonemasons were erecting a more substantial wall. It looked to Minna that it would soon be impregnable.

"Looks like we won't need you soon."

Minna turned to find Sigurn giving her a knowing smile. The boy's ability to read her mind was unsettling.

When Minna looked away, Sigurn asked, "When are you leaving?"

"Leaving?" Minna asked. "What makes you think I'm leaving?"

"See it in your eyes," Sigurn answered. "Every time we talk about Alar or Tove." When Minna looked at him again, he added. "And your mother."

Minna held his gaze. What would it hurt to tell him? Everyone would know soon enough. "I'm telling Aron at the war council today."

Sigurn didn't react at first, but then he looked down into the Cut and said, "He won't be happy about that."

Minna waved her hand at the obstacles the *Alle'oss* were constructing. "The Imps won't get past all this. They won't need me here anymore. I stand around here doing nothing while they're devastating the rest of Argren. We need to find out if my mother actually had a plan."

She blurted it out without thinking. It felt like a confession, and it surprised her how relieved she felt. It was the first time she told anyone what she was thinking, though she knew others were thinking the same thing. The reports of what was happening in the rest of Argren were affecting morale. No one said it to her, but she had the impression many were beginning to believe Ragan left them in the lurch. She could see it in the eyes turned her way as she walked through the camp. But Minna wasn't ready to give up on her mother. Worried how he would respond, she peeked at Sigurn out of the corner of her eye.

Sigurn simply nodded, then looked up at a raven approaching from the south. "You'll need a guide."

Minna stared at him. With Ulf gone, it never occurred to her she wouldn't have to go alone. She followed Sigurn's gaze as the raven flew overhead. News from Keelia or just a bird about its own business? When Sigurn gave her his open smile, she couldn't help returning it. "You?" she asked.

"Of course."

"What will Lief think?"

He frowned, watching the raven dip below the tops of the trees that hid the headquarters. He glanced at her and said, "It was his idea. Come on, let's go see what that's about."

* * *

The atmosphere in the headquarters had become increasingly tense over the past few weeks, but today, it was as taut as a drawn bow. As usual, everyone gathered around the map table. But the room was as silent as a graveyard. Only the mutterings of the recently arrived raven disturbed the quiet. Minna glanced up at the bird as Linea rose into the rafters to investigate the newcomer. A glimmering eye and a shawl-like collar of white feathers across its shoulders were visible in the shadows before Linea cast her light on it.

Sigurn nudged her forward, and the two of them joined the others at the table.

Zaina glanced up, handed her a thin scrap of paper, and said, "Message from Keelia."

With a deep sense of foreboding, Minna took the paper, glanced at *Helala* on the map, then read the message.

1000 Union mercenaries 30 leagues east of Helala. Headed north. Suspect they intend to attack your rear. Suggest you set up a blocking force at 20x36. We'll attack them in the rear after they engage. Scouts report three witches with the mercenaries.

Minna turned the paper over, hoping for more information. There was a date, but nothing else useful. Exchanging a look with Sigurn, she handed him the message, then found the number 20 on the top margin of the map and followed a line down to where it intersected a line from the number 36 on the left margin. It was the spot where the Imperial Highway turned south and squeezed between the eastern end of the Kalana Valley and a spur of the mountains. She and Ulf stopped for a quick meal near there on their journey to Brennan.

"If Keelia is right about what they're up to, that's good ground to meet them," Lief said.

"It's going to be tricky coordinating that plan," Zaina said. "For it to work, Keelia will have to stay hidden until they attack. If she's too slow… We might be able to hold out for a while, but without Minna, I don't like our chances against Union mercenaries. If Minna is there, she won't be here." She looked at Minna. "And there are the three witches. I think we know what they're there for."

Everyone cast furtive looks at Minna, but she ignored them. She was remembering the insane witch she fought the previous winter. Aife. The outcome of that battle was a near thing and left her insensible. What could she do against three women like Aife?

Lief picked up the message Sigurn set on the table, flipped it over to show the date. He put his finger on the coast thirty leagues east of *Helala* and traced a path to the spot of the proposed ambush. "We have time to prepare strong defensive positions. We'll be able to hold them in place long enough for Keelia to strike them in the rear."

"Could work as long as everything goes right, but like I said, a lot has to go right," Zaina said. "The timing has to be perfect. A lot of moving pieces. A lot of uncertainty. Hard to coordinate."

"Minna, there's nothing you can do with the spirits to… I don't know… talk to Keelia or keep an eye on the mercenaries?" Aron asked.

Minna blinked and looked up from the map to the hopeful faces turned her way. "I'll… I'll ask Linea," she said. Aron nodded slowly. Minna looked from him to the others, whose expressions were now a mixture of expectation and confusion. She pointed toward the door. "Um, I'll just step outside." Turning away without waiting for a response, she opened the door, paused until Linea slipped through, then stepped onto the porch. Ignoring the people waving to her as they passed, she welcomed Linea into her center, sank onto the bench beside the door and allowed herself a moment to enjoy Linea's company.

Did you understand what we were talking about? Linea looped. Minna smiled. *Is there a way for me to communicate with Keelia?* Linea didn't respond. In the past, when this happened, Minna concluded the question was too complicated for Linea to answer with the methods available to her. *Is there a way for me to keep an eye on the mercenaries?* An image of the raven perched in the rafters of the headquarters came into her mind. While Minna was considering what this meant, another image of the raven passing overhead while she and Sigurn were talking appeared. *Can I… talk to the raven?* A swoop. *And the raven will do what I ask?* A vague sense of uncertainty. Minna took that to mean Linea didn't know. Couldn't hurt to ask.

She rose and entered the headquarters, bringing the conversation to a halt. Looking away from the faces turned toward her, she looked up at the raven. *Linea.* Linea swooped and left her center. Minna closed her eyes, preparing herself to encounter the new spirit. If it was like the airy *luft'and,* she would need to concentrate to detect its presence. When Aron asked her a question, she put her hand up to silence him.

It wasn't like any spirit she encountered before. Rather than an individual presence she sensed in her center, the spirit blanketed her mind in a warm serenity. Opening her eyes, she looked up at the raven watching her. She closed her eyes again, considering how she might ask the spirit for what she wanted.

And then she felt her awareness flowing outward from herself. Disoriented, she put out a hand and caught herself on someone's shoulder. As her awareness extended outward, she sensed other beings. Bright, furtive presences in the eaves of the roof. A family of mice? Sleepy presences in burrows beneath the building. Some nocturnal animals? There were others. No humans. She couldn't sense the people in the room with her, but there were many other animals, including the raven.

She opened her eyes. It was like being pressed on all sides by a large number of people, everyone talking at once. The multitude of simple thoughts created a low buzz in her mind, like being in a crowded room alive with conversations. It was too much. On instinct, she sought the serenity of her center, and suddenly, she was outside the clamor, observing it from a comfortable distance. And just as you could focus on a single conversation in a crowded room, she found she could distinguish individuals.

When she focused on the raven, she sensed curiosity, but not surprise. She twisted her lips. How do you talk to a raven? *You're not surprised.* A rising sense of curiosity. The raven hopped out of the shadows to a nearer rafter. Minna glanced at the people gathered around the table, who watched her with worried expressions. Taking a step and turning so she could put them out of her sight, she looked up at the bird and mumbled,

"You've talked to another human?" An image of an old woman sitting on a log in front of a hut appeared in her mind. "Beadu!"

Aron appeared beside her. "You can talk to the raven?" he asked urgently.

"Yes," she said. "Kind of."

"Can you communicate with Keelia?"

"I don't think so," Minna said. "I think Keelia would have to be able to talk to it… him, too."

"Can it keep an eye on the mercenaries?"

"How do I even ask that?" Minna asked.

"Maybe… picture what they look like," Zaina said from the other side of Aron.

"I don't know what they look like," Minna said.

"Big, ugly and dour," Lief said from her other side. When she lifted a brow at him, he shrugged and added, "They wear brightly colored leather armor."

"I don't think that will be enough," Minna said. "Besides, I would have to tell it where to go look. I don't think I can communicate anything complex."

"Try," Sigurn said.

Minna considered, then tried to picture a large dour man with colorful armor. The result was Agmar without a beard. The raven didn't respond. "No," she said.

"There must be some way this could be useful," Aron said.

"Beadu," Minna said.

"Beadu?"

"He's talked to Beadu before. Maybe she would know how to tell it what to do."

"But the ravens are trained to fly to a specific place. How would you send it to *Helala*?" Zaina asked.

"Can you tell it to find Beadu?" Aron asked.

"Can you take a message to Beadu?" Minna asked, picturing the old *saa'myn* in her mind as she asked.

A warm, happy feeling.

"I think that means yes," Minna said.

"Quick, write a message," Aron said. Everyone but Minna and Sigurn gathered around the table, arguing about what the message should say.

Minna looked at Sigurn, who was watching her. When he lifted a brow, she said, "Don't say it."

"What?"

"Whatever you were going to say," she said.

"I was *not* going to say anything about the legendary wi — *saa'myn,* who knows all spirits," he said. "Never crossed my mind."

She elbowed him in the ribs. Distracted by all the presences, she pulled the spirit back and her mind was quiet again.

"You can't leave now," he said. "Sorry."

Minna bit her lip and looked up at the bird, who was still watching as if it could understand what they said. She may never get to find out what her mother wanted. "It may not matter," she said. "I doubt my mother considered me having to fight three of Hoerst's witches by myself."

Sigurn leaned toward her, glanced at the others and whispered, "I may have a plan for that."

Before Minna could ask what he meant, Aron spoke.

"Minna, come help us figure out what to tell Beadu."

• • •

Minna watched the raven climbing laboriously into the air before veering southeast toward *Helala.*

"Lief, take as many as you need to prepare the ambush."

She turned to see Lief nod to Aron, before he headed back to the *Oss'stera* campsite with Sigurn in his wake. Sigurn gave her a smile over his shoulder before he disappeared into the trees.

She was idly returning people's waves, considering what she would do the rest of the day, when the thunder of approaching horses caught at her. Her heart lurched as two horses approached on the path from the direction of the highway. The horses were lathered, having been ridden hard. The rider of the lead horse was Raif.

"Ulf," she muttered.

The horses pulled up, and the riders dismounted.

"What's happened, Raif?" Aron asked.

In the brief glance Raif gave her, she saw in his face the worst had happened.

"Rangers found a way out of the valley," Raif said. "We were on a training exercise when we stumbled onto them." He glanced at Minna again. "It was a chaotic situation, but considering how green our recruits were, they did well. We've canceled the training and assigned them to patrol the rim of the valley."

Minna watched Raif talking, saw his mouth moving, but wasn't listening to the rest of his report. Aron and Zaina looked at her sadly as they returned to the headquarters. When the door closed, Minna faced Raif, having to lock her knees to stay upright. Before Raif could speak, Minna asked, "Ulf?" She saw the answer in his face before he spoke.

"Ulf was involved in heavy fighting," Raif said. "He was just assigned to be leader of his squad. We believe they saved the lives of many men and women."

"Dead?" was the only word Minna could get past her tight throat.

"We don't know," Raif said, forcing a reassuring smile on his face. "We didn't find a body, but he and most of his squad are missing." He rested a hand on Minna's shoulder. "There's always hope."

Hope. Minna nodded vaguely and mumbled, "*Tok*." Raif looked as if he would say something else, but Minna walked away. She didn't know where she was going. She just didn't want to share her grief with all the people gawping at her exchange with Raif. Disappearing down the same path Sigurn took, she slid into the trees before the gaggle of children who followed her caught up. Once she was out of sight of the path, she sank to her knees, bent forward and pressed her hands to her mouth so her sobs wouldn't betray her.

When she finally gained control of herself, she straightened, let her hands fall into her lap, and stared numbly at nothing through watery eyes. The anger came on so quickly, it overwhelmed her defenses and burst out through gritted teeth. "Ulf, you stupid —" Horrified, she clamped her mouth shut and pressed clenched fists against her thighs. The rage passed almost as quickly as it came, leaving her feeling deeply ashamed. Rolling onto her side, she wept quietly and whispered, "I told you not to fight."

Linea drifted down into her line of sight and Minna welcomed her into her center. With her spirit guide soothing the raw edge of her grief, Minna felt herself drifting and allowed Linea to ease her to sleep.

Chapter 30

The 27th Day of the Month of Ungemon

Ulf

Ulf, Mikaela and Helga had been walking for days with little rest and only a few berries and mushrooms to eat. Mikaela's home sat beside the Kalana River, twenty leagues from where the valley divided the escarpment and opened onto the plains. The river made its lazy way through the center of the valley from the highlands in the east until it merged with the Odun River south of Hast.

They'd only caught glimpses of Imps in the distance. Even so, what they saw worried Ulf. It seemed the *Alle'oss* chose to guard the few exits to the valley, leaving the residents of the valley to their own fate. He could tell Helga was thinking the same thing. Given what they knew the Imps were doing in the rest of Argren, what were the chances Mikaela's village remained untouched?

"Come on," Mikaela urged. They walked in silence for most of the trip, reserving their energy for putting one foot in front of another. But as they neared Mikaela's village, she perked up, pointing out landmarks and telling stories about her childhood.

Now, within a league of her home, Mikaela roamed ahead, stopping occasionally to wait for Ulf and Helga to catch up. Ulf was looking down, picking his way on wobbly legs over the tricky ground that descended to the river bottom, when Helga caught his arm. She leaned toward him and whispered, "Something's wrong." She pointed to the sky above the trees.

Black smoke. The wrong color and more than would normally be expected from a village the size Mikaela described. Ulf looked at Helga and shook his head. When she didn't let go of his arm, he whispered, "We don't know for sure."

Helga held his eyes for a moment, then let go and pushed past him. By the time they caught up with Mikaela, she had discovered for herself that all was not right.

She stood still, peering through the trees toward the village. "Something's wrong," she said when Ulf and Helga stepped up beside her.

Helga caught Ulf's eyes behind Mikaela's back and asked, "How can you tell?"

"It's so quiet," Mikaela said. "And the smoke doesn't smell right."

"You want us to go check?" Ulf asked. When she didn't answer, he touched her arm. "Mikaela?"

She started, then said, "No, let's all go." Without waiting for a response, she set off.

The ground flattened out a hundred paces before they saw the first burned-out houses. Ulf strung his bow and lifted their last arrow from Mikaela's quiver. They crept toward the river. Mikaela's home would have been a typical *Alle'oss* village before the Imps burned it to the ground. The fires that consumed the small houses were more smoke than flame by the time they stepped into the community space that abutted the languid river.

"Probably happened last night," Helga said, turning in place and peering into the surrounding forest.

Ulf, watching Mikaela closely, only nodded. He put a hand on Mikaela's shoulder, but she walked away, sinking to her knees next to the ashy remains of a small house on the eastern edge of the village.

Tearing his eyes from her, Ulf gazed around at the rest of the village. "There aren't many bodies. Hopefully, most of them left before..." He looked at Mikaela. Her face was buried in her hands and her shoulders were shaking.

"What are we going to do?" Helga asked.

When he turned back toward her, Ulf found a worried expression on her face. Somewhere along the way, even Helga started to look to him to make decisions. "We're…" He paused and looked around at the smoldering remains of the houses. "Right now, we're going to look for anything we can use. Food, arrows. Not sure how they do things here, but a lot of people in Fennig have root cellars. See what you can find." Helga nodded. "I doubt the Imps will be back soon, but we shouldn't linger. I'd feel safer in the forest."

"Right," Helga said. "Me, too."

"I'll check on Mikaela, then I'll help."

Mikaela had quieted by the time Ulf sank to the ground beside her. He searched the ruins of the house, looking for bodies. "This was your home?" he asked.

She nodded.

"Maybe they got away," he said.

She stood, looked down at him, her mouth set in a determined line. Without speaking, she walked to the shore of the river, where two bodies lay halfway in the water. With a sinking sensation, Ulf followed.

Even in death, Ulf saw the resemblance between the woman and Mikaela. This was her mother. The woman and the man who lay beside her bore wounds from cutting weapons, probably swords.

"Mikaela," Ulf said, lifting a hand that hovered above her shoulder before he pulled it back. "I'm sorry."

She nodded again, then turned and put her arms around his neck. He held her while she wept, trying to dismiss awkward memories of holding a weeping Minna atop the ridge after the attack on the *Alle'oss* camp the previous winter.

Pulling away, she wiped tears from her face and asked, "Will you help me bury them?"

He hesitated, his eyes going to the surrounding forest, but when he saw Mikaela's expression, he said, "Of course."

They found a spade and dug shallow graves in the soft ground behind the remains of their home. By the time they finished, Mikaela's eyes were red-rimmed, but dry. Ulf was trying to think of something to say when she said, "Let's go help Helga," then turned away from her parents' graves.

Ulf tossed the spade to the ground and followed.

• • •

A half hour later, they gathered in the community space and took stock of what they scavenged. As it turned out, the homes did not have root cellars. Mikaela explained the water table was too high because they were close to the river. They stored food in pantries that burned with the houses. Still, they recovered two cheeses and some smoked fish. Helga found a quiver with ten arrows beside the body of a man who was shot in the back as he fled. They divided the arrows and the food among themselves. Hefting distressingly light packs, they looked at one another.

"Now what?" Helga asked.

Ulf was anxious to get out of the village, but the question was which direction they should go. Mikaela, who trailed along behind him while he searched, gazed absently across the river. He leaned over so he could look her in the face. "Mikaela?" he asked gently. When she focused on him, he asked, "How do we get out of the valley?" She just stared at him. "Mikaela!" he said sharply.

She started and blinked.

"We need to get out of the valley," Ulf said. "Where is the nearest exit?"

She pointed south, across the river.

"That's the wrong way," Helga said.

"The longer we stay in the valley, the more likely we run into Imps," Ulf said.

"But the army is north of here," Helga said.

"Part of the army is south of the valley," Ulf said. "They're guarding — It's not important what they're guarding, but there are *Alle'oss* soldiers south of the valley." Helga looked uncertain. "Once we're out of the valley, we can go the long way around to get back. It will take longer, but it will be safe." Noticing Mikaela was following the conversation, he asked her, "What do you think, Mikaela?"

"I agree with Ulf. I want to get out of the valley."

Before Helga could protest, they heard men's voices coming from the direction they entered the village

"Imps," Helga said. She headed toward the river, but Ulf caught her.

"They'll see us swimming," he said. "Let's head upriver until we're out of sight."

They headed east until they rounded a shallow bend in the river, putting the village out of sight.

"This is the nearest ford," Mikaela said dully. "The next one is ten leagues farther east."

Ulf looked back toward the west. "They might be able to see the far shore from the village," he said. He looked up at the sun, which was edging toward the western horizon. "Let's wait until after sunset to cross."

Three hours later, Ulf held his pack and bow above the surface of the water with one hand, allowing Mikaela to help him up the muddy bank on the south bank of the river. They hurried into the trees and looked back toward the village. The rangers made camp in the village community space. As he watched, a sentry passed between him and a small fire.

"What do you think they're doing?" Helga asked.

"Scouting for a way out of the valley. Tracking down survivors. Not sure," Ulf said. "Which way, Mikaela?"

She took one last lingering look at her home before pointing to the south. Then she turned away and started walking.

• • •

Ulf's face must have given him away, because a small smile curved Mikaela's lips. The first since they found the ruins of her village.

"You don't like fish?" she asked.

"Never had it before," Ulf said, and forced himself to swallow.

"You don't eat fish in Fennig?"

"Some people do," he said, examining the remaining portion of his meal, considering how hungry he really was. "There's a river east of the mountains, but mostly the only people who eat fish are the farmers out that way."

"Well, it's this or nothing," Helga said.

"Yeah," Ulf said. He gathered himself, stuffed the rest in his mouth, chewed as fast as he could, then washed it down with a gulp from his water bottle. Fortunately, there were enough streams feeding the river that finding water wasn't an issue. "How much farther?"

"We should be there before dark," Mikaela said, taking a bite. "We should probably wait until morning before climbing the cliffs."

"What if there are Imps like there were at the bottom of the stairs?" Helga asked.

"Then we'll have to come up with another plan," Ulf said.

Someone stepped into the clearing. They leapt to their feet, scrambling for their bows before they noticed the man's red hair. He was *Alle'oss.*

"Who are you?" the man asked.

"I'm Ulf Lothan," Ulf said, intercepting Helga's angry retort. He introduced the others, then said, "We're in the army. We got separated from the rest of our unit and are trying to get back." When the man didn't respond, he asked, "Who are you?"

"Hakon," he said. "You said you're in the army?" When Ulf nodded, the man asked, "The *Alle'oss* army has decided to defend the valley?"

"No," Ulf said, choosing not to respond to the man's challenging tone. He nodded to Mikaela and said, "We were hoping to get supplies at Mikaela's village, but we were too late."

Hakon eyed Mikaela's hair. She had the deep burgundy curls common in the valley. "You're from the valley."

She nodded and said, "Helenatok."

"Where are you going?" Hakon asked.

Before Mikaela could answer, Ulf said, "Hold on." He noted the man's longbow and full quiver of arrows. "You're from the valley?"

Hakon nodded. "My village was burned weeks ago." He raised the hand holding the bow and gestured toward the east. "We've been moving west, picking up survivors and avoiding the rangers."

"We?"

Hakon eyed Ulf, then turned and nodded toward the trees behind him. Ten people stepped out of the dense brush. "We're all from villages at the eastern end of the valley," Hakon said. "We're on our way to climb out of the valley."

Ulf studied the men and women, noticing how thin they were. They returned his regard silently. "We're on our way to join the army south of the valley," he said. Noting the looks they gave one another, he said, "You can come with us, if you want."

"Ulf is our squad leader," Helga said.

Surprised, Ulf looked at her.

"Squad leader?" one of the women asked doubtfully.

Ulf smiled and said, "Yeah. Welcome to the misfits."

Alyn

Knowing Alyn wouldn't be able to tame the swarm, Beadu worked with her to coax the small spirit that showed her the first vision into the open. To no avail. Every time she opened herself to the spirits of *annen'heim*, the swarm flooded her center, leaving her overwhelmed and terrified. Having Beadu at her side helped her recover, but Alyn and the old *saa'myn* made no progress sorting through the horrifying visions the spirits allowed her to see. In fact, the episodes left Alyn so dispirited and pessimistic, she stopped eating and was finding sleep elusive.

With Beadu's encouragement, she returned to translating her mother's journal. Though she found nothing to help her with the *sjel'and*, after Beadu pointed out Alyn's similarities with her mother, Alyn saw her in a new light. Whatever she thought of the morality of Ragan's quest, it was clear to Alyn she loved her daughters and her husband.

She found the description of her birth in the last pages of the journal. Everyone else in *Helala* had long since gone to their beds. She could barely keep her eyes open, but the gripping narrative held her in place. She was astonished to discover she was born in a small *Alle'oss* village near Richeleau, rather than in Fennig. Her mother lied to her father about the due date and undertook the arduous journey despite being eight months pregnant. It was yet another one of her efforts to steer the course of events, this time to save the life of Harold Wolfe.

Head planted firmly in the palm of her hand, Alyn traced the text with her index finger to help her tired eyes focus. Ragan wrote that Union mercenaries attacked the village while she was in labor, and that she and a newborn Alyn were pulled from the flaming wreckage of the hut soon after she was born. But it was when her mother described a very unusual encounter with a *sjel'and* during the birth that Alyn sat up. Something about the incident tugged at her mind, but she was so exhausted, it fluttered out of reach when she grasped after it. She backtracked, intending to translate the passage again. But she finally reached her limit. Her mother's scrawled runes bled together, no matter how hard she tried to focus.

Sighing, she picked up the ink-stained rag she used to wipe the nib of her quill, then realized she already set the quill aside. Tossing the rag on top of the desk, she rose, stowed the journal in the cabinet, extinguished the lamp and made her slow way to the house she shared with Deirdre.

• • •

Alyn woke with a start. She fell into her bed in the wee hours, not bothering to undress. Morning's gray light was already leaking through the windows of her bedroom before she fell asleep, and it wasn't much past dawn now. But she rose from her bed, feeling more energized than she had in days. Something she read in Ragan's journal the day before was the reason. But what? She stood still, listening to the community coming awake, grasping after the dream that pulled her from sleep.

It was no use. All she knew was it was something she translated the previous day. Forgetting her tangled hair and bare feet, she yanked the door to her room open, brushed past a sleepy-looking Deirdre and rushed out the door of the house.

Stopping on the small porch, she looked up the hill and was gratified to find Beadu already sitting on the log in front of her house. Ignoring the stares, she sprinted across the community space and ran up the hill.

"Beadu!"

"You have found something."

Alyn dropped to sit in her customary place and said, "Yes, maybe, I don't know."

When she didn't continue, Beadu asked, "Something in your mother's journal?"

"I think so," Alyn said. "Something I translated yesterday. It woke me up, but I don't remember what I was dreaming."

"Tell me what you translated."

Alyn propped her elbows on her knees and stared into the fire, trying to arrange what she read into chronological order. "There was something about a woman, a friend of Ragan's, a Seidi sister who ran away, like Ragan. She died, and I think it really affected my mother. There was something about an *Alle'oss* witch." She gazed into the fire. "I don't think that was it." When she looked up at Beadu, the old woman was gazing into the distance.

"There was something about the *Alle'oss* rebels in Richeleau rescuing Harold Wolfe. *Oss'stera.* Then there was —" She stopped with her mouth open.

"She described your birth," Beadu said.

"Yes," Alyn said. That was it, but what about it woke her up? She looked at Beadu again and found her smiling at her. "What?"

"I don't know why I didn't think of this before," Beadu said. "I can only claim age has softened my memories."

"What?"

"Did your mother describe what she experienced when you were born?" Beadu asked. "A very unusual encounter with a *sjel'and?*"

"Yes!" That was it. The very last passage she translated the night before. "Ragan wanted to know the *lan'and* which would be my spirit, so she tried to prolong her labor. But before I was born, a *sjel'and* appeared and… she was afraid what it would do to my spirit, but the *sjel'and* and my spirit… well, she didn't really describe it well. It was like they greeted each other. It didn't really sound like a *sjel'and*, at least not the ones —" She stared at Beadu.

"Yes," Beadu said. "I think you have encountered this unusual *sjel'and* on more than one occasion."

"The vision of Minna and me on the ship when I was in prison," Alyn said. "And the vision of Minna facing the three witches."

Beadu nodded.

"So, this spirit shows me helpful visions, because it met my spirit before I was born?"

"Perhaps," Beadu said. "It would be an explanation for the inexplicable. But I think it may be more than that."

"What?"

The old *saa'myn* gestured up to the *lan'and*. "The *sjel'and* are not so different from the *lan'and*. But for the fact the *sjel'and* are burdened by the sins they accumulated in life, they are the same. Some carry a heavier burden than others, and it is difficult to see the similarities. But for those who carried less into *annen'heim* with them, one can sense something of their true selves."

"What are you saying?"

"Perhaps this *sjel'and* is burdened far less than many others, and so it retains some of the joyful qualities of the *lan'and*."

Beadu gazed at Alyn expectantly, but a rising sense of dread kept Alyn mute. She started to shake her head even before Beadu spoke.

"I don't see any reason that a *sjel'and* can't be an *and'reoime*," Beadu said.

Alyn gaped at her. Her first response was revulsion. "No," she whispered. "That can't be." She looked at Beadu hopefully, but she saw in her face, she was serious. "My spirit guide is one of those awful spirits?"

"Perhaps," Beadu said. "The spirit chooses the *saa'myn*. This spirit gives all indications it has chosen you."

"No, that can't be," Alyn said, but she knew that was what woke her this morning. "How do I even…" She looked up at the *lan'and* flitting playfully around Beadu's hut, remembering Minna's descriptions of her joyful interactions with Linea. The thought that she would be denied that was devastating. "Oh, no, no, no," she moaned. She looked up and Beadu. "How would I know?"

"You must ask it to introduce you to another spirit."

Alyn's head swiveled to look down the hill at a group of children approaching for their morning lessons with Beadu.

"I…" She shook her head. "I can't even call it without calling all the others. I've been trying."

"But the first time, when it showed you the vision of Minna and the three witches. *You* called it then," Beadu said. "There must have been something different that time. Think on it and come back this evening."

• • •

Alyn couldn't bring herself to work on the last pages of her mother's journal. Days with little sleep left her listless and exhausted, and the idea that her spirit guide might be a *sjel'and* sapped her of all motivation. She dropped onto a small bench in the shade across from the building where she worked on her translations and absently watched the community coming to life.

She wondered about the odd looks she was receiving until she remembered she never managed to put herself in order after bursting out of her bed. After attempting to run her fingers through her hair, she decided it was a lost cause, and pulled it back and tied it into a tail with a thong she wore around her wrist. When she looked up, Deirdre was striding across the village square toward her. Her instinct was to flee, but Deirdre knew she saw her coming. If she fled, she would eventually have to explain why. So she tried to compose herself, even trying on a weak smile.

"Good morning," she said brightly, trying to gain the initiative.

Instead of answering, Deirdre shooed her over so she could sit on the small bench. Alyn was surprised to see sadness on the former Malefica's face.

"Deirdre?"

"You and Beadu must think I'm an idiot," Deirdre said.

"No, of cou —"

"Don't even try to deny it," Deirdre said, anger edging her words. "I can *see* you two together, and you are both so secretive. I would think I deserved —" She slammed her mouth shut.

Alyn watched her struggling with her emotions, wanting to deny the accusation. But Deirdre was right, so instead, she sagged against the older woman and lay her head on her shoulder.

Deirdre started, but then she took Alyn's hand.

Tired of lying, Alyn sat up and said, "Beadu has been helping me to communicate with the *sjel'and* that showed me the vision of Minna and the three witches. We've been trying to find something that would help the *Alle'oss*. Beadu says the war isn't going well. She didn't tell anyone, because she thinks the children would know something was wrong."

Deirdre looked across the square to a group of children gathering for their lessons with Brother Xander. "And?" she asked. "Have you?"

"No. There is always the swarm, showing me so many horrible things, I can't make any sense of it." She paused, chewing on her lip. "I'm sorry."

Deirdre only nodded, but some of the rigidness in her postured softened.

Alyn watched her for a moment. She couldn't bring herself to mention that Beadu thought the foul little *sjel'and* might be her spirit guide. "You read my mother's journal." When Deirdre nodded, she asked, "Do you remember when she described my birth? The part about the *sjel'and?*"

"Yes."

"Beadu thinks that might be the same *sjel'and.* The one who showed me that first vision." Alyn watched Xander herding the children into the community building and returned his wave. "She thinks there might be something I did different the first time I called it."

"Well," Deirdre said, shifting around to face Alyn. "The first time, no one knew what you were doing. It was before you told me about the vision, and you weren't withholding it from Beadu."

"Right," Alyn said. "Sorry."

"No," Deirdre said. "I'm not trying to make you feel bad. Ragan said the *sjel'and* sense fear and weakness. They're predators. Something you're doing after that first time might be signaling you're prey to them."

"*Tok*, Deirdre," Alyn said thoughtfully. "That helps." Deirdre nodded, hesitated, then rose and crossed to the community building. Alyn watched her until she disappeared, then rose and crossed the square. As she neared the far side, her pace quickened, and by the time she neared the edge of the village, she was sprinting. Minna was older, and in many ways her spirit sense was far more developed. But Alyn's time as a prisoner of the Inquisition taught her much about her own spirit. She thought she knew why the ugly little *sjel'and* came the first time without the swarm. She needed to find a place she could be alone, so she could make sure. Waving to a group of the older students hanging out of the school's windows, she headed into the forest.

Chapter 31

The 28th Day of the Month of Ungemon

Alyn

Alyn bent over, resting her hands on her knees, gazing down on *Helala* from her favorite spot in the mountains behind the village. Low clouds moved in after she left the village, leaving the water in the bay a flat grayish green. Though it was hard to tell, she guessed it was late morning. Normally, she found the climb refreshing, but today, it left her trembly and weak. The grumbling of her stomach reminded her she hadn't eaten anything today. But sleep and food could wait. Sustained by nervous energy, she straightened, wiped sweat from her face and sank to sit cross-legged.

It was something Deirdre said that triggered her memory. The first time she called the *sjel'and* was before she read her mother's description of the swarm. She wasn't afraid, but more importantly, she communed with her own spirit before reaching out to the *sjel'and*. They called together. If the little *sjel'and* and her spirit knew one another, maybe it was her spirit it responded to. She needed to be clear about what she wanted and let her spirit call out to the *sjel'and* it knew from the moment of her birth.

Taking a deep breath, she sighed it out, closed her eyes and sank into her center, expanding her connection to *mid'heim* until she sensed her spirit's cheerful presence. Despite her excitement, she settled into her center, seeking serenity, letting her worries go and pushing her hunger and fatigue into the background. Not until her jangly anticipation quieted did she take her emotions by the reins and allow her spirit to call out to the *sjel'and*.

The sudden appearance of the repulsive spirit, as if it had been waiting in the wings, took her breath. When she recoiled instinctively, as one would from an awful odor, the *sjel'and* froze and lay utterly still. Trying not to think of her sister's description of Linea's joyful swooping presence, Alyn suppressed a shudder and forced herself to reach out to the little spirit. To her surprise, she sensed fear. No, not exactly fear, more like trepidation. Was it worried about her reaction?

Alyn and the spirit regarded one another. Catching herself chewing her lip, Alyn blew a breath out and shook herself. *This is ridiculous.* At a loss, she focused on her own spirit and sensed bemusement.

Laughter, pure and spontaneous, bubbled up out of her. The ice broken, the *sjel'and* swooped suddenly. Alyn startled, but conscious of its reaction, she forced herself to relax. As the spirit swirled around her center, its obvious relief brought a small smile to her face.

Suddenly, she was somewhere else. A vision, but without the crystal clear clarity of other visions. She was peering through a drifting mist at a girl sitting on a stool at a high desk. The girl bent over a book that lay open on the desk, forehead resting on the palm of one hand, fingers of the other hand idly rolling a quill back and forth. With a start, she realized she was looking at herself working at translating her mother's journal. Was it a vision of the future? Suddenly, terrifying howls sounded from the murk. Her point of view left the girl, who remained unaware of the unfolding drama, and plunged into the shadows, horror lending it speed.

And then she was back in her center, stunned, panting, but alone with the little *sjel'and* and the comforting presence of her own spirit. It *was* a vision, but not of the future. Minna told her Linea could show her things the spirit saw when she was away from Minna. They used that connection to find safe routes through the Fallows when Minna was lost in Brennan. Did the *sjel'and* just show her its realm, *annen'heim*? Aron told her the physical realm was veiled by a mist when he was in the realm of the dead. The *sjel'and* must have been watching her while she worked, and the monsters that chased it were other *sjel'and*, the spirits which gleefully tortured her in the swarm.

Returning her attention to the little spirit still swooping around her center, she saw it in a different light. "You're safe here," she murmured.

But was the spirit her *and'reoime*? That it could show her a vision like Linea showed Minna suggested it was, but Beadu said she would know it was her spirit guide if it could introduce her to other spirits. Her time in *Helala* taught her far more about the spirit realms and the spirits that resided within them than Minna knew. Still, her first thought was of one of Minna's favorites, the *fjel'and*, the spirits from *fjel'heim* that sometimes manifested as fire. Alyn focused on an image of the fire that burned perpetually in front of Beadu's hut and whispered, "Can you introduce me to spirits that make fire?" Nothing happened. Was the little *sjel'and* not her spirit guide? Did it mean she had no affinity for the *fjel'and*? Or was that the wrong way to ask?

She was considering how else she might ask and thinking she should have done this with Beadu present, when the spirit looped and disappeared. Alyn's breath caught. Linea behaved in exactly the same way when she introduced a new spirit to Minna. Holding her breath, Alyn waited, all of her attention on her center. Her sister told her the fire spirits were fidgety and shy at first.

When the spirit appeared, she had the impression it was hiding and peeking at her. "Hello," she whispered. As if encouraged, the spirit edged more into her consciousness. Alyn swallowed a sob, afraid of frightening the little spirit. But instead of fleeing, the spirit, encouraged by her joyful response, surged into her center, swirling chaotically, as if it were bouncing off the inside of her mind.

Alyn restrained herself, forcing herself to allow her spirit and the *fjel'and* to become acquainted. When she couldn't wait any longer, she reached out to the spirit and whispered, "Fire." She pictured Beadu's fire again and held her hand, palm up. The spirit paused in its erratic flight, as if considering, then it was gone. Before Alyn could feel disappointed, warmth flowed down her arm.

Her eyes flew open. "Oh, oh, oh," she breathed and held her hand away from her body just as a small flame appeared above her palm. She gaped at the flickering spirit made watery by her tears. Swiping at her eyes with her other hand, she rotated her hand, watching the little spirit curl around her wrist, then she thrust her hand toward the sky, releasing a gout of flame to singe the leaves of the maple tree that shaded her spot.

Weeping openly now, she held her hand up and welcomed the spirit back into her center. "*Tok*," she said. The spirit caromed off the inside of her head twice, then returned to its realm.

Alyn allowed herself to settle, taking slow breaths, feeling the anxieties she accumulated since returning to *Helala* drain away. The dangers her family and the *Alle'oss* faced were the same, but she was no longer useless. She knew it wasn't fair to think of herself that way, but feelings weren't always easily dispelled by reason. She didn't know how she could help, but she would find a way.

When her *and'reoime* edged into her awareness, she laughed. The little spirit *was* repulsive, but it couldn't help it. Responding to her happiness, the spirit swooped around her center. "*Tok*," Alyn whispered.

•   •   •

Alyn took her time returning to *Helala*, allowing herself to enjoy the soft mellowness left by the easing of her worries. She was exhausted and famished, but when she arrived in the village, it was to Beadu's hut she went, rather than the dining hall. She was relieved to find only Deirdre sitting with the old *saa'myn*.

The former Malefica spotted her trudging up the hill. Alyn returned their greetings and sank bonelessly onto a log across from Deirdre. When Beadu saw her expression, she returned her smile and said, "You have found your *and'reiome*."

Alyn laughed, nodding. Throwing her arms above her, she said, "*Da!*" Beaming, she held a hand up to forestall their questions and produced a small flame that hovered above her other palm.

Laughing, Deirdre sprang up and came around the fire. Alyn just managed to close her hand and stand before Deirdre wrapped her arms around her. When she leaned back, still gripping Alyn's arms, she frowned and searched Alyn's face. "The *sjel'and?*"

Alyn nodded. "*Da.*"

Deirdre stepped away from her and turned toward Beadu. "How can this be? Have you ever heard of such a thing?"

"No," Beadu said. "But it is not so outlandish if you think about it. The *sjel'and* are merely *lan'and* which carry the sins of the people they once were. For those who lived an exemplary life, they are very nearly the same."

The news delivered, the excitement keeping Alyn upright fled, and she sat heavily. "It doesn't feel the same." She gestured to the cloud of *lan'and* swirling above them. "As the *lan'and*, I mean."

"Is it awful?" Deirdre asked.

"Yes, no," Alyn said. She focused for a moment on her spirit guide, drifting languidly around her center. *Was it awful? No, it wasn't awful. Just different.* The spirit vibrated briefly. Laughter?

A flutter of wings interrupted her thoughts, followed by a caustic cry. Alyn looked up, startled, to find a large raven, black as coal except for a shawl of white feathers across its shoulders, peering down at them from the low branches. Before she could remark on its odd behavior, Beadu spoke.

"You are looking for me." The crow fluttered down and perched on the old woman's knee. Beadu scratched beneath the feathers behind the raven's head and said to Alyn, "Your sister has an affinity for the *alver'and.*"

The spirits of the forest. "Minna sent the raven?" Alyn asked.

"Just so," Beadu said. The raven offered a leg and Beadu removed a small packet tied to it. "And he has delivered a message." She removed a roll of paper from the packet and unrolled it.

Deirdre watched Beadu, brow furrowed, fingers over her mouth. "What does it say?" she asked.

"The mercenaries from the Union are moving north to attack the *Alle'oss* from behind." Beadu glanced at Deirdre and said, "Willa must have notified them."

"You knew about this?" Alyn asked.

"Yes," Deirdre said. "That woman, the scout, Willa, informed us when the mercenaries landed on the coast east of here."

Alyn frowned, but decided knowing the rest of the message was more important than her pique. "What else does it say?"

Beadu handed her the slip of paper and resumed scratching the raven behind its head. "They ask whether I can have the raven watch the mercenaries."

Alyn took the message, scanned it quickly, then let it hang from her hand. "Can you?"

"Yes," Beadu said. "Though it may not be as useful as they are hoping. Ravens are quite intelligent, but their concerns are not the same as ours. One must think carefully how to ask for their assistance, and they don't speak a human language, so the answers they give are not always what you expect or want. The ravens already know about the mercenaries, but they will not know how to tell us where they are."

"But the raven came to you to deliver the message when Minna asked it to," Alyn said.

"Just so," Beadu said, "but it knew where to go because we are old friends." When she removed her fingers from the raven's neck, it returned to the limb and tipped its head to watch the three women. "This will take some thought."

"This is how you know what is happening," Alyn said. "In the war."

"Just so," Beadu said absently.

Deirdre returned to her seat and asked, "What is like to talk to a raven?"

"Memories and emotions," Beadu said. "They have remarkable memories, and they have strong opinions about many things." She pursed her lips, adopting a rare expression of disapproval. "The war and the carnage it brings has been of utmost interest to them. The mercenaries are already much talked about among their kind."

While Beadu and Deirdre considered, Alyn gazed up at the raven, her mind drifting on waves of fatigue, wondering idly what Minna was doing and how she came to reach out to the *alver'and*. Suddenly alert, she sat up. She didn't have to wonder at Minna's affinity for the spirits anymore. Shutting her eyes, she focused on her spirit guide, which responded instantly to her attention. *Can you introduce me to the alver'and, the spirits that let me talk to the raven?* The spirit rose, paused, then swooped and disappeared.

Alyn waited for the new spirit, expecting it to appear in her center like the *fjel'and* had. When it came, however, she didn't sense a presence like she did with others. Instead, she felt her perception expanding beyond the narrow confines of her own mind. "Oh!" she uttered. Her eyes flew open, her fingers gripped the log beside her, grounding herself in her own body.

The thoughts of hundreds of creatures in the forest assailed her. A raucous clamoring, full of the baser needs and desires of primitive minds, the curiosity, calculation and awareness of more sophisticated minds. Disoriented, she squeezed her eyes shut and was about to send the spirit away when Beadu's voice cut through the buzz.

"You must sink into your center and focus on the raven."

Alyn opened her eyes and found Beadu smiling at her. "Focus on the raven," she said and nodded up to the bird.

Alyn let herself sink into her center, tuning out the riot of other minds, then focused on the raven. "It's curious?" Alyn asked.

"Just so," Beadu said. "They are very good with human faces, and he recognizes your sister in you."

Suddenly, Alyn saw her sister looking up at her, a quizzical expression on her face. "Minna!" Her sister was in a large room, surrounded by people all looking at what Alyn guessed was the raven. She recognized Aron and Zaina, but none of the others.

"Yes, it appears your sister is well," Beadu said. "Now, we must decide how to answer their question."

"You can see what they've seen?" Deirdre asked. When Beadu nodded, she said, "But they have no way of telling humans where they saw something."

"That is the problem," Beadu said. "Humans like to draw maps, hemming the world in with imaginary lines, identifying places with names. These are foreign concepts to other creatures. They have their own ways of organizing their world."

"But if Minna could describe what the raven has seen, someone might recognize it," Alyn said.

"That might work," Deirdre said. "But what reason would the ravens have to help the *Alle'oss* instead of the Empire?"

"We would be foolish to expect them to," Beadu said. "The ravens, as well as all other creatures, have their own priorities. They may align with our own for a time, but that is the best we can expect." She peered up at the raven. "I allow myself the small conceit that some creatures and I have known one another long enough to have developed some small affection for one another, but we should not rely on that. We can but ask and hope." She shooed Alyn with one hand and said, "We must send our response. Alyn, I know you need rest, but first, run, get some paper and a quill."

Reluctantly, Alyn let the spirit of the forest return to its realm, losing her connection to the raven's mind. She rose and walked as quickly as she could down the hill.

Chapter 32

The 28th Day of the Month of Ungemon

Macha

It didn't take long after they left the beach for Eriu to begin testing the three *Alle'oss* scouts. When they looked more amused than afraid, Macha went on high alert. Fortunately, Svend, the lead scout, set a punishing pace through the rugged terrain, leaving Eriu little time for her usual antics. They started early and stopped late, gnawed on hard biscuits and dried meat, then wrapped themselves in their bedrolls on the hard ground as the sun set.

Not that Macha would complain. She was used to meager rations and, though she was as exhausted as her sisters at the end of the day, the ground was far softer than her narrow stone bed in Narvik. Neiman endured everything stoically, giving no outward signs of what she thought of it all. Eriu, on the other hand, complained bitterly, which Macha took as a good sign. As long as she focused on her own discomfort, she had no interest in tormenting the *Alle'oss*.

Each night, Svend planned potential routes for the mercenaries, and each morning, one of the scouts ranged ahead, returning to report at nightfall. Another scout would track back and make contact with the mercenaries. In this way, they made their way northwest, avoiding the small, scattered *Alle'oss* villages which were not plotted on their map. Svend explained they avoided the villages to ensure surprise when they appeared in the *Alle'oss's* rear.

Macha nodded when he explained it to her, but she already knew it was pointless. They were being shadowed by the *Alle'oss*. She suspected the main *Alle'oss* army already knew they were coming. When Svend asked her whether they were being followed, she lied. After all, the Father tasked her and her sisters with killing the three *Alle'oss* witches and what better way to draw them out than to alert them that the mercenaries were coming. If the attack came as a surprise, there would be no guarantee the witches would be present. Macha had no intention of getting caught in a messy battle for no reason.

The fast pace, and the fact that none of the scouts other than Svend were present most of the time, contributed to comparatively cordial relations between them and her sisters. That was until an evening two weeks after they set out. They were becoming accustomed to the strenuous hikes, so when they stopped earlier than usual, they had time after their meal to relax around a small fire. One of Svend's companions shot a brace of grouse, a welcome change from the usual monotonous fare. After eating a small portion, Neiman sat quietly, drawing her knife across her scalp, scraping away the stubble that had begun to obscure her tattoos. Eriu sat cross-legged, back straight, humming softly while she picked meat from a grouse leg with dainty fingers.

Seeing her sisters were occupied, Macha turned her attention to Svend, who studied a map which he tipped toward the fire's light. Taking advantage of a rare quiet moment, Macha asked the question she had been contemplating since she met him. "Why are you helping the men who are attacking your people?"

The scout who shot the grouse looked up sharply and became very still. Svend didn't respond at first, but she could see his jaw muscles working. She expected an angry response, but when he sat back, folding the map, he only grinned as if he had been expecting the question. "You're Andian."

Neiman, who was in Macha's line of sight, lowered her knife and focused on him.

"Andian?" Macha asked.

Svend searched her face, as if trying to decide whether she was putting him on. "You don't know who your people are?" he asked finally.

When Manfrid said that word in the Father's office, it was the first time she heard it. She wasn't sure exactly what he meant when he said it. She looked down at her hands resting on her knees. In Narvik, there were people who lived in a village outside the fort. The woman who raised her told her they were Tituun. They were the only other people Macha knew with dark skin. When she was young, she thought perhaps they were her people, but their skin was a slightly different shade, their hair straighter, their noses narrower. She looked into the fire, allowing herself to recall fragments of memories from her previous life. They were too soft and misty for her to recall individuals, but she was sure they were people who looked like her. When Svend started talking again, she returned her attention to him.

"—Eriu is clearly *Alle'oss,*" he said.

Eriu, suddenly alert, stopped humming and focused on Svend, the grouse leg still held aloft.

Worried about Eriu's response, Macha watched her carefully, but her sister merely studied Svend as if she suddenly found something interesting. Deciding Eriu was safe, Macha asked Svend, "What are you saying?"

He frowned at her, then waved his hand to encompass her and her sisters. "None of you are Volloch, yet you do the emperor's bidding. The Empire is going to exterminate the *Alle'oss* the same way they did your people, the Andian." Svend stowed the map in his pack and said. "Yet, here you are."

Though his expression suggested he thought he answered her question, Macha wasn't fooled. He was deflecting. But before she could challenge him, Neiman asked in a soft voice, "What about my people?"

Svend glanced at her, then said to his comrade, "Not Volloch."

The man shook his head. "Ferol," he said. "It's the eyes. In the sunlight, you can see they're dark gray, not black."

Neiman gazed at him. "That's what Manfrid told the Father," she said quietly. She set the knife aside, dropped her gaze to her hands folded in her lap and whispered, "Ferol."

Svend watched her for a moment, brows knitted, then he turned to Macha and said, "There are more Ferol left than Andian, but that's only because there were more to begin with."

"The Empire killed them?" Neiman asked.

"Yes," Svend said. "That's what they do." He turned a wide grin on Macha as if he proved his point, though it still wasn't clear to Macha what that was.

To give herself time, Macha looked from Neiman to Eriu, who had lost interest in the conversation and returned her attention to the grouse. When Svend stood and hefted his pack onto his shoulder, she said, "You haven't answered my question. You know all this, about how the Empire exterminated our people, and yet you would help them do the same to your own."

Svend gazed down at her, his face shadowed. "We all have our stories." He picked up his bedroll and headed into trees, beyond the light of the fire. Before he slipped from view, he looked over his shoulder and said, "You can take first watch."

When the other scout followed Svend, Macha moved over to sit next to Neiman. Her sister smiled at her and said, "Ferol."

Macha returned her grin, retrieved Neiman's knife and set to removing the last of her sister's stubble.

Neiman let her head fall to the side and pulled her hair over her shoulder to get it out of the way. After a time, she asked in a small voice, "Are we doing the right thing, helping those men attack the... the *Alle'oss*?"

Before Macha could answer, Eriu said, "We're not helping those men. The Father told us to kill the witches who killed our sister, Aife."

"That's right," Macha said. She looked at the side of Neiman's face and was relieved to see a small smile turning up the corner of her mouth.

"Right," Neiman said. "It's for Aife."

•　•　•

Early the following afternoon, Macha and her sisters were following Svend, when the scout that went ahead that morning appeared at a run. He huddled with Svend, speaking urgently, then returned in the direction from which he came. Macha caught up with Svend and asked, "What happened?"

Svend glanced at her, then retrieved his map and studied it. He hadn't spoken to her since the previous evening, and she was thinking he was going to continue his petulant silence when he spoke. "There is a village up ahead that looks as if it was recently evacuated. We were going to bypass it, but it appears they knew we were coming." He slipped the map into his pack and looked at her expectantly.

"We're being watched," Macha said.

"And you didn't tell me because…"

Macha shrugged, holding his gaze. "You have your mission, we have ours, and for us, it's better that the *Alle'oss* know we're coming." She shifted around so she was facing him. "What would you have done if you knew they were there?"

"You could have taken care of them," he said. "You are witches, aren't you?"

"They already know we're coming," she said. "Killing their scouts would not change that."

"Well, now they know where we're going."

"Where else would you be going?" Macha asked. "All this secrecy has been foolish since they saw you on the beach."

He stared at her, then turned and followed the other scout.

The first signs of the village were small houses constructed of uncut stone, nestled among the trees. Only enough of the forest had been cleared to allow the inhabitants to plant gardens around their homes. There was no movement, no human sounds, no smell of smoke. Only the birds disturbed the silence. She found Svend conversing with the other scout in an open space in what she assumed was the center of the village. She checked to ensure her sisters were following, then walked across the space toward Svend.

Svend was pumping the handle of a well when she neared. He put both hands under the last gush of water and splashed it on his face. When he saw her, he said, "They left at least a day ago." Lifting the strap of his leather water bottle off his shoulder, he worked the pump handle again and held the bottle under the flow. "They're probably evacuating all the villages ahead of us." Replacing the stopper of his bottle, he settled the strap on his shoulder and looked at her. "How many are out there?"

"Three," she said.

"Are they watching us now?"

She nodded.

"Well, this simplifies things. If we can't surprise them, we can at least get there before they're ready. No more need for stealth. Be ready to move out in a half hour."

Macha watched him walk away, then turned to find Neiman watching Eriu dance around the well, her arms extended to her sides. When she saw her sisters watching, she pirouetted and sang, "What a beautiful day." She scooped water from the trough in two hands and threw sparkling droplets into the air. "Not cold and dreary like Narvik, right, Neiman?" She extended her arms again and walked, heel-to-toe, away from the trough. "You think the Father would move our home here, Macha?" She twirled slowly again, her face turned to the sun. "He might if *you* ask him?"

Macha was used to all manner of antics from her volatile sister, but there was something different about this. Her usual lilting tone sounded stretched and brittle, as if the mania gleaming in her eyes would burst through at any moment. And Macha wasn't the only one who noticed. Frowning at her sister, Neiman put a hand on Macha's arm. Macha called her spirit guide to her, wanting to be ready for whatever Eriu might do.

Before she could decide how to approach her sister, Svend exited a house that bordered the square, his pack bulging. He came to a stop when he saw them, sensing their tension.

Eriu spun toward him and crouched as if she were about to spring at him. He startled and appeared ready to flee, until Eriu relaxed, filling the square with her tinkling laughter. "Hello, story man," she said. It was her sing-song voice, but the brittleness had hardened into something dangerous. When she leaned toward him and spoke again, there was no longer music in her voice. "What's *your* story, story man?"

Macha was moving before she felt Eriu opening herself to the spirit realms.

Svend backed away, his eyes cutting to the sides, looking for an escape.

Eriu strolled after him. "What you got in the pack, story man?" she asked.

"Bread and cheese," he responded, trying and failing for nonchalance. "So, we have something more interesting to eat."

Eriu was lifting her hand when Macha inserted herself between the two of them. Eriu startled. She hesitated, her hand still held with her palm facing Macha and Svend.

"Eriu," Macha said.

Eriu dropped her hand and lifted her arms languidly above her head, but her smile retained an untamed quality. "We all know *our* stories, Macha. All our sisters. Our stories are what the Father made for us." She threw a glance at Neiman. "Right, Neiman. We know why *we're* here. The Father told us why." She let her arms fall and stared over Macha's shoulder at Svend, her smile hardening. "But what's *your* story, story man?"

"Eriu —" Macha started, but Eriu cut her off.

"Why are you protecting this man?!" she screamed.

Before Macha could think of a good reason, Neiman crossed the short space between her and her sister and rested a hand on Eriu's shoulder. Eriu jumped.

"Sister," Neiman said gently.

Eriu's face quivered. She met Macha's eyes, a pleading look in her expression, then her face crumpled and she wept. Neiman pulled her around and led her away, throwing Macha a worried frown.

The crisis apparently passed, Macha turned toward Svend, who was watching Eriu with a horrified expression. "She doesn't like you," Macha said.

"No *sheoda!*" he said. "What did I do to her?"

Macha shrugged.

He stared at her, obviously expecting more. When it became clear she wasn't going to offer an explanation, he said, "You can't come with us. You'll have to make your own way."

"That won't work," Macha said.

"She was going to kill me."

"I'll protect you."

"Who's going to protect me when you're asleep?"

Macha pursed her lips. It was aggravating, but it wasn't the first time she was forced to accommodate her sister's erratic behavior. "I'll keep watch while you sleep."

"No, no, that won't work. You'll just have to make your own way."

When he turned away, Macha lifted her hand and released a shield in his path. He ran into the obstruction, dropped the pack, and took a step back. She lifted her other hand and released another shield, angling them so that they met behind him. Spirit light glittered and sparked where the shields met.

He stared at her with wide eyes, pressing himself back into the corner. Seeing the fear in his eyes, his chest rising and falling rapidly, Macha grinned and brought the shields together, squeezing him. Not enough to hurt him, but enough for him to understand where they stood.

"We're going to proceed just as we have been," she said calmly. "I will not let Eriu hurt you." Before she let him go, she said, "I have a feeling *your* people will take care of that for her." She released the shields, and he fell to his knees. "We leave in a quarter hour," she said, turned her back on him and looked for her sisters.

Neiman and Eriu sat cross-legged beside the well. Neiman, smiling and more animated than normal, was talking, accenting her words with her hands. Eriu, arms crossed over her chest, rocked slowly forward and back, a soft smile on her tear-streaked face.

Macha caught Neiman's eye as she neared. Her sister gave her an almost imperceptible nod. Macha sank to sit. "Eriu?" she asked. When her sister looked at her, she asked, "Are you okay?"

Eriu nodded.

"Do you want to talk about it?"

Eriu shook her head.

Macha wanted to know what triggered her sister, but she knew from hard experience, Eriu couldn't be pushed. It would come out, but only when Eriu felt safe enough to talk about it. "We need to get going. Can you walk?"

Eriu nodded.

"And you aren't going to hurt Svend?" Macha asked. "At least until we find the other witches."

"For Aife," Neiman said softly.

Eriu's smile was reassuringly sane. "Okay," she said.

Macha returned her smile. "Come on, let's fill our water bottles."

Chapter 33

The 32th Day of the Month of Ungemon

Ulf

Ulf looked out over the Kalana Valley from atop the southern rim. Though he couldn't see the Imps beneath the forest canopy, the thick black smoke rising near the north rim was evidence they were there. The Empire held sway over the entire valley now, the inhabitants massacred, enslaved or fled, their villages abandoned or razed. Around the rim, squads of *Alle'oss* guarded the exits against increasingly insistent probes by rangers. To the east, where the valley rim curved north, the Ishien River arced out into space, the mist glittering orange in the sunset. He thought he could see the spot he and Minna paused for a quick meal on the second day of their journey to Brennan. But maybe that was wishful thinking.

What could Minna be thinking? He knew how she felt about him joining the fight, but she swallowed her fear because she knew how important it was to him. It was her expression the day he left, masking her fear behind a tremulous smile, that he saw each night before he fell asleep. She probably thought her worst fears were confirmed, that he was dead.

"They were a lot better today," Mikaela said.

Ulf grinned and turned to find his second in command smiling at him. "They were," he said. He looked over her shoulder at the misfits busy making camp.

When the *Alle'oss* they met in the valley discovered Ulf, Mikaela and Helga were soldiers, more emerged from hiding, swelling their ranks to twenty. The following day, they climbed out of the valley and encountered one of Keelia's squads guarding the exit. From them, they learned about the games of cat and mouse they played with rangers south of the valley. They also heard the rumors of an impending battle east of their position. This, they dismissed as preposterous. How could there be a battle in central Argren unless the *Alle'oss* lost the Wollen Cut?

Once they were all safely out of the valley, they had to decide what to do. Some of the newcomers argued for joining Keelia's forces, but Ulf, Mikaela and Helga were dead set on rejoining the *Alle'oss* army at the Cut. To Ulf's surprise, all the newcomers acquiesced.

Buoyed by their escape from the valley, they made good time, at first. Argren's summer bounty was nearing its peak, and with no Imps in the forest, they could forage and hunt to feed themselves. It wasn't long, however, before reality intruded. Like Mikaela, all the newcomers lost their homes, and most of them lost friends and loved ones. Grief's heavy shroud cast a pall over the group. Their pace slowed, their hunting and gathering became listless, and arguments broke out over small matters.

It was Ulf's idea to continue their training as they moved east. He explained to Mikaela and Helga it would allow them to focus on something other than what they lost. And it worked. The training kept their minds occupied, and the prospect of striking back at the men who destroyed their lives instilled a sense of urgency and cohesion.

Surprisingly, having learned all the wrong ways to carry out the various squad level maneuvers, the original misfits proved the perfect instructors. Each morning, they started with a lecture, then broke up into squads and spent the morning training. After a debrief at midday, they resumed their eastward march, hunting and foraging as they went. In this way, they made their slow way east.

Now, standing on the rim of the valley with Mikaela, Ulf watched the misfits engaged in light conversation, joking and laughing as they made camp and prepared the evening meal. Tragedy and loss had left their marks, but the past few days forged their grief into a shared sense of purpose and resolve.

"They're starting to feel it," Mikaela said.

"Yeah," Ulf said. "Even Helga." The third member of the original misfits complained about the training at first, wanting to return to the Cut as quickly as possible, but it didn't take her long to change her tune. Ulf suspected she appreciated the respect the others showed her as a member of the *Alle'oss* army. He watched her drawing in the dirt as she explained something to two members of her squad.

"Sort of gives you hope," Mikaela said.

"Hope?"

"Yeah. Like maybe we *can* learn to fight back," Mikaela said. "I mean, here in our mountains." She grinned, bumped him with her shoulder, and went to join the group.

Ulf watched her go, feeling vaguely guilty for a reason he couldn't put his finger on.

• • •

"Let's hear a tale," Mikaela said.

They sat in a big circle around a fire, pleasantly tired and full, having finished a meal of turkey, mushrooms and blueberries. It was their custom to tell a tale before going to bed.

"Does anyone know the tale of Minna and Aife?" a small woman named Inger asked. She arrived as they climbed out of the valley, half-starved, limping and with the entire left side of her face mottled by fading bruises. Ulf didn't think he heard her say one word until the second day of training, when a flood of questions poured forth during the morning lecture. Though she arrived without a bow, they acquired one of the spare bows for her from the squad guarding the exit. It was obvious she never handled one before, but she worked at it with an intensity that bordered on mania. This may have been the only time Ulf heard her speak outside of training.

"Oh, I've heard that so many times," Helga said. "Does anyone know any other Minna stories?"

Ulf dropped his gaze and plucked a twig from the ground, grinning at the phrase 'Minna stories,' when Mikaela spoke.

"Ulf does," she said, nudging him. "Don't you, Ulf?"

Startled, Ulf looked up to find her smirking at him.

"Yeah," Helga said. "You must have some stories we haven't heard."

"Why?" Inger asked.

Helga waved a hand at Ulf. "Because this isn't just *any* Ulf, this is *the* Ulf."

Ulf gaped, feeling the blood drain from his face. Seeing realization dawning in everyone's expressions, he dipped his head and snapped the twig between tightly clenched fingers.

"Wait," Hakon said. The man who was the first to approach them in the valley was lounging on an elbow, but he sat up and sat cross-legged at this news. "You're *that* Ulf?"

Mikaela elbowed Ulf. His head pivoted toward her. She smiled, hitched a brow, and nodded toward the others.

Ulf sighed and raised his head. "Yeah." In an instant, the easy familiarity he was beginning to feel with these people changed. No longer was he just another member of the group. Now, he was *that* Ulf, the Ulf from the stories. He could see their faces transform as realization set in. Speculation, appraisal, doubt and a touch of awe. Was this what Minna experienced all the time?

Looks were exchanged, whispers shared, shuffling, then Inger worked up the courage to ask, "So… did she really fight that witch, Aife?"

They grew still, a sort of hunger coming into their expressions. "Yeah, she did," Ulf said uncomfortably.

"Was it like the stories?" Hakon asked. "The lightning, fire and everything?"

"I heard Aife was a monster, like she wasn't even human," an older man said.

"No, she was human," said a young man, "but her face was all scarred so she *looked* like a monster."

"That's not the way I heard it," the other man said with a scowl.

"It was in the middle of a blizzard, the wind howling, and Minna put her arms out and said, 'Wind be still,' and it just stopped," Hakon said.

"Wind be still?" Mikaela asked with a laugh. "No, she doesn't *say* anything. She puts her arms up, that's true, but she sort of directs the wind spirits with her hands." She held her hands up and swished them from one side to the other.

"How would you know?" Hakon asked.

"Because we saw her do it, at the Cut, before we left," Helga answered.

Even as uncomfortable as he felt, Ulf couldn't help a small grin at the pride in her voice.

"When the Imps attacked." Helga lifted her hands in front of her, pantomiming as she spoke. "She sort of swept her arms to the side, then back. When the wind hit the Imps from behind, she lifted her hands and they went flying." She mimed shooting her bow. "Then we just... picked them off."

Silence descended as they considered this. It was probably the only firsthand account they had of a 'Minna story,' and Ulf could see them savoring it. Everything they heard before were stories passed around through many ears, stories that grew so fanciful they were easy to doubt.

"So, what was the battle between Minna and Aife *really* like?" Inger asked, for once, her voice animated by her eagerness.

Ulf gazed around, the silence suddenly taut. They wanted to believe, especially after what the Empire made of their lives. They wanted him to tell them it was true, to confirm their hopes. But he couldn't.

"I couldn't tell you," Ulf said. "I wasn't there."

As much as he didn't enjoy being the center of their attention, their disappointment was far worse. After a moment, people looked at one another, muttering and throwing veiled glances at him.

"But you were with her in Hast," Mikaela said. "I heard someone tell the story, and they said you were there."

"Were you?" Inger asked, unwilling to give up her hopes.

"Yeah, I was there." Ulf said, feeling a swelling of gratitude for Mikaela.

"Yeah, yeah, I heard that story," Hakon said, nodding and glancing around for confirmation. "You spun some yarn with all the brothers standing around, and they almost let you go, so she didn't even have to fight."

Ulf chuckled. "Yeah, that's partly true. I did tell them a story, but I'm not sure how much they believed."

"Did she nearly burn the city down?" Helga asked. "I heard she threw fire all around."

"No, it wasn't fire," Ulf said. "She didn't meet the fire spirit until the next day. It was wind."

"Wind?" Helga asked. "Like with the soldiers?"

"Sort of, but much bigger. Bigger than the most violent thunderstorm you ever saw." He saw in their distant expressions they were trying to picture it. But there was no way they could. "It was terrifying."

"Tell the tale," Mikaela said.

Ulf was about to decline, but seeing the sudden hope in their faces, he let his gaze drop. "Where do I start?"

"At the beginning," Inger said.

"No, you *wota,* we'd be here all night," Hakon said.

"I mean *after* they got to Hast."

"I'll tell you how we *escaped* Hast," Ulf said. He thought for a moment, then started to speak. Fumbling at first, he was forced to restart more than once, not sure what to tell and what to skip. Noticing his listeners looking uncomfortably at one another, he felt his face heat.

And then he told them about the wind spirit destroying the storeroom at the tavern where they hid. Hearing a chuckle, he looked up, and found people glancing at one another and suppressing smiles. The memory of Minna's face after she finally got the spirit under control came into his mind and he laughed. Given permission, the others joined him and soon they were all laughing.

"Not the legendary hero you've all heard about," he said when the laughter subsided.

"She's not?" Inger asked.

Hearing the fear behind her words, Ulf hurried to reassure her. "Oh, she is. She's everything you've heard about and more." His voice gained strength as he continued the story. He caught Inger tracing her finger along her temple when he described Minna's fake tattoo, designed to disguise her as a Seidi novice. There was more laughter when he described Minna's surprise when he asked her name while he was spinning his yarn. Gasps greeted his description of the brother yanking Minna off her horse and dropping her onto the cobbles.

"I thought she was dead," Ulf said, nodding. He paused, spreading his hands, palms down above the leaf strewn ground. "She lay as still as a corpse. But when the Imp reached down, she just... flicked her fingers." He mimed the motion. "And the giant went flying." This was greeted with satisfied exclamations. "She stood. The Imps were all closing in on her and she looked up at me, all calm, and said, 'Hide.'"

"What did you do?"

"I hid." More laughter. "I'd seen what she could do. I took her horse's reins, busted through the men closing in on me and got away." He paused, finding himself enjoying their anticipation. "So, the brothers were closing in on her, and one of them yelled, 'Get her!'" Ulf rose into a slight crouch and spread his arms. Growing up, he heard his father, Fennig's loremaster, tell tales countless times, and as he continued, he adopted what his mother called his father's storytelling voice. "She lifted her arms and twisted, like this." He twisted, then slowly swept one hand across the gathering, giving them time to picture the scene as they hung on his words. "And the air just exploded. WOOOOSH!" He gesticulated wildly. "People thrown around, those big coal wagons tipped over, the coal whipped up, smacking people, horses throwing their riders and fleeing." Gazing past his upraised hand at the memory, he said, "When I looked back, the wind circled her, like she was at the center of a tornado. Hair and cloak flying, head back, arms out." Straightening, he mimicked Minna's posture, then he dropped his arms to his side and focused again on their rapt faces. "I watched her disappear —"

"She can become invisible!?"

"No," Ulf said with a grin. "The wind picked up the snow and whipped it around, so it was all white, like a blizzard." He paused for a beat, then said, "Then it stopped. Sudden. Just like it started. I rode back, bringing her horse." He swayed drunkenly on his feet. "When she uses a lot of magic, she gets really weak. I thought she was going to pass out. Wasn't sure what I was going to do. Then she sort of shivered, and she was okay."

"Then you left? Did they chase you?"

"No." He gestured with his hand and mimed searching. "She looked around, searching. She found the inquisitor cowering behind a tree. She strode over, stood over him and said…" He bent over Helga and lifted a finger. "'If you come after us, I'm going to LOSE MY TEMPER!'" Gasps. "'If I have to come back here, you'll be picking up *pieces* of your men!'"

"*Sheoda*," Hakon breathed into the hush.

"*Da*," Ulf said, straightening. "She's scary when she gets mad." He returned to his place between Mikaela and Helga and said, "Then we rode awa —" He scanned their taut faces. "Well, I probably shouldn't tell you this…"

"Tell us!" Mikaela said to a round of eager nods.

"I don't think she would mind." He paused, letting them think he was considering, then he leaned forward and spoke in a confidential tone. "She was walking back to her horse and… I could see the problem right away."

"What?"

"Well, these were big Imperial stallions, see, and —"

"Minna's short," Helga blurted, eliciting some twitters.

"Yeah," Ulf said. "So, while she's walking to the horse, she makes this fog, so no one could see her, and when she gets near her horse, she…" He looked around again.

"What did she do?" Inger asked.

"She said, 'Ulf, help me get on my horse.'"

There was silence, everyone staring at him, then they were all laughing, snorting, slapping one another on the back, rolling on the ground.

When the laughter died down, Mikaela wiped tears from her eyes and asked, "What did you do?"

Ulf interlaced his fingers. "I got off my horse and boosted her up." He smiled at the memory. "We both laughed about it later."

A comfortable silence settled on the gathering. Ulf could see them painting their own versions of the story for their memories.

"Did they come after you?" Inger asked.

"No. I guess Minna scared them pretty bad," Ulf said. "But they *were* waiting for us in Brennan." He looked around, returning their grins, and said, "But that's a tale for another night."

Chapter 34

The 34th Day of the Month of Ungemon

Aron

Aron gazed at the small pool of light the single lamp cast on the drawing of the Imp camp. Zaina waited beside him, her usual stoic exterior masking the frustration he knew she must feel. They were alone in the headquarters. It was late. They were exhausted, and their argument had been circling for hours. Normally, Imp officers made liberal use of Brochen servants while in the field. Aron hoped to use this vanity to insert spies into the camp, but General Prather's security had been much tighter than expected. The question of how to find out what Prather planned had occupied them for days.

He straightened and said, "There's no way around it. I have to visit the camp in *annen'heim*." As a realm walker, Aron could enter the realm of the dead, *annen'heim*, and return. While he was in *annen'heim*, time appeared to slow in the physical realm. This allowed him to pass unseen and appear to cross distances in the blink of an eye.

Zaina didn't answer right away, but Aron knew her well enough to interpret her silences.

"I'll be careful," he said. "If there are any *sjel'and* in the vicinity, I come right back." The *sjel'and*, the soul spirits, that inhabited *annen'heim* were not fond of trespassers. If he were to encounter one, it would rip the spirit from his body.

"You're reckless," Zaina said, "and there are too many people depending on you."

Aron gave her a sad smile. "Far less reckless than I once was," he said, "and I understand all too well what's at stake. There is no one else who can do this. We need to know Prather's plans. If you have an alternative — a viable alternative — let me hear it."

"What if you can't get away from a spirit while in *annen'heim*? You'll have to return to the physical realm no matter where you are. You could be inside Prather's headquarters."

Aron stared at her, visualizing the moment he appeared in front of the famously pompous general. Then the ridiculousness of the scene unlocked something inside him. He managed to suppress his giggle, but it must have left its mark on his face. Zaina's frown deepened. Aron drew himself up, tucked his chin, lifted his eyebrows and pruned his lips.

"What's that?" Zaina asked.

Adopting an affected elite Volloch accent, he said, "Who let this *l'oss* in my headquarters?" He flicked his fingers and said, "Jeeves, do something with this. Immediately!"

Zaina's face went slack. Then her cheeks quivered and reddened. She bent over, caught herself on the map table, her body quaking.

Aron reached out and asked, "You okay, Zaina?"

She straightened abruptly, the tips of her hair whipping across Aron's face. She drew in a deep breath, paused, then gales of laughter spewed forth.

Aron watched, fascinated. This was something he had never seen before. A chuckle from his taciturn friend was as rare as summer snow. The sight of this hardened warrior laughing helplessly broke a hard knot that had grown inside him. He chuckled, then he laughed, then he put his hand on her shoulder and let the current of her humor sweep him away.

Containing her laughter, she brushed his hand off and straightened. Clearing her throat, she pursed her lips, planted a hand on her hip and gestured with the other. "Jeeves, what did I tell you about leaving the door open?"

Aron laughed so hard, he thought he might crack a rib. He stumbled backwards, held up a hand and said, "Wait, wait." Drawing himself up again, he said, "And you know, Jeeves, if you see one *l'oss*, there must be a hundred you don't see." He pointed to the bed in the corner. "Quick, check under the bed."

Zaina leapt onto a chair and screeched, "Eeek!"

Before Aron could respond, the door to the headquarters slammed open and the man standing sentry duty burst through, sword drawn. Zaina, standing on the chair, and Aron, hands above his head, gaped at him. Then they dissolved into laughter again. The sentry stared for a moment, then turned away, mumbling something unintelligible, and pulled the door shut as he left.

Zaina spluttered, tipped over, and fell into Aron's arms. They tumbled to the floor where they sat, leaning into one another, Aron's arm across her shoulders, shaking with laughter.

The laughter faded, leaving them breathless and weak. Aron withdrew his arm and gave her a soft smile. "I needed that," he said.

Zaina returned his grin and asked, "Me too." She wiped a tear from the corner of her eye and sighed. "You'll be careful?" she asked. When Aron nodded, she said, "You hear any *sjel'and,* you come right back, even if they aren't close. You can always try another day."

"I'll come right back."

.   .   .

Aron looked down from the top of the escarpment at the stockade that blocked the entrance to the Cut. A westerly wind lifting his hair muffled the voices of the squad of *Alle'oss* descending the Cut toward the barrier.

"Here they come," Zaina said and pointed to the squad. The soldiers would patrol the forest at the base of the escarpment, ensuring the Imps kept a respectful distance.

There were rumors among the *Alle'oss* that he was a realm walker, but it wasn't officially known and Aron Zaina kept it that way to reduce the opportunities for the Imps to learn his secret. So, the first puzzle was how to get him beyond the stockade at the bottom of the Cut. He couldn't walk through walls and having the commanding general wandering beyond the wall would lead to the worst kind of speculation and rumor. The solution was for Aron to slip out when they opened the gate for one of their patrols. Since time in the physical realm slowed while he was in *annen'heim*, all he had to do was to make his way down to the stockade and walk out.

When the gate was open, Aron glanced behind him to make sure no one was paying attention. They juggled the sentries to make sure no one was posted at the top of the Cut. Seeing no one, he gave Zaina a reassuring smile and stepped into *annen'heim*.

The realm of the dead was as silent as the grave. There were no spirits nearby, so he set off.

The men and women of the patrol were still passing through the gate when he made it to the stockade. Their expressions had the intensity of those about to put their lives on the line. He paused briefly, wishing them luck, then set off down the highway.

He encountered the Imp patrol two hundred paces from the stockade. They were hiding in the underbrush beside the highway, their attention focused on the *Alle'oss* patrol emerging from the gate. An ambush? He stared at the leader of the Imp squad, then glanced over his shoulder toward the camp. If he hurried, he might get back in time to the warn his people.

He made it as far as the eastern gate in the perimeter of the Imp camp before he encountered the spirit. He couldn't see its dark bulk drifting in the murk, but he heard its rumbling groan nearby. It hadn't detected his presence. He gazed down the east-west thoroughfare that bisected the camp to the pavilion, which was Prather's headquarters. It was so close.

But he promised Zaina he would be cautious. He could try again another day.

The gate was nearly closed when he made it back to the stockade. The *Alle'oss* patrol was still in the open space at the base of the scree below the cliff. They wouldn't hear him if he tried to shout from the top of the Cut. He slipped through the gate, walked ten paces up the highway, then crossed the boundary. The attention of everyone on the stockade was on the recently departed patrol, so they didn't see him.

"Lieutenant!" he said.

All the men and women manning the stockade whirled around. The young lieutenant nearly toppled off the ledge at the top before her fellow soldier caught her. "Sir?" she said once she was safely on her feet.

Aron climbed the ladder and stood beside her. He pointed to where the Imps waited. "There is an Imp squad waiting in ambush just before the bend in the highway. Send someone after that patrol that just left to warn them."

She hesitated, then gave the order.

Aron watched the man until he caught up with the squad just before they melted into the forest. "*Tok*, Lieutenant," he said, then turned to go.

"Sir," she said. "How did you know?"

"Spies," he said with a smirk.

•   •   •

It wasn't until his sixth attempt he made it as far as Prather's headquarters. He stood outside the pavilion, holding his breath and listening for spirits, but the realm of the dead was silent. Not believing his luck, he studied the flaps that made up the door of the pavilion. They were closed, but he could just squeeze through the narrow gap. He would survive if he touched the fabric, but it would be unpleasant, leaving the part of him that made contact numb.

Safely inside, he paused and marveled at the number of men on Prather's staff. In contrast to his own spartan headquarters, Prather's pavilion was luxurious. Woven rugs covered the ground. Canvas sheets partitioned the space along one side into offices where men worked at desks. Prather sat in one of a pair of cushy chairs in one corner, a teacup in one hand and a sheet of paper in the other. About to sip his tea, his pursed lips made him look remarkably similar to Zaina's imitation.

Aron grinned and let his gaze sweep across the scene until he found what he was looking for; the map table. Weaving carefully through the men gathered around the table, he found a space and studied the map. It was similar to the one in his own headquarters, except there were small markers scattered around the map on which someone had written, in a precise hand, the designations of various units.

The Imps put two markers atop the Cut. On one, the number two thousand was written, followed by a question mark. They had underestimated the *Alle'oss* forces, but not by much, unfortunately. On the other marker, someone wrote Minna's name.

He checked the eastern end of the Kalana Valley and was pleased to find there were no unit markers for the *Alle'oss* units preparing to ambush the mercenaries. They didn't know about the ambush. A marker representing the mercenaries was on the map, a third of the way from the coast to the site of the ambush. How accurate was that?

The *Alle'oss* had already identified the units facing Keelia in the south and *Oss'stera* in the north. Nothing new there. But he found another thing he was looking for east of the Imp camp. On the highway, near the Cut, the designations of some of the Ninth Legion's cohorts were arranged in a long line. An order of battle for the great assault Keelia predicted. The Imps would attempt to overwhelm the *Alle'oss* defenses with waves of men.

Aron stared at the ten small, carefully rendered numbers, each representing 500 lives. Five thousand men. Half the Ninth's strength. There was no secret to how the *Alle'oss* would survive the coming battle; they would have to kill enough of these men that the Imperials decided the cost was too high. How many would it take? The actual order of the units wasn't very helpful to the *Alle'oss,* because they didn't have any intelligence on the makeup of the cohorts. Still, he spent some time memorizing the numbers.

When he looked up, he noticed four women standing at the back of the tent. He didn't need to see their tattoos to know who these women were. No other women would be allowed in an Imperial military headquarters. They were Seidi sisters. He came around the map table and studied them.

The elaborate tattoos at their left temples sent a thrill of fear through him. They were full sisters of considerable rank. But their well-tailored clothes, more suited to the ballroom than the battlefield, offered a ray of hope. They didn't look like women who battled the Kaileuk. These were hot-house flowers who languished in the Seidi. He had seen their kind strutting arrogantly around Brennan, but they would find themselves out of their league here. Still dangerous, but no battle winners.

He gazed at their haughty expressions, then wandered the tent, looking for anything else that might give him a clue to what Prather intended beyond a massed assault. In particular, he wanted to know what role the sisters would play. After a half hour, he decided there was nothing helpful.

He was preparing to leave when he heard the spirit. It was close. He usually heard their plaintive wails from far off, but this one was close enough to sense him. He hurried to the door and came to an abrupt stop. Time in the physical realm didn't completely stop while he was in *annen'heim*. It just slowed sufficiently that it appeared to be frozen. While he searched Prather's headquarters, the opening between the flaps of the door, perhaps caught by a gust of wind, narrowed. He could not squeeze through.

The spirit huffed, so close, it vibrated in his abdomen. It detected his presence. Throwing caution to the wind, Aron crossed the boundary. A startled shout followed him as he plunged through the tent flaps. Breath coming in ragged gasps, he dashed across the face of the pavilion, then entered a lane between two rows of tents.

More shouts rose behind him, the alarm spreading. He sprinted down the lane, swerving between two tents when someone burst out of a tent ahead of him. Stumbling over a guy line and ripping the stake from the ground, he sprawled on his stomach as shouts converged on his position. Praying to the Mother he was far enough from the soul spirit, he crossed the boundary, leaving the rising clamor behind, and plunging into silence.

He lay still and listened. A low wail started below his hearing and rose in an undulating cry. The spirit was searching for him, but it wasn't near. He rose to his feet and dashed away from the sound, heading to the perimeter of the camp. Despite the fear racing his heart, he couldn't help grinning, imagining Zaina's face when he told her what happened.

• • •

The conversations ended abruptly when Aron entered his headquarters. He greeted everyone and came around to his usual place beside Zaina.

"Did you make it to Prather's headquarters this time?" Zaina asked.

"I did," Aron said.

"What did you see?"

He gazed at the drawing of the Imperial camp. "They have sisters of the Seidi," he said. "Four of them."

"What kind of sister?" Zaina asked, her voice suddenly taut.

"Based on their clothes, I'd guess they are the kind that sit comfortably in the Seidi most of the time. I can't imagine they're too happy Briana sent them here."

"That's a good thing," Lief said.

"Yes," Aron said. "Still, even if they aren't powerful, they can probably produce shields and spirit waves."

"We will have to do something about them," Zaina said. "Anything else?"

He pointed to where he'd seen the marker for the mercenaries. "They had the mercenaries here."

"They're moving slowly," Lief said.

"If it's accurate," Aron said. He bent over the map and wrote what he could remember about the order of battle in front of the Cut.

"Those are the designations of cohorts in the Legion," Lief said. "Not sure that helps us much. We already know *where* they'll attack."

"We could send these to Keelia," Zaina said. "Maybe she knows something that would be useful. Which ones are engineers, archers, infantry."

"Good idea," Aron said. "The only thing we didn't already know about is the sisters, but I saw nothing that would change our preparations."

"That, by itself, is good to know," Zaina said.

"So, it's just a question of timing," Leif said.

"Right, but I think we can guess when they will attack if Keelia is right about them assaulting everywhere, all at once," Aron said. "The Ninth should attack at the same time as the mercenaries. I assume the mercenaries and Prather are communicating via bird, so the timing wouldn't be precise. Maybe plus or minus a day." He pointed to the site of the planned battlefield with the mercenaries on the eastern end of the Kalana Valley. "Lief meets the mercenaries here. That will be three or four days earlier than Prather expects. We defeat the mercenaries, then Lief returns to the Cut with everyone who can still walk —" He glanced up and noticed for the first time Minna was absent. "Where's Minna?"

"She's… taking some time," Lief said.

Aron took in their worried expressions. "How much time is she going to need?"

"She has a lot on her shoulders and she's had a shock," Zaina said.

Aron let his eyes fall to the line of Imperial cohorts, an arrow pointing at the Cut. Only half the Ninth Legion, but they dwarfed the *Alle'oss* army facing them even so. In a flash, he saw the Imps brushing their pitiful resistance aside and rampaging through Argren. All their preparations, sacrifices, Ragan's plans — it was for nothing without Minna. He straightened and gathered himself, giving himself time to force his despair back where he hid it from everyone save Zaina.

When he was sure his voice would be steady, he said, "This is war." He paused, swallowed, and looked up at the ceiling. He lowered his gaze and gestured to all of them. "Losing people and shouldering more than you're capable of is part of it." He wiped his mouth with the palm of his hand. "I don't know what my mother wanted us to do, but I'm pretty sure she expected Minna to be a big part of it." He put his finger on the cohorts he listed near the Cut. "We won't survive the first battle without her." When no one responded, he said, "Someone needs to go talk to her. Soon."

Chapter 35

The 34th Day of the Month of Ungemon

Minna

Minna's eyes fluttered open. It was morning. *Bless the Mother.* She slept. At least for a couple of hours. It was more than she slept any night since Ulf —

Rolling onto her back, she gazed at dust motes drifting in a shaft of sunlight. Her stomach grumbled, but it was never satisfied lately. It complained when she didn't eat and rebuked her when she did. She let her head fall to the side and gazed numbly at the bed she refused to sleep in. It felt too… final. She preferred to sleep on the cloak spread on the ground, where she and Ulf slept together. She should get up, but the thought of facing the people who wanted so much from her was overwhelming.

Linea appeared, swooping under the door and swirling around the small space.

"Go away," Minna mumbled. Linea swooped down within an inch of Minna's nose, then rose out of reach. Growling, Minna flapped her hands at the spirit. When Linea obstinately continued to circle, Minna let her arms flop to her sides.

"Okay!" she said finally. "I'll get up." She dragged her boots over and pulled them on. With an effort, she rolled onto her hands and knees, gathered herself, then pushed herself upright, and stood swaying, staring blearily around. Apparently losing patience, Linea's circuitous route narrowed until she was buzzing Minna's face. Minna swatted at her, ducked away and shouted, "I said okay!" Glowering at the spirit, she wrestled her tangled hair into a ponytail, waved at the door and said, "Well?"

Linea swooped under the door. Minna followed and stood, blinking in the bright sunshine, ignoring the parade of people who always seemed to find a reason to take the path in front of her hut. Her stomach grumbled again. "I heard you the first time," she mumbled and followed Linea to the kitchens.

It was too late for breakfast, but her mother saw her coming and met her with some cheese and bread.

"*Tok*," Minna said, keeping her eyes on the food rather than endure the concern in her mother's gaze.

"Haven't seen you at mealtimes lately," her mother said.

Minna heard the worry in her voice, so she tried a smile and braved her mother's scrutiny. "Just busy," she said. Her mother frowned, reached out and rubbed Minna's arm. She started to speak, but something in Minna's expression must have made her change her mind. Her parents tracked her down when they heard about Ulf. It was all Minna could do to act like she appreciated their condolences, but it was excruciating. Ever since, though she felt guilty about it, she avoided them.

"I've been busy," Minna said. The effort of maintaining her smile hurt her face.

"Your father should be home from his hunting trip today," her mother pressed on. "You should come sit with us after dinner tonight." When Minna nodded, her mother added, "You don't have to talk. We'll just sit." She lifted her hand again, let it hang between them for a moment, then let it drop.

The worry in her mother's voice almost overwhelmed Minna's defenses. She needed to get away before she felt something. "That sounds nice," she said hurriedly. "I'll… I'll see you." She gave her mother a quick nod and turned away.

The tables were almost deserted, but she went as far as she could from the kitchen before sitting. Eying the cheese and the bread, she decided the bread was less risky and took a small bite. Dropping her head back, she closed her eyes and let her mind drift. A northeasterly breeze, having wound its way through mountain peaks still capped by snow before finding its way to the camp, lifted goose bumps on her exposed neck.

"You missed the war council yesterday."

Minna startled and opened her eyes to find Sigurn dropping onto the bench across from her. "Let me guess," she said. "Things are bad. The Imps are winning." Minna never saw Sigurn so much as miffed before. She watched, fascinated, as a struggle played out on his face. She anticipated an angry response, but she was disappointed.

"Listen, you don't know Ulf is dead. They searched the area and didn't find his body."

That was true, but it didn't help. The Imps might have captured him. The horrors that prospect conjured in Minna's imagination visited her every night. Not trusting herself to say anything, she shrugged and took another small bite of bread.

Finally, losing his internal war, Sigurn spat, "You think you're the only person who lost someone?"

That was more like it. "No, I'm *not* the only person who lost someone, but no one expects those people to win the war all by themselves."

"Yes, none of the rest of us have anything to do with it," he said coldly.

Minna's heart raced, anticipating his anger escalating. Unfortunately, he settled himself with an effort.

"Your moth —"

"My mother is dead," Minna said flatly. "She died without telling anyone what she planned, because she *had* no plan." There it was. That was what she needed him to goad her into saying. She stared at him, willing him to contradict her, but all she saw was her own uncertainty in his expression.

Leaving the bread and cheese, she pushed herself up, stumbled extricating herself from the bench, then hurried away.

Head down, to avoid the troubled expressions of the people she passed, she walked until she was sure Sigurn wasn't following her. Turning slowly, she cast about for a place she could go where she could be alone with her grief. Somewhere that didn't remind her of Ulf. There was nowhere. Not in the *Alle'oss* camp. Everywhere she went now, people she didn't know offered their condolences. It was all she could do not to snap at them. Their sorrow was for their own crumbling hopes. Not for Ulf.

Turning abruptly, she returned to her hut, shut herself in, lay down, and imagined she could still detect Ulf's scent on the cloak they lay on each night. Linea entered the hut and drifted slowly. "I don't know what to do," she whispered. "And you'll never be here again to help me figure it out."

Alyn

"Are you ready?" Beadu asked, one eyebrow arched.

Alyn sat in her customary place outside Beadu's hut, hands flat on her knees, gazing into the fire. When she looked up and caught Beadu watching her expectantly, she took a breath and blew it out. "Yes," she said with a quick nod, trying as much to convince herself as her mentor.

She let her eyes slide shut and reached out to her spirit guide. The little spirit appeared instantly, swirling joyfully around her center. *Do you watch me all the time?* A loop that Alyn was beginning to recognize as confirmation. Remembering the vision in which other *sjel'and* chased the spirit, she pictured the spirit following her around, waiting for her to call it and free it from its dark prison. *Can you come into my center without me calling you if you needed to hide?* A loop. She pondered the spirit's predicament, and how its appearance was affecting her life, then gave herself a shake. She was delaying again.

It was Beadu who pushed her to use her spirit guide to peer into the future. As hard as Alyn worked for it, one would think she would jump at the opportunity. But now that seeing the future was within her grasp, she found herself reluctant. The horrid visions the swarm showed her left their mark on her. Would she see Minna dying at the hands of the three witches? Would she see the Empire ravaging Argren, burning villages and murdering her countrymen? She didn't believe her spirit guide would intentionally try to frighten her, but the spirits could not lie.

To put the moment off a little longer, Alyn opened her eyes and found her apprehension reflected on Deirdre's face. She paused when she saw Beadu's knowing grin. How was it the old *saa'myn* knew exactly what she was thinking all the time? Ignoring the twinkle in the old woman's eyes, Alyn said, "How far spirits can see into the future depends on how long they've been in *annen'heim*."

"Just so."

"And my spirit guide, because he…" He? How did she know that? "Because he is very nearly a *lan'and*, he doesn't have the sins that would keep him in *annen'heim* very long."

Beadu nodded.

"So, he wouldn't be able to see very far into the future."

"Just so," Beadu said. "This is what the *saa'myn* of the past believed, and was confirmed by your mother. She believed the *shehdi'enun*, the cause and effect of creation, is laid bare to the *sjel'and,* but to truly understand the subtleties, to follow the path of cause and effect far into the future, requires an eternity of experience."

"Only the spirits of people who were truly evil can see far into the future?" Deirdre asked.

"Just so."

"In mother's journal, she said it was difficult to get the spirits to show you what you wanted to see, that they showed you only what they thought would be most painful," Alyn said.

"That is true," Beadu said. "Your mother spent long hours learning to coax the spirits into revealing what she wanted to see." She paused and gave Alyn a pointed look. "But she did not have the advantage of having a spirit guide, which was also a *sjel'and.*"

Alyn pressed her lips together and gazed at the trees behind Deirdre. Finally, she asked, "How far would my spirit guide be able to see?"

Beadu pursed her lips and shrugged. "Let us see." Her tone was soft, but the gentle admonishment was unmistakable.

Unable to think of any more questions, Alyn could delay no longer. Glancing at Deirdre, she quirked one corner of her mouth, sighed and closed her eyes. Her spirit guide slowed. She could sense it quivering with anticipation and dreaded what that meant. They regarded one another while Alyn worked up her courage. *Can you show me the future?*

The vision appeared so suddenly, Alyn was momentarily disoriented. She was looking down on three women, sitting on logs arranged around a fire. She recognized herself, Beadu and Deirdre. The Alyn in the vision opened her eyes and said, "Very funny!" The vision faded as quickly as it came, leaving her spirit guide swooping through her center. Alyn opened her eyes. "Very funny!" she said. The spirit vibrated. Laughter.

"What?" Deirdre asked anxiously.

"He showed me this moment," Alyn said. "He listened to us talking and is trying to be funny." When she noticed the two women suppressing grins, Alyn narrowed her eyes.

"Clearly, having a *sjel'and* spirit guide has unique challenges," Beadu said with a chuckle. "What did you ask it to show you?"

"I just asked it to show me the future."

"Perhaps you can be more specific."

Catching herself chewing her lip, Alyn blew out a breath and closed her eyes. What did she want to see? It wasn't the battle between Minna and the witches. She wasn't ready for that. She didn't know enough about what was happening outside *Helala* to ask anything specific enough to be useful in the war. Then it came to her. It was the question on everyone's mind. What was their mother's plan? What future did Ragan see that made her so confident Argren could defeat the Empire? That was what they all needed to know. But how could she ask for that?

Before she could decide, her spirit guide slowed to a stop. It was so unusual, Alyn forgot the question of what to ask it. *What's wrong?* The spirit disappeared.

Her eyes flew open.

"What happened?" Deirdre asked.

"He's gone," Alyn said. "My spirit guide... he just left."

"What did you say to it?" Deirdre asked.

"Nothing!" Alyn said. The note of accusation in Deirdre's voice brought heat to Alyn's cheeks. She turned to Beadu. "I was trying to decide how to ask it to show me what my moth —"

Her spirit guide reappeared, but it wasn't alone. When Deirdre spoke, Alyn lifted a hand to forestall her and squeezed her eyes shut. Another spirit accompanied her spirit guide. But it was not a *sjel'and*, or at least not like any other *sjel'and* Alyn encountered. It glittered like a *lan'and,* only brighter. Stunned, she *watched* the new spirit and her spirit guide swooping around her center, chasing one another, weaving together and apart again. Alyn's spirit sang a greeting so joyful that Alyn laughed out loud.

Suddenly, her spirit guide disappeared again, and the other spirit swirled to a stop. Alyn hesitated before cautiously extending her awareness toward it. "Oh!" she breathed. She hugged herself, her head fell back. Tears, leaking between her closed eyelids, streamed across her temples. Deirdre's concerned exclamation was a distant sound.

Her center dissolved into a vision so clear, it was almost as if Alyn were in the small, dimly lit room. A woman with black hair knelt beside a crude bed. Another younger woman with dusky blond hair, someone Alyn didn't know, knelt beside the black-haired woman. Alyn couldn't see the black-haired woman's face, but somehow she knew who it was. It was her mother. Ragan. This was a vision of the past.

The vision zoomed toward the women. There was a confusing shift of perspective. Then she was seeing a *lan'and* and a *sjel'and* swooping together. With a start, she realized she must be seeing Ragan's center. Lost in the vision, Alyn fell forward onto her thighs, her hands over her mouth, weeping from a joy that was too powerful to be just her own.

The vision shifted again. Her mother was still kneeling by the bed, but the blond woman was holding a baby, a shock of blond hair visible between her arms. Just before the vision dissolved into chaos, Alyn realized the baby must be her. This was the moment Alyn was born.

An instant later, she was looking down on her father. He cradled a baby with blond hair in his arms. It was Alyn, not much older than the previous vision. A toddler with black hair clung to his pants leg. Minna. The vision rotated and zoomed in to focus on her father's face, dragging a gasp from Alyn. It was hard to believe this was the man who was the bedrock of her childhood. Bringing his daughters to giggles with his silly songs, filling them with wonder with his tales of distant places by the fire at night. The man her mother, the woman who raised her, Vada, loved. Always steady. Never failing to provide for his family. This man looked broken. Red-rimmed eyes looked out from a haggard face. The expression of a man crumpled and lost. No child should see their parents in such a state. Realizing she stopped breathing, Alyn gasped, sucking in air that escaped as a sob.

The vision pulled back and rotated until she was seeing what caused her father's misery. At first, she had the confusing impression it was Minna riding away on a horse. Then she saw the woman's tattoo and realized it must be Ragan. She never met her mother, but she knew from everyone who knew her how much she resembled Minna. Ragan was accompanied by a blond girl on another horse. They were riding away on the Imperial highway that passed in front of their home near Fennig. Her mother was looking back, but before they rounded the bend and disappeared, she turned away. The vision faded to black, leaving her alone with a sorrow so profound, she knew it wasn't just her own. She was experiencing the spirit's emotions. Alyn gave into their combined grief and wept.

A swirl of confusing images passed so quickly, Alyn could make no sense of them. When they slowed, she was looking at a familiar sight. It was her and Minna on the ship that brought them to *Helala* after Alyn escaped the Inquisition. A rush of pride and love overwhelmed her. She sat up, wrapping her arms around herself. She knew who this spirit was.

The vision faded, and for a moment, she was alone with the glittering spirit. She kept herself closed, afraid to reach out and find out she was wrong, that it wasn't who she thought it was. Another vision appeared. It played out in a series of scenes involving people she never met at places she never visited. The one constant was her sister, Minna. It was what they wanted to know, what she wanted her spirit guide to show her. It was the future Ragan foresaw. But even as it played out, she sensed from the spirit the tenuousness of the *shehdi'enun* that bound the moments together. Something had gone wrong. One of the threads which tied the tapestry together had frayed.

After the visions faded, she was alone with the spirit. They regarded one another quietly, Alyn spent, wrung out by their combined emotions. *You waited until I was ready to see that.* The spirit bobbed. *You're leaving, now.* Another bob. *Can't you stay until it's all over, when we've won? Just in case?* A sideways slide and back again. Alyn didn't know what that meant. Wanting to bathe in the spirit's loving glow for as long as she could, she sat quietly. The spirit didn't move, but Alyn felt another wave of love so overpowering, she gasped again. She opened herself fully to the spirit and gave in to an emotion so powerful, she felt she would lose herself. Then it faded, leaving her feeling vaguely empty. *I love you, too, Mother.* And then the spirit was gone. Alyn was alone.

The wave of emotions ebbed, washing away months of uncertainty and worry. Her mother did have a plan, and Alyn had seen Minna's part in it. Someone sat beside her, draped an arm across her shoulders and supported her when she sagged. Beadu and Deirdre were waiting for her to explain what happened, but she needed a moment alone in her center with the comfort of her own spirit.

Her spirit guide appeared and drifted slowly. *It was you. In my mother's center, when I was born.* A loop. *You and my spirit.* Another loop. *Have you followed me all my life?* Alyn saw two girls chasing a man in the yard in front of a small house. It had the veiled quality of the vision her spirit guide showed her of her working at her desk. This was a vision of something the spirit saw from *annen'heim* long ago. The two girls were Minna and her, of course, and the man was their father. She glimpsed her mother sitting on the bench on their porch, laughing at their antics. It was Vada, the woman who raised her, not Ragan. This was from a time before Minna changed. A happy time. The vision faded, leaving her alone with the *sjel'and.* The little spirit watched her her entire life. *What were you doing while I slept?* Laughter.

Alyn opened her eyes to the women's worried expressions. She leaned into Deirdre. After a moment, she said, "I need to send a message to Minna."

Chapter 36

The 34th Day of the Month of Ungemon

Alyn

"You met your mother's spirit?" Deirdre asked.

Reading the longing Deirdre was trying to hide, Alyn said gently, "Yes."

"And she was… what, like a *sjel'and?*"

Alyn heard the horror behind the question and understood it. The *sjel'and* carried the sins of the people they were into *annen'heim.* While Alyn was repeatedly enduring the swarm, part of what kept her awake at night was wondering what sins Ragan must have accumulated as she twisted people's lives to her vision of the future. Beadu told her and Minna that she hoped the gods called Ragan's spirit to *gud'heim,* the realm of the gods. Until today, that sounded like wishful thinking to Alyn. She assumed, as Ragan's dearest friend, Beadu just didn't want to think of Ragan's spirit suffering the torment of *annen'heim.*

"No," Alyn said. "She wasn't a *sjel'and.* More like a *lan'and,* but that wasn't it either. I don't know what she was."

"A *gud'and,*" Beadu said matter-of-factly. "As I told you and your sister. She is a god spirit. Your mother sensed the presence of the gods in *annen'heim,* though none ever made themselves known to her so clearly."

Beadu smiled at Alyn. "You have been granted a rare gift, Alyn. You have been shown the mind of the gods."

They sat in silence for a time, then Deirdre asked, "What did she say to you?"

"She showed me her plan. At least, the part for Minna." Deirdre's frown surprised her, but her next question revealed her thoughts.

"Do you… do you think she will… return and speak to you again?"

Alyn shook her head. "I don't think so." When she saw Deirdre trying to hide her disappointment, she added, "I'm sorry."

A sad smile replaced Deirdre's frown. "No matter. I'm just happy Ragan will not have to suffer *annen'heim* for eternities." Her smile widened. "And it is very heartening to know that she did have the support of the gods. That is a hopeful sign."

"Just so," Beadu said. "It is indeed. Now we must decide what message to send to Minna."

"What message did Ragan ask you to send?" Deirdre asked Alyn.

"My mother told me Minna stepped out of the proper current. She didn't say exactly what happened, but…" She lifted a hand, palm out, and made a pushing motion. "…she wants us to *nudge* her onto the right path."

"Proper current?" Dierdre asked.

"Yes," Alyn said, suppressing her impatience. "You read her journal. You must have read the part she talked about this." Scrunching up her face and peering up at the sky, she said, "The river of time finds its path, and some courses are more likely than others, some currents irresistible."

"How can that be? How could some series of events be set in stone and others aren't? Especially when it relies on people's choices." Addressing Beadu, Deirdre said, "I thought you said the *shehdi'enun* of people was especially volatile. It's impossible to predict what people do."

"That is true, but I think Ragan is putting much stock in the character of the people involved."

"Right!" Alyn said. "She knows what choices Minna will make, no matter what others do or say."

"Why?" Deirdre asked.

"Minna has a forthrightness…" Beadu said. She squinted up at the sky, then started again. "She has a certain willfulness…" She stopped again and stared at Alyn.

"You're trying to say she's honest to a fault and stubborn as a mule," Alyn said.

"Just so," Beadu said with a chuckle.

"She also has a strong sense of justice," Deirdre said, nodding. "I haven't known her that long, but you can tell someone instilled a deep sense of morality in her." She hesitated and looked at Alyn. "In both of you."

Alyn dropped her eyes, feeling suddenly warm.

"Okay," Deirdre said. "Say I get the *proper current* idea. Why didn't Ragan just tell someone what she intended? If she did, we wouldn't have to rely on this…" She waved a hand. Before Alyn could answer, she added, "I mean, if the current is irresistible, why not just tell everyone what to do?"

"It's not like it's set in stone," Alyn said. "It's just that events resist being changed from the proper course for certain people. Ragan tried to put the right people on the proper paths. She believed they would end up where they needed to be." She shrugged. "But the future is never set. Things can always change, and something has happened to distract Minna."

"She didn't tell anyone what she intended because that would change their *shehdi'enun* and change the future in unpredictable ways," Beadu said.

"This is where it gets fuzzy for me," Deirdre said.

"No, Beadu's right!" Alyn said, tapping her knee with a fist. "See, if you think you know what the right thing to do is because someone tells you they know the future, you stop making your own choices. BUT, the future Ragan saw depended on our choices, the ones we make for our own purposes."

They sat silently for a bit, until Deirdre said, "I'm lost."

Alyn rested her elbows on her knees, tapping her palms together. She caught herself biting her lip, pictured Minna doing the same, but ignored it. "Okay," she said. "Let's say Ragan had a vision of you visiting your friend when their barn caught fire. You were there, so you helped rescue all the animals." She sat up and waited until Deirdre nodded. "So, she tells you this and you decide to go straight to your friend's house." She held up a finger. "*But* before, in the future Ragan saw, you took a different, more indirect route, because you liked the scenery or something. Now, because you know you have to be there, you go straight there." She thrust her hand out. "Straight through the village. On the way, you get run over by a wagon full of turnips." She smacked her hands together. "So, you never make it, and all the animals burn up in the barn."

Alyn and Deirdre stared at one another, until Deirdre asked, "Couldn't she just tell you to take the scenic path?"

"Well, sure," Alyn said. "But maybe the scenic route is along the top of a cliff and, because you're hurrying, you fall and die." When Deirdre started to speak, Alyn waved her hands. "This is a simple example. The point is there *might* be another future in which you save the animals, but it *wouldn't* be the one Ragan saw. It would be a different one, *because* in the future she saw, she didn't tell you anything." She paused, then spoke deliberately. "This future Ragan saw, the one everyone wants to know… It's the *only* one where the *Alle'oss* win the war and transform the Empire." She held up a finger. "And in this *one* future, Ragan *doesn't* tell anyone what to do. If she did, it would no longer be the future she saw."

Deirdre stared at Alyn for a moment, then the furrows on her brow smoothed. "I get that," she said. "But you have to tell Minna… something to nudge her into the proper current. It's okay to do that? "

Alyn shrugged helplessly. "Ragan thinks so," she said.

"You said she showed you the entire path. Why, if you can't tell Minna anything else?"

"We have to trust she has her reasons that will become clear in time," Beadu said. "We have put great trust in Ragan. Now is not the time to question her."

"If we don't get Minna where she needs to be, everything falls apart." Alyn paused, letting that sink in, then she said, "Then we're on our own."

"What message do we send?" Deirdre asked. She glanced up to the empty branch where the raven often perched. "And how do we send it?"

Chapter 37

The 2nd Day of the Month of Heulomon

Minna

Though Minna ran from Sigurn, she heard his message. She knew what was at stake and how many people were counting on her. Later that day, she roused herself and took up her mother's invitation. To her relief, her mother was true to her word. Her parents allowed her to sit quietly and listen as they chatted and exchanged camp gossip. There was a comforting familiarity to it. Slowly, the walls she hid her pain behind crumbled and she wept. Her parents didn't press her to talk about her pain or cajole her into being happy. Minna lay her head on her mother's shoulder and let her tears and her parents' quiet acceptance soothe the raw wound Ulf's disappearance inflicted.

That night in her hut, she allowed Linea into her center and let her spirit guide show her memories of home, hearth, and happier times. For the first time in days, she slept soundly. The next day, she ventured out for a time and allowed people to see her smiling and confident around camp. When she returned to her parents' fire that night, she ate a bit and even asked her father about his hunting trips. She knew she had a long, rough path ahead of her, but she was functional again. And just in time.

•   •   •

Slouching on the bench on the headquarters porch, arms crossed, Minna watched *Alle'oss* soldiers filing past. Spirits high, they joked and waved to her as they passed. When Agmar saw her, he waved a massive hand, pointed at her, then pounded another man on the back so hard, he nearly threw him to the ground. These men and women were the last of the soldiers going to meet the Union mercenaries. They were excited about applying their new skills with the long spears they carried. Eager to strike a blow against the enemy. Their high spirits wouldn't last once the killing started.

"You're going to drive yourself crazy, thinking about it."

Startled, Minna looked up to find Gyda, one of Sigurn's *Oss'stera* comrades, looking down at her. Taller than Sigurn, Gyda wore her blond hair in the style most of the younger members of *Oss'stera* did; the right side of their head shaved to fuzz. She had always been nice to Minna. Until recently. Minna scowled and resumed watching the soldiers filing past. "How do you know what I'm thinking?"

Gyda sat on the bench, forcing Minna to sit up and slide over to make room. She leaned her bow on the seat between them, then lifted a hand, thumb extended. "It's either the three witches coming to kill you." She extended the index finger. "Your mother's mysterious plan." Another finger. "Tove and Alar." She dropped her hand, met Minna's eyes and said, "Or it's Ulf."

Minna slouched back, crossing her arms again, and returned her attention to the soldiers. "You don't think any of that is worth worrying about?"

"Oh yeah, I worry," the woman said. She gestured to the last of the long line of soldiers. "We're all worried." Gathering her bow, she stood and said, "Especially when our big hero is moping around like she thinks we've already lost."

Minna hitched a brow, preparing a withering retort, when she noticed the bow. It was longer than any bow she ever saw, including her father's. The limbs were wide and as thick as her thumb. "What kind of bow is that?"

Caught off guard, Gyda glanced at the weapon. "Longbow."

"Not like any longbow I've ever seen."

Understanding animating her face, Gyda retrieved a bowstring from a small pouch attached to her belt. With great ceremony, she let the string unroll, slipped the loop on one end over the nock, then flipped the bow so she could attach it to the other end. The thick limbs made the bow so stiff, she had to put all her weight on it to bend it. When she was done, she plucked the string and offered it to Minna.

Minna stood and took the bow. It was a good foot taller than she was and the draw was so hard, she could barely deflect the string. "How do you shoot this?" she asked, easing off the tension.

With an expression like a proud mother, Gyda took the bow, stepped off the porch and held it up at arm's length. "You have to use your back and hip." She took the string with her other hand, leaned slightly forward, then twisted her body and pulled the string to her chin. When she released the tension slowly, she smiled at Minna. "Not everyone can do it."

For the first time, Minna appreciated how powerfully built Gyda was, with broad shoulders and bulging arms.

"It's our secret weapon," Gyda said as she unstrung the bow. "The Imps use short bows and crossbows. They don't have nearly the range or punch, and they haven't seen these yet. They're in for a surprise."

"What about the Union?"

"Lief says they use short bows. Least they did the last time he tangled with them. He's got a plan. They won't stand a chance, don't worry." She finished rolling the string and tucked it into her pouch. "As long as we don't have to worry about *witches* spoiling the party," she said with a pointed look, then she stepped onto the porch and rested her hand on the latch. "You coming?"

Minna watched her enter the building, then said to Linea, "I think I've just been chastised."

Linea bobbed.

Before Minna could respond, Sigurn brushed past her, paused in the open door and asked, "You coming?"

Minna watched Linea follow him, then entered and closed the door. The first thing she noticed was a familiar raven hopping among the rafters and muttering to itself. "It's back!" she said.

Aron and Zaina looked up. "We've been waiting for you," Aron said.

Minna caught Gyda's arched brow before she bent over to study the map. It wasn't like Minna didn't know her recent funk was on everyone's lips. She noticed them tiptoeing around her, was annoyed by it, though not enough to rouse herself until now. They knew about Ulf and wanted to give her space, but apparently, with the battle approaching, their patience was wearing thin.

Turning away from their unvoiced accusations, Minna looked up at the bird and opened herself to the spirit, which allowed her to speak to it. Instantly, her mind filled with the presences of many animals. Sinking into her center and focusing on the raven, she found him returning her attention. She crossed to the corner of the building where the raven perched.

"You've seen Beadu," she murmured. An image came into her mind, but it wasn't only Beadu. The *saa'myn* was joined by Deirdre and her sister. "Alyn!"

"It was with your sister?" Zaina asked.

Minna glanced over her shoulder at the group gathering behind her.

"Ask it about the mercenaries," Aron said.

Minna returned her attention to the raven. *Do you know Alyn?* An image of Minna looking up in this room came into her mind. It was the raven's memory of the first time she talked to it. *That's right, she's my sister.* An image of Alyn returned, but this time, her expression was of astonishment and Minna heard her say, "Minna!"

Minna's mouth dropped open. She didn't hear other sounds in the raven's memory. Maybe she heard only what the bird thought was important. And her sister said her name while she was looking at the raven. What did that mean? Minna turned around suddenly and pushed through the crowd. "The message," she said. "What did it say?"

Zaina returned to the table and handed her a slip of paper. Though Minna only saw Alyn's handwriting a few times while they were in *Helala* together, she recognized it. Her sister wrote the message.

Ravens can't tell us where the mercenaries are. Ask him to show you his memories of the mercenaries and look for recognizable landmarks. Minna, I found my and'reoime!

Holding the slip of paper in both hands, Minna rubbed her thumbs along the text, before setting it on the table and staring into space. Alyn had only eleven summers, but she found her spirit guide. And Minna wasn't there to share her joy.

"Minna," Aron said, startling her out of her thoughts. He picked up the message and said, "They said to ask it to show you the mercenaries."

Minna focused on his face, noticing how haggard he appeared. How had she not noticed that before? "Right," she said. Returning to the corner, she looked up at the bird and murmured, "Have you seen the Union mercenaries?" Someone, probably Beadu, must have gotten across to the raven what she meant when she thought of the mercenaries. In the vision, she was looking down at a long column of men making their way through rugged terrain. The view shifted constantly as the raven's attention shifted, but there was no doubt these were the men Zaina described to her. They were enormous, wider and taller than Agmar, and though they didn't wear it, she saw bundles of the colorful leather armor strapped to their backs. "Yes," she said. "I see them."

"Where are they?" Zaina asked. "Do you see anything you recognize?"

"No," Minna said. "It's rugged, but the mountains are lower than central Argen. Pine trees, maples." She ignored Aron's mumbled disappointment. The raven passed the front of the column and the view changed as the raven looked toward where it was headed. "Wait," Minna said. "They're climbing a pass between two mountains." She heard shuffles as everyone gathered around the map, but the raven's memories continued to spool in her mind. He rose toward the top of the pass, the scene rising and falling with the beat of the bird's wings, until it was flying between the peaks on either side. She glimpsed people below her, then the raven descended to perch on a boulder beside the trail. When it turned around, three women came into view.

Minna's breath caught. Though she never saw them before, she knew who they were. Aife didn't shave the sides of her head, and these women didn't have the black stains around their eyes, but there was no doubt they were Hoerst's witches. A woman with mahogany skin smiled and approached the raven, reaching into a pouch at her belt and producing a bit of dried meat. Minna felt the raven's anticipation.

"Aren't you a pretty one?" the woman murmured. She held up the meat, but when the raven moved to pluck it from her fingers, she drew it back. "You're looking for us," she said. She gazed at the raven for a moment, then she bent toward the bird and said, "Minna Hunter."

Another woman with blond hair appeared at her shoulder. "It's seen the witch who killed Aife?" she asked.

The first woman nodded. "She's looking for us." She lifted a hand and waggled her fingers, a gesture Minna was sure was meant for her, then she held out the morsel as the vision faded.

Minna let the spirit return to its realm, cutting off her connection to the bird. She and the raven regarded one another for a few more moments, then she said, "I don't have anything for you." Returning to the table, she forced herself to focus on the conversation.

Aron tapped the map. "It had to be here," he said. "They're moving much faster than they were when they set out. The question is, how long ago did the raven see them?"

"Hasn't Keelia been telling you where they are?" Minna asked. If she didn't already know how frustrated they were with her, the embarrassed glances they gave one another made it obvious.

"The scouts Keelia sent only have one raven trained to return to Keelia," Zaina said, not taking her eyes off the map. "There are no ravens that go the other way, so they have to rely on riders most of the time."

It was obviously something everyone already knew. Only Sigurn gave her a smile.

"There's too much delay between when the scouts report to Keelia and it's relayed to us," he said to her, "so we're not sure exactly where they are." He let a familiar smirk slide onto his face. "Timing is everything."

Sigurn gave her space after their argument, and he harbored no lingering animosity. A grateful smile appeared unbidden on her face, surprising her and watering her eyes.

He let his eyes linger on hers for a moment, the small secret smile he gave her before on his face, then he looked down at the map. He traced a line from the pass where the raven saw the mercenaries to the Cut. "Assuming it saw the mercenaries while returning from *Helala*, and it came straight here… it saw them a day ago, maybe two."

The room grew quiet until Zaina said, "We have a week at the most, maybe five days."

"Right," Aron said. He looked at Gyda, who was representing Lief.

"We'll be ready," Gyda said.

"What about the witches?" Aron asked.

The quiet room grew even more still. Even the raven was silent for once. Suddenly the center of everyone's attention, Minna saw worry and doubt. "I saw them," she said.

"The witches? You did?" Sigurn asked. "With the mercenaries?"

Minna shook her head. "They were already at the top of the pass." She caught the look Sigurn threw Gyda, but couldn't guess what it meant.

"Right," Aron said. "Are you…" He stopped, let his head drop before looking at Zaina.

"Ready?" Minna asked.

"Yes," Aron said. "This is entirely on you. We'll do what we can to help, but we have no hope without you."

"I'm ready." It was a lie, but she saw relief in their expressions.

Without hesitation, Aron said, "Good. Gyda, you better get going. You can take Minna with you."

"I… uh… we'll take Minna," Sigurn said. When Aron started to object, Sigurn said, "We," he gestured to himself, then Gyda, "have some ideas that might give Minna an edge."

Aron hesitated. "Okay, that's… good. You're leaving right away?"

"Of course," Sigurn said.

Aron rested his hands on the map table and gazed around at everyone. "We're as prepared as we can be for this. You all know what's at stake." He started to say more, dropped his head for a moment and swallowed, then he straightened, clasped his hands behind his back, and said, "*Andsutra.*"

A chorus of subdued responses answered him. As the others filed out, Sigurn and Gyda approached Minna. "You have ideas?" she asked.

"Come on," Sigurn said. "We'll tell you what we're thinking."

•   •   •

Eight people waited for them in the *Oss'stera* camp, sitting quietly around the cold firepit. Minna knew them all, had laughed with them, swapped tales with them and considered them friends. But they greeted her with solemn nods now. She took a seat between Gyda and Sigurn and waited expectantly.

"The raven showed you the witches?" he asked.

Minna glanced around at everyone hanging on her answer. "Yes."

"And there were three of them?"

"Yes."

He looked past Minna to Gyda, then he asked Minna, "Can you win? Against three of them?"

Minna almost lied and told him yes, but these were the people who befriended her when she needed them. She couldn't lie. "Maybe, I don't know." She was relieved she didn't see disappointment in Sigurn's expression. "If they're like Aife…" She waggled her head.

"And you said they were ahead of the mercenaries?" Gyda asked.

"Yes, a couple of hours."

Sigurn reached into a shirt pocket and withdrew a roll of paper, which he placed on the ground and unrolled. It was a copy of the map in the headquarters, but only the part around the expected battlefield. After the others gathered around, Sigurn pointed and said, "This is the pass you saw." Minna nodded. He traced his finger to the spot where the Imperial Highway bent around the eastern end of the Kalana valley. "This is where we laid our trap for the mercenaries," he said, "but they don't know that."

"They know we're watching them," Minna said.

Sigurn gave her a blank look.

"The witches do," Minna said. "One of them said my name."

"What do you mean?" Gyda asked.

"When I saw them in the raven's memory, one of the witches said my name. I think she saw me in its memory. She also asked if the raven was looking for them."

In the silence, a squirrel barked its outrage at some threat. "It changes nothing," Sigurn said finally. "The plan is the same. Even if they know we know they're coming, they won't expect this." He pointed to a spot on the map between the pass and the battlefield. "We'll have to move fast to get there in time, but we want to ambush the witches here."

"Ambush?"

"Yeah, an ambush is when —"

"I know what an ambush is!" Minna said, sharply. "I meant…" she looked around at the small gathering. "All of you?"

They all nodded and Sigurn said, "Of course. All of us but Gyda. She'll be with the army."

"But…" Minna said.

"But what?" a woman asked.

"What were you planning to do?" Sigurn asked. "Were you going to go out and meet them by yourself?"

That was exactly what she was planning. Not that she had an actual plan. But there would be no way for her to defend herself and protect others from all three of the witches amid the chaos of a battle.

Before she could respond, Sigurn said, "Listen, if we can catch them unaware. Get shots off before they can defend themselves, we might even the odds for you. If we get lucky, maybe we take out all three before the fight starts. Even if we don't, while they're busy with you, we'll be on their flanks."

"And if you miss or if they catch wind of the ambush?" Minna asked. "I won't be able to protect all of you." When Sigurn protested, Minna spoke over him. "If I have to protect you, I won't…" She waved a hand and said, "It will be easier if I don't have to worry about anyone else." She was surprised when this elicited some chuckles.

"This isn't just your fight," Sigurn said. "We may not be able to toss around fire and lightning, but we've been in this fight for a long time. We know what we're getting into."

It was true, *Oss'stera* had been fighting the empire longer than Minna, though she doubted they really knew what they were volunteering for. But before she could protest, she took in their determined faces. Some of them wore the evidence of a lifetime resisting imperial violence on the outside. All of them bore scars that were not visible, scars earned through trauma and loss. The tough, twisted growth on one's soul left behind when one took another life. It was why they accepted her as an equal when others lifted her onto a pedestal. It was why this was the only place she felt comfortable. They shared the same scars.

She felt a knot she hadn't noticed before, loosening in her chest. Swallowing against tears welling in her eyes, she looked up as Linea appeared, followed by a swarm of *lan'and*. They poured into the clearing, swirling and illuminating the surrounding forest in glittering spirit light. Minna smiled, stood and lifted her hand to allow Linea to hover above her palm. "*Tok*," she whispered. "You knew I was ready to wake up, didn't you?" Linea bobbed once and rejoined the joyous cloud. Minna watched her go, closed her eyes and took a breath, then gazed around at the others who waited patiently. They had grown accustomed to her conversing with her spirit guide. "What are we waiting for? Let's go," she said.

Part III

The Storm

Our mother's plan was never so tenuous as when the storm broke. The sacrifices our people made to give Minna a chance to follow her clues will never be forgotten.

From Alyn Hunter's commentary on The Book of the Witch by Ragan Hunter

Chapter 38

The 2nd Day of the Month of Heulomon

Flynn

The small sloop that carried Flynn from Ulm to Lubern arrived a day early on steady winds, so she took the opportunity to spend a night in one of her favorite taverns. An appreciative audience kept her on stage spinning tales until the wee hours. She considered telling the new story, the one about the *Alle'oss* witch, but she didn't feel confident with it yet. The next morning, she caught the barge that brought her up the Odun river to Hast. Even with the late night, pleasant weather and comfortable bunks had done wonders. She felt more rested than she had in years.

She waved to the captain of the barge, then stepped onto the busy quay of the Imperial port. As she set off toward the Ninth Legion's camp, the first thing that struck her was the lack of traffic on the highway which bisected the city. Normally, there was a constant stream passing through Hast to and from Argren. Where was the Empire finding coal to fuel its forges?

She stepped onto the bridge that spanned the river, noting how quiet the *Alle'oss* sector, north of the highway, was. With the war against Argren heating up, the *Alle'oss* in Hast had either fled, were lying low, or the Empire was keeping a clamp on them.

She found the Ninth's camp abuzz, men laughing and joking boisterously, strapping on armor. It was a familiar sight; the nervous bravado of soldiers before a battle. The Ninth was apparently done sitting on the outskirts of Argren. She fought alongside some of these men. When they recognized her, they waved and shouted her name. Word spread ahead of her and she walked the last few paces to Prather's tent between rows of cheering men. Buoyed by their admiration, she picked up her pace, smiled and returned their waves. But there was something unsettling about the relief she saw in their expressions.

General Prather's headquarters pavilion was just as busy as the rest of the camp, though there was a marked difference in mood. None of these men would find themselves in harm's way today. She entered the tent, letting the flap drop, muffling the tramp of men heading east toward Argren.

A prim young man approached her. "You must be Nara," he said, trying and failing to hide his indignation at her rumpled appearance

Looking him up and down, she couldn't help smirking at the man's spit and polish and the gold embellishments on his uniform. Prather's influence, no doubt. The general had a mania about that sort of thing.

"*Sister* Flynn," she said. "And you are?"

He blinked, looked as if he would ask her a question, then decided against it. "I am General Prather's adjutant," he said.

"Ah, good. Perhaps you can tell me why the Ninth, one of the emperor's more powerful legions, needs my help ravaging Argren, instead of allowing me to protect the Empire from the Kaileuk."

The adjutant's eyes widened, but instead of answering her directly, he said, "Well, I'm sure the general will explain your assignment."

"I'm sure," Flynn said. She followed the man, weaving among the staff officers about the complex business of organizing an army on the move.

"General," the adjutant said to Prather. The general, a tall, thin man, with short graying hair and a precisely shaped goatee, turned away from berating two junior officers and snapped, "What is it?"

"Sister Flynn, general."

Flynn ignored the general, stepped up to the map table and studied the disposition of the Imperial units. She nodded a greeting to four Seidi sisters, who eyed her from the other side of the table. All of them were Briana's good girls of middling talent. When the tent grew quiet, she looked up from the map and glanced around. Everyone was watching her. Turning to the general, she said, "Oh, right. General Prather. It's been a long time. I have to say, I'm surprised to be here, you know, after the last time."

Prather's mouth worked as if he were chewing a particularly bitter herb. "I can assure you, it was not my choice."

"Well," Flynn said. "That makes more sense."

"The Malleus insisted."

"Hoerst?"

You would have thought from the man's expression, Flynn slapped him. He cleared his throat. "The *Malleus* felt some insurance was necessary."

Flynn glanced at the four sisters and couldn't help smirking at their sour expressions. "Insurance?" she asked. When he just stared down his nose at her, she added, "Sir."

"There is an… *Alle'oss* witch with some talent —"

"Minna Hunter?" Flynn asked in surprise. Was there some truth to the story?

The general looked surprised. "Yes, quite." He paused and looked her up and down. "In any case, that is why you're here."

Flynn heard a sniff from one of the sisters and didn't bother to suppress her grin. *That's gotta sting.* "Yes, sir. Just point me at her," she said crisply and snapped a salute.

The general paused, looking as if he wasn't sure whether she was mocking him, then he bent over the map and pointed to a spot where the highway crossed the escapement. "The *l'oss* erected a stockade across the entrance of the Cut. We could take it by storm, at a cost. But we've decided to use a tortoise to burn it to the ground. He gestured to the four sisters. "Your sisters will go forward with the tortoise to ensure it reaches the wall unmolested. Once the wall has been eliminated, the infantry will go forward. You will accompany them, offer your…” He clenched his teeth. “Gifts to provide support. If the witch appears, you will remove the threat.”

“Excellent plan, General,” Flynn said. “I’ll just step outside. I need to freshen up after my trip.” Before the storm gathering in his expression could break, she said, “Don’t worry, I’ll be ready.” Ignoring his affronted utterances, she stepped from the gloom into the bright sunshine. One perk of being one of the most powerful women in the Empire was she didn’t have to suffer fools. Not too much, anyway.

Absently returning the waves of the soldiers marching past, she considered the implications of what she heard. Despite her low opinion of his competence, she couldn’t imagine Prather didn’t probe the *Alle’oss* defenses. He knew what he was up against. If Hoerst felt it necessary to bring her here, it meant it was likely Minna was a real person. Flynn didn’t believe everything in the story she heard in Ulm. She knew better than most how events were embellished in the retelling. But she was isolated for the past two years in the south. Who knew? Not that she was worried about meeting this witch. She would deal with it when the time came.

Deciding it would be a while before the show started, she followed her nose toward the kitchen. As she walked, Marshal Storm’s words popped, unbidden and unwelcome, into her mind, as they had since he uttered them. At first, she tried to give him the benefit of the doubt. He wasn’t explicit, so maybe she misunderstood. But the more she thought about it, the more she was forced to conclude her initial reaction was correct; it was treason. He was talking about overthrowing the Empire’s power structures. But what would that mean? The Inquisition, the Seidi, the emperor, would all have to be swept away or supplanted. Who would be left to impose order? The army could, but who would keep the Kaileuk at bay? It was a crazy notion, entirely out of step with her image of the brilliant but stolid marshal.

Even if it were possible, there was the personal cost she would pay. As the only daughter of a wealthy Volloch family and one of the most powerful Seidi sisters in the Empire, she led a charmed life. At least, until they sent her to fight the Kaileuk. And though she wasn't as carefree as she appeared, wealth, power and a naturally buoyant disposition allowed her to float above most of life's obstacles. She sat at the pinnacle of the Empire's elite. She and her family stood to lose everything if the Empire fell.

Still, she hadn't been able to stop ruminating on it. And as she watched the might of the Ninth Legion marching past, she finally understood why. She held on to her idealistic fantasies of what a sister of the Seidi was while she fought the Kaileuk. After all, she was protecting the Empire from barbarians. But who was she protecting from the *Alle'oss*?

Arriving at the kitchen, she decided she was no longer hungry. Instead, she lifted her gaze to the sheer cliffs of the escarpment in the distance, remembering the times she traveled to Argren. It was a beautiful country, its people warm and generous, if a bit rustic. She wasn't alive when the Empire wiped Ferol and Andia from the map, but she heard the stories. As a novice, she'd seen, firsthand, the devastation in Styria. Even if the story she heard in Ulm was true, the *Alle'oss* would need more than a single witch to avoid the same fate.

As she often did when she faced difficult choices, she thought of her father's words on the day he bade her farewell; remember the stories and always do what is right. "I will, Father," she whispered. The trick was knowing what was right.

Keelia

"Bad news?" Bjorn asked. Keelia's second in command handed the raven to Siv and leaned in, trying to get a glimpse of the message.

Keelia handed him the slip of paper and gazed out over the camp. "Unexpected, is all."

"The Union mercenaries are arriving sooner than expected," Bjorn said and handed the message to Siv, whose hands were already full with the raven. "Do we have time to get there?"

"Just enough if we hump it," Keelia said. It was her plan. They would wait until the Union mercenaries engaged the *Alle'oss* army, then strike their rear. If they weren't there, the *Alle'oss* would be forced to engage with the mercenaries in brutal hand-to-hand combat alone. Keelia knew, firsthand, the savagery the mercenaries were capable of. The emperor employed a handful in the war against the Kaileuk. It was a battle the inexperienced *Alle'oss* weren't likely to win. "We move out in an hour. Get everyone organized." She was ducking into her tent when someone called her name from the far side of the camp. She turned, her heart thumping at the panicked tone. A man was sprinting up the hill toward them. She didn't need to see his stricken expression to know something was wrong. The fact he wasn't carrying his bow was enough.

He slid to a stop, scattering debris, jostling Siv and sending the raven into the low branches of a nearby tree. "Sir, the Imps are attacking," he said breathlessly.

"What do you mean, attacking?" Bjorn asked before Keelia could respond.

The man glanced at Bjorn, but spoke to Keelia. "We were patrolling the frontier when a whole bunch of Imps appeared. We… we ran… scattered, but Linton and Greta got —"

"Soldier!" Keelia snapped. "Pull yourself together."

He snapped to attention, his head bobbing.

"Where did you see them? Exactly?"

"Four leagues west and a league south from here, sir."

"Which direction were they heading?"

"This way," the man said.

"How many, and don't say a whole bunch."

His eyes squeezed shut, his lips moving. When he opened his eyes, he said, "Two, three hundred, at least."

"Sound the alarm," Keelia said to Bjorn. "We've drilled for this. Get everyone moving and send out scouts. We need to know where they are."

Bjorn took off at a run. "Tell Jason I want him," Keelia said to Siv. When she took off, Keelia said to the messenger. "Good job, son. Go get yourself a bow. We're going to need everyone." She ducked into her tent and donned her brigandine. It was the only armor she wore and was a concession to Jason. She never wore armor when she fought for the

Empire. She only agreed because the sleeveless vest left her arms free and the small iron plates weren't too heavy.

When she emerged, the camp looked like a kicked fire ant nest. Men and women climbed the ridge to the west of the camp, already coalescing into their squads. Jason met her as she descended the hill. "You heard?" she asked.

"Yeah," Jason said, falling in beside her. "You think this is revenge?"

"Maybe," Keelia said. She flagged Siv down and said, "Get that raven. Send Aron a message and tell him we're going to be late."

"Yes, sir," she said and sprinted up the hill.

"Could be revenge," Keelia said. "Or something bigger." She looked up at the spirits, who seemed oblivious to the unfolding drama below them. Letting her center open, she reached out and hesitated. A lone *lan'and* broke away from the others, spiraled down and orbited around her and Jason. Keelia turned, trying to keep it in view.

"Keelia, what's…" Jason said. "Are you okay?"

"It can't be," she whispered. Ignoring Jason and forgetting the surrounding chaos, she closed her eyes and threw her center open.

"Whoa," she heard Jason say.

The *lan'and* burst into her center. She never had a single *lan'and* in her center before. It was always a swarm, overpowering in their ecstatic celebration. Like the choral in the Great Cathedral, their songs blended in such perfect harmony, it was hard to distinguish individuals. This little spirit's song was no less joyful, but she heard its voice and it called out to her. Her spirit responded, a delicate counterpoint that sent shivers through Keelia's body.

"Keelia?" Jason asked. "What's going on? We need you here."

Moisture forced its way through her eyelids and beaded in her lashes. No sister ever had a spirit guide, not in living memory. But she was no longer a sister, and more importantly, she was *Alle'oss*. She opened her eyes, turned to find Jason's worried face, and giggled like a younger, more innocent version of herself. Jason stepped back, alarm replacing his worry. Keelia grasped his broad shoulders, gave him a shake, and laughed the full-throated laughter of a woman accustomed to throwing fate's dice.

"Let's go teach the Imps a lesson they'll remember," she said. She laughed at Jason's wide-eyed shock, turned and strode through the camp, calling more *lan'and* to join her spirit guide.

Ulf

"What do you think?" Ulf asked Hakon. They stood on the path that ran along the southern rim of the Kalana Valley, where it narrowed to squeeze between the valley and the low mountain called *Shonum Chonum*.

The man's lips pursed as he studied the terrain. "Good place for an ambush," he said, the slight rise in his tone indicating he was gauging Ulf's reaction. When Ulf didn't respond, he pointed to the wooded slopes of the mountain on their right. "Someone could hide up there." He gestured to the narrow path that squeezed between the mountain and the valley rim. "Catch us there and we have no place to hide. There's no place to retreat to and it would be hard to counterattack up the slope."

Ulf nodded. The rest of the misfits gathered around to listen. "So, what should we do?"

"Scout the slopes?" Inger suggested. "Make sure they're clear, maybe find another way, so's we don't have to follow this one."

Ulf grinned at her and gestured up the slope. Hakon and Inger took off.

"This could take hours," Helga said. "And the path is right there."

"There's a path about a hundred paces up," Ulf said. "My brothers used to hunt this area," he added when Mikaela raised a brow.

"Where'd you learn all that stuff?" Mikaela asked. "About ambushes and stuff."

"You didn't listen to Raif's lectures when we were training?" Ulf asked.

"Yeah, I listened," Mikaela said. She gestured to the path. "He never talked about this."

Ulf stared at the path. She was right. Raif never talked about this specific situation. "He talked about avoiding being caught out in the open, especially where the enemy could be hiding nearby." He shrugged and added, "This seems like that situation."

She wrapped her hand around his upper arm, squeezed, and gave him a shake. "You got a good head for this. Pretty soon…" She trailed off as Inger came sliding down the slope. The woman, who was so quiet when she appeared, battered and beaten, out of the forest on the valley floor, flourished over the past weeks with the support of their tight-knit group.

As she neared the bottom of the slope, her feet slipped out from beneath her and slid the last few paces on her bottom. Taking Ulf's hand, she stood, wiped the dust off, and said breathlessly, "There's a path." She pointed. "About a hundred paces up. Winds around the mountain. The ground above it is too steep for anyone to hide."

"Good job," Ulf said. "All right, misfits, let's move out."

Inger took off, followed by the rest of the misfits.

"That looks steep," Helga said. "It's hot today," she added as she mounted the slope.

Ulf winked at Mikaela and followed.

Alyn

Thanks to Ragan's spirit, Alyn knew what message to send Minna. The problem was they had no way to send it. The raven had not returned from the Cut yet. So, to distract herself from watching the skies, Alyn and her spirit guide explored the future. Or the near future anyway. He could only reliably see a few days into the future.

She sat cross-legged on the bed in her small room, the little spirit swooping around her center. Seeing him like this, it was hard to remember her initial reaction to him. Sure, he was a bit scruffy compared to the glittering *lan'and*, but he was lovable and had shown a sense of humor Alyn found appealing.

You ready? The spirit swooped and slowed.

In the vision, Alyn soared over *Alle'oss* soldiers at one end of a long, narrow field. They carried spears or bows and were deploying into a long line across one end of the field. It looked like they were readying for a battle, but this wasn't the Cut. Looking for a recognizable landmark, she noticed the Kalana Valley opening out toward the western horizon on her right. A battle in central Argren within days! Leaving the soldiers behind, she crossed the field and flew over a forest. She slowed when a meadow cradled between the shoulders of two low mountains appeared. She didn't see why her spirit guide was showing her this place until Minna came into view, standing at the edge of the meadow. A boy she saw with Minna in the raven's memory stood beside her. Minna pointed across the field.

Alyn's fingers dug into her knees when three witches emerged from the trees on the far side of the meadow. They were the same witches she saw in her first vision. Two of the witches released flames onto the slopes at each end of the meadow, flushing *Alle'oss* men and women hiding in the brush. Alyn flinched as she watched the witch in the center thrust her hands toward Minna.

"Look out!" she shouted.

Minna's shield lit up with spirit light as the spirit wave crashed into it. Her sister rocked back under the impact. She lifted her arms, as if she were calling a spirit, but before she could attack, all three witches released spirit waves, sweeping Minna's hurried shield aside and throwing her and the boy backwards.

The image of Minna's crumpled body faded, leaving Alyn breathless in her room. She leapt from her bed, careened off the jamb of her door, sprinted out on her porch and looked up the hill to Beadu's hut.

Deirdre, surrounded by a group of children, waved. Her hand slowed, and a frown appeared on her face when she saw Alyn's expression. Alyn waved both arms and pointed toward Beadu's hut, then took off across the square.

Beadu's last morning class passed Alyn as they headed toward the square. Two of the oldest girls recently produced spirit waves and their joy infected the entire village, but Alyn ignored the girls' greetings.

When she skidded to a stop outside the logs that ringed Beadu's fire, Beadu glanced down the hill and held up a hand before Alyn could start. "Deirdre will want to hear this."

Alyn clamped her mouth shut, crossed her arms tightly over her chest, and paced. Noticing a familiar raven watching her from a nearby tree, she blurted, "It's back!"

Deirdre arrived at a run and fell, panting, onto her usual spot beside Beadu.

When Beadu nodded to her, Alyn spoke in a rush. "Minna will fight the three witches I saw in my first vision! Soon!" Their response was disappointingly subdued. They stared at her, then glanced at one another. Alyn threw her arms out to her sides. "We have to do something!"

"You've seen this?" Deirdre asked.

"She dies!" Alyn said. "We have to get her to run away!"

Beadu frowned. After a long frustrating moment, she said, "Running away does not seem to be in Minna's nature."

"It's the only way! She can't fight three witches at once!"

Deirdre glanced up at the raven. "Couldn't you just send her a message?"

"She's not at the Cut," Alyn said impatiently, "and the raven will never get there in time."

"The raven would not be able to find her if she is not at the Cut," Beadu said. "There are only a few places we can send the raven that it will recognize. Where will this battle take place?"

"It's near the eastern end of the Kalana Valley," Alyn said. "But there's no time, anyway."

"Then you must get her to go to *honua*," Beadu said. *Honua* was a spot the *Alle'oss* resistance used as a rendezvous and to shelter from the weather.

"But how?" Alyn asked. "How do we tell her that?"

"Do you remember how Ragan sent Minna a warning last winter?"

"The *sjel'and*! It showed Minna a vision to warn her Ulf was in danger," Alyn said. "My spirit guide can send her a message."

"Yes," Beadu said. "He can show her visions of the future. We must find futures that convey a message she understands, and we have little time." She glanced up at the raven. "The raven will need some time to make it to *honua* so we must send it immediately. Go! Bring paper."

Alyn leapt up and dashed down the hill. *You ready?* Her spirit guide swooped.

Minna

Minna swayed comfortably in the saddle as they headed south on the Imperial Highway. They rode hard to arrive at the intended battlefield on time, but they slowed as they grew near to rest their horses. She searched the side of the highway where it pressed up against the rim of the Kalana Valley. The spot where she and Ulf stopped for a quick lunch on the second day of their journey to Brennan was somewhere around here.

"Minna!"

Minna startled and turned toward Sigurn. "What?"

Sigurn smirked. "When you focus on something, it's hard to get your attention."

"Sorry," Minna said. "What did you want…" Her voice trailed off as she noticed the tents pitched in a field east of the highway. *Alle'oss* soldiers about the business of a military camp moved among the tents.

Sigurn waved a hand in front of her face to get her attention and pointed south to where the highway bent to the east. A familiar figure waited beside the road, watching them approach. Behind Lief, a long, narrow field extended to the south, bordered on the west by the rim of the valley and to the east by bluffs that rose to *Shohnem Chithana*. The valley and the mountains formed the bottleneck where the *Alle'oss* planned to meet the mercenaries.

"*Lehasa!*" Sigurn called, and Lief lifted a hand in greeting.

As they neared him, Gyda dismounted and took Lief's offered arm.

"Looks like you're just in time," Lief said. "Scouts say they're less than a day to the south."

"Any word on the witches?" Minna asked.

"Nothing," Lief said, shaking his head. "But our scouts haven't gotten very close. You got a plan for them?" he asked Minna.

Minna nodded. "Sigurn's idea."

"We go out ahead and set an ambush," Sigurn said. "See if we can take one or two out to even the odds for Minna."

Lief nodded slowly. "Can't say I'm not happy keeping that chaos out of the middle of our battle." He cocked his head and asked Minna, "You think you can handle them?"

Minna nodded without hesitation.

"You better get going then," Lief said. He turned and pointed to the east. "Best make your way down that side. We've made the field a bit of a swamp."

They rode along the highway until they reached the spot where the land climbed *Chithand's* shoulders, then turned south and made their way along the eastern edge of the long, sloped field. Shallow trenches crisscrossed the field, like the irrigation ditches the farmers in Argren dug in their fields. Water diverted from the Ishien River to the north trickled through the trenches.

Sigurn leaned toward her and pointed at the trenches. "Saturates the ground. When the mercs attack over this ground, they'll be ankle deep in mud. Gives the archers more time to thin them out."

Minna thought of the longbow Gyda showed her and peered down the hill toward the forest. She guessed it was four hundred paces from the forest to the *Alle'oss* camp. Twisting in her saddle, she looked back at Lief and Gyda and noticed an orange stick driven into the ground.

"That's a hundred paces," Sigurn said, pointing at the stake. He pointed to the south. "The yellow one is two hundred paces, the red one is three hundred."

"That longbow," Minna said. "The one Gyda had."

"Four hundred paces," Sigurn said with a wide smile. "A little less for the newcomers, so they'll wait until the mercs reach three hundred paces."

Minna gazed at the treeline that bordered the battlefield on its southern end, trying to picture the coming battle.

"They'll come out of the trees so they can form up," Sigurn said, sweeping his hand across the treeline. When Minna gave him a questioning look, he said, "Very important to keep formation in battle, so they'll have to be out of the trees to form a straight line."

"They'll send their archers forward to soften us up," said a small man, who always seemed to have a smile on his face. "They think they're out of our range, so they won't be in a hurry."

"But before they can get in range," Sigurn said. He mimed loosing an arrow. "They won't stand a chance."

"So, they'll send their foot soldiers charging up the hill," the smiling man said. "And when they hit the boggy ground…" His smile widened as he drew a finger across his throat.

"So, we'll win?" Minna asked.

Sigurn shrugged. "Funny things happen once a battle starts, so you never know. But Lief made a good plan. We have a good chance." He leaned toward her and grinned. "That is, if we can do something about those witches."

Minna twisted in her saddle as they entered the trees. Lief was talking to Gyda and gesturing broadly toward the prepared battlefield.

·   ·   ·

"I've never seen your hair in a braid before," Sigurn said.

Minna tipped her head and gave him a sideways glance, letting her hands work. "It's going to get windy." She ripped a leather tassel from her belt and secured the braid. Flipping her hair over her shoulder, she planted her hands on her hips and gazed around at the spot they chose for the ambush.

Three hundred paces south of the battlefield, the ground fell sharply and opened up into a wide grassy lea. The steep wooded slopes of *Shonum Chona* and *Shonum Chonum*, the twins, guarded the eastern and western borders, forcing the witches and the mercenaries to come cross the field to head north. The *Alle'oss* who accompanied them took up positions on the slopes from which they could hide and have a clear shot at the open ground.

"You ready?" Sigurn asked.

"Yes," Minna said. Now that she was here, and the waiting was over, she was ready to get on with it. Her concern for Ulf and the fate of Argren were still there, but this confrontation with the approaching witches was something she controlled. She glanced up at a flock of crows flying south, black against the blue sky.

Chapter 39

The 2nd Day of the Month of Heulomon

Aron

"They're coming," Zaina said.

"Looks like it," Aron said, trying to match Zaina's calm tone despite his jangling nerves. Earlier that day, when scouts reported heightened activity in the Imp camp, Aron and Zaina activated their plans for defending the Cut. Now they stood on the rim of the escarpment, surrounded by silent *Alle'oss* archers. A freshening westerly wind brought the scent of approaching rain and drowned out the sounds of the Ninth's heavy infantry forming up in a long column beside the highway just out of bow range.

"They're early," Aron said. "Prather shouldn't expect the mercenaries in our rear for two or three days."

"Prather apparently doesn't want to share the credit," Zaina said. "He probably thinks he can take care of us on his own. Not sure what his plan is for Minna."

One of the squat tortoises separated itself from the army and made its slow way toward the stockade the *Alle'oss* built at the bottom of the Cut. Four people walked beside the tortoise, two on each side.

"Those would be the sisters," Zaina said.

"That would be my guess," Aron said. Though they were too far away to see their tattoos, they dressed like the sisters he saw when he visited the Ninth's camp.

As Aron turned away from the edge of the escarpment, Zaina grabbed his arm. "Where are you going?"

Aron gave her his widest smile. "They've done us the courtesy of giving us an opportunity to take care of the sisters. I'm going to take it."

"You're in command now. We can't afford to let you run off recklessly."

Aron's grin fell away. "Listen," he said. "They're going to come, and we won't be able to stop them without Minna and the rest of the army. We have to do whatever we can to slow them down. The best time to take care of the sisters is before the *sjel'and* swarm. Once the battle starts, death will draw the soul spirits like crows." When Zaina didn't let go, he said, "I'll be careful. I'll take care of the sisters and come right back. I won't linger."

"You see a *sjel'and*, you come right back," Zaina said.

"Of course," Aron said with a grin.

Zaina gazed at him for a moment longer, then let go. "Be careful."

"Be careful," Aron mumbled to himself as he made his way along the edge of the Cut, smiling and greeting the *Alle'oss,* waiting anxiously for the Empire's attack. "We're long past being careful," he said to himself as he strode toward the back of the stone wall that spanned the highway near the top of the Cut. The young captain in charge of the wall's defense eyed him nervously.

"You ready, Captain?" he asked.

"Yes, sir!" she said, a little too loudly.

"Excellent," Aron said. He glanced at the men and women on the top of the wall. "They'll likely get past the stockade at the bottom of the hill, but they'll have to get through the gauntlet of the Cut and that'll weaken them." When he paused and studied her face, she nodded. "You can't let this wall fall. You understand?"

She snapped to attention. "Yes, sir!"

"Good," Aron said and rested his hand on her shoulder. "We've given you this responsibility because we trust you." Letting his hand fall, he said, "Now, open the gate. I'm going to reconnoiter."

"You?" she asked uncertainly. "That is, I mean, by yourself? Sir?"

Aron smiled. "Don't worry, Captain. I'm under orders to be careful." He waved at the gate. "Now, time is pressing, so if you would."

She gave the orders, and soldiers sprang forward to open the gate.

Aron slipped past the abatis, which was now embedded in the road surface, then set off at a jog down the slope, dodging the obstacles in the road designed to impede tortoises and cavalry. As he approached the wooden stockade at the bottom of the Cut, he heard Zaina shouting down at him. He looked up and found her waving at him. Cupping his hands to his ears, he could just make out what she said.

"Two hundred paces."

He waved an acknowledgment, then turned toward the young man commanding the defense of the stockade.

"Sir," the man said. "Have you seen the tortoise?"

"Yes."

"And the sisters?"

"Yes," Aron said. Before the man could speak again, Aron grasped his shoulders. "Calm yourself." The soldiers lining the top of the stockade were trying to hear what was going on below them while keeping an eye on the approaching threat. "Let us see what we can do about that tortoise," he said and waved at the gate. "Open the gate."

As he slipped through the narrow opening, he looked back at the young man and said, "Make sure you keep it open so I can get back in." He waited until the lieutenant nodded, then wormed his way through the abatis and stepped into *annen'heim*.

Aron looked up at the horrified expressions of the men and women lining the top of the stockade and couldn't help grinning. What they must be thinking, seeing their commander standing outside their defenses as the tortoise approached. But he could guess what they thought when he stepped into *annen'heim*. These men and women would be much in demand after seeing the stories about him being a realm walker confirmed. If they lived.

He took one last look at the young lieutenant watching him over the sharpened end of the logs, his face not yet revealing his astonishment at Aron's disappearance, then turned and peered into the murky realm. There were *sjel'and* in the vicinity, but they were not near. As he set out to intercept the tortoise, he wondered how much the *sjel'and* were aware of what was about to happen here. The carnage would draw the spirits in droves. Once the fighting started, he could no longer safely cross the boundary into *annen'heim*.

The sisters walked alongside the tortoise, two on each side. Frozen in mid-stride, they held their arms extended as they were now in range of the archers on the escarpment. The archers were under orders to refrain from firing at the tortoise or the sisters. It was a waste of arrows. But not everyone could ignore such a tempting target. An arrow hovered a pace above where Aron assumed the first sister's shield would be.

He walked past her, not worried about the shield, which didn't extend into the realm of the dead. The woman wore a grim expression. He noticed when he visited the Imp camp, these sisters didn't have the rough-and-ready look of the sisters who labored to hold back the Kaileuk. These were ornaments of the Seidi's lost power. He wondered if they were aware they were about to die. This woman didn't know her executioner was close, but she must know the storm she was approaching. They were no Minna, nor even a Deirdre. They were sacrificial lambs.

Aron gave her a last look, then headed to the sister walking on the same side at the back of the tortoise. With their focus on the threat ahead, he might kill them all before any of them were aware he was there. Stepping to within a few inches of the sister's back, he drew his knife, reached around her neck, rested the blade a hair's breadth from her neck and crossed the boundary.

Flynn

"What was that?" Flynn didn't need the benefit of General Prather's spyglass to tell something odd occurred. There was a flicker of motion behind the sister walking along the left side at the back of the tortoise, then the woman simply dropped to her knees and flopped onto her stomach. Flynn snatched the spyglass out of Prather's hands, took a step forward, and put it to her eye. It took her a moment to find the sister on the other side, and by the time she did, the woman was already dead. She lifted the spyglass just in time to see someone appear out of nowhere behind the sister in the front. There was a quick motion, a bloody knife flashed in the person's hand, then they were gone.

Prather retrieved his spyglass, leaving Flynn to gape as the last sister met the same fate. It all happened so fast, the sisters didn't have time to react, even if they noticed what was happening. A realm walker. That could be the only explanation. But though Flynn only saw the person briefly from the back, she had the distinct impression it was a man. That made no sense.

Prather grabbed her arm and pulled her around. He stooped over her, putting his face so close to hers, she could smell his breath.

"What happened?" he shouted. "What was that?"

"Realm walker," Flynn said vaguely. "The *Alle'oss* have a realm walker."

"A realm walker?" he blurted after a pause. "How can that be?"

Flynn peeled his hand off her arm, took a step back, and said, "Another myth come to life, General. This Minna is apparently Ione reborn, and now the *Alle'oss* have realm walkers."

The general's face went still. He straightened and turned toward the Cut, his spyglass hanging limply at his side. Flynn followed his gaze as the door to the stockade swung open, disgorging a squad of soldiers who wrestled heavy casks past the abatis. The tortoise was still trundling forward fifty paces from the entrance to the Cut, the crew undoubtedly unaware they lost their protective escort.

"You're about to lose your tortoise, General," Flynn said.

The soldiers walked as fast as they could with their heavy burdens toward the tortoise. Another person carrying a torch emerged from the gate. Flynn took the spyglass from the general's limp fingers and held it up to her eye. She only saw him from the back before, but if she had to bet, she would say the person with the torch was the realm walker. And he most definitely was a man.

She let the spyglass fall as the *Alle'oss* splashed the tortoise with the contents of their casks. The realm walker waited until they were clear, then threw his torch. Even from far away, Flynn heard the whump as the tortoise went up in flames.

The general finally overcame his shock. "Captain!" he shouted to his adjutant. "Give the order for the vanguard to go forward. Tell them to scale the wall with ladders."

Flynn held the spyglass out to the general. When he didn't seem to notice it, she turned and handed it to another member of the general's staff.

"Well?" Prather said. His head swiveled around so he could glare down his nose at her.

"Yes?" she asked, sweetly. She knew what he wanted, but she wasn't going to make it easy for him.

He threw his arm toward the flaming tortoise. "Go do your job, Sister *Nara*." Spittle spattered Flynn's blouse. A tic as the corner of his eye forced his eye closed and sent ripples down his cheek.

Flynn gazed up at him, then around at the glares of the officers on his staff. None of them were any better than Prather. For a flickering moment, she imagined them scrambling to escape her flames, their faces melting, emitting the high-pitched screams that haunted her nightmares.

She returned her gaze to the general. Prather was no better than the sisters who hid in the Seidi tower, letting her and her sisters carry their load. He was only here because he had experience committing genocide against the Ferol. His one brief stint on the southern front ended in disaster. Flynn didn't regret saving him from his incompetence then, because many good men would have died if she didn't. But this wasn't the first time she wondered how much longer she would cover for the likes of Prather and Malefica Briana.

She snapped to attention, affected a crisp salute and walked away without a word.

Chapter 40

The 2nd Day of the Month of Heulomon

Alyn

"It's almost time," Alyn said.

"Your spirit guide knows what to show her?" Deirdre asked.

Alyn nodded. "It's the only future we found in which she survives and gets away."

"Let's hope Minna understands," Deirdre said.

"She will," Beadu said. "It's time."

Alyn focused on her spirit guide. *You heard?* The spirit swooped. *Are you ready?* He swooped again and was gone.

Alyn opened her eyes and sighed.

The three women exchanged worried looks. "How will we know if it worked?" Deirdre asked.

"My spirit guide will watch and show me what happened," Alyn said.

"How long?" Deirdre asked.

"A few hours," Alyn said. She stood, hesitated, then said, "I can't sit still. I'll come back when I hear something."

Macha

"They're waiting," Macha said, dangling a bit of meat for the crow to pluck from her fingers.

"Who?" Eriu asked.

"Minna Hunter and a handful of *Alle'oss*," Macha said.

"That's all?" Svend asked. "No army?"

"The army is waiting three hundred paces behind them," Macha said. "The witch hopes to ambush us." Macha was relieved. She would rather not encounter the witch in the middle of a battle. "Are you ready?" she asked her sisters.

Neiman nodded.

Eriu lifted her arms above her head and twirled. "Finally," she said. "I'm so tired of traipsing through these mountains. What do you think, story man? You think they'll tell stories about this?"

Ignoring her, Svend asked Macha, "How many in the army? What is their disposition?"

Macha turned her gaze on him. She was tempted to ignore him, but he was true to his word and led them here without complaint after their dispute in the *Alle'oss* village. "Five or six hundred in a line at the north end of a long narrow field," she said.

He blinked. "Five or six hundred? That's all? You're sure?" When she didn't respond, he nodded, then set off to convey the news to Chagan, who was now minutes behind them with the Union army.

Macha watched him go, then faced her sisters. They had planned how they would confront the black-haired witch. They knew she must be powerful because she defeated Aife. But there was only one of her. "She has archers with her," she said. She squatted and sketched the scene the crow showed her in the dirt. Pointing to each side of the lea, she said, "They're hiding in the hills."

"Fire?" Eriu asked.

Macha nodded. "You two sweep the forest on each side of the field with fire, then fan the flames. I'll keep the witch occupied." She stood. "Then we all turn our attention on her. Spirit waves." She opened her arms and welcomed her sisters into her embrace. "For Aife," she whispered, and her sisters echoed her vow.

Minna

"Can you…" Sigurn asked, peering down the hill from where they crouched in the shadows of the trees. "You know, use that speaking to animals thing to find out where they are?"

Minna bit her lip and looked up at the birds in the trees above them. "If they're close, they'll sense me." She watched Linea, who had taken an interest in a meadowlark, dipping in and out of the tall grass. She could send Linea to search for the witches, but she was reluctant to let her spirit guide out of her sight. "They have to come this way," she said. "We just have to be patient."

Sigurn hesitated, then nodded and crawled forward once again to check on their companions. When he returned, he glanced at Minna. Seeing her smile, he asked, "What?"

Minna shook her head. Sigurn hadn't been able to sit still since they arrived. She gazed down the hill to find Linea lost interest in the bird and was zooming up the hill toward them. She let herself open only enough for Linea to squeeze into her center. *You ready?* Linea swooped, then froze.

"What?" Minna said aloud, relaxing her center in her surprise.

"What?" Sigurn asked urgently, peering across the field. "Are they here?"

Minna gave her head a small shake. Linea was never still in her center. Even when she tried to keep Minna warm while they were lost in Brennan, she drifted slowly, never coming to a complete stop. *What's wrong?* But before Linea could respond, another spirit appeared. The sudden appearance of the *sjel'and* sent a shudder through Minna. Her hand went to her mouth.

Linea and the *sjel'and* hovered, as if eying one another uncertainly. The *sjel'and* surged toward Linea suddenly, then stopped. Linea shot backward. The *sjel'and* vibrated briefly and started a slow circuit of Minna's center. Linea hesitated before following. After two circuits, the two spirits came together, then separated, swirling slowly around Minna's center in an intricate dance.

"Stop it!" Minna said aloud. "Who are you?"

"Um, I'm Sigurn," Sigurn said. "Is this some kind of *saa'myn* thing? Should I be worried?"

Minna held up a hand to forestall his questions as the *sjel'and* came to a stop. Linea left Minna's center, appearing in the air in front of her, but before Minna could ask why, a vision filled her mind. She froze. Her mother used a *sjel'and* to warn her about Ulf being killed in Brennan. But her mother was dead.

"Minna?" Sigurn asked quietly.

The vision was as clear as if she were there. She was looking down at herself and Sigurn from behind. Her hair fell down her back in a braid. It was now, or only moments from now. Across the lea, the witches she saw in the raven's memory emerged from the forest. Minna watched the vision, horrified as the two at the edges of the field on the left and right sent gouts of flame into the forest where the *Alle'oss* waited in ambush, then swept their arms in a familiar gesture, bringing forth whirlwinds that fanned the flames.

"They know about the ambush," Minna whispered.

"How do you know?"

The witch in the middle, the one with dark skin who said Minna's name to the raven, thrust her hands toward Minna and Sigurn. Though she couldn't feel the power of the spirit wave, Minna could see its effect. The grass in the field rippled with the passing of the wave. Minna's shield lit up with spirit light. The trees and bushes around her and Sigurn bent, branches snapped, leaves were stripped and scattered.

"Do something," Minna said aloud to the future version of herself.

And the Minna in the vision did. She lifted her hands and brought forth lightning which splashed against the shield of the witch, who released the spirit wave. Before Minna could raise her shield again, she and Sigurn were struck from the left and right by waves from the other witches. Minna watched, horrified, as she and Sigurn were tossed, broken, back into the forest.

The vision faded, leaving the *sjel'and* motionless in her center. Minna opened her eyes and stared at the forest across the field. They were all going to die. She couldn't defeat the witches if they could come at her from different sides at once. What was she thinking? But what could she do? If she fled, the witches would attack the army. If she stayed, everyone who came to set the ambush would die.

But before she could decide what to do, a new vision appeared. Once again, she was looking down at herself and Sigurn, but this time, as she watched, Sigurn blew the retreat signal on his horn. Though her field of view prevented her from seeing all the edges of the field, she glimpsed the *Alle'oss* waiting in ambush, responding to Sigurn's call. The witches appeared as before, sending flames into the forest. Minna saw one man succumb to the fire, but others escaped.

"Show me what to do," Minna said.

"Minna, I'm getting worried," Sigurn said, taking hold of her arm.

The Minna in the vision caught the black witch's spirit wave as before, but instead of responding with lightning, she raised her arms, crouched and swept her hands down.

The image lurched as if someone jostled the vision. A rumble, so deep she imagined she felt it in her chest, followed. Sigurn, in the vision, was thrown into the air and landed on his side. Across the field, the witches were thrown from their feet. A tree at the edge of the forest tipped and fell across the witch in the center. Stones dislodged from the flanks of the mountains, tumbled down the slopes, picking up momentum until small avalanches raced down in clouds of dust.

The Minna in the vision dragged Sigurn to his feet and fled into the forest as the vision faded.

For a moment, she was alone in her center with the *sjel'and,* then a new vision appeared. It took her a moment to recognize the place through a heavy downpour, but then the vision drifted forward until her point of view emerged from the rain and she could see herself and Sigurn, soaked to the skin, facing one another and arguing. She recognized the place. It was *honua,* the place where she and Ulf stopped on the first night on their journey to Brennan. Watching the vision, Minna leaned forward, as if it could help her hear what the Minna in the vision and Sigurn were saying, but rumbling thunder and the steady roar of falling rain drowned their voices out. Both Minna and Sigurn startled when a familiar-looking raven burst through the driving rain and landed in front of Minna. Minna held her breath as the Minna in the vision retrieved the message and unrolled it. Her point of view drifted closer until she could hear herself when she spoke.

"It's from Alyn," she said as the vision faded.

Minna opened her eyes to find Sigurn's worried face only inches from her own. Alyn used the *sjel'and* to send her a warning, just like Ragan did. She wanted Minna to run away, but that would leave the *Alle'oss* at the mercy of the witches. And as if the *sjel'and,* still in her center, was waiting for that thought, a new vision appeared. She saw the three witches. Behind them, the mercenary soldiers streamed across the lea. One of the witches, the one with black hair, lay on her side, curled in on herself as if she were injured. The others knelt beside her, their expressions showing their concern for their wounded companion.

Minna's eyes flew open. "Tell the others to retreat," she said.

"What?" He glanced over his shoulder across the field. "The witches could be here any moment."

"I can't explain right now," Minna said. "I've just had a vision of the future. We're all going to die! You have to get everyone out of here!"

"You want us to run away?" Anger edged his words.

Before Minna could respond, a motion in the shadows of the trees across the field caught her eye. They were here.

Minna shut her eyes. The *sjel'and* was still there. *Tell Alyn I got the message.* The spirit bobbed, then disappeared. Linea appeared in her center. Minna recalled the vision of her sweeping her arms down. *Do you know what to do?* Linea swooped. She opened her eyes, grabbed the horn tied to Sigurn's belt and ripped it free. "Tell everyone to run! Now!" Turning to face the oncoming threat, she stepped into the open, threw her center open and called the *lan'and* to her.

Sigurn sounded the retreat as the witches emerged from the treeline.

Ulf

"Ulf!" It was Helga, who was at the head of the long line of misfits spread out along the narrow path.

Head down as he navigated the uneven ground, Ulf looked up sharply at the urgency in her voice. The faces of those in the line ahead of him turned toward him and pressed themselves against the rock wall to allow him to squeeze past.

Helga was standing on a broad flat space, which bent around the shallower eastern slope of the mountain. When he stepped up beside her, she pointed down to a field at the base of the slope and said. "Isn't that Minna?"

"Minna?" Ulf blurted. The first thing he noticed when he looked down the slope was a handful of *Alle'oss* archers hiding among the trees below them. Raising his gaze to where Helga pointed, he saw Minna. Though she was nearly two hundred paces away, there was no mistaking her. Minna and the boy named Sigurn stood just outside the forest at the northern edge of the field. While he watched, Minna turned toward Sigurn, snatched something from his belt, held it up and shook it. The urgency in her motion, the familiar tension in her body, the concealed archers —

"Misfits!" he shouted. "String your bows! Spread out and take cover." The misfits exiting the narrow path and spreading out on the shallow slope around him sprung into motion.

"What's going on?" Mikaela asked, squeezing past the line of soldiers. A horn sounded the retreat. "I think those rumors of a battle we heard are true," Ulf said. "And we've stumbled into the middle of it."

Chapter 41

The 2nd Day of the Month of Heulomon

Minna

The *Alle'oss* lying in ambush emerged from their hiding places, responding to Sigurn's signal and fled north, away from the oncoming threat. A witch with blond hair appeared out of the forest on the eastern end of the field, raised her hands and released flames that swept the lower slopes. Sigurn's warning saved everyone on that side of the field. Knowing what was coming, Minna lifted her arms, stepped closer to Sigurn and released her shield just in time.

The wave from the black witch was every bit as powerful as it looked in the vision. Minna rocked back, her knees nearly buckling. Her center rang, sending the *lan'ands'* swirling dance into chaos. For a frightening moment, she was sure she would swoon. Then Linea's song rose above the discordant notes and found the right harmony.

She could only hope her spirit guide understood better than she did what Alyn expected her to do. *Linea! Now!* Her first indication there was a new spirit in her center was when the swarm of *lan'and* deserted her, leaving Linea alone. Nearly defenseless against another spirit wave, Minna stared across the field at the witches. The black witch approached cautiously. The blond witched emerged from the smoke, swirled by whirlwinds she released. *Linea?!* Linea swooped. Minna raised her shield, knowing it was useless. The witches' combined attack would sweep it aside.

Her eyes were on the witches, but her attention was inward, waiting, hoping for some sign of the new spirit. But no spirit appeared. She sniffed, inhaling smoke, shook her head and blinked, glancing up at the swarm of *lan'and* that still swirled around her, wondering if she should call them back. Pressure spiked in her sinuses, as if she suddenly had a cold. And then the pressure spread, pouring from the space behind her eyes to fill her entire head, until it felt as if her head would burst.

Just when she thought she couldn't stand it any longer, Linea swooped. Minna lifted her arms, crouched, and with a scream, she swept them down, hoping the new spirit understood.

A deep grumble emanated from the ground beneath her feet. The ground dropped, then lurched upward, thrusting her into the air. She landed in a crouch, remaining standing only because she'd seen herself in the vision. A ripple spread out in a circle, as if the earth were a pond and the spirit was a stone. A deep rumbling growl reverberated off the surrounding hills and vibrated in her legs. Shouting in alarm, Sigurn was thrown a foot into the air. The ripple dragged his feet from beneath him, so he landed on his side.

Minna shuddered in relief at the instant release of pressure in her mind. She fought to keep her eyes open, watching the ripple race down the hill toward the witches. The black witch, the one who released the immensely powerful wave, was tossed into the air, then disappeared beneath a tree uprooted behind her. The blond witch turned to flee, but the earthquake caught her before she took two steps and threw her into the shadows of the trees.

Ulf

The misfits spread out across the eastern slope of the mountain, arrows nocked, searching for the threat Ulf's urgent command implied was nearby. Ulf watched, horrified, as a witch with black hair appeared at the near edge of the meadow. She released gouts of flame onto the slope below them, engulfing an archer who emerged from hiding at the sound of the retreat. Sweeping her arms, she released wind that fanned the flames and swirled the smoke.

Another witch appeared in the center of the field and thrust her hands towards Minna. Ulf saw Minna make that gesture before and knew it was a spirit wave. The grass flattened along the path of the wave. He couldn't see it impact Minna's shield, but he could see its power in her reaction and in the trees behind her.

He glimpsed the black-haired witch, who started the fire below them through smoke and flames, turning her attention to Minna. Minna wouldn't stand a chance against all the witches at once.

"Minna!" he shouted, but wind and the roar of the flames snatched the words away. Drawing his bow, he aimed at the witch below him.

A deep rumble rose from below the wind's whistle, as if a giant were grinding stones together. Before he loosed his arrow, the earth lurched. The ground, which had been sure and solid only moments before, tossed him up and dragged his feet from under him. Earth, stone and the scrubby pines that dotted the slope, slid down the slope, carrying him along with it. Bow held free of the debris, he caught a tree still anchored to the ground with his free hand and ducked behind the trunk to shelter from the avalanche.

Before the last pebbles slid past him, he pulled himself upright, crouching lest the ground betray his trust again. Rubble doused most of the flames, but raised a dense cloud of dust that obscured what was happening below him. The misfits he could see were scattered across the slope. Eyes burning from smoke and dust, he coughed to clear his throat and peered into the cloud. He glimpsed Minna pulling Sigurn to his feet. Searching for the black-haired witch, he found her below him, getting to her feet, her attention on Minna.

He reacted without thinking. Drawing his bow, he took aim. The witch was one hundred paces below him. A shot he should be able to make. She lifted her hands as he loosed. The arrow struck her low on her side and she crumpled.

Minna and Sigurn disappeared into the forest, but before he could feel gratified, Helga shouted, "Ulf!"

She appeared out of the cloud of smoke and dust, legs churning as she fought her way up the slope on the loose ground. When she saw him looking, she pointed south and shouted, "Imps!"

Men were pouring out of the forest along the southern edge of the field. They didn't look like Imps, or not like any Imps he saw before. They were all bigger than Agmar, the largest man Ulf knew, and they wore colorful leather armor. But regardless who they were, their intent was clear. As he watched, a squad broke off and headed toward the base of the slope on which the misfits were scattered.

Ulf scanned the surrounding terrain. They could traverse the slope to the south, but that was where the enemy was coming from. To the north was the narrow path they arrived on. He didn't want to fight there. They wouldn't be able to concentrate their fire standing in single file. As the slope rose behind them, it became steeper, but there was a shoulder, a relatively flat area, fifty paces above them. A good place to make a stand. While he was assessing the situation, Mikaela appeared beside him.

"Sound the retreat," he said to her. "Up the slope." He pointed to the spot he had in mind.

Without hesitating, she licked her lips, put her fingers to her teeth and blew the signal.

Already climbing the slope, the misfits redoubled their efforts. Ulf waited until Helga passed him, then turned and followed, pulling Mikaela with him. The giants were only thirty paces behind them, close enough for Ulf to make out their disturbingly blank faces.

"The shoulder!" he shouted, stumbling and pointing as his legs pumped in the loose scree on the steepening slope. "Make a stand on the shoulder." The first misfits to reach the refuge, turned and loosed over their comrades' heads.

Heavy breaths and rumbling grunts from the men laboring up the slope behind him urged him to greater effort. He glanced back and saw

Mikaela struggling. A man five paces behind her was reaching toward her with a halberd. Ulf snatched up a fistful of gravel and flung it at his face. It was enough to distract him and slow him down.

Ulf took Mikaela's hand and together, they struggled up the last few feet to join the rest of the misfits who were raining arrows down on the approaching enemy. By the time he got to his feet, the enemy was retreating.

The misfits, stunned by the sudden violence, didn't cheer. Some dropped where they stood, panting and staring wildly around. Others checked on their comrades, consoling those who needed it and treating minor wounds.

Ulf looked down at the men in their colorful armor streaming north across the field. They were heading in the same direction as Minna.

"Two missing," Helga said.

Ulf ensured the Imps who attacked them weren't coming, then turned around. Helga told him the names of the missing.

"We don't know what happened to them," she said, but he could hear his own resignation in her voice.

Ulf swallowed and licked dry lips, then spat out the dust that coated them. All he wanted to do was sink to the ground and weep. But then he caught Mikaela looking at him and recognized the signs of shock and impending panic on her face. He couldn't afford to let the misfits see him sink.

He put his arms around her. She buried her face against his chest and sobbed softly. "We're okay," he whispered. Most of us.

After a moment, she pulled back, swiped the moisture making tracks in the dust on her cheeks and said, "It's war."

It *was* war. It had been on his mind since he left Minna weeks ago. People died in war. Jora died on top of the ridge in their first skirmish. But these were his people. "Yes, it is," he said. "Not what we wanted, but it's what we have."

"What do we do?" Hakon asked.

"Go back?" Helga asked. "The way we came?"

Ulf wasn't sure what they should do, but that didn't seem right. "No," he said.

"You're not thinking we should go after them?" Mikaela asked.

Go after Minna. That's what he wanted to do, but Mikaela's unspoken warning was right; there were too many of those strange men for the misfits to fight. He looked up at the sun, then looked down the slope to where what remained of the squad of soldiers who attacked them still waited. He gazed around at the misfits. Most of them watched, tense, waiting for Ulf to decide. It was late in the afternoon, and he could see in their faces, they needed to process what happened to them.

"We camp here tonight," he said. The tension went out of the group. "But we need a scout to track those soldiers."

"I'll do it," Inger said and shot to her feet.

"Don't get too close," Ulf said. "Just find out where they go. Be back by morning."

"Yes, sir," she said and set off.

He looked down the slope, at the Imps looking back at him. "Keep an eye on those Imps," he said to Hakon. "If they leave, let me know so we can go look for our missing."

"Yes, sir."

Ulf turned away and began to checking on his misfits.

Minna

Minna pulled Sigurn to his feet and dragged him into the forest behind them.

"What in the Father's name was that?" he asked, stumbling over tangled feet, trying to keep up.

"Earthquake spirit," Minna said. It was as good a name as any.

"You had them down. The witches," he said, finally getting himself all the way upright and pulling his arm free. "Why are we leaving?"

"My sister sent me a message, a vision. If we stay, everyone will die, including you." She didn't know for sure that was true. Part of her agreed with Sigurn, but Alyn's intent was clear. She didn't want Minna to fight the witches, not now. She trusted her sister, Beadu and Deirdre.

"So, we just run away?" Sigurn asked as they entered the clearing where they left their horses.

The *Alle'oss* who survived the witches' attack startled when they burst into the clearing.

"What was that?" the man they left to tend the horses asked. Only two horses remained. The rest obviously fled.

Ignoring the question, Minna took the reins of the first horse, but before she could mount it, Sigurn caught her arm.

"You're running away," he said.

Minna saw the shocked expressions of the others over his shoulder when they heard. She shook his hand off and mounted the horse. "We, you and I, have to go. I don't have time to explain. Get on the horse."

"What about the army?" Sigurn asked, throwing his arm toward the north where the *Alle'oss* army waited. "Those witches will devastate them."

"No, they won't," Minna said. "The witches will come after me." She didn't know that was true either, but she was sure Alyn wouldn't allow the army to be massacred. Or she hoped not. "They'll be coming soon. We need to get moving. Now!"

Sigurn glanced back the way they came, then peered up at her. "You sure about this?" he asked her.

"I trust my sister."

Sigurn hesitated another moment, then mounted the other horse.

"What about us?" someone asked.

Sigurn looked at Minna, who shook her head. "Just us."

"Go back and join the army. Hurry!" Sigurn said. "*Andsutra!*"

Minna wheeled her horse around and set off at a gallop, with Sigurn behind her.

Macha

Macha knelt beside Neiman, drew her knife and cut away her sister's shirt to expose where the arrow penetrated her side. The wound was four inches below her rib cage. Neiman lay on her side, panting, eyes bright, fists clenched.

Eriu fought her way through the mercenaries streaming past and looked down at her sister. "She's alive," she said. She fell to her knees and took Neiman's hand, worked her fist open and twined their fingers together.

"For now," Macha said. "Her spirit guide won't be able to heal her with this arrow in her." She looked up as Svend and Chagan appeared.

"She's a goner," Chagan said.

If Eriu saw the twitch at the corner of his mouth when he said it, he would be dead. Macha saw it and would remember it, but they needed to take care of their sister. When he saw her expression, he turned hastily away and followed his soldiers.

"I hate to tell you," Svend said. "But he's right. If the arrow didn't penetrate her guts, the iron will cause an infection that will kill her eventually. She'd be better off if it killed her outright."

Eriu stood.

"Eriu!" Macha shouted, bringing her sister to a halt. "You, stop!" she said to Svend, who started backing away as Eriu rose. When he hesitated, she said, "We have to get the arrow out."

"You can't pull it out," he said, his eyes not leaving Eriu. "The barbs will cause more damage if you do."

"How do you get it out?" Macha asked.

"I can get it out," he said. "But like I said, she's a goner, and it won't be an easy death."

"Just get it out!" Eriu said.

He looked from Eriu to Neiman. "This is going to hurt," he said, catching Macha's eye and nodding toward Eriu.

"Eriu, you need to let him do this," Macha said. When Eriu nodded, Macha said to Svend, "She'll be fine."

"Hold her down," Svend said and crouched beside Neiman.

Macha knelt next to Neiman's head and grasped her forearms. Eriu straddled her legs, pinning them in place.

Lifting the strap of his water bottle over his head, Svend poured water on the wound and wiped blood away with his hand. "You ready?" he asked Macha. When she nodded, he drew a knife and put the tip of the blade to Neiman's skin at the base of the arrow and plunged it into her side.

Neiman screamed and jerked.

"Hold her still!"

When she was still again, he cut an incision an inch from the bow shaft. Then he repeated the cut on the opposite side. With the fingers of one hand, he pulled the skin apart, then felt inside the wound, searching for the arrowhead. "That was lucky," he murmured. Holding the wound open, he grasped the shaft near the skin and worked it slowly out of the wound.

Standing, he tossed the arrow aside, then washed his hands with water from the water bottle.

Macha waited until Neiman relaxed, then stood and said, "Thank you."

"For what it's worth," he mumbled.

As he turned away, Macha said, "I hope you find whatever you're looking for."

He turned back, started to speak, stopped, then said, "I don't know how all of you ended up here. My guess is it wasn't your idea. But whatever the reason, you can make your own choices."

Macha didn't answer, and after a moment, he nodded, turned and walked away.

Eriu watched him go, then sank to sit beside her sister and took her hand. "What do we do now?"

Macha gazed across the field, to where the witch disappeared into the forest. Minna Hunter. The witch who killed their sister, Aife. That hadn't changed. "We wait, for now," she said, sitting beside Eriu. "Neiman needs time to let her spirit guide fix her."

Eriu lay her head on Macha's shoulder.

Chapter 42

The 2nd Day of the Month of Heulomon

Aron

Returning to the safety of the stockade, Aron glimpsed the lieutenant's wide eyes peering at him through the narrow gap in the gate. He was afraid, and Aron couldn't blame him. The tortoise ground to a stop as soon as the men inside became aware they were on fire. They escaped out the back, only to be shot down by archers standing on top of the stockade. Aron held out a slim hope this attack was like the previous ones, that after the *Alle'oss* blunted the initial foray, the Ninth would retreat and lick their wounds. But the Ninth Legion wasn't giving up this time.

From the top of the stockade, Aron watched the heavy infantry approaching, their red and gold shields illuminated by the flaming tortoise. Already, the archers on top of the Cut were pouring arrows into their ranks, but few found their way past the shields.

Aron turned to the lieutenant. "Don't wait too long," he said. "Loose a volley or two, then get your people up the slope so you can harass them as they come over the wall." When the man gave him a nod, Aron said, "No unnecessary heroics. Get everyone to the other side of the stone wall alive."

The man gave him another nod. He started to speak, but had to swallow and lick his lips before he could say, "Yes, sir."

Aron took one more look at the oncoming threat, then climbed down to the road's surface and jogged up the slope. The gate in the wall at the top of the Cut stood wide. Zaina stood in the opening, thumbs hooked into her belt.

"That was well done," she said.

"Not sure what good it did," Aron said. "You saw them coming?"

Zaina nodded. "Least we don't have to worry about the sisters."

"Right," he said.

She caught his arm as he passed her and said, "No unnecessary heroics."

Aron grinned at her use of his own words to the lieutenant. "I've a feeling heroics will be necessary today," he said, glancing up as the first few raindrops pattered down. "Let's get into position."

From the top of the Cut, Aron watched cohorts of heavy infantry, each comprising five hundred men, approaching the stockade, sheltered by their heavy shields. After the first salvo of arrows proved ineffective, the archers watched in silence. They could just hear the tromp of thousands of feet above the wind and rain. A flash of lightning glimmered on the shields' gold paint.

When they neared the barrier, Zaina shouted, "Arrows!"

The archers nocked arrows, waiting for the moment when the soldiers would be forced to expose themselves as they neared the wall. Four paces from the stockade, the infantry paused. Archers on top of the Cut and on the stockade drew and took aim.

Suddenly, the cohort moved forward until their shields extended over the abatis. From the top of the Cut, Aron couldn't hear the saws, but he knew they were dismantling the abatis to make room for their ladders. The *Alle'oss* already used the oil behind the stockade on the tortoise, so all they could do was loose arrows into small gaps between the shields.

All at once, the shields in the front parted. Men with ladders emerged. They planted them on the ground, lifted them against the stockade and threw their weight against them to hold them in place. Arrows rained down. Screams punctuated the staccato thunks of arrows striking shields. As soon as the men bracing the ladder fell away, others replaced them.

Imps flooded up the ladders. A few, protected by their armor, made it to the top, only to be cut down. For a few moments, Aron thought they may stop them at the stockade, but then two men withstood the deluge long enough to throw the gate open before they succumbed.

The gate open, the infantry continued their slow march, protected beneath their shields. Forced to trod on the bodies of their comrades until they were clear of the stockade, they resumed their tight, protective formations and mounted the slope. The archers held their fire, watching for small gaps caused by stumbles when the tightly backed columns encountered the obstacles embedded in the highway.

When the legionnaires reached the halfway point, filling the roadway from wall to wall, Zaina shouted, "Boulders!"

Squad leaders relayed the command along the both sides of the Cut. Men and women set down their bows and bent to roll large stones toward the rim of the cliff.

"Now!" Zaina shouted.

The *Alle'oss* shoved the stones over the edge, then returned to retrieve more. Though the heavy shields stopped their arrows, they offered little resistance to the heavy stones. Men fell, their bodies and shields becoming impediments to those following them. Archers exploited the resulting openings. The *Alle'oss* continued to rain death down on them until the dead and wounded carpeted the highway.

It wasn't enough. Though many fell, there were still many more climbing the hill. As the Imps neared the top, the height of the cliffs on either side of the highway diminished, reducing the effectiveness of the stones.

"Oil," Zaina shouted.

The *Alle'oss* tipped casks of oil, pouring the contents onto the Imps' shields, then flaming torches were thrown into the mass.

Aron raced to the top of the Cut, hurried up the ladder behind the stone wall, and squeezed between two archers.

The flames felled many of the enemy, but not enough. Heavy rain diluted the oil and quenched the flames. The unstoppable tide still approached, trampling the smoldering bodies of their comrades. The stone wall was their last chance to stop them.

The enemy used the same tactics to clear the abatis they used in front of the stockade. Men with saws attacked the spikes while their comrades attempted to shield them. Archers found gaps, felling many of them, but there were always others to take their place. Aron waited, knowing what was coming.

The shields shifted as the men beneath them prepared for the assault.

Aron drew his sword and shouted, "Draw!"

The archers on the wall drew.

Suddenly, the shields in front of the cohort parted.

"Loose!"

Arrows struck home, felling the first rank of the enemy. Abandoning their methodical approach, the enemy surged forward with a roar. Ladders were thrown against the wall and braced. Imps raced up the rungs. Arrows felled many, but a few survived their wounds to reach the top. Despite the *Alle'oss's* best efforts to avoid a fight they couldn't win, a desperate hand-to-hand struggle erupted on the parapet of the wall.

Lightning flashed, freezing a moment of the titanic struggle. The flow of Imps arriving on top of the wall slowed, and the *Alle'oss* regained lost ground. But it was only a temporary respite as the Imps adjusted their shields, creating a tunnel which allowed men to approach the ladders at a run unmolested. They burst out of the tunnel and flew up the rungs of the ladder in a well-drilled choreography.

Slowly, the Imps established themselves on top of the wall, pushing the *Alle'oss* back and creating space for more Imps to arrive. Legionnaires dropped to the ground behind the wall. Archers behind the wall cut the first few down, but more arrived until some could raise their shields to protect their comrades while they opened the gate.

Aron fought desperately at the end of the parapet, back against the granite wall. When the gate opened, a roar rose from the legionnaires and the men pressed against the wall poured through the opening.

Blocking a strike aimed at his head, Aron misplaced his foot and fell from the wall. He landed amid a mob of Imps forming up to counter the *Alle'oss* counterattack. He looked up at Imps glaring down at him and crossed into *annen'heim*. The murky underworld writhed with the shadowy *sjel'and* driven into a frenzy by carnage and death. The glittery spirits of the recently dead fled through the dark, only to be engulfed by the soul spirits. He had only moments before the *sjel'and* detected his presence.

Working his way through the mass of men emerging from the gate, he made it into the clear then hurried across the space separating the Imps from the *Alle'oss* reserves who had formed up, pikes raised twenty paces behind the wall.

When he appeared in their midst, they barely noticed, distracted by the oncoming threat. Grabbing the arm of the woman commanding the last reserves, he shouted, "Attack now! Drive them back!"

For a moment, he wasn't sure she would obey. But then she turned to her soldiers and shouted, "Charge!"

As if shot from a bow, the *Alle'oss* charged across the space. Aron joined the headlong rush.

Seeing the oncoming threat, the Imps instinctively formed ranks, raising a line of interlocking shields just before the *Alle'oss* crashed into the barrier. The Imp line sagged under the impact and for a moment, Aron thought they might regain the gate, but the unrelenting pressure of the legionnaires coming from behind arrested their momentum. The mass hovered for moments, men and women hacking at one another, then the *Alle'oss* slowly gave way. They were too few, their lines too thin, and the mass of the enemy too great.

Aron stepped back behind the front line, searching desperately for options. But there were none. Even the archers arriving from their positions along the top of the Cut weren't enough to stem the tide. If the Imps broke through, they would rampage through the *Alle'oss* camp, then all of Argren. His only option was to sound the retreat. If he could save some small part of the army, they could fight another day.

He cast about for someone with a signal horn, then a guttural roar drowned out the growls and screams. He looked past the mass of struggling men and women at flames leaping into the sky on the far side of the wall. Fire illuminated the archers on the rim in yellow and orange.

The Imps pouring through the gate, silhouetted black against the bright flames, stopped and turned to look back.

The pressure on the *Alle'oss* line eased all at once. Sensing the catastrophe unfolding behind them, the Imps in the front line glanced over their shoulders. The line wavered.

Aron rushed forward, screaming, "Now! Drive them back." His sword rose and fell as flames licked at the gate. Faced with the furious assault in their front, and the mysterious inferno at their back, the Imps' shield wall broke. Unable to flee back through the gate, they scattered. Their formation broken, they became vulnerable to pikes, swords, and arrows.

Aron paused, allowing his soldiers to mop up the last of the Imps and looked toward the gate. The flames were dying. Smoke swirled, caught up in whirlwinds spun up by superheated air. Into the opening, a small figure appeared. A sister. She gazed around at the carnage for a moment, swayed on her feet, then collapsed and lay still.

Flynn

Flynn trudged up the hill. Spirit light spidered across the shield she held above her head as arrows struck it. While the cliffs provided the *Alle'oss* a safe vantage to fire down on the Imperials, it was much easier for her to protect herself than in the wild melees she was used to with the Kaileuk. She only had to hold her shield aloft. She was ready to face the *Alle'oss* witch, but when the witch didn't appear immediately, Flynn guessed she was elsewhere. Why else would she allow her countrymen to be slaughtered?

Despite the piles of dead legionnaires on the road, without the witch to bolster the *Alle'oss* defense, the outcome was inevitable. The Empire was willing to accumulate a mountain of bodies to break through at the Cut because they knew the *Alle'oss* defense was a thin shell. Once the Cut fell, Argren would be laid bare.

But when the Imperial assault on the wall slowed, the surge of hope she felt surprised her. She watched the struggle on top of the wall and whispered, "Come on, *Alle'oss*."

Then the gate was thrown open. It was over. There was nothing to stop the flood of Imperial infantry now. So what? Why should she care about the *Alle'oss*? Why were they different from the Andian, the Ferol, the Styrians and all the Empire's victims before them that history forgot?

Men jostled her as they rushed to get through the gate, eager to end the battle and reap the victor's spoils. She watched the tide flooding past her and whispered, "The trick is knowing what is right."

Before reason could dissuade her, she lifted her hands and let the fire spirits loose. Fire was her greatest gift. It was why the legionnaires revered her and the Kaileuk feared her. She turned, releasing flames that spiraled away from her, splashing against the walls of the Cut and engulfing the men pressed tightly together on the highway. The cohort coming up behind her couldn't react before being consumed. The following cohort fled, stumbling over one another to distance themselves from the conflagration. Losing their discipline, gaps appeared between their shields which the *Alle'oss* archers exploited.

Her back safe, she turned toward the top of the Cut. The men pressing to get through the gate turned at the sound of the flames, gaping at her and looking uncertainly at one another. One of them threw a sword, which Flynn caught on her shield. When she lifted her hands, the men turned to flee, but there was nowhere to run.

She knew she was leaving herself open to arrows from above. Knew she would pay the price for channeling the spirits so liberally. She didn't care.

When she felt a familiar euphoric oblivion blanketing her mind, she let her flames go. Stumbling forward through the stinking smoke, arms up to allow the spirits to return, she made it to the gate in time to see the *Alle'oss* finishing the last of her former comrades. Men she risked her life to save in the past. Then she allowed herself to sink into darkness.

Aron

"Up on the wall!" Aron shouted to the stunned survivors. He found the captain in charge of defending the wall, staring around, dazed. "Captain! Get your people organized. We need to get defenders on the wall, and we need to take care of the wounded."

She stared at him blankly and glanced at the smoldering embers of the gate. "But the gate —"

"Archers on the wall! Now!"

"Right," she said, coming to herself.

Aron watched her gathering up the survivors and getting them moving in the right direction, then he picked his way through the carnage to the open gate. Kneeling next to the sister's body, he rolled her onto her back. Though she looked young enough to be a novice, the complexity of her tattoo told a different story. The only sisters who earned such adornment now were those fighting the Kaileuk. Noting the slight rise and fall of her chest, he stood and gazed down the hill.

Corpses, blackened and smoldering, carpeted the highway from the wall to the remnants of the stockade. He couldn't see much past that because of the rain and smoke. Sensing someone step up beside him, he turned to find Zaina looking down at the sister.

"You ever seen her before?" he asked.

"No," she said. "You didn't see her when you visited the camp?"

"No. If I had, I would have been a lot more worried."

"It had to be her," Zaina said. When Aron glanced at her, she gestured around. "She saved us."

Aron looked down at the sister. "It certainly appears that way." He turned and found the captain organizing the treatment of the wounded. "Captain!" When she hurried over, he gestured to the sister and said, "Tie her up." He pressed his elbows and palms tight against one another and said, "Like this. Wrap her arms from her elbows to the tips of her fingers. Tight." When she nodded, he said, "Take her up to the headquarters and leave three guards to watch her."

Aron turned and strode back through the gate, with Zaina beside him. They made their way along the top of the Cut, smiling at their shaken soldiers and giving words of encouragement. The men and women gathered at the opening of the Cut made way for them.

Beyond the tortoise, which smoldered disconsolately in the rain, the remnants of the cohorts that stormed the wall straggled back toward the Imp encampment, passing the unbloodied cohorts still formed up on the highway. A flash of lightning illuminated the general and his staff, safely out of range, sitting on their big Imperial stallions.

"If they come again, we can't stop them," Zaina said.

Aron glanced at her. Noticing blood on her forehead, he rubbed a thumb through the blood and was relieved it didn't appear to be hers. "No," he said. "But even if Prather doesn't know exactly what happened, he has to know a powerful witch was involved. He doesn't know the witch in question is currently passed out and in our custody."

"Is he a gambling man?"

"Prather?" Aron said and grunted. "Prather is a man who prefers massacre to actual fighting." Another flash of lightning revealed the general gesticulating violently to his staff. Despite his assurances to Zaina, Aron's legs wobbled as the tension drained out of him when he saw the general wheel his horse around and head back toward the Imp camp. He turned to the officer who commanded the archers on this side of the Cut. An *Oss'stera* veteran from the far north, her dusky skin revealed her Tituun ancestry.

"Sir?" she asked, sounding as relieved as he was.

"Take care of your people, but keep an eye on the Imps," he said.

"Yes, sir," she said. "Did you…" She glanced at Zaina. "Did either of you see what that sister did?"

"No," Aron said. "What happened?"

"She was just standing there, the infantry streaming past her." She lifted her hand above her hand. "Had a shield up so we couldn't hit her." She let her arm fall. "All of a sudden, she turned around and torched all the men behind her. When she was done with them, she turned toward the gate and just started walking and burning her own men." She glanced around at her soldiers, who were listening and nodding. "It was terrifying. Who was she?"

"One of Deirdre's?" Zaina asked.

"Good question," Aron said. "Let's go find out. Well done, Captain," he said, with a grin. As he and Zaina made their way to their headquarters, he watched the *Alle'oss* coming to terms with the battle. There was trauma, both mental and physical, but there was also a realization they survived and defeated the Empire. At least on this day.

Chapter 43

The 2nd Day of the Month of Heulomon

Gyda

Clouds, black with portent, towered over the plains to the west. The fresh scent of impending rain competed with the sour odor of mud the *Alle'oss* made of the meadow. Rain was not good for their bowstrings. Gyda's stomach rumbled along with distant thunder, reminding her she forgot to eat today.

Not for the first time, she found herself wishing the Union would get there already. The tension building in the *Alle'oss* for weeks was near the breaking point. She felt it and she could sense it in the archers shuffling quietly around her. No matter how bad the battle was, it couldn't be worse than the waiting.

"You think the plan will work?"

Gyda turned her head toward the man who spoke. Frigg. He was as battle-hardened as anyone here. Wore the scars of someone who had been fighting the Imps since the beginning, when Alar led *Oss'stera* into the mountains to loot the Imperial supply caravan. And he turned to Gyda for reassurance. Not that Gyda blamed him for being uncertain. Though she hid her own doubts better, she caught herself glancing over her shoulder, planning her retreat should it become necessary. The *Alle'oss* were used to skirmishes. Hit and run attacks designed to exploit surprise and cause as much damage as possible while minimizing their casualties. They never fought a set piece battle before. She didn't know whether Lief's plan would work, but that wasn't what this man and the other archers waiting nervously for her answer needed to hear.

"Of course, it's going to work," she said, raising her voice so everyone could hear. She turned to face the forty archers gathered around her, lifted her bow and shouted, "*Ērtsa jīla Alle'oss, da?*"

"*Da!*" they shouted in response.

"*Otsuna!*" she shouted *Oss'stera's* battle cry, and they answered. Acknowledging the grins the familiar ritual produced with one of her own, she peered over their heads toward where Lief stood on a low rise behind the thin *Alle'oss* line. His staff gathered around him, all of them looking toward the storm clouds on the western horizon. Two squads of *Alle'oss* soldiers stood off to the side. Their only reserves. The giant, Agmar, towering over the others, caught her eye and gave her a wide smile.

As she turned to face the front, a low rumbling from the south quieted the nervous chatter. "What was that?" she asked.

The trees on the far end of the field shivered, as if some giant shook them. Then the earth near the treeline convulsed. She squinted, unsure what she was seeing. It appeared as if a wave raced across the field toward them. It wasn't large, only a riffling in the grass, but it squeezed the saturated earth, forcing burbling water to the surface where it remained in pools. Most of the *Alle'oss* stepped over the ripple as it passed. Gyda put out a hand to brace herself on Frigg's shoulder and let the disturbance slide under her feet. She felt a slight lift, then turned and watched it peter out a few paces behind their line.

"What in the Father's name was that?" someone asked.

Gyda gazed south. "Earthquake?" She glanced at the ominous clouds reaching out from the western horizon. She wasn't a superstitious person, but between the approaching storm and the earthquake, it certainly seemed like the gods were sending a message.

"Probably something those witches did," Frigg mumbled. "Hope it was Minna."

Gyda did too. In her more optimistic moments, she admitted Lief's plan had a chance against the mercenaries. But no amount of planning would prepare them to face witches. "Steady," she said, talking to herself, but raising her voice so everyone could hear her. "Just an earthquake. *Na'lios* letting us know she's with us, is all."

They gazed across the field in silence. Even the birds, huddled against the coming storm, were quiet. The mountains held their breath. Another crashing rumble, thunder this time, elicited sheepish grins from the startled *Alle'oss*. As the last bass notes of the thunder faded, a small group of *Alle'oss* burst out of the forest on the southern end of the battlefield.

"Steady," Gyda said again.

The newcomers raced across the field on the relatively dry strip along the eastern edge, shouting and gesticulating. Gyda leaned out and looked along the line of *Alle'oss* soldiers, many of them pointing at the newcomers. As they neared the far end of the line, she recognized them as some of the soldiers who accompanied Minna. Why so few, and where were Minna and Sigurn? She cupped a hand behind her ear to hear what they were saying. The mercenaries were coming.

Her breath suddenly thready, she squinted into the shadows beneath the trees on the far end of the meadow. Hints of color became movement which resolved into the enemy. The moment they had been planning for, for weeks, was upon them.

Lief told them what to expect. Told them how frighteningly enormous the Union soldiers were. But it didn't prepare her for the reality. She felt shock and fear ripple through the men and women under her command as the mercenaries emerged. As soon as they spotted the thin *Alle'oss* line spread across the northern end of the field, they slowed. The scene was eerily silent until shouted orders, muffled by distance, urged the enemy into ranks. They spread across the field, a forest of wicked-looking halberds extending above their heads.

"So many," Frigg muttered.

"Lief said a thousand," Gyda said. She couldn't help glancing down at her arrows protruding from a hole gouged into the ground in front of her. It seemed so many only moments before. Now she wondered if it would be enough. "They die like anyone else!" she shouted. "They have to come a long way under a hail of arrows!" To herself, she whispered, "Make every arrow count."

The steady beat of drums rolled across the field. Distant thunder offered an accompaniment. *Now, Lief!* But the signal didn't come as the first rank of the enemy's line parted, allowing a company of archers to file through and deploy into ranks in front of the main line. Just before they moved forward, the horn finally sounded.

Gyda jumped, then glanced around, but everyone was too concerned with their own nerves to notice their commander startling.

"Pikes!" she shouted. The archers scrambled to lift sharpened poles. Though they drilled endlessly on this maneuver, curses rose as people mishandled weapons, tripping and whacking their neighbors. They shuffled forward and thrust the blunt end of the poles into prepared holes arranged in an arc in front of the archers. When everyone returned to their places, they peered through a wall of six-foot spikes that leaned toward the enemy. The barrier would protect the archers and funnel the enemy to the pikemen in the center of their line. The portable abatis in place, Gyda shouted, "String bows!"

This was something they all knew, and she could feel the jitters of her fellow archers steady. Setting her anxiety to float, untethered, she let her body take over, performing the motions she had thousands of times before. Hefting the reassuring weight of her long bow, she glanced left and right and found her archers looking back at her, the signs of panicked flight no longer in their eyes.

"Arrow!" she shouted.

As one, they drew arrows from the bundle at their feet and nocked them. She waited until the enemy archers neared the three hundred pace marker and shouted, "Draw!"

The reassuring creak of bows being drawn momentarily drowned out the roll of the enemy's drums. They angled their bows to ensure the arrows fell in a cloud at the proper range. She waited a moment, then just before she heard the command from the archers on the far end of the *Alle'oss* line, she shouted. "Loose!"

Bows twanged, and arrows from both ends of the line arced into the air. "Arrow!" she shouted and plucked up another arrow. As the first flight was bending toward the earth, another was chasing it.

Before the Union archers even nocked their first arrows, death fell among them. The yard long, iron-tipped *Alle'oss* arrows passed through the mercenaries' leather armor as if it were tissue paper. The first flight felled nearly a third of the enemy archers. By the third flight, the few still able to run streamed back toward their own lines.

"Cease fire!" Gyda shouted, watching the last flight falling uselessly among the bodies left scattered across the ground before glancing down at her diminishing supply of arrows.

A cheer rose all along the *Alle'oss* line.

"Thank the gods!" Frigg said. "It worked!"

That was the easy part. Soldiers in the Union lines shuffled aside to let their archers pass through, then closed up.

"They're coming!" Gyda shouted. "Ready yourselves. They'll be coming fast. Don't waste arrows."

The drum's cadence picked up, and the long, colorful line rippled. Four ranks of men, four hundred in all, started walking, shoulder to shoulder, small flags fluttering from halberds pointing toward the sky. After a few steps, the drum's tempo increased, and the enemy picked up their pace to match.

"Arrow!" Gyda shouted, trying to gauge the mercenaries' pace. She needed to time it so their salvo fell at the right spot. "Draw!" As the mercenaries neared the three hundred pace marker, she shouted, "Loose!"

As soon as she gave the order, the drums sped up again, and the enemy surged forward. "Zut!" Gyda muttered as arrows fell behind the line of men.

"Arrow!" she shouted.

As they approached the two hundred pace marker, she shouted urgently, "Draw! Loose!"

The drum sped once more, and the mercenaries increased their pace again just as they reached the pools of water left behind by the earthquake. The ripple churned the wet earth, leaving it soft and sticky. Despite their increased efforts, the enemy's pace slowed as they sank to their ankles in mud.

Gyda timed it perfectly. Arrows fell on the ranks and the mercenaries fell in droves. The entire line slowed as the fallen jostled and tripped their comrades.

"Fire at will!" Gyda shouted.

Arrows dropped from the sky as the first raindrops pattered down. Still, the mercenaries came on. Distantly, she heard the horn signaling the infantry to prepare. The *Alle'oss* infantry stretched out between the two groups of archers raised their pikes. Glancing to her left, she saw a bristling barrier that would surely stop the remnant of the enemy's charge. Then she looked south toward the other end of the field. Four more ranks of mercenaries were moving forward. Looking down at her few remaining arrows, she shouted, "Hold fire!" just as the first wave of mercenaries crashed into the center of the *Alle'oss* line.

Agmar

Agmar stood in the center of the two squads that made up the reserve. From the small rise behind the front line, he had a good view of the oncoming threat. He squeezed the smooth shaft of his pike and glanced up at the steel point, gray against a darker gray sky.

He watched the first four ranks of the enemy falling to the hail of arrows, marveling that any of them survived. As they neared the two ranks of *Alle'oss* soldiers that made up the line between the archers, he noticed more than a few of the *Alle'oss* glancing over their shoulders. Whether they were looking to Lief for reassurance or looking for a way out, he couldn't tell. The fear on their faces suggested it was the latter.

Agmar sympathized. He had never been afraid of physical confrontation, but the sight of the mercenaries charging across the field was like nothing he imagined before. They were easily as imposing as he was. He glanced at Lief and his staff. They looked as calm as if this were a drill. Catching the panicky frown on the face of the man next to him,

Agmar clapped him on the back and grinned widely when the man lurched forward. "Won't be long now," he shouted.

Since coming west to join the army, Agmar found something he never had before; a sense of purpose and belonging. He enjoyed farming, enjoyed working the land with his hands, seeing what he put into the ground grow. But in soldiering, he found something suited to his natural aggression. He was twice the fighter as anyone else in the army. That was why they put him where he was. If the enemy broke their line, Agmar's squad would close the gap. Lief told him so himself, and Agmar took the responsibility seriously.

He gazed south at the enemy struggling across the swampy ground. They were getting close. For a moment, he considered the possibility the archers would finish them to the last man. He knew he shouldn't feel disappointment, but he did. After weeks of training, of honing skills he was proud of, he wanted to get into the action.

The horn sounded. Men and women on the front line lifted their pikes. The first line rested the butt ends of their pikes in prepared holes, angling the tips to create a wall of sharp points. The second rank lifted their weapons and held them horizontally between the gaps of the first rank's pikes. It was hard for Agmar to see how anyone could penetrate that spikey wall. "Steady!" he called, wanting to rush forward to fortify the line. "They's thinned out, but they're still comin."

Somehow, nearly forty mercenaries survived the hail of arrows. When they reached the relatively dry ground near the top of the hill, they bellowed in their rough language and surged forward.

"Brace!" The command rolled down the line and Agmar answered with a roar.

The relentless surge of the enemy crashed into the *Alle'oss* lines. Some were caught on the sharp ends of the pikes, but others brushed the obstacles aside with their halberds and bulled into the soldiers holding them. Screams, splintering wood, roars, growls, a violent cacophony erupted.

The line sagged in the middle where the enemy concentrated their attack. Agmar took a step forward before he caught himself. He glanced at Lief, who looked as calm as he had before. Men on the second *Alle'oss* rank stumbled backward, impaled on the sharp points of the enemies' halberds or cut down by the wide axe blades. A gap opened, revealing the mercenaries in their brightly colored armor.

Agmar was moving even before the horn sounded the attack. With a bellow, he charged down the slope, his pike held out in front of him. A mercenary standing in the center of the gap saw him coming and set himself, halberd up to parry Agmar's thrust.

At the last second, Agmar lifted his pike vertical, using it to sweep the halberd aside. He lowered his shoulder and drove it into his opponent's chest. He expected to drive the man back into his comrades, but he only took a step back and swung the long handle of his halberd at Agmar's head. Only the fact that Agmar stumbled to one knee saved him.

Throwing out his arms to catch his balance, Agmar dropped his pike. When the halberd swept over his head, he let out a feral growl and thrust himself upward. Grasping the mercenary's head in both hands, he drove his forehead into the man's face, flattening his nose with a satisfying crunch. The halberd went flying and before the man could recover, Agmar drove his knee up between his legs, then drew his knife, expecting his opponent to be incapacitated. Instead, the man's hand wrapped around Agmar's wrist, trapping his hand against his side. Agmar's vision blurred as something struck his face. Seeing his opponent pulling his knobby fist back for another punch, Agmar stepped forward and wrapped his free arm around the man. With another growl, Agmar twisted and kicked the man's feet from under him. They fell, Agmar landing on top.

Driven by his weight, Agmar's knife pierced the mercenary's abdomen. Agmar's face was inches from his opponent's. In the moment before the light left his enemy's eyes, Agmar was sure he saw relief replacing the mercenary's blank mask.

He backed away from the body, got to his feet, and stood in a small void among the struggling men and women. The few remaining mercenaries battled the *Alle'oss* to keep the gap open. The next four ranks of mercenaries were on their way. If the *Alle'oss* didn't reform their line before they arrived, it would be a disaster.

Agmar dug the fallen mercenary's halberd from the mud and turned toward the oncoming threat.

Gyda

Impossibly, Gyda saw the center of the *Alle'oss* line give as the enemy crashed into it. How could so many have survived to reach their lines? Setting her archers to firing at the next group of mercenaries, she grabbed Frigg and pulled him into motion.

They bypassed the makeshift abatis, drew their swords and fell on the backs of the mercenaries, applying pressure to the *Alle'oss* infantry. Their attention on the pikemen in front of them, the Union men didn't react to the attack coming from behind until it was too late. All at once, the ferocity went out of the mercenaries and they turned and fled.

Gyda took a swipe at the last one, then rushed to return to her command. Retrieving her bow, she gazed across the battlefield. The next rank was coming on, but the ground, churned by the passage of men, slowed them even more than the first group. Gyda plucked an arrow up, nocked and loosed. She continued to fire until she reached down and discovered she was out of arrows. Looking around, she saw others looking back at her. They were all out of arrows.

The mercenaries were still coming, but there were fewer than there were in the first attack.

"Pikes!" she shouted. The archers dropped their bows, rushed forward and pulled the pikes from the holes where they placed them. "Form up!" she shouted, and they formed a rough line around her.

The mercenaries were thirty paces away when the horn sounded the charge.

Gyda's voice joined the rest of the *Alle'oss* as the entire army flowed down the slope. The row of pikes struck the remaining mercenaries like a tidal wave, engulfing them and driving them back. After burying her pike in a man's stomach, Gyda let it go, pulled her sword and cast about for another victim. But only her fellow *Alle'oss* looked back at her. The last of the Union soldiers were fleeing back the way they came. She took a step, intending to chase them down, but then fatigue and overwhelming relief crashed down on her. *They won!*

She looked around at her countrymen, disbelief on all their faces. Despite their bluster about Lief's plan before the battle, they all harbored doubts.

Gyda lifted her sword above her head and shouted, *"Otsuna!"*

Frigg looked at Gyda, his face trembling, a series of emotions trying to pull it into some recognizable expression. Then a wide smile split his lips. Throwing his arms above his head, he answered her. *"Otsuna!"*

And then all the *Alle'oss*, those who had been shouting *Oss'stera's* battle cry from the time they were children and those who only recently joined the fight, were shouting, clapping one another on the back, hugging, sinking to sit weeping in the mud. Gyda wrapped her arms around Frigg, rocked back and forth until they fell in a heap into the mud.

The horn sounded the assembly. Slowly, they pulled themselves together and trudged up the hill to their original line.

As Gyda took stock of the health of the men and women under her command, she saw scouts heading south to check on the enemy's whereabouts.

"We won," Frigg said quietly. Those standing close enough to hear him smiled at one another.

"Yes, we won," Gyda said. "Today," she added to herself, gazing at the broken bodies of her countrymen lying in the mud.

Chapter 44

The 2nd Day of the Month of Heulomon

Keelia

The *Alle'oss* met the rangers a league from the *Alle'oss* camp four hours earlier. Unlike previous encounters, the Imps pressed their attack after the initial skirmish. It was the first time Keelia commanded a large force in such a dynamic engagement, and it showed. She spent most of the battle confused and a step behind events. The only reason they hadn't been overrun was because she trained her soldiers well. They were comfortable acting independently and fought tenaciously.

But little by little, the ranger's superior numbers and experience began to tell. Displaying all the skill and cunning of their kind, the rangers repeatedly outmaneuvered the *Alle'oss* and drove them backward. Keelia's command was now arranged in a loose arc in front of their camp. They didn't have the numbers to form a continuous line and were forced to rely on movement and knowledge of the terrain to fill the gaps.

Though Keelia repeatedly tried to take the initiative, the enemy knew her weakness. Every time she entered the fight, the rangers faded away before she could come to grips with them. Her lightning had limited range in the forest and she couldn't pursue them because she couldn't protect herself from all sides. They were baiting her, willing to sacrifice a few men to draw her out, force her to tap into the spirits, then retreating before her presence was decisive.

And their tactics were working. Keelia was reaching her limit. There was no heavy infantry to accept her into their protective embrace here. Chewing the inside of her cheek to help herself focus, she guessed she had maybe one more major effort left in her.

"I think they're gone," Jason whispered.

Keelia peered through the brush toward the top of a ridge which a company of rangers defended tenaciously for the past two hours. There was no movement and there hadn't been for the past half hour. "I agree," she said. "But where did they go?"

"Want to send a scout up the ridge?"

She shook her head. She had been so overwhelmed, she hadn't taken advantage of the fact she had a spirit guide. Remembering Minna telling her how she and Linea found their way through the Fallows the previous winter, she focused on her spirit guide, who was gleefully communing with the other *lan'and* in her center. *I need to see on top of that ridge.* The spirit looped, then disappeared. Keelia peered around the ancient elm she and Jason hid behind and watched her spirit guide disappear into the undergrowth.

"We could give up the camp," Jason said. "Fall back and hope surprise gives us enough time to get organized before they catch us."

"We'll have to abandon the wounded," she said. "Besides, if we lose the camp, we might as well keep going. We'll be out of arrows soon. If I knew they would chase us east, I'd consider it, but they might head south and find *Helala*." She bit her lip. Was it time for her to take matters into her own hands? She couldn't attack them from a distance, but if she could get close enough —

"No, you don't," Jason said as if he read her mind. "You'll never be able to protect yourself in the forest. They'll come at you from all sides."

"I could take two squads to protect my flanks. Make sure no one gets behind me."

"They'll overwhelm us down here, and you'll be alone."

They fell silent. For the first time in hours, the forest was quiet. No shouts, no screams from the wounded or dying.

"Wish I knew what they were up to," she said. Her spirit guide reappeared. Keelia closed her eyes and welcomed it into her center. Minna told her about the visions Linea showed her, but when it appeared, she was startled by how clear it was. It was as if she were flying north to south along the spine of the ridge. Only two men from the company remained.

"They're gone!" she said.

"Where?"

Shouts on the *Alle'oss* left erupted, signaling a renewed attack. Keelia stood and listened as the shouts died down. It was too brief to be a serious attack. Was it worth gambling? Yes. She was tired of letting the rangers dictate the course of the battle. It was time to take to initiative. "They're moving around our left flank," she said. Before Jason could ask her how she knew, she stood and signaled to the commander of her last reserve squad.

"Sir?" the man said.

"Get your squad to Siv's bluff," she said, pointing to the southeast. They named features in the surrounding terrain after soldiers in her command. "Don't let it fall. No matter what."

He glanced over his shoulder, then saluted. "Yes, sir."

"What's going on?" Jason asked.

"The rangers in our front pulled back and are working their way around our left," Keelia said. She gestured to the sound of fighting to the south. "That's to screen their passing."

"So, we should send more than a squad to meet them," Jason said. "There was an entire company in front of us."

"No," Keelia said. "They've left us an opening, and we're going to exploit it. Pass the word, we have to move quickly."

Jason turned to comply. When he returned, he asked, "What's the plan?"

"We cross over the ridge, get behind their line, then turn south and hit the Imps pressing our left flank from behind."

Jason gave the signal that sent the four squads up the slope.

Climbing the brush covered face of the slope, Keelia said, "Leave a squad on the top to block any Imps coming from the north. We don't want anyone hitting our backs."

"Yes, sir," Jason said.

Show me the top of the ridge again. Her spirit guide looped. When it returned, the spine of the ridge appeared again. The two men who remained were scouts to ensure the *Alle'oss* didn't do exactly what they were intending to do.

"Sound the halt," she said.

Jason put his fingers to his lips and blew a mountain bluebird's warble.

"Wait here," she said. She picked her way along the slope until she was below the spot where the two men peered down on the *Alle'oss* lines. Five more paces up, she would emerge from the thick brush and be visible. She sent her spirit guide up one more time, and once she was sure where the men were, she rushed up the last few steps and burst from the undergrowth. One of the men put a signal horn to his lips before Keelia's spirit wave threw them backwards.

She climbed to the top of the ridge and made sure the Imps were dead, then sounded the advance. When the rest of the soldiers joined her, she gathered them around and said, "We need to hurry, but stealth is essential." She waited, scanning their faces as they nodded. "We descend to the bottom of the ridge, head west for forty paces, then turn southeast. When I give the signal, we spread out, line abreast, and attack east, then we roll them up. Speed is the key. Don't give them time to melt away." She waited for questions, and when none came, she said, "Alright, move out."

Even as the faint sounds of fighting from Siv's bluff reached them, they kept to a stealthy pace. Her spirit guide found the enemy, drawn up behind a low hill. Most of them lined the top of the hill, watching the *Alle'oss* lines. The commander and a squad gathered at the bottom of the hill, looking as relaxed as if they were in camp.

Keelia used hand gestures to signal the enemy's disposition. When her soldiers were in position, they moved forward. Their appearance was such a surprise, the Imps barely reacted. Crowded together in the small hollow below the hill, they made an easy target for her lightning. The soldiers spread out on either side of her targeted the Imps lining the top of the hill. It was over in moments.

"Move!" she shouted. "Roll 'em up." Without waiting, Keelia turned south and plunged into the underbrush, searching out the Imp lines. Though the rangers could hear her lightning, they had been hearing it throughout the battle and couldn't know the *Alle'oss* were behind their lines. By the time they understood, there was not enough time to redeploy to face the new threat. Keelia and her soldiers rolled up the Imp lines, inflicting far more casualties than they suffered.

When they reached Siv's bluff, the squad Keelia left to hold it was near collapse. The Imps were so intent on breaking through the wavering *Alle'oss* resistance, they weren't paying attention to Keelia approaching them from their left flank until her lightning buzzed and crackled among them.

The last few Imps fled into the forest. Keelia sent her soldiers in pursuit, then searched for Jason, but somehow, they became separated in the confusion. Unfortunately, there was a sea of details to see to, so she returned to camp. They still had to contend with the Imps on their northern flank, who, not knowing the catastrophe that befell their comrades, still pressed the *Alle'oss* lines. They needed to tend to the wounded and track the fleeing Imps to make sure they didn't turn and resume their attack.

Go find Jason, she told her spirit guide. A vision of Jason, his soft smile inches from her own in the dim light of her tent, came into her mind. *Yes, that's him.* Keelia felt her cheeks warm. When Minna described how intimate her relationship was with Linea, it left Keelia wondering if it was something she wanted. Naturally reticent, Keelia let few people past her outer layers.

While the spirit set off, Keelia pushed the thought from her mind and got to work.

"Can we get more supplies from our contacts in Kartok?" Keelia asked Siv a half hour later. The largest city in Argren was an Imperial stronghold and only a few leagues east of their camp. A big part of the *Alle'oss* operations involved keeping an eye on the Imp garrison in the city. Fortunately, it appeared the Volloch elite who lived there were too concerned with protecting their own property to allow the garrison to cause mischief for the *Alle'oss*.

"Already sent a squad to make contact," Siv said.

Keelia looked up as her spirit guide zoomed across the camp. It stopped and hovered two paces in front of her. Keelia let her center open, but the spirit didn't move. "What's wrong?" she asked, a dank sense of dread spreading from her stomach.

Behind the guide, a man burst out of the brush on the far side of the camp and raced toward Keelia. He came to a stop, saluted, but before he spoke, Keelia could see in his face what he would say.

•   •   •

Jason lay on his back, eyes open, staring unseeing at the forest canopy. It happened early in their counterattack. Keelia hadn't noticed. There was so much confusion and she was so intent on the attack, she forgot to protect the one person in the world she should have.

"I'm sorry, si — Keelia." Siv's voice, a distant echo, though she was standing right behind her. Keelia didn't answer. Couldn't find the breath to speak if she wanted to. Not caring about the squad that insisted on accompanying her, she sank to her knees in the damp litter. She reached out, wanting to touch his face one more time, but then she let her hand fall to rest on her thigh.

It was just war. It's what happened when men fought. She, more than most, knew the costs of men's hate. Faced with the choice of throwing herself on his body and weeping uncontrollably, to Daga with what her soldiers thought, or allowing the callouses she earned against the Kaileuk to encase her heart once again, she chose to protect herself.

Rising, she turned to Siv and said, "We'll bury him on top of the bluffs south of the camp."

Siv gazed uncertainly at her, tipped her head to the side, looking as if she would speak, then she gave Keelia a crisp nod and said, "Yes, sir." Keelia hesitated for a moment, fighting the urge to turn and look down at the only man who ever pried her heart open, then returned Siv's nod, pushed her way past the squad and returned to her duties.

Chapter 45

The 2nd Day of the Month of Heulomon

Flynn

She was a prisoner in the *Alle'oss* camp. A murmur of voices rose momentarily, enough so she could tell they were speaking *Alle'oss*. She lay on her back. Her arms were wrapped from her elbows to her fingertips, her palms pressed together. It was clever. She didn't know what would happen if she called on the fire spirits. She usually didn't have to worry about them burning her. They might free her from the rope, but who knew? Not that she wanted to escape. It was just that she was curious and her fingers ached.

She opened her eyes and looked up at shadowy rafters and roughly cut planks lit only by lamplight.

"Ērtsi sa elera."

It was a woman's voice. Flynn craned her neck and saw a woman with blond hair and sapphire blue eyes approaching the bed. Her face fell into shadow as she neared. A man with blond hair appeared beside her.

"Hello," he said.

Flynn licked her lips and swallowed to moisten her mouth. "Hello," she croaked.

The woman retreated for a moment and returned with a waterskin. She helped Flynn sit up and let her drink, then lay her down. It was all handled much more tenderly than Flynn expected.

"I'm Aron Hunter and this is Zaina," the man said and gave her an expectant look.

"Nara Flynn," Flynn said. "But people call me Flynn."

The man pulled a stool over and sat. "*Sister* Flynn, and an accomplished sister, judging by the tattoo."

"Yes, well, I'm not sure about the sister part. Not after..." She fell silent and stared up at the ceiling, trying to piece together the moments before she erupted. What exactly was she thinking? The man and woman watched her, letting her think. "I..." Flynn started, then stopped. "I really couldn't tell you why I did what I did. Just snapped. Had enough of people like Briana and Prather. Maybe." That was as good an explanation as any. What would her father have thought? "I'm not sorry for it." She was surprised she said it, and even more surprised she believed it. It would take time to sort through her feelings, to come to terms with cutting her ties to everything she knew, including her family. But she didn't regret it, not much, anyway. And that was enough. For now.

"Can you..." She lifted her hands. Her fingertips protruding from the rope coils were a deep red. "I think I might lose my fingers."

"You see our predicament," Aron said. "You saved our army, and quite a few others as well. We owe you a great deal. But..."

"If you're worried I'd turn on you, I can assure you I have no intention of harming anyone here."

"We want to believe you," Aron said. "But the stakes are rather high."

"I've cut any ties I had with anyone in the Empire," Flynn said. "No matter what you think, they'll never forgive me for what I did. I could burn all of Argren to the ground and it wouldn't be enough." She swallowed and examined Aron's face. "Besides, you're a realm walker. I'd be dead before I could channel the spirits."

Aron and Zaina exchanged a look.

"We saw you kill the sisters," Flynn said. "If it was supposed to be a secret, the cat's out of the bag."

Aron stood and drew a knife from a sheath at his belt. "Would have come out sooner or later." He leaned over her and started working on the ropes.

Flynn grimaced as blood returned to her fingers, a far more painful imitation of the fire she was known for. She curled her fingers into loose fists. "Daga, that hurts."

"Sorry about that," Aron said.

As Zaina took her arm and helped her to sit on the edge of the narrow cot, Flynn noticed Aron didn't sheath his knife. She let her hands rest in her lap, the pain ebbing to fiery prickles, and stared around the room, which was obviously the *Alle'oss* war room. "Now what?"

"Up to you," Zaina said.

"You'll just let me go?"

"Well, our choices are to let you go or kill you," Aron said with a disturbingly wide smile. "It's not practical to keep you prisoner for long. You might resent that, and eventually, we'd slip up. We could ransom you. I'm sure the Imps would pay handsomely to have you back. For their own reasons." He flipped the knife and caught the blade. "Seems impolite to give you back to them after what you did for us."

Flynn flexed her fingers experimentally.

"You're welcome to stay with us," Aron said. He flipped the knife again, caught the hilt and returned it to its sheath.

"Fight for the *Alle'oss*?"

"We would, of course, welcome that possibility," Zaina said. "But we can't force you to fight."

Could she fight against the Empire? Beyond what she already did? She gave her head a shake. That was a whim, a momentary lack of judgment. She thought of the men who waved to her when she arrived in the Ninth's camp. Men she bled with, celebrated victory with. Men with whom she mourned the passing of friends. How many of them did she murder on her whim? She gave her head another imperceptible shake and shoved the memories aside. "I don't know what I'm going to do."

The room was silent for long moments, then Aron asked, "How well did you know Sister Keelia?"

Flynn's head snapped up. "Keelia?" She knew Sister Keelia. One of the good girls. They were novices together. Keelia was devout, eager to please the older sisters, especially Briana. When she turned up at the front, Flynn was sure it wouldn't end well. And she was right. It was a miracle Keelia survived her first encounter with the Kaileuk.

It was Flynn who helped her shrug off the effects of the cleansing that robbed her of her spirit sight. Flynn was gratified when Keelia proved to be one of the most powerful sisters at the front, and they became fast friends. But it disgusted her and her fellow sisters that Keelia was called back to the capital, hailed a hero, and held up as evidence the Seidi wasn't a shadow of what it once was.

Aron nodded. "She's in command of our forces in the south. You should go talk to her." He glanced at Zaina, who nodded. "It's a place to start."

Keelia was alive. Flynn squeezed her fists, letting the pain sharpen her focus. "Yes," she said, nodding. "I would like to see Keelia again." She looked up at the two *Alle'oss* and said, "That's what I'll do."

Gyda

"So, we just let the mercs go?" Gyda asked Lief, trying to keep the anger from her voice. They were in his headquarters. Rain battered the canvas, forcing them to stand close and raise their voices.

"We don't have a choice," Lief said. "Aron is expecting everyone who can walk back at the Cut. But you're right, we can't just let them roam through Argren on their own. Willa is still tracking them." He drew her attention to the map of Argren and pointed to a village. "Last we heard, she had her HQ here." He met her gaze. "I want you to take two squads, link up with Willa, and keep an eye on the mercs." He traced a line connecting the scribbled notes on the map that represented the sightings of the mercenaries along their path from the coast. "They'll probably return the way they came. If they do, don't interfere. Just track them and keep us informed." His face took on an uncharacteristic intensity. "But there's always the chance they'll head south to the coast before turning east."

Gyda stared at him, not sure what caused the tension in his voice.

He glanced around at his staff, who were busy with other tasks, and leaned close to her. "There's a village on the coast called *Helala*," he said and pointed to a blank spot on the map. "The Union cannot find that village. Do you understand?"

She started to ask why it was so important, but it only mattered that Lief said it was, so she asked, "What do we do if they head that way?"

"Whatever is required."

Two squads. The *Alle'oss* mauled the mercenaries pretty badly, but what remained would swat two squads aside without slowing down. "Yes, sir," Gyda said and saluted.

Ulf

The misfits stood on the shoulder of the mountain where they made their stand and watched soldiers streaming south across the field below them. Their armor's bright colors appeared duller in the downpour, but it was unmistakably the army they saw moving north in such good order earlier. They were crossing the field in the opposite direction and appeared to be in much worse condition than before. Many of them bore wounds, some of them carried wounded on stretchers.

"What does it mean?" Hakon asked.

"It means the *Alle'oss* won the battle," Ulf said.

"We beat them?" Helga asked. "Was it Minna?"

"I don't think Minna was involved," Ulf said. "I didn't see or hear anything like the fireworks she usually creates."

"So, we won without Minna?" Mikaela asked.

"Looks like it," Ulf said. He looked around at the others, rain water pouring down their grinning faces.

"Where *was* Minna?" Helga asked.

It was a good question, but Ulf was not about to encourage Helga's negativity.

"I can't wait to hear that story," Mikaela said, ignoring the question of Minna's whereabouts. "The *Alle'oss* army defeated an army of monsters. No one will believe it a hundred years from now."

Helga frowned, but found no one willing to pursue the question of where Minna went.

Noticing the enemy who were keeping an eye on them from the bottom of the slope leaving, Ulf said, "Someone needs to go check on our two missing misfits."

"I'll go," Hakon said. When he returned, he shook his head. "They didn't make it. Should we —"

Inger appeared out of the deluge, chugging up the slope. Mikaela moved aside to allow her room beside Ulf.

She saluted, her chest rising and falling. "We won," was all she could get out before she had to pause for breath.

Her words were passed to those standing too far away to hear. A few ragged cheers rose, then as the news sank in, a full-throated celebration erupted. Ulf put his face close to Inger's and asked, "Did you see Minna?"

"No," she said. "It was just the army. But we won anyway!"

Ulf let go of her arms and gazed north. If Minna wasn't there, she had a good reason. Or she wasn't able to be there.

"So, we go meet the army, right?" Helga asked.

Ulf blinked and gazed at her blankly. "Meet..." he said vaguely, then with an effort, he put thoughts of Minna aside. Taking his upper lip between his teeth, he watched the last of the enemy army emerging from the trees along the north end of the meadow. They would likely return south the same way they came. Still. He closed his eyes and brought to mind the map of Argren Minna showed him. As the celebrations subsided, he turned south, trying to picture where they stood in relation to *Helala*. Opening his eyes, he gazed toward the coast. *Helala* was almost due south from where they stood.

"What's the matter, Ulf?" Mikaela asked.

Ulf focused on the faces around him. "We have to make sure," he said.

"Make sure of what?" Mikaela asked.

It wasn't his place to divulge the location of *Helala,* but how could he ask the misfits to put themselves at risk without telling them why?

He retreated from the rim of the slope and motioned for everyone to gather around him. Raising his voice so everyone could hear him over the steady beat of the rain, he said, "There is a village south of here on the coast called *Helala.* It's a refuge for children like Minna. Children the *Alle'oss* rescued from the Inquisition."

"I've never heard of it," Hakon said.

"The resistance kept it secret," Ulf said.

"So?" Helga asked.

"Those men are heading south. We don't know if they're going toward *Helala,* but if they are…" He swallowed and said, "We have to make sure."

They all looked down as the last of the enemy army crossed the field below them. They were battered, but there had to be three hundred of them still walking.

"Ulf," Mikaela said. "What are we supposed to do to stop them?"

She was right, but they had no choice but to try. They needed help.

"Helga, go contact the army. They should be sending some soldiers to keep an eye on this lot." He gestured to the meadow below them. "Tell them what we're doing and see if you can get them to send help." He thought a minute, then said, "We'll keep to the west of the enemy army. If they send help, you'll find us there."

She nodded, hesitated, then saluted and turned to go.

Surprised, Ulf watched her making her way down the slope.

"What about the rest of us?" Mikaela asked.

Ulf turned to look at his soldiers, who watched him expectantly. "Someone has to race ahead to *Helala,* to warn them."

"I'll go," Inger said.

"I'll go with her," Hakon said.

"Okay," Ulf said. He knelt and sketched what he remembered of the map in the mud. Inger and Hakon leaned over to block the rain. Pointing at the spot where *Helala* would be, he said, "Just head south to the coast. There's a powerful *saa'myn* there named Beadu and the former Malefica, Deirdre. They can help defend the village."

"The Malefica?" Hakon asked. "A Seidi sister?"

"Yeah," Ulf said. "She helped us escape last winter." He shrugged. "She's supposed to be powerful." When no further questions came from them, Ulf added what he remembered from their hikes in the terrain north of *Helala* to the map. "They'll have to go through this pass to reach the coast."

"Good place for an ambush," Mikaela said with a grin.

Standing, Ulf returned her grin and used the rain to wash the mud from his fingers. "We'll send someone ahead to let you know the plan when we come up with one. Just tell them to get ready."

"Yes, sir," they chorused, saluted and took off.

"What do we do?" Mikaela and the other misfits waited for his answer.

"We keep an eye on the… Imps or whatever they are," Ulf said. "Make sure they don't go toward *Helala*. We don't want to fight unless we have to, but if we have to, we slow them down to give Hakon and Inger time. Any questions?" When none came, he said, "Let's go."

Minna

By the time Sigurn and Minna made it to *honua*, they were soaked through to the skin and shivering. Even in summer, *na'lios* could be chilly. Water poured down the granite edifice that gave *honua* its name; the shelter. Minna led Edda through the torrent into the sheltered overhang, flicked the moisture from her fingers and wiped her hands down her face. When she opened her eyes, she was looking at the firepit where she and Ulf spent the first night of their journey to Brennan. She stared, frozen in place, until Edda nudged her and nickered softly.

Minna blinked, looked up and rested her hand on Edda's nose. She led her over beside Sigurn's horse and set to loosening the girth. Sigurn dropped his horse's saddle and blanket, walked away without speaking and dropped onto a log beside the cold firepit.

"Light a fire," Minna said as she heaved the saddle from Edda's back and let it fall.

"Why don't you light the fire?" Sigurn asked, staring morosely into the rain. "Isn't that one of your *gifts*?"

"We don't *use* the spirits that —" Another traitorous memory of Ulf suggesting the same thing to her the previous winter stole her voice for a moment. But cold, exhausted, worried for the *Alle'oss* army, and tired of Sigurn's griping, the anger she suppressed surged. "We need a fire to dry everything!" She snatched the saddle blanket from her horse's back, held it up and shook it at him, before dropping it on top of the saddle. "Unless you *like* moping around in wet clothes."

He thrust himself upright and stomped over to the woodpile at the back of the shelter, grumbling under his breath. Minna watched him, teeth clamped against the invective she wanted to hurl at him. All Sigurn did since they left for *honua* was complain and question her motives. Between his gripes and the rain, she didn't have a moment to think about the vision. Ulf would have listened to her, would have trusted her, would have helped her understand.

Sensing weakness, the despair which hovered so close to the surface since Ulf's disappearance pounced. Caught by surprise, she sucked in a breath and took a stumbling step backward.

When Sigurn glanced at her, she bent over to retrieve a curry comb, disguising her efforts to wipe traitorous tears from her cheeks. She straightened, turned her back on him, panting with the effort to put the blackness back where it wouldn't hurt her. When she was sure she had control of herself, she put the comb to her horse's back, and took advantage of Sigurn's silence to think. She was sure it must have been Alyn or Beadu who sent the *sjel'and*. She was less sure she interpreted the message correctly, but she wasn't going to admit that to Sigurn.

"No telling what happened to the army with those witches alive," Sigurn said under his breath.

Minna clenched her teeth. That was it! Whirling to face him, she said, "I told you —" She gestured violently with the hand holding the comb. It slipped from her grip and flew out into the rain. Ignoring it, she shouted, "I told you already. One of the witches was injured and the other two were taking care of her."

"How did she get injured? It wasn't something you did. *You* ran away."

The heat roiling her thoughts and spurring her tongue cooled in an instant. She stared at him, studying his face as if seeing him for the first time. "I know worry and fear are behind your words," she said. "I can forgive that." He started to argue, but she held up her hand. "What I can't forgive is that you abandoned me when I needed you most." She waved a hand. "You're here. You didn't run away." She pointed to her chest with her thumb. "But I need more than your churlish presence. Too much is at stake for you to surrender to pique." His expression shifted. She could hear the apology coming, but didn't want to hear it.

"You would think," she said, cutting him off, "after everything I've done, you would have a little more faith in —"

The raven burst through the torrent of water cascading down the granite edifice above them, and landed on the ground in front of Minna. Looking as disgruntled as a raven could, it ruffled its feathers and turned one black eye on Minna.

It was the raven with the shawl of white feathers. When she recovered from her surprise, she called the spirit that let her talk to animals. The forest came alive with the presences of creatures huddling in their dens against the rain. Ignoring all of them, she focused on the raven and was rewarded with an image of her sister attaching the message to his leg. Relief flooded through her, loosening her joints and emerging as laughter that echoed in the small space and brought a small grin to Sigurn's lips.

After the last time she encountered this bird, when she saw the black witch dangling a bit of dried meat, she made sure she was ready for the next time. Dipping into a small pouched attached to her belt, she withdrew a bit of dried venison. She knelt and held up the treat. "Thank you for bringing my sister's message." The raven hopped toward her and allowed her to remove the message. It plucked the meat from her fingers, fluttered as far from Minna and Sigurn as it could in the shelter, then set to picking at the morsel.

Minna unrolled the damp paper.

If you're reading this, then you heeded the message from my spirit guide. I know, a sjel'and is not what I would have chosen for a spirit guide, but I've grown quite fond of him. I don't have much space, so you will have to trust me and wait for explanations. I met our mother's spirit. Ragan. She told me to tell you to get Sigurn to take you to meet Ecke.

Minna flipped the message over. That was all? Couldn't they just use a bigger scrap of paper or use both sides? With a sigh, she sank to the ground and sat cross-legged. She held the message in her lap and gazed into the rain. Alyn's spirit guide was a *sjel'and?* She couldn't imagine it. She saw Sigurn shift out of the corner of her eye and glanced down at the scrap of paper. For better or worse, they were tied together now. Would he agree to take her?

"What does it say?" Sigurn asked and sank to sit beside her.

Minna handed the message to him. "Who's Ecke?" she asked after he read it, turning it over as she had.

"Ecke is a wi —" He looked up at her and amended his statement. "A *saa'myn.*"

"A *saa'myn?*" Minna asked, the still smoldering embers of her anger stirring. Another secret Beadu and Ragan kept from her. "Where has she been? I thought Beadu was the last *saa'myn.*"

Sigurn handed the slip of paper back to her. "She's not old like Beadu. Alar rescued her from the Inquisition nine or ten years ago."

"How come I haven't heard of her?"

"She's been abroad," Sigurn said. He waved his hands in imitation of Minna channeling the spirits. "She can't do all the fire and wind stuff. She's more a healer. Been in Tsada studying medicine."

"Tsada?"

"It's across the Eastern Sea."

Minna huffed and immediately felt like a child. Wasn't she just angry with Sigurn for not trusting her? Beadu and Ragan earned her trust. If they didn't tell her something, they had their reasons. She rubbed her nose and asked, "Why do you think Alyn wants me to meet her?"

"How would I know? I don't know Ecke very well and I have no idea where to find her. The last I heard, she was still in Tsada." He picked up a small stone and flung it into the rain. "Visions and prophecies. It's all very mysterious to me. All I know is you're our best chance at defeating the Empire, and you're running off chasing… whatever."

With an effort, Minna bit back her first response. For better or worse. She cupped her hands around the message in her lap and took a slow breath. "I can't defeat the Empire by myself," she said. "I don't understand it, but Alyn said she met my mother's spirit. Do you realize what that means?"

He stared blankly at her.

"It means she *did* have a plan."

His frown fell away, and a small smile curved his lips. "Right, right," he said, his voice growing more animated. "And talking to Ecke is the first step of this plan." He paused, his smile fading. "Why didn't she tell you the whole thing?"

"I don't know." Minna held the message up and said, "But this is the best chance we have to find out what she wanted us to do. It's the only chance we have to defeat the Empire."

She let her hand fall into her lap and stared into the rain. The burden of anxiety and uncertainty she bore for weeks fell away, leaving behind a hope she thought lost. Putting aside, for the moment, the enormity of the task ahead of her, she let exhaustion and the first tentative warmth from the fire ease her into a mellow lethargy. The raven's soft grumbles brought a small smile to her face.

"Maybe, if I knew what happened at the battle," Sigurn said. "It would help."

"It would help me, too."

"Can you tell the raven to go check?"

They turned to look at the bird, which was busy preening its wet feathers.

"I don't…" Minna called to the raven and brought back memories of riding past the battlefield the day before, focusing on landmarks the bird might recognize. Suddenly, her mind was full of an image. She was looking down on the forest, obviously from the raven's point of view. Lightning illuminated the scene, followed a moment later by the bark of thunder. The scene was obscured by a heavy downpour. The image disappeared as quickly as it appeared, leaving her with a profound sense of disgust. She recalled the spirit. The raven resumed preening.

"It doesn't want to fly in the rain," she said.

"Can't say I blame it for that," Sigurn said.

Minna returned his tenuous grin. She opened her center and called to Linea. Her spirit guide, who was orbiting the grumpy raven, swooped over and appeared in her center. *Can you go find out what happened in the battle?* Linea bobbed and zoomed into the rain.

She cut her eyes to Sigurn, who was working the fire, a small frown on his face. "So, you don't know where we would find Ecke?" she asked carefully.

"I haven't seen her in years," he answered as he added another log to the fire.

"Surely, we don't have to go to Tsada," Minna said.

Sigurn shrugged. "I hope not." He sat and brushing his hands together. "The war would be over by the time we got back." He looked up, a small grin curving one corner of his mouth. "Wish I brought some food."

Minna smiled, rose and retrieved her saddlebag. She sat, unrolled an oilcloth bundle, then handed Sigurn a small pot. "Water," she said, then set to chopping potatoes.

Sigurn took the pot and held it in the rain. "Well, aren't you the prepared one?"

"I learned the hard way last winter. Don't go anywhere without enough food to keep yourself alive for a while." She plopped the potatoes into the pot, tossed in a handful of dried mushrooms, herbs and added slices of sausage and a handful of barley flour. When she was ready, she set the pot on a rock beside the fire, tossed a bit of sausage to the raven and sat beside Sigurn, close enough that their knees touched.

After a few minutes of silence, Sigurn said, "I'm sorry."

"Me too," Minna said. "I don't really understand what's going on either. I'm worried, too. All the time, about everything. I'm just trying to do my best." She met his eyes. "I need someone I can talk to. Someone I can rely on."

His face froze, and she worried their argument might flare anew. But then a ghost of his smirk appeared, and he nodded. "Deal," he said. He reached out tentatively and rested his hand on her back. Minna grinned at him, and he let his hand fall.

• • •

"That wasn't half bad," Sigurn said as he rinsed the pot in the rain, which had slowed to a surly drizzle.

"Not half bad, huh," Minna said. "It was amazing, given the circumstances."

Sigurn shook water from the pot and gave her a crooked smile. "Amazing might be going a little far."

Minna stood abruptly as Linea appeared. She let the spirit into her center and closed her eyes. "The battle is over," she said.

Sigurn remained silent.

"There are a lot of bodies lined up at the bottom of the field," Minna whispered. "They're digging a really big grave."

"We won!" Sigurn shouted and threw his arms over his head.

Minna's eyes flew open. "How do you know?"

"The Union couldn't stop to bury anyone if they were heading to the Cut," Sigurn said. "We did win, didn't we?"

Minna returned her attention to the vision. "The bodies are Union. The people digging the grave are *Alle'oss*." Her eyes opened again, and she started bouncing. "The *Alle'oss* camp is still there!"

"Waa!" Sigurn shouted. He reached out, took her hands and before Minna knew it, for the second time in her life, a boy was leading her in a dance she only saw from afar at festivals from her perch on the hill outside Fennig.

"We won! We won!" They shouted. The raven squawked and flew out into the rain.

They danced until they were breathless. When they spun to a stop, Sigurn relinquished one of her hands, but held onto the other. His grin shifted, a brow lifting ever so slightly. Suddenly warm, Minna wanted to pull her hand free of his fingers, but she hesitated. She dragged her gaze away from his face and stared into the gathering darkness. Light from the fire glittered on rain drops, adding to the fireflies' flickering summer dance.

"We… we better get some sleep," she said. When she looked at him, his smile had softened. She glanced down at their hands and pulled her hand free. "We should start early."

"Right," Sigurn said, his eyes lingering on her hand before rising to gaze into her eyes. "We should… sleep."

Minna turned away and added wood to the fire. "Right," she said. "Tomorrow, we start looking for Ecke." She hesitated, returning Sigurn's gaze. "I'll… uh… take first watch."

Macha

Macha ran her fingers through the soft fuzz on the side of Neiman's head. They moved so fast after the incident in the *Alle'oss* village, they hadn't bothered keeping their heads shaved. Her sister slept peacefully, her slow, even breaths signaling the crisis was past. Eriu was asleep, curled up with her head on Neiman's thigh.

When the rain started, she and Eriu found a relatively dry spot further into the forest, beneath an old spruce. They were out of the downpour, but they had to endure the drips that found their way through the prickly boughs. Eriu remained uncharacteristically quiet despite the miserable conditions. It wasn't until the rain slowed and it became clear Neiman would survive that Eriu relented and fell asleep.

They saw nothing of the battle, but it drew corvids from far and wide. Ravens, crows, magpies all streamed to the sight of the feast. From the ravens, Macha learned the fate of the Union mercenaries. She watched the battle play out in the birds' memories, the images tinged by their delight. She glimpsed the birds gorging themselves and felt their chagrin when the victors shooed them away so they could start the grisly task of burying the dead. She watched the Union army retreating south and a small band of *Alle'oss* set off in pursuit from the mountain to the west.

None of that interested her. She only wanted to know the fate of Minna Hunter. To her surprise, the black-haired witch was not involved in the battle. Macha glimpsed her fleeing north after the earthquake and assumed she left to aid the *Alle'oss* army. She didn't know why Minna fled when she had the advantage, but she was confident it wasn't because she was afraid. She easily absorbed Macha's strongest spirit wave and produced the earthquake. Though Macha and her sisters had access to many texts the Inquisition purged from the Seidi's libraries, she never read anything about a spirit that could produce an earthquake.

She let her gaze fall to Neiman's peaceful face. Her bookish sister would know if the Seidi sisters ever knew of such a spirit.

They still needed to find Minna Hunter, but Macha wasn't worried about that. She didn't know why the witch ran away today, but the *Alle'oss* would need her to win this war. She would have to show herself, eventually.

Damp and shivering, Macha lay on the thick mat of spruce needles and scooted back until she felt Eriu's warmth. Her sister moaned in her sleep, draped an arm over Macha and tugged her closer. Macha slid her fingers between Neiman's thighs, let her eyes close and drifted until she fell asleep.

Sera

Sera and Nicola sat beside one another on the bed in the room where they met Harold and Nia. Worried that Nicola would be recognized, they hadn't been allowed to leave the small apartment. Harold promised them they would move to better accommodations soon. Not that Sera minded too much. She was still marveling at the fact they escaped. She looked at Nicola who gazed unseeing at the wall. "What are you thinking?"

Nicola blinked, seeming to come back from distant thoughts, and looked at Sera.

When she didn't speak, Sera asked her, "Are you having second thoughts?"

A small smile curved Nicola's lips, and she shook her head. "No. I'm so happy to be here, away from the Imperial District. With you."

"But?"

"I don't know. It's just, I feel like we've stepped into something much bigger than we imagined. The rebels. The monastery. A secret mission."

Sera returned her grin. "Just like in my mother's books."

"A real adventure," Nicola said softly. "I've always wanted to travel. To see the world. And now I get to see it, or part of it, with you." She grew serious. "It's just so amazing."

"Are you afraid?"

"Yes."

Sera leaned toward her and brushed her lips with her own. "I'll protect you, princess."

"I know, Sera Storm."

Chapter 46

A Destitute Woman in Ulm

Pushing her hair behind her ears, the woman bent over the man's body, rummaged in his pockets, and was gratified to find an expensive-looking leather purse. Kneeling, she released the clasp and peered inside. It was too dark to see the contents clearly, but it was heavy and when she shook it, the coins clinked pleasingly. Shoving the purse into a pocket, she returned her attention to the body. Some jewelry, but nothing she could use.

Standing, she patted the coin purse in her pocket, peered up into the rain and considered her options. There were few places a bedraggled *Alle'oss* woman could find a meal in Ulm. Not the kind of meal she wanted, anyway. She was tired of garbage and what passed for street food in the slums. In fact, there was only one decent tavern she knew of that served Brochen.

She glanced up at the small spirit hovering nearby, then without another glance at the body, she said, "Let's go," and set off down the alley.

She walked through the rain ruminating on how she came to this sad state. When she arrived in Ulm months before, she had nothing. No coin. No past worth returning to. No future worth living for. The first few weeks, she wandered the seedier streets, scrounging what she could from the garbage pails behind taverns. She had no plans beyond satisfying her gnawing hunger. Only slowly did she consider how she might better her situation.

Afraid of being discovered in the teeming Imperial city, she was reluctant to call on the spirits, and without the spirits' gifts, what was she? She had no skills she could sell. No friends or family to call on. Her only option was to steal what she needed. Even in that, she was at a disadvantage. She didn't know what she could steal and how she would use it. She never used money before, but watching the exchange of coins in the markets unearthed dusty memories from her childhood. It was coin that granted power in the civilized world. She followed the men who tucked coin purses into their pockets, but had no plan for how to steal them without being caught.

Then she noticed well-to-do men, tourists to the bad side of the town, disappearing down dark alleys with the women who walked the streets. Instinctively, she knew what it was about. She had no experiences that would allow her to visualize what they did and no interest in finding out. Still, she recognized the possibilities. The men were rich, and they were alone with the women down a dark alley.

It surprised her how reluctant she was to kill with her own hands. Somehow, it was more intimate than using the spirits. But need finally overcame her squeamishness. She watched the women and copied their flirtatious come ons. Still, it surprised her when a man paused and looked her up and down.

"How much?" he asked.

"What is it worth to you?" she asked, not having any idea what a reasonable amount would be.

Her naiveté and desperate circumstances only seemed to fan his eagerness. The predatory leer that appeared on his face eliminated any chance he would survive the encounter. When he followed her, hoping for a quick toss, she found herself anticipating what was to come. It was easier than she expected. And now she had some coin.

She stood in the rain staring at the back door of the tavern a long time before she worked up the courage to knock. When no one answered, she nearly decided to give up. But patting the pocket with the purse restored her resolve, and she knocked again.

The door opened, startling her. When the Imperial man who emerged saw her, he scowled and said, "Get lost!"

He was pulling the door closed when she extracted the purse from her pocket and jingled the contents. He hesitated, giving her the opportunity to say, "A bath, a meal and a dry place to sleep. That's all I want."

He glanced at her red hair, then his eyes trailed down her ragged clothes, lingering on a tear in her shirt.

The way he looked at her decided it for her. If he said no, she would blast him back into the kitchen she saw behind him. She didn't care that people might sense a witch.

Fortunately, he made the right choice. Stepping back, he motioned her inside. When they were standing in a pantry behind the kitchen, he said, "You're lucky we cater to your kind here."

She would have burned the tavern down to the ground if it weren't for the tantalizing aromas coming from the kitchen.

He led her into the kitchen, then down another hallway to a room that looked like a storeroom. Amid the mops, brooms, broken crates, empty barrels and other detritus was a tub only large enough for her to sit in.

He quoted her a price, she suspected wasn't fair, but she wasn't in a position to bargain. Turning away, she dumped the contents of the purse into her hand. Fortunately, they had little numbers on one side. She handed him a collection of coins that added up to the amount he quoted and was annoyed when his eyes widened slightly. It was okay. She was desperate, and she still had a few coins left. Besides, she could always get more.

"Someone'll bring the water," he said, tucking the coins into his pocket. "Brochen eat up in the balcony. After you eat, you can sleep in here. When you're done here, come back to the kitchen and I'll show you the way."

She watched him leave, then followed the progress of her spirit guide exploring the small, cluttered room. It was a pit, but it was also the nicest room she had been in since she arrived in Ulm.

•   •   •

Dropping her fork onto the clean plate, she let her hands fall into her lap. The meal was basic — beef, boiled potatoes and a crusty bread — but it may have been the best meal she ever ate. Her clothes were damp. The other Brochen on the balcony peered at her ragged clothes and tangled hair as if she were a wild animal. But she felt wonderful. She was safe for the moment and could look forward to a dry place to sleep. At least for one night. She was about to return to the storeroom when someone on the main floor shouted, "A story!"

She perked up. How long had it been since she enjoyed something as simple as a story? Amazed at her turn of luck on this day, she crossed her arms on the balcony rail, propped her chin on her hands, and watched her spirit guide orbiting a portly man with long white hair stepping onto a small stage below her.

Eyes misty with a joy she hadn't felt in years, she watched him sip from a tankard and gaze expectantly out at the crowd.

Then someone shouted, "The battle of Minna and Aife!"

Cheers erupted from everyone. Everyone except Aife, who stared down at the storyteller, too stunned to move.

Look for the exciting conclusion of
Spirit Light, Book 2 of the Spirit Song Trilogy
in *Spirit Light Volume 2*

Characters

Alle'oss

Minna Hunter	Daughter of Thomas and Vada Hunter, sister of Alyn Hunter
Thomas Hunter	Father of Minna and Alyn Hunter
Vada Hunter	Mother of Minna and Alyn Hunter
Aron Hunter	Commander of the *Alle'oss* army
Zaina	Aron Hunter's second in command
Karl Siegling	Friend of Thomas Wolfe
Agmar Ericson	Farmer from Fennig. A member of the Alle'oss army
Torsten Junge	Member of the Alle'oss resistance
Svend	Scout for the Union mercenaries

Helala

Alyn Hunter	Daughter of Thomas and Vada Hunter, sister of Minna Hunter
Beadu	The last *saa'myn*
Deirdre Breasal	The former Malefica of the Seidi. Runs the school in *Helala*

Keelia's Command

Keelia Darrah	Former sister of the Seidi
Jason Smyth	Friend of Keelia
Bjorn	Keelia's second in command
Siv	Keelia's adjutant
Willa	An *Alle'oss* rebel
Ogden	In Willa's command
Halfdan	In Willa's command

Oss'stera

Lief Admundson	A founding member of _Oss'stera_
Sigurn	A member of _Oss'stera_
Gyda	A member of _Oss'stera_
Frigg	A member of _Oss'stera_

The Misfits

Ulf Lothan	Soon to be a Minna's promised. The commander of the misfits
Mikaela	One of the misfits. Ulf's second in command
Helga	One of the misfits
Hakon	One of the misfits
Inger	One of the misfits

Imperials

Victor Storm	Marshal of the Imperial forces fighting the Kaileuk
Lyra Storm	Victor Storm's spouse
Sera Storm	Victor's and Lyra's daughter
Ludweig II	The emperor
Crysta	The emperor's spouse
Roderik	Ludweig's and Crysta's oldest son. The heir apparent
Kari	Ludweig's and Crysta's oldest daughter
Nicola	Ludweig's and Crysta's youngest daughter
Werner	Victor Storm's weapons instructor

Brothers of the Inquisition

Harold Wolfe	Inquisitor. Left as a spy in the Inquistion by Ragan
Hoerst Bernston	The Malleus, leader of the Inquisition
Stefan Schakal	Inquisitor, right hand to the Malleus
Henrik Matison	Sergeant in Harold Wolfe's escort

Joseph Weidner	Former member of Harold Wolfe's escort
Raif Alundson	Former member of Harold Wolfe's escort. Now part of the *Alle'oss* army
Fenton Wynton	Former member of Harold Wolfe's escort. Now part of the Alle'oss army
Eckehart Baumann	The Malleus's assistant
Manfrid	In charge of the Malleus's program to brainwash witches
Otto	Manfrid's closest confidant

Sisters of the Seidi

| Briana Darragh | The Malefica, leader of the Seidi |
| Nara Flynn | One of the 'bad girls' fighting the Kaileuk. Friend of Keelia. |

Others

Louisa Brukman	Bar maid in the Monk's Habit
Renard Faust	Bar maid in the Monk's Habit
Xander Mendler	Bar maid in the Monk's Habit
Lika	An orphan living on the streets of Brennan
Gimlet	Gravedigger
Hawthen	Gravedigger
Di	Gunther's spouse
Macha	An Andian. One of Hoerst's witches
Neiman	An Ferol. One of Hoerst's witches
Eriu	An *Alle'oss*. One of Hoerst's witches
Chagan Koutman	The commander of the Union mercenaries

Thank You

Thank you for reading *Spirit Light. Volume 1*. If you liked the story, please consider leaving a review on Goodreads or your favorite online retailer. Reviews are one of the most important ways to show an author support and spread the word.

If you would like to hear about upcoming books, short stories, and other news from the Spirit Song world, sign up for my newsletter at rosshightower.com.

While you wait for *Spirit Light Volume 2*, consider reading one of the other novels in the Spirit Song Saga.

About the Author

Somehow, after spending most of his life in the south, Ross Hightower found himself living in Milwaukee and loving it. One cold, snowy morning, not too long ago, he woke with a story stuck in his head. That wasn't unusual, but what happened next was unprecedented. He wrote it down. That small story grew into his first novel, *Spirit Sight*. Ross and Deb, his partner of 35 years, had so much fun talking about stories, they decided to write a prequel to *Spirit Sight* together. The result was the award-winning novel, *Argren Blue*. There will be many more books to come. Some might wonder why it took so long to find his calling in life, but Ross is just grateful he has.

Other Titles by Ross Hightower

Note from Ross Hightower

Word-of-mouth is crucial for any author to succeed. If you enjoyed *Spirit Light*, please leave a review online—anywhere you are able. Even if it's just a sentence or two. It would make all the difference and would be very much appreciated.

Thanks!
Ross Hightower

We hope you enjoyed reading this title from:

www.blackrosewriting.com

Subscribe to our mailing list – *The Rosevine* – and receive **FREE** books, daily deals, and stay current with news about upcoming releases and our hottest authors.
Scan the QR code below to sign up.

Already a subscriber? Please accept a sincere thank you for being a fan of Black Rose Writing authors.

View other Black Rose Writing titles at www.blackrosewriting.com/books and use promo code **PRINT** to receive a **20% discount** when purchasing.